MLIRF

Praise for Raymond A. Villareal's
A People's History of the Vampire Uprising

—*Literary Hub*

A PEOPLE'S
HISTORY
OF THE
VAMPIRE
UPRISING

A NOVEL BY
RAYMOND A. VILLAREAL

TITAN BOOKS

A People's History of the Vampire Uprising
Print edition ISBN: 978 1 789 09188 5
E-book edition ISBN: 978 1 789 09189 2

Published by Titan Books
A division of Titan Publishing Group Ltd
144 Southwark Street, London SE1 0UP

First edition: April 2019
1 2 3 4 5 6 7 8 9 10

A CIP catalogue record for this title is available from the British Library.

Printed and bound by CPI Group (UK) Ltd, Croydon, CR0 4YY

For Mom and Dad

"The only hope for the doomed,
is no hope at all…"

—Virgil, *The Aeneid*

A
PEOPLE'S HISTORY
OF THE
~~VAMPIRE~~ UPRISING

FOREWORD

When I was approached to compile a recent history of the Gloamings and their entrance into society, I initially thought, *Too soon*. Events continue to change at a rapid pace. But it's exactly these changing conditions—we are still trying to figure out how we got here—that caused me to realize: now is the perfect time to compile the beginning, middle, and…if not the end, then that place that occupied the in medias res of our current conflicts.

Some historians may consider other, more eminent or notorious individuals than the ones I've documented here—but I believe the individuals in this text affected the course of events most profoundly. In fact, I view those other accounts of this period with suspicion. Their research is negligent at best, their prose too concerned with the salacious details of irrelevant events.

This book is also for the martyrs who sacrificed their lives to the cause—no matter what side. Other historians have attempted to subvert these deaths to their own cause. It is ironic that the Gloamings' emergence occurred during what was generally considered our empire's finest days—*"Un grand destin commence, un grand destin s'acheve,"* as Corneille stated of the Roman Empire. Those other historians labor under this misconception.

Not I. I decline.

In spite of the great personal sacrifice, I have labored to be impartial. I have been threatened and attacked during my research for this book. As a result, and after frequent hospitalization, my quality of life has been severely, negatively affected. Yet I pass no judgments on those responsible. These pages are compiled for everyone: those who lived through this time, and those who did not survive.

I hope, reader, that they give you meaningful perspective.

[REDACTED SIGNATURE]
April 22

New York Post — March 13[1]: Last night, the home of wealthy trial attorney John Hatcher in the Flatiron District was robbed by three unknown persons. The house was empty while Mr. Hatcher attended a performance of "Nixon in China." The thieves stole an undetermined amount of gold rumored to comprise a worth of more than $10 million. Sources with the New York City regional office of the FBI indicate Mr. Hatcher's extensive and professional surveillance system was not sabotaged, yet the video was not usable to authorities. A spokesman for the FBI stated that the Agency has no current suspects but the investigation continues.

---

[1] Page 2, Metro section.

CHAPTER 1

Dr. Lauren Scott
Research Physician, Centers for Disease Control

"Let the dead bury their own dead." That's what my dad used to say, when faced with a losing proposition. Of course the blood, which dominated so much discussion during the time of this investigation, was heavily on my mind as well. Strange to admit as a doctor, but since birth I've been terrified at the sight of blood. Have you ever seen a bird fly straight into a window and drop to the ground? Kind of like that. As a kid, my heart rate and blood pressure would drop suddenly, and *bam!* The darkness descended, lights out. I would wake up on my back.

Then, when I was fifteen, a new doctor kindly told me about applied tension, where you tense the muscles in the legs, torso, and arms, raising the blood pressure to the head, thereby counteracting the response to pass out. It was ingenious. I spent years working on the response—tensing all these muscles until it was second nature—since I needed to be able to handle the sight of blood.

15

Even as a child, I already wanted to be a doctor.

I know every doctor says that. But it's true. My dad fixed refrigerators for a living and I often tagged along during the summer. I was fascinated by the spectacle of him carefully taking apart the back cover to expose the innards of the refrigerator's engine. He pulled the wires from the adapter and condenser, stripping them with the care of a surgeon. He burned the soldering metal to clean and replace the shattered cords. Even in a bird's nest of wires, my dad knew exactly which ones to pull out and fix. I considered him a refrigerator doctor, and I daydreamed he was performing surgery on old robots. I wanted to be a doctor like my dad—but to fix humans, not refrigerators.

My mom was similarly precise, although in a decidedly less productive style. She would maniacally rearrange all desk and home objects to *get them in order!* Between the two of them, I grew up with an extremely disciplined personality, well suited for a medical occupation. My younger sister, Jennifer, was the exact opposite. By the time she was twelve, Jennifer had run away from home more than ten times. But it wasn't running away to leave home; it was more leaving home to go to the lake or a concert or even the mall. After a while, my parents realized Jenny just wanted to experience life. "Tell us where you want to go next time," my dad yelled at her the time she vanished for three days to go hiking. "I'll drive you there myself." To his credit, until she got her driver's license—an epic battle in and of itself—he often did.

In medical school I soon realized anything too invasive led to an audience with blood. That led me to a concentration in virology. The first time I became aware of the…*the* disease, I had just started at the Centers for Disease Control and Prevention [CDC].

The CDC is a government agency whose goal is to protect public health and safety through the control and prevention of disease, injury, and disability. I had recently graduated from medical school with the intention of becoming a research physician. After my residency, the CDC came to my university to speak about the procedures involved when doctors are confronted with new and unusual symptoms out in the field. I was fascinated by the deductive reasoning involved—like being a detective searching for microbes and living cells. My background in research, plus my experience working in a biosafety level three lab with pathogen and lethal agents, made my résumé a natural fit for the agency. By then, too, I had internships with the World Health Organization in various third world countries, mostly in West Africa. So it was an ideal first job.

Young and inexperienced in the ranks, I was usually sent to cover not-so-dangerous health alerts around the country. Which is why on April second, when we received a strange but vague report from Nogales, Arizona, my older colleagues didn't even blink. It seemed even less than routine.

So the CDC sent me.

The request from Arizona was slightly more expedited than usual because Nogales is a border town, and, well, you never know what you're getting so close to another country. Of course, that was also the week of the solar flare panic, which only added to the tension. Unusual solar flares had been causing disruptions with satellite transmissions, radio signals, and transformer blowouts in the power grid. I mean, it wasn't as bad as the cable networks made it seem—watching Fox News or CNN, you'd think the entire world had gone dark, when really the country was just experiencing some blinks with some Internet service and GPS providers. My sister Jennifer and I, who texted often, resolved to stay in touch despite the Internet troubles. We took to sending each other the cheesiest postcards we could find—preferably one bought from a gas station or restaurant. But it was enough that, en route to Arizona, I didn't have much to go on other than a few phone calls with officials in Nogales to discuss the incidents.

I arrived on a scorching Tuesday afternoon, hot air slapping my face as I left the airport to look for a taxi. My contact in Nogales was Dr. Hector Gomez, head of the city's health department and also its coroner—and we agreed to meet at the coroner's office complex so that I could view the bodies in question. I lugged three suitcases, two of them holding my equipment, including my hazmat suit and other protective gear. CDC rules stipulated that an investigator conducting an initial on-site review should procure a fully encapsulating chemical-resistant suit. I considered bringing a self-contained breathing apparatus with a level A suit, but I figured that might be overkill. It was also heavy as hell.

The coroner's office was a small modular office with greenish drab colors, utilitarian furniture, and cheap leaded paint. In the small lobby, I saw a young man who I assumed to be Dr. Gomez, and another man in a police uniform, nervously awaiting my arrival.

I held out my hand, trying to sound older and more experienced than I felt. "Hi, I'm Lauren Scott."

The man with the dark bushy mustache over pursed lips took my hand. "Dr. Gomez. Pleased to meet you, Dr. Scott. I'm glad you're finally here. This is Sheriff Wilson."

The tall figure in the uniform tipped his cowboy hat. The fixed gaze on his lined face told me he was ready to get down to business. "Pleasure."

"Nice to meet both of you," I replied. "And please, call me Lauren."

"We should get started immediately," Dr. Gomez said as he fidgeted with the small notebook in his right hand. Almost as if he were tempted to take notes on our conversation. "Let's go to the morgue and we can review our notes and the body."

I followed them through a long hallway, then down a flight of stairs to the basement. It smelled like formaldehyde and alcohol, and there were fluorescent lights that blinked in the freezing temperature. It was hard not to crack a joke or run away; this old building looked like a scene right out of a TV show. I saw a body already lying on the slab, covered with a green sheet. As Dr. Gomez lifted the sheet, I briefly wondered if I should be wearing a suit or at least protective headgear. I was still new and obsessed with not catching any disease I encountered, unlike the older grizzled veterans who showed up to hot zones with barely any gloves, much less a protective suit.

I stepped closer to the body and noticed there did not appear to be any obvious signs of trauma.

"How long has the body been here?" I asked.

Dr. Gomez paused and glanced at the sheriff with his bottom lip sticking out in a scowl. "Twenty-four hours."

I should have called for help right then, but I simply turned to Gomez, surprised. "You called three days ago about a body exhibiting unusual hemophilia bruising and intradermal contusions over ninety percent of the body. I thought this was that body. I need to see the other body."

Sheriff Wilson and Dr. Gomez exchanged another agonized glance. "That body is not here anymore."

I stared at them for a moment and I'm pretty sure my mouth was open. "What do you mean?"

"Apparently it was stolen from the morgue," Sheriff Wilson answered, a pained look on his face. "We're still investigating. Frankly, we have no idea how it got out, or who in their right mind would want to steal it. I hope it's some damn college students looking for a prank."

"Oh," I said. I pointed at the body on the slab. "So who is this?"

"This is another body we found at the ravine, which exhibited the identical intradermal bruising over the torso as the previous one," Dr. Gomez replied.

I leaned over the body. Incisions had been made already on the scalp. I glanced over at Dr. Gomez.

"We sort of felt that we needed to get a jump on everything," he said. "But then we thought better of it and stopped. Sorry."

"That's really not what I anticipated when I emailed the protocol." I was pissed, but what could I do? I moved on to the external examination. This would have to be a cursory exam for the moment. I placed my iPhone on a small table and clicked on the recording app.

"No obvious signs of trauma that would indicate the cause of death. Appears to be a woman in her thirties in moderate shape. One hundred and forty-five pounds. No distinguishing marks or tattoos. Turning the head of the body I see two circular wounds—openings—of equal-millimeter diameter—maybe a bite—close to the carotid artery and extending an undetermined length into the skin."

I leaned closer and smelled something faint. A floral scent? Sweet yet strangely not pleasing. Cheap perfume, most likely. I rubbed my nose with the back of my hand. The scent lingered far longer than I was comfortable with. I continued.

"A dissection would need to be performed. However, a cursory glance doesn't seem to indicate that this would be the cause of death unless a poison was injected. But the wounds do resemble teeth marks at first glance. However, they do not resemble any teeth wounds I am familiar with from either a human or other mammal. I am going to examine the body under magnification. No blood or tissue under the fingernails, although a swab will be performed for further testing. Teeth seem to be in good shape, but two top molars seem to be loose. Can't speculate on that cause yet. An examination of the full body shows no signs of obvious trauma. A chemical analysis of hair and blood will need to be performed immediately. The eyes show no signs of hemangioma or petechial rash. The dissection and brain examination will proceed tomorrow morning."

Dr. Gomez handed me the syringe. I took blood and saliva samples and placed them in the biohazard containers. I had some trouble extracting a usable amount of blood. A simple touch indicated that the body was unusually devoid. Premature coagulation, perhaps. "Where can I take these samples for a quick chemical analysis?"

"University of Arizona, Santa Cruz, has a small lab," Dr. Gomez said. "I can get someone to drive it over tonight, and the lab techs there owe me. They can put in the rush. It won't be as detailed but it's a start."

I stopped in the hallway and turned to the sheriff. "I'm wondering: did you rule out a human cause before calling me?" I asked. "I mean, like a murder or something."

Sheriff Wilson nodded. "Sure, but the first body—the female— was dead. I mean, it had no vital signs. Then it gets up and leaves! Hector sent a sample of hair to the state crime lab and they told us there were some unidentifiable substances or some sort of thing and they wanted us to call our state board of health. We had to call someone. Someone federal. Hector here—I mean Dr.

Gomez—thought we should call the CDC. Next on the list was the FBI." He smiled. "We may still do that."

"Thanks," I said, still trying to gather all the ideas bouncing around in my mind. "I guess I'll go back to my hotel room to settle in. Then let's head out to the ravine where the bodies were found."

Sheriff Wilson and Dr. Gomez just nodded as they each scratched the side of their faces.

I checked into a dingy La Quinta not too far from the Mexican border. There weren't many choices in this town. I threw my bags on the bed and attempted to take a nap, even with the window-unit air conditioner growling like a busted muffler. I was going to have to be up for the results of the toxicology—hopefully sooner than later.

Even then, in those early hours, the situation felt weird. Who steals a body from the coroner's office? I was struck, too, by the bite marks. And where was all the blood? All those years trying to avoid blood, and now I was wishing for it to be there. Always, it was about the blood. I thought of Macbeth: "The near in blood, the nearer bloody." I think my father taught me that. It seems so apropos in hindsight, as I've felt covered in the blood ever since.

I transferred the pictures to my iPad and tried to consider what type of animal could leave that mark. I attempted to find significance in the loose upper molars and what systematic disease could cause this. Diabetes and cancer were obvious ones, but the body looked to be in good health, so I eliminated those possibilities. Another type of autoimmune disease could be a contributing factor, but that would take more tests. I made a mental note to get a tissue sample sent to Atlanta. This was my first solo assignment; I needed to cover all the bases.

I had pretty much just laid my head on the flat pillow when a knock on my door almost caused me to leap out of my skin.

"Dr. Scott? It's Sheriff Wilson and Dr. Gomez."

I unlocked and opened the door. They stood there, looking like a mixture of shame and frustration. "Sorry," the sheriff said. "We tried calling but your phone must be on silent—"

"What happened?" I cut him off. I was probably overtired by this point. "Did we get the results already?"

Wilson glanced at Gomez like neither of them wanted to talk. The sheriff won the silent battle. "The body is—well, it's not in the morgue anymore," Dr. Gomez said.

On the way back to the morgue, Sheriff Wilson tried to explain. "We've never been broken into before," he said. That was an ambiguous accomplishment at best, I thought. "It's a bit more than that," the sheriff continued. "The guard at the back door says the woman walked up to him and hit him with a surgical hammer. He doesn't remember much after that."

"I'm sorry. What woman?"

"The woman you saw. The corpse on the table."

I laughed. "What? That can't be true."

The car was silent for a moment, until the sheriff said, "He swears it." I glanced out the window again and it was like a movie on repeat, the identical saguaro cactus every few miles with its crooked arms locked in a permanent wave at random tumbleweeds along for the ride.

When we arrived back at the morgue, a deputy surveyed the scene we had left just hours earlier, as if looking for his keys. I saw the empty table, and then the materials from the shelf strewn across the floor as if an earthquake had hit. My eyes became fixated on a roll of gauze and scissors on the table.

Wilson saw what I was looking at. "The deputy says that the woman's head was bandaged," he said.

I exchanged a glance with Dr. Gomez. All he could do was shrug. We walked into the other room and another deputy, who looked all of nineteen years old, sat on the floor, his head bandaged. He recounted the story to us as he held an ice pack to his head. He said, "One minute I was by myself, and in a flash that girl—"

"The presumed corpse," I said.

He nodded slowly. "Yeah. Her. She was standing next to me. I was eating a Twix bar. The girl, she—"

"The presumed corpse," I said again.

The deputy paused. He looked nervously at the sheriff, then continued. "Yeah. The presumed corpse. She was wearing pants. Also, a sweatshirt. No shoes."

Sheriff Wilson said, "There's a locker down the hall. Used by techs and deputies assigned to the morgue. Broken into—missing those exact clothes."

"I wanted to ask her what she was doing but it's like the words wouldn't come out," the deputy said with a frown on his thin face. "Then, when I just about found the words, my head caught the end of that hammer."

I nodded and tried to keep my face from looking disgusted. "Now the other body that disappeared yesterday. Were there any—"

Sheriff Wilson completed my sentence. "Clothes were missing out of the locker also."

I couldn't help thinking that the deputy himself looked like someone half dead, and maybe on meth. And it wasn't the recent hammer to his head. I suppose good help was hard to find. Without anything else to do—no preliminary tests back, no body to examine, and everyone wide awake—we decided to head out to the desert area where the bodies were found.

The desert was still dark, but I cannot describe how dark the desert gets close to the border. We were only a ten-minute distance from the morgue, and it was like our vehicles' headlights had led to another world, one closer to the black sky. We ended up on a slight hill near an eight-foot metal fence with barbed wire strewn on top and with concrete bollards every couple of feet. A cold wind blew in from the south with not a bird or animal in sight. I guessed this was the border—it was a bit anticlimactic. Stepping out of the police van, I was surprised to see the ground covered in grass. Not desert sand.

Sheriff Wilson slapped a hand on the fence. "On the other side of this you'd be in Mexico. Doesn't look much different, does it?"

As far as I could see over the fence, it appeared pretty much the same, albeit farther from our lights. I couldn't shake the feeling something was staring back at me from somewhere in that murky distance. My eyes strained to see into it. I felt years of nothingness scattered across these plains and it made me shiver and cough.

The headlights from the van illuminated the shallow hole nearest the fence. The cold desert wind tickled a chill down my back. I knelt down in front of the hole but I saw only wet dirt. Dr. Gomez, hunched in a catcher's position next to me, ran a hand through the dirt.

The corpses had been found by a trucker whose engine had burned out on the side of the road while transporting salvaged computer parts. No one could determine why he took such an indirect route, although the sheriff said suspicion was that he may have been carrying illegal cargo. The trucker was waiting on the side of the road for a wrecker to arrive when he spotted what he said looked like a figure running away at a high rate of speed. Then he noticed a hand, some distance away. When he went out into the field to investigate, he found the body.

"Border Patrol showed up before the wrecker," Sheriff Wilson said with a voice disembodied from the headlights. "Then they stayed with the body while checking the fence. They called our office. The rest you know."

I shined my flashlight over the area. I placed some dirt into a plastic bag for testing. I shined the light on the plastic bag. The dirt appeared reddish. I looked over at Sheriff Wilson. "Is that dried blood?"

He took the bag, pushed back his cowboy hat, and studied it with his small flashlight. "Might be." He handed me back the bag and shined the light onto the ground. He pushed his hand into the ground and put the light on it as he rubbed his index finger and thumb together. "Damn. Looks like wet blood also."

Wondering about Border Patrol protocol, I poked a finger in the same spot as Wilson. Dried and wet blood mixed on my fingers. In hindsight, of course, the whole area looked like a dug-up shallow grave, but in the moment that early morning it simply looked like loose dirt near a fence. At the time, none of us knew about the mass grave on the other side of the fence.

I arrived back at my hotel at about five in the morning. I leaned back on the hard pillow and thought about emailing an update to the CDC, but they were wrapped up in another Ebola scare in Africa, and there were potential carriers in Minnesota. No one would read my report for another two weeks, if even then.

I must have slept for an hour before my phone began to buzz. It was Dr. Gomez, and his tone was urgent, although to be honest in the short time I had known him, he always sounded like he was beside himself.

"The lab called," he said quickly. "They want to see us immediately."

At the science lab of the University of Arizona, Santa Cruz—about a thirty-minute drive from Nogales—I grabbed coffee from the cramped office, stirring in lumpy sugar as I introduced myself to the med student and professor waiting for us. Gomez looked like he hadn't slept in two days. He shook Professor Chen's hand as if they had met before. Chen was a skinny, animated older man with professor hair and rumpled clothes. His assistant, Jimmy Morton, looked like a hipster out of central casting. He wore a red flannel shirt and a mustache that sprang off his face like a twist tie. He must have left the monocle at home.

Chen waved us over to the computer. "Okay, so we did a preliminary test of the blood. It's been pretty slow around here so we were able to do it quick, but let me just say, we really need a hematologist to look at this." His eyes sparkled like fireworks. "Prepare to have your mind blown." He clicked the mouse on the computer and a 1000x microscopic HD image appeared on the screen in neon green and red looking like an animated video game. "A light microscopy image would be better but we obviously do not have access to that equipment here." He pointed a bony finger at the red circles on the screen. "See the platelets. At first we thought it was some type of sickle cell anemia—one that we weren't familiar with—but look over here. It's like a classic case of leukemia. But even that didn't register in our further tests. And it has a distinct hypercoagulable state at times, and then it adapts again."

Sheriff Wilson raised a hand. "What is a hyper...whatever?"

"It means that the blood has a tendency to clot very easily," Jimmy answered. I secretly prayed he might start twirling his mustache as he talked. "It's not a good thing because it can cause life-threatening blood clots in a person. A person with blood this advanced would have clots throughout their veins."

Professor Chen continued as he rubbed his calloused hands together. "Honestly, this is what probably killed the person, I would think."

"She's alive," I told him. I glanced at the sheriff. "Allegedly."

Chen and Morton stared at us and exchanged a glance. "How? That's absurd," Professor Chen said. He didn't wait for an answer before he continued. "But then you're not going to believe this, but the blood thins to a level—and what I mean is the blood-clotting cells begin to mutate to a level akin to Ebola. I'm serious."

"He is," Jimmy concurred.

"It's like a type of essential thrombocytosis that I'm not familiar with at all," Chen said. "This needs to be sent to the University of Arizona and their lab for more testing. In all honesty we should probably be wearing level A hazmat suits or be looking at this in a level four biosafety lab. I would love to see if Niemann-Pick C1 cholesterol transporter is essential in the transmission as in Ebola."

"I need to get a sample to the CDC as soon as possible," I said, entranced by his computer screen. I started to feel the rush of adrenaline. Had this dusty old town actually birthed a new virus?

Sheriff Wilson's phone rang. He stepped away to answer it.

"Hematology is not my specialty, obviously," Dr. Gomez said, "but can a body survive long with this particular condition?"

"Not likely," Professor Chen said. "I suppose there are outliers for every disease, but I wouldn't think that a body could withstand any of the conditions. I mean, for example, Ebola will kill a body in a short period of time, and this is as bad—if not worse—from all appearances. I can only imagine that was the cause of death. But now you're telling me this woman isn't dead? I find that unreal, to be exact."

"I find it unreal too, but it happened," Dr. Gomez said with a shrug.

Sheriff Wilson walked back to the computer. "Well, good news, you see. We have an actual lead. A girl named Liza Sole was reported missing by her roommate and she matches the description of our former dead body."

"Mind if I tag along?" I asked.

"I was just gonna ask you the same thing," Wilson said.

We ended up at an older apartment complex only three miles away. The sun had come up and I could feel my body drained of energy. I was itching for another cup of coffee but I was pretty sure that wasn't going to happen anytime soon. Strangely enough, I used to hate the smell of coffee. Reminded me of going to my aunt's house in Florida in the summer, which always smelled like coffee, and was so god-awful hot and humid. Coffee used to smell like boredom and mosquitoes to me, but medical school will make you change every habit and attitude you hold dear.

I counted about twenty units in the complex—not big by any means. Two floors and some parking—that was it. We walked up the stairs looking for apartment 221. Sheriff Wilson's face darkened as we reached the top steps.

"What's wrong?" Dr. Gomez asked.

"One of my deputies was supposed to meet us here. He should be waiting for us already. He said he was here already." He frowned and looked around. "You know, we're a small county here. I expect my deputies to be available when requested."

Wilson rapped on the door a few times, waited, thought for a moment, then grabbed the handle and twisted. The door swung open. But he didn't walk inside. We glanced at each other. With a long sigh, Sheriff Wilson stepped into the apartment.

"Thought I heard someone in distress," he said without much conviction.

We stepped inside and I was struck by the peculiar familiar smell. At the time I couldn't place it, but of course I now know that it was the same sweet tinge from Nogales not six hours before. And of course we should have been wearing masks before we walked inside. I had violated so many protocols so far this visit, it's a wonder I still had a job later.

The apartment looked like it had been vacated in an emergency. The television was tuned to some celebrity reality show. Two plates of half-eaten sushi sat on the living room table with two glasses of wine near the edge. Wilson and Gomez looked inside one of the bedrooms while I moved over to the kitchen. Nothing seemed amiss. I saw a piece of floral cardboard tacked to the refrigerator with a SpongeBob SquarePants magnet. In block letters at the top it stated, "LIZA'S THINGS TO DO THIS YEAR!!" Without thinking, I pulled it off the fridge and stuck it in my jacket pocket. The sheriff strode back into the den and looked around again. "No sign of the roommate or the dead girl," he said. The roommate who made the report was Glenda Jones. Not that it matters now. He looked at me. "The presumed corpse."

I didn't even try to hide a smile—and the smile hadn't left my face when a yell from Dr. Gomez cut through the moment. We both rushed to the hallway and almost ran into Gomez, who was running in the other direction. He pointed behind him, as Sheriff Wilson pulled out his pistol.

"In the bathroom," Gomez cried.

Wilson took the lead and ordered me to stay back, but I was right behind him as we approached the bathroom. Wilson waved his gun as he stepped inside. It was a small bathroom, so I parked at the doorway.

"No, God, no," Wilson said. He knelt next to the bathtub and holstered his revolver. I stepped inside and looked over his kneeling figure. A young man in the same uniform as Wilson lay in the bathtub. His face was white. His eyes open.

He was obviously deceased. For now.

That's how it really started. A back-from-the-dead girl, a dead deputy, and a missing roommate. Later, I would hate myself for not calling the FBI and ordering a quarantine of the area immediately. But things were moving too quickly. From that moment in Liza Sole's bathroom, it was a cascade of action from the police and the CDC—meaning myself.

Of course I wanted to take samples in that apartment, but there was nothing to be found. Strangely enough, no blood. An autopsy by Dr. Gomez determined that Deputy Shawn Miller died from exsanguination. Gomez spent hours on that autopsy attempting to find another cause of death, but the only cause could be a draining of all of his blood.

I made my own examination but came to the same conclusion.

Two holes in the carotid artery were determined to be the only source of the exsanguination. No trauma, bruising, scratches, or lacerations whatsoever.

Dr. Gomez couldn't believe it. Not even a butcher knife could have drained the blood in such an efficient manner. I spent that first day with him, trying to hash out how those two holes could have drained an entire body of blood in a matter of minutes. Deputy Miller had arrived at the scene not more than an hour before we did, took his report, called it in, and waited for us. It didn't seem possible.

The trace amounts of blood Dr. Gomez and I found on the body bore the same indicators as the samples from the escaped body from the morgue. The sample was sent to Galveston, Texas, and the University of Texas with their level four biosafety lab; it indicated the same structure as the previous sample. However, when studied through an electron micrograph, it showed a mutation of what they identified to be the Marburg virus, a hemorrhagic fever virus considered as serious as Ebola. My supervisors still did not recognize the importance of these findings, yet they ordered me to stay in the field, in the event that other persons reported symptoms indicative of the virus. I could only imagine what my apartment back in Atlanta would look like after another month away from home. And as if on cue, my mom called me, hysterical. "Lauren, thank goodness! What's going on? Why does your apartment look abandoned?" she sputtered. I had asked my sister if she would check on my apartment every few days, but it's never good to ask a twentysomething girl with a new boyfriend to remember anything important.

It was only a matter of a month before more bodies started to show up in Arizona and then New Mexico. All the exsanguinated bodies were accompanied by another person from the same household disappearing. All the dead bodies either had their blood drained or they exhibited the same blood characteristics that the original dead girl—Liza Sole—had in her system.

Liza Sole was a twenty-eight-year-old woman from Dallas, Texas, who worked various retail jobs and went through a few marriages before she decided to return to school to finish her degree at the University of Arizona. That didn't last too long: she met another man and moved to Nogales, Arizona, where she worked at a Pizza Hut. As with many of her previous relationships, this one did not last long, and soon she moved out of his house and rented an apartment with various Craigslist roommates who stayed for short periods of time and then moved on.

Clearly, the CDC should have been more involved, given the growing scope of the virus, but the center was still enthralled by Ebola ravaging Africa and then being carried into the United States by returning health-care professionals and tourists. My blood cell disease was getting no attention, no real funds. I was made the head of the Nogales team a month after the initial event, but "team" was a stretch. It was still just me, filing reports back to Atlanta. No support staff.

I started calling it the Nogales organic blood illness on my field reports. NOBI for short. I had Sheriff Wilson send out an addendum to his APB on Liza Sole that the CDC would like to be informed about any leads or similar cases because of the possibility of illness related to the condition of the suspect.

But I still couldn't get my superiors at the CDC to issue a warning on the disease. A warning would have required the FBI and other federal law enforcement to issue an immediate alert on the spreading disease, and on Liza. A warning would have sent information out to every law enforcement agency in the country. I'm not saying we could have stopped NOBI if that had been the case, but it would have made a huge difference in how far the disease spread before it became a national emergency.

It would have saved lives.

About a month after the initial Liza Sole event, Dr. Gomez took a leave of absence from the Nogales Department of Health to devote himself to my investigation. At his own expense, he followed me to different cities in the Southwest as we tracked the disease and the wake of bodies and those missing. He soon rode with me in the car I rented on the government's tab and was a great help in tracking the people and the virus. And in keeping me company.

In the beginning, we followed Liza's and the disease's trail through Arizona. It felt like a spur-of-the-moment road trip for two college roommates piling all of our random belongings into a compact car. All we were missing was a cooler of cheap beer. Every small town seemed to blend into another, our files growing, our space for clothing shrinking. Ten miles to the next motel and I could hardly wait.

I was beat up and could only drop my bags to the floor as I stared at the motel's rumpled bed. Dr. Gomez—Hector—had long since blown through his budget and was sleeping on the floor of my room. He dropped to the ground and puffed up his thin pillow against the torn wallpaper of the motel. I felt sorry that Nogales County would not pay for his research, and he had to front it all from his savings. His dedication to solving this unfolding crisis, like mine, only grew with adversity.

He looked pretty uncomfortable trying to make the hard floor into a bed. "Hey, Dr. Gomez," I said. He looked up with tired eyes.

"What's up, Dr. Scott?"

I cocked my head at the bed. "First of all, why don't I call you Hector and you call me Lauren? Secondly, you look like crap on the floor. Why don't you sleep on the bed? There's room enough for both of us and I'm pretty sure I can trust you by now. And if not, I'll beat the crap out of you. Pretty sure I could."

He stared for a moment, as if he might not even want to get up from the floor. Maybe he was one of those ascetic individuals, abstaining from any indulgent behavior and preferring to deny himself any comfort.

Hector rose up without a word and flopped down onto the comforter. He flipped onto his side and gripped the pillow like a life preserver. In no time, he was asleep. I lay down on the other side of the bed in all my clothing, and was dreaming of leeches within minutes.

A month in, we had eight confirmed dead, devoid of blood, and ten people missing. The missing people were the most perplexing part of this investigation. I couldn't come up with a plausible theory as to why some people who came in contact with Liza Sole went missing: if they had acquired this virus, wouldn't they be dead after a short time? Did she kidnap them? Did they follow her willingly? Did she kill them and bury them somewhere remote?

But then Liza Sole finally made a mistake, became more than a myth, and every bulletin that we'd sent paid off.

At the time, we had seven dead bodies that were autopsied and found to be devoid of blood. It was almost as if all the blood had been drained and the rest incinerated within the body. Therefore, we could autopsy the body but we couldn't find the most important aspect of the death: the blood, and how it compared to the sample we had from the previously dead Liza Sole.

We received a call from the El Paso police department about

an eighth body, found near the border crossing with Ciudad Juárez, Mexico. A police officer was in his car on patrol near a back alley behind some abandoned warehouses when he saw a person crouched over another body lying on the ground. The officer shined his spotlight on them. The crouched figure jumped up and started to sprint away at great speed. The officer couldn't believe a person could run so fast.

The officer approached the figure on the ground: it was a man with blood spurting from the neck, from his artery. The man on the ground didn't last long enough for the ambulance, but at the morgue a technician remembered the notice from the Nogales police department. When Hector and I arrived, Hector convinced the coroner, an old medical school classmate of his, to let him sit in on the autopsy. He came to the conclusion, based on the postexposure condition of the body and the internal organs, that the body was probably exposed to the same virus as Liza Sole, but for some reason his body could not handle the physical changes.

Of course, we still hadn't determined how Liza Sole carried this virus with no obvious ill effects. I had a disease with a mortality rate, albeit unofficial, of about 50 percent, if not more. A disease that presented with bodies disappearing and others coming back to life after being deceased. And a disease that also drained the blood from the truly deceased bodies.

Dr. Gomez and I had been so busy chasing bodies that I really hadn't had the time to compile thorough statistics. Everything was haphazardly noted in my iPad and Moleskine notebooks, which I lugged to every city, but my notations were weeks behind the current cases. I'm not making excuses for the blame that has been thrust upon me; I'm simply stating facts.

And then. We finally caught a break there in El Paso.

We caught up with Liza Sole.

* * *

Dr. Gomez and I decided to go eat some real Texas Mexican food. Yelp brought us to a place called El Capitan. Supposedly it "didn't get any better!" Of course, it took all my persuasive powers to get Hector out of his room given his monk-like devotion to figuring out Liza Sole's path.

"It's good Mexican food," I said, pushing the door to our motel room open.

"I have work to do," he replied.

I glanced around at the hurricane of files around him. Hector had a pretty thick beard now and he looked to have lost about ten pounds since we started this journey. He sat in his boxers and a dingy T-shirt.

"You seriously want to eat Dairy Queen or McDonald's again? Or maybe there are some new items on the menu at the vending machine." I did the best thing I knew to scare a man: I crossed my arms and channeled my mother. "Seriously: get your fucking clothes on and let's get some Mexican food!"

He stared at me for a moment.

Then he walked over to the bed and grabbed his pants.

Soon enough, we were sitting in a corner booth sipping margaritas and working on chips and salsa. The restaurant was pretty old and worn, with red lights above the tables casting an eerie glow over the booth. The seats' vinyl covers were old and ripped from end to end. We sat in silence, left to our own thoughts while we nursed our drinks and ate greasy chips. My phone buzzed and I answered it before the second vibration. I didn't get a word out before—

"Where have you been?" It was Jennifer. I should have checked the caller ID. I could tell she was looking for an argument.

"I'm on the road, Jenny," I replied. My irritation vanished when I heard her raspy voice. It had been far too long…

"Are you still chasing that bug?"

"Virus," I corrected. "So what's up?" Although I already knew the answer.

"Well…I'm gonna be a little short this month and I was wondering…"

"What was it this month? Music festival?"

Silence on the other end. "Stuff. You know."

"Okay. I'll send you five hundred."

I heard a sigh on the other end. "Thanks. And call Dad. He always complains he never knows where you are."

"I will," I replied. When she hung up, I regretted not calling her more often. I had so much to ask her but never had the time.

Hector looked at me but didn't ask. And I didn't answer. "I wonder when they'll call us with another body," he said.

I thought for a moment while I savored an especially salty chip. "If the pattern proceeds to schedule…probably in two days. That seems to be the routine." I laughed to myself. My dad would be appalled at all the sitting around and thinking. He would demand that I get my hands dirty and grab something real!

"I agree."

"Where do you think it'll be?"

Hector shook his head. "Who knows? Could be anywhere."

My mind raced. "Not anywhere. Somewhere. Has to be somewhere. I mean, all of this is proceeding like a pattern. Let's see if we can figure it out."

Hector ignored his enchilada plate as he tapped his fork on the table. "She doesn't go very far from the last city. Probably hitchhiking or by some other means—God help us if she has a car."

"Exactly. I think we can safely say she's not in El Paso anymore," I declared as I took a big bite of my flauta. The grease dribbled off my chin. Heaven.

"We need a map," he said.

Instinctively we each took out our cell phone and hit Google Maps. "She's not going to Mexico or she would have gone there from Nogales," I said. "I think she's going to stay in the Southwest."

"She's going to stick to towns off major highways. She doesn't have a choice. Carlsbad, Las Cruces, Van Horn. Has to be one of those. But which one?"

I thought for a moment as I sipped on my second margarita. I tried to remember the inventory of Liza Sole's apartment. Papers, receipts, notebooks…The search of her computer history. I slammed my hand on the table. "She's an artist! Or someone interested in art."

Dr. Gomez gave me a sideways look. "So what?"

I leaned over the table toward Hector. "Listen. She's going to a city or area where she feels familiar or interested in…the type of people she wants to meet. She had a list of things she wanted to do that I found on the refrigerator! One of them was to check out the art scene in Marfa, Texas."

"Hmm. Seems tenuous. Very." He stared at the map on his phone as he pointed his finger at the various cities spread out from El Paso. He shook his head before biting off almost half of his enchilada. "But damn. It would be easy for her to get there with minimal effort, and it's off a highway but not a major highway, so it lessens the opportunity to be seen."

Hector looked up and we held our stare for a moment.

* * *

We reached the Marfa Motor Inn as the sun came up. It was cheap enough for Dr. Gomez to have his own room, and we decided to grab some much-needed sleep until noon and then get to work. Of course, noon rolled into three in the afternoon. Angry and muttering to myself, I knocked on his door. He answered with sleep covering his face.

"Seriously. We need to get moving."

Hector nodded. "I know. Sorry. I needed it, though. And I'll bet you did too."

From there we stopped by the local sheriff's office—Sheriff Langston Lamar—to present our credentials and discuss the current situation. He looked to be in his forties and was built like a linebacker. There had not been any suspicious activity or injuries in the past couple of months other than a few bar fights. He told us he did not have the manpower to assign any deputies to the investigation, but if anything came up he would certainly take it seriously. He gave us his cell phone number.

Back at the hotel, we brainstormed various options in Marfa that night. Hector searched his phone. "Okay, so there's an art show, a live country band, and a couple of dinner events in the center of town," he said.

"I think we should start at the art gallery. And then move on to the others if we have the time. She could be at any of them."

We changed our clothes, although neither of us had anything even resembling art opening–wear. Jeans and sweatshirts it would have to be. I put the hazmat suit in the trunk just in case. We walked in the cool night air to the end of the long main street block to the Hi-Times Gallery, a converted gas station from another era, now captive to hipster art patrons. The sun had already fallen away and the gallery was full—I bet the town population doubled at this gallery. The crowd flaunted their beards, flannel, and black garb—cowboy chic—and mingled with drinks in their hands, all but ignoring the art on the walls.

Hector and I kept to ourselves near the door. Every so often we checked a picture of Liza Sole on our phones, as a reminder. The lead was solid—I could feel it. This had to be the place and town. But after an hour and three glasses of wine I began to lose hope. I looked over at Hector. Was he having the same doubts? I saw him glance over at the people and the art, almost ignoring the front door. I knew his doubts were starting to surface. Had we made a huge mistake? What the hell was I still doing on this wild-goose chase…

Then a woman walked in by herself.

She wore a pair of faded and torn Levi's 501 jeans that hugged her hips and legs—and a black turtleneck. It was as if she didn't care that no one wore turtlenecks like that in Texas. An old beat-up tan Stetson cowboy hat was perched on her skull like she had grabbed it off her lover's head as he lay in bed. Scuffed old black punk rock boots completed the image. She looked like a young Patti Smith busking in front of the Chelsea Hotel in seventy-three, screaming mad at society for not conforming to her vision. The hat tilted down about to her nose so it covered her face. My eyes were automatically drawn to her and I saw others in the gallery staring in the same manner.

She had a presence. A tingling in the back of my neck made me shudder. A sweet smell drifted into my nose and only made my thoughts scramble and bounce around in my head. It was like a car accident where you see your life as if in a flip-book of pictures scrolling too fast for you to even catch a memory. It only made me sad.

There was a magnetism I couldn't put into words.

Temptation in human form.

She took measured strides over to the first wall aisle of paintings. The woman made no eye contact with any person, but her gaze—shaded as it was—cut across every occupant as if each were prey. I looked over at Hector and he was transfixed. I mean, he looked like he wanted to devour her. "Take a picture—it'll last longer," I told him with an elbow to his ribs.

He about jumped out of his skin. "Damn! Sorry. I mean, she's a pretty girl. Although I can't really see her face."

I don't know if it was the hat or the face or the fact that the hat covered her face—or simply a vibe. But it clicked. My picture of Liza Sole and this girl were not an exact match—this girl in the gallery was a bit thinner—but I felt my heart beating faster and faster.

I leaned in to Hector. "I think that might be her."

He looked over at me. "Her?" He raised his arm to point. I yanked it down.

"Look at your picture. The nose on down."

Hector clicked on his phone and studied it before leaning over to me. "Fuck!"

I was still distracted but I concentrated. "I'm going to stay here. You go outside and call the sheriff."

"Are you sure?"

"It's her. I'm certain."

"No, I mean are you sure you want to stay here instead of waiting outside?" Hector asked.

I gave him a hard look. He walked outside to call the sheriff.

With the studied focus of a professor, the woman was considering the painting of a white bird in an oak tree with its roots spreading out everywhere under the ground. I was so engrossed trying to see what she found so interesting about the painting...that I didn't notice she had turned away.

She was staring at me.

I caught my breath, even from across the room. All I wanted to do was look into her eyes. It was as if she knew the reason I was there and that I was looking for her.

She moved like a cat. She was lurching toward me before I even realized it. I stepped back but she had already sprinted toward the back of the gallery, to a back room.

The gallery was almost empty save for a few stragglers trying to convince the bartender to open back up. I screamed for Hector as I chased Liza Sole toward the back door. I reached for the handle to the back room, and the door blew open and knocked me to the floor. Liza leapt over me as Sheriff Lamar sprinted inside and drew his Taser. He yelled at her to stop and she did for a moment, baring her teeth like an animal, then she lunged toward the front door of the gallery.

She made it to the front door just as the sheriff yelled a second time for her to stop. Surprisingly, she did, bared her teeth again, and then surged through the doorway.

The Taser wires made contact with her back just as Hector tackled her waist. In a single swiping movement, she swept loose the Taser darts and Hector both, but as she made it outside she was tackled again, now by the sheriff and three deputies.

She scratched and swung, but quickly they were able to cuff her wrists. The sheriff screamed for leg-irons but Liza kicked her heel into his face. All of a sudden, Liza jumped up and spread her legs. The handcuffs snapped off like wet paper. She took off in a sprint into the street, where a large pickup truck immediately hit her head-on.

She bounced off as the truck screeched to a halt, rubber smoke hovering in the air.

We all stood there in shock.

"Another day at the office," the third deputy grumbled.

"Are you taking her to jail?" I asked.

"No, honey, I thought I might take her back to the art gallery," Lamar said.

More of this bullshit. "I meant—"

"I know what you meant," Sheriff Lamar replied. "We have a holding facility in the office until we can get her transferred to Alpine, which has a proper jail, and maybe to El Paso. Pretty sure Arizona will come for her in record time."

"Is it okay if I come with you? I need to make a determination about whether there is a danger from any virus."

Sheriff Lamar shrugged. "You started the show. Feel free to play it out."

The trip to the sheriff's office only took about two minutes. I rode in the front of the police car, with Liza Sole in the back behind the bars. When I glanced back at her, she stared at me with sparkling blue eyes and pale skin. Her lips were bright red even in the darkness of the vehicle, and as she moved her body in and out of the shadows it was almost as if she disappeared and reappeared.

Liza allowed the deputies to walk her into the police station. She showed no signs of violent behavior or resistance. They placed her in a small cell with bars—like from an old western movie. I think Sheriff Lamar sensed my amazement. "Original forged steel," he said. "They don't make them secure like this anymore." Let's hope it's as secure as he claims. A window to the outside sat on the wall opposite the cell, moonlight streaming inside.

Years later, when I was debriefed extensively by a multitude of federal authorities, I would sometimes question my own recollections from that night. For example, I don't know how long I watched Liza in that cell, or when Hector joined me, but I held her eyes for what felt like hours. Liza stared silently back out at us. There was something hypnotic in her movements and eyes. A strange gracefulness in her manner, like a gentle migration from one space to another.

A distinct sense of hopelessness enveloped me in those minutes or hours. But I had to get through all these psychological flashes in my brain—I felt a certain responsibility to understand this person, in spite of my fear. I felt that the prison bars were a mere curtain that Liza could push aside with a wave of her hand. An hour, maybe more, passed.

"How do you feel?" I asked her with a cracking voice.

Silence.

Then: "I feel awesome."

I didn't expect that answer with such a blank face.

"I only ask because I believe you have acquired a new type of virus into your system and you may begin to exhibit symptoms."

Silence.

And she never said another word to me.

Even today, I can recall the feeling of something attempting to put thoughts in my mind or look into my consciousness. The Nogales organic blood illness, we now know, reached each victim or recipient through a previously unknown virion attached to specific cell-surface receptors—such as C-type lectins, DC-SIGN, or integrins. The virus then entered by fusion of the viral envelope with cellular membranes. Even their virions had a mind of their own. So those affected with the virus, essentially, could tap into a consciousness on even a cellular level.

But that night, I, and eventually Hector, simply watched her through the bars in amazement. Finally, Sheriff Lamar pulled us away. The FBI and federal marshals would be arriving soon to transport her back to Arizona, and he urged us to catch a nap in his office.

I don't know how long I slept. I may have dreamt of people stoning me for transgressions, like waking up late for class, forgetting the answers on my medical boards, not sending my mother a birthday card, or not lending my sister five dollars.

What woke me was the most vengeful shriek I had ever heard. Animalistic—like something from a bad sci-fi movie.

Liza Sole sat in the corner of her cell, screaming, as her arm and part of her face emanated smoke. Were they...burning? The skin almost dripped off her face. I thought it might be some type of dermatitis or eczema, a by-product of the blood disorder, until I realized the window across her cell—

"The sun," I whispered to Hector.

Given my credentials, the Feds graciously allowed me to ride along in the helicopter. Hector said he would meet me at the hospital.

It was a longer trip to the university medical center than I would have liked. Liza had screamed like a trapped animal the entire helicopter ride, and when we landed on the hospital's roof, the doctor administered a sedative as the nurses rolled her gurney across the roof in the morning light.

Liza still screamed.

When I met Dr. Jenkins, the hospital's burn specialist, near the quarantine ward, she shook her shoulders in exasperation. "I have no idea what this is. Her blood has certain attributes that shouldn't fit, but that's not my expertise. It appears to have been a significant allergic reaction to exposure to the sun, but the molecular composition of this reaction needs to be studied."

"Is she any better?" I asked.

"She's stabilized. We have her in a windowless room with soft lighting. It doesn't help that there are police everywhere, but she's still in intensive care. We've just got to wait."

I nodded. "I need to get a sample of her blood."

"We have that for you."

As I sat in the cafeteria making calls to the University of Texas at El Paso to get a team together, I saw cameras and reporters descending on the hospital outside. My phone buzzed with a blast of emails: similar cases of dead bodies with the same carotid wounds had spiked in the last few days. The NOBI virus, it seemed, had finally made it to the top of the CDC agenda.

But that didn't mean that my efforts were being recognized or encouraged. My research was disputed and questioned down to every minute detail. Some scientists insisted that the bite marks were in fact made from a needle and a syringe. Others insisted that there was no new virus—the conditions were simply circumstances and consequences of environmental factors related to injuries from various assaults. And others felt that any possible virus was so limited in the apparent infection rate that it didn't warrant any expenditures of funds.

I was on my third cup of coffee when Hector shuffled into the hospital cafeteria looking worse than myself. I glanced down after hearing another buzz from an email. This one was from my supervisor at the CDC. I read it three times in the time it took Hector to make it to the table.

He collapsed into the Formica chair. "So what's the verdict?"

I wanted to laugh. The email seemed to confirm my madness, and I didn't know if that was a good or bad thing, but I knew it would change my life forever.

And it has. My old man also used to say, "I'd be ahead by now if I could quit while I'm behind." I thought about that a lot as, for many years, we searched for the Nogales organic blood illness cure. We'll never know how or why Liza Sole ended up at that mass grave site on the border. No one knew where the bodies went or who retrieved them. But I always suspected they were somewhere out there, re-created for some purpose. And in spite of the many accusations that my work was unethical, I believe my work had—still has—merit.

That day, I sat in the hospital cafeteria and gave Hector a sad smile.

I handed him my phone, so he could read the email too. I said, "I think we found the first vampire."

I needed to see Liza Sole one more time before I went back to Atlanta. If only to monitor her condition and make certain observations—or more likely to see if I could look into her eyes and have a conversation without my mind becoming fractured. As a scientist, I needed more time with this subject—the most important carrier of this virus.

I took the elevator up to the third floor, and as the doors parted, a scream and crash rolled down the hallway. I brushed against the tide of people running away from the drama. I tripped into the room in time to see Liza Sole launch herself into the closed window and fall out with a hail of glass shards and onto the pavement below.

I suppose it was a stroke of luck that I arrived a few moments after the sun went down, because that was when Liza Sole broke out of her restraints and killed two federal marshals and one nurse, before breaking the window and leaping silently from her third-story room onto the pavement.

She was never seen again and still remains on the FBI's ten-most-wanted list.

But I had her blood.

Boston Herald

July 19[2]: Early this morning, in the South End historic district, the Ellison Corporation, an independent gold distributor for the Northeast, was robbed of over $5 million worth of gold bullion. The Ellison Corporation traded in other precious metals but most of those were kept on the first floor—the gold was kept exclusively in the basement. The FBI has determined that the surveillance systems of the building were disabled and other surveillance cameras on the block malfunctioned with no usable video made available. The two guards on duty were incapacitated by unknown means, rendering them unconscious. The FBI has no current leads on the perpetrators.

---

[2] Page 2, Metro section.

CHAPTER 2

Father John Reilly
Ordained Catholic Priest and Jesuit

Department of Defense—DIRECTIVE:

SUBJECT: High-Value Detainee Interrogation Group interview with Father John Reilly

Detainee was captured in **REDACTED** by agents of the Federal Bureau of Investigation. Detainee was transferred to a holding facility at **REDACTED**. After four days, interviewed by the High-Value Detainee Interrogation Group.

Detainee was not subject to extraordinary conditions before his interview.

Transcript tracks with video recording.

Interviewer is a younger man with Gucci joggers and a gold bomber jacket with a black snapback cap. He chews gum at a rapid pace in between puffs on a cigarette.

Detainee is a man in his early thirties without any visible signs of nervousness.

Interviewer: Are you comfortable? Coffee? If you need a bathroom break let us know. We're not here to waterboard you or anything. That's not funny, is it? **[Pause. Loudly.]** Let it be known that the subject shook his head in dissent.

Interviewer takes a drink of water.

Father Reilly: Actually, if you're not too busy, maybe you can start a GoFundMe page for me. Kinda like, "Save me from getting tortured by the U.S. government."

Interviewer: That's hilarious. So, how are you feeling?

Father Reilly: Well, if every Shakespeare tragedy has five acts, let's just say I'm probably sitting here in act five. I used to think of Shakespeare as more of God's word than the Bible, but then I realized Shakespeare's work was just better made.

Interviewer claps!

Interviewer: I feel that! Okay, so the bad thing for you is you weren't exactly caught on American soil. That makes you subject to extraterritorial measures. Let me break it down to you this way. These men sitting and standing in front of you are from the High-Value Detainee Interrogation Group. They have put together a plan for our interrogation. It's what they do. I will carry out that plan. It's what I do.

Father Reilly: Shouldn't I be read my rights? I mean, for appearances.

Interviewer: We have an emergency exception due to extraordinary circumstances—a "public safety" exception to Miranda. Members of the task force have not yet decided whether to assign your status as an "enemy combatant." I'll give you the quick history lesson. Under the Geneva convention guidelines—

Father Reilly: Yes, yes. I know all that.

Interviewer: Then needless to say, you don't prefer that option. Agreed? **[Pause.]** Good. Let it be known again that subject nodded in assent. Why don't you start by telling me what brought you to the priesthood?

Father Reilly: Okay. Yes. I never entertained thoughts of becoming a priest when I was growing up. My hometown was pretty small, and kind of backwards—at least to a teenager. "The kind of place where people still point at planes," my sister used to say before she left for college. Or the kind of place where directions were given through local landmarks: "Take a right at the third Olive Garden, then a left at the Red Lobster." You get the idea.

My parents were Catholics but never whipped a heavy hand when it came to religion. We were expected to make our sacraments of baptism and confirmation, but to be honest, I think it was enough for them that we never got arrested or hooked on drugs.

I never had friends growing up. It sounds kind of offhand when I say that, but it was true. Literally. No. Friends. I wasn't what is now called Asperger's, but I was certainly diagnosed many times during my childhood as a loner. I spent years in waiting rooms of doctors' offices with their medicinal scent, uncomfortably hard couches, and stale music. Answering a series of questions. Waiting on the examination table with the disposable, thin, and crinkled sheet. Then watching the doctor explain the diagnosis to my mother as she nodded in agreement.

I had "a distinct detachment from social interconnections," with the exception of close family members. As well as "a confined range of exposition of emotions in interpersonal settings." In layman's terms, I hated people—solo and in groups.

Interviewer: You know, at a party, someone might call that a sob story.

Father Reilly: Don't feel badly. I actually developed a pretty elaborate fantasy life. I could sit outside on the driveway with my comic books and become any superhero I wanted to be. Or lie on my back in the front yard, count every star, and blast off into space. I liked it that way—all by myself.

Perhaps I never thought to feel badly for myself, because of my father: he had a pretty hard time of life, and it was sort of the defining aspect of our family.

Interviewer: What do you mean?

Father Reilly: He was born with an extremely large jaw and eyebrow ridge as part of his acromegaly illness—where the anterior pituitary gland produces excess growth hormone. Sort of like gigantism. Not only was his face aggressively distinctive, but he was so tall. You couldn't miss him if you tried. As a result, he had a perpetual cloud of low self-esteem that seemed to follow him through every encounter. I didn't realize this for many years. As a kid, he was just my big dad. But as I got older, I saw that any event that required him to leave the house became a stressful circumstance. Even for simple excursions to the grocery store or my baseball games, his anxiety permeated our house for days before and after. He found solace in his garage work space and playing with us in the backyard behind our tall privacy fence.

My father was almost like a monk in his religious devotion—I suppose he thought he could cure his afflictions with prayer, or more likely, he preferred to spend his days at church or at home, to avoid being in public. He began to save money to make a pilgrimage to a shrine in France. There, my dad was certain he would be granted a cure. My dad would take me with him as we went in his truck to pick up junk and scrap metal from different neighborhoods. No matter the heat, we dug through boxes and garbage bags, slime covering our hands, gagging from the smell of rot.

We took what we could find and held a garage sale every Saturday. Our neighbors soon loathed us, although they were too nice—or just felt sorry for my dad—to complain to the police about it. It took forever to accumulate even close to enough money for the pilgrimage. Even then, he ended up having to sell his truck.

So on a warm June day, we all boarded a plane for France—specifically Rocamadour, in southwest France, where the shrine to the blessed Virgin Mary was located. The shrine of Our Lady of Rocamadour.

The church and shrine were located high up on a plateau of a jagged mountain with the basilica built up against a cliff that overlooked the Alzou, a tributary of the Dordogne River. We stayed at a hostel in the Hospitalet village closest to Rocamadour. The next morning, as the sun rose, we made our way to the main street of the village and to the Place de la Caretta. My father stopped in front of the steps that led up to the shrine.

Interviewer: You've stopped. Was that it?

Father Reilly: No. This is difficult.

At last my father said, "You all go ahead."

"What do you mean?" my mom asked. "What are you going to do?" I still recall her fearful expression.

"I'm going up the steps like you but I'm going on my knees while praying the rosary."

Me, my mom, and my sister all looked at him as if he had lost his mind. "Richard," my mom said. "You can't do that. There have to be, like, five hundred steps. You're in no shape to do that, much less in this heat."

"I'm doing it," he said. He wasn't going to give this up, even if he ended up in the hospital.

So my mom pivoted to make a bad situation better. She pointed to me. "Johnny, you and your sister go find a store.

Buy ten bottles of water and some healthy snacks and bring them back here. We need to keep your dad hydrated."

It was hard to watch, but certainly even harder for him to do. Two hundred and sixteen steps to the top. Each step he took on his knees with the pocked and uneven granite that dug into his skin and radiated through his entire body up his spine. Ready to give penance with despair on each step. Twice he leaned over as if he were going to collapse or fall back down the stairs, and we rushed to hold him up. Mom didn't ask him to quit, but after a hundred steps I was certain he would not make it to the top. I saw the blood seeping through his pants at the knees. His enlarged face twisted in agony. His spine curved to dissipate the needles that poked through his back.

But he kept going.

Interviewer: Did he make it?

Father Reilly: I don't know if it was the hand of God, but something led him up those stairs. At various points along the route were the fourteen Stations of the Cross, with the cross of Jerusalem staring down from the top of the stairs. With ten steps to go, his hand that held the rosary cramped like a bushel of tree branches after a lightning strike. He crawled on his hands and knees, sweat soaked through his pants and shirt.

He took the last step with a slight grunt—the only time I heard him make a sound during the hours of crawling. I didn't know if it was a cry of pain or accomplishment.

He sat at the top of the stairs staring up into the sky, as if he saw something no one else could. We sat next to him and wrapped him in a hug. I felt exhausted, like I had also climbed the steps.

Even then, he wanted to visit each of the seven churches located at the top. And then, as we helped my dad stand upright, we walked inside the Chapel of Our Lady towards the smell of candles and incense. We knelt before the Black Madonna and even I could feel something inside my body, like a tingling. Something inside of me wanting to be let out.

I was so happy he had made it. I did not think he could, but he did. I felt the tears fall down my face and I prayed—it was the first time I had ever truly prayed. I wanted this feeling to last forever. When we returned home, nothing about my father's condition had improved and I would eventually go back to skateboards and surfboards as my saviors. But that day before the Black Madonna, as I prayed with my father, it would have taken an army of a thousand to pull me away.

Interviewer: Okay, jump forward a bit here. Let's go to college.

Father Reilly: I discovered a newfound interest in the church when I left for college. Well, truth be told, I discovered a newfound interest in a girl, and she sparked my interest in the church again. She was God's conduit.

Christine and I dated my senior year at UCLA. She was my first serious girlfriend, after a long series of bad dates and one-night stands. She was tall and lanky, with brown hair and cute dimples that radiated when she decided to throw a smile my way. Christine seemed to accept and even enjoy our long silences together. And oddly enough, the more silence she gave me the more I wanted to open up and actually engage her in a conversation. She was the first non-family member I could do that with. Christine was a Catholic who attended mass on a regular basis, but I was more of a once-a-month attendee if we had decided to go to brunch that day too.

One day Christine mentioned we should go to midnight mass on Christmas Eve. It's a long mass and I'm not saying I was overcome with the Holy Spirit or something like out of a movie, but I enjoyed the mass and the ceremony— the incense and chanting, the whole spectacle of it all. The things that stir the soul and mind of any Catholic. They were the same feelings that had overcome me in Rocamadour. The next week, I was the one who suggested we attend mass. After that, I returned to church again and again—and eventually I started attending the student ministry and I felt I had found a purpose. Like I had returned home from a long banishment.

And then my father died.

He had endured two transsphenoidal surgeries through his nasal cavity, after a round of growth hormone receptor antagonists had no appreciable effect on his condition. Neither procedure lowered his GH levels in any way. While recovering from his latest surgery, he acquired meningitis and died almost immediately.

I was devastated. What kind of life would place such burdens on one person?

As graduation day came closer, I began to think where life would lead me after college. Christine seemed obsessed with business school applications, but we never talked about plans if she left town. The prospect didn't bother me all that much. And one day, when I was about to leave the parish office, I saw Father Thompson changing into his daily mass attire, donning his clerical shirt and placing his white collar. And in that moment I saw myself doing the same thing. Perhaps in some way I could continue the long periods of prayer that my father had begun and construct it all into something substantial.

I took to spending time at the Dominican School of Philosophy and Theology—the seminary for Catholic priests about fifty miles from where I lived at the time. As I grew more interested in the priesthood, my relationship with Christine suffered; I was spending all of my time at the seminary and none with her. One day she wrote me an email: she reminded me I once told her I'd had enough of drama in my life. Apparently, she continued, I loved drama and could never own up to my part in it. So much for staying friends.

I became a candidate and entered the seminary. I completed my seminary education early, after three years, received the sacrament of Holy Orders, and became a priest. But then my religious life took a definite alternate route. I decided to become a Jesuit.

Interviewer: I think I need another cigarette. Tell me about the Jesuits.

Father Reilly: As you wish. A better explanation about the Society of Jesus, as it is called, is in order here. It is a Catholic congregation—a society within the church that conducts ministry work. It was founded by Saint Ignatius and approved by Pope Paul III in 1540. So it's been around awhile, you could say. We took vows of poverty, chastity, and obedience. Within the Catholic Church, Jesuits have always been a source of controversy and suspicion. We are referred sometimes derogatorily as the Soldiers of God. We've been linked to assassinations, violence, coup attempts, and other political intrigue. We've also been accused of outright lies and moral ambiguity in reasoning to justify our goals. There has always been a conflict between the Jesuits and the Holy See—the Pope and his bureaucracy—but we've always wanted what is best for the church.

Interviewer: So you say.

Father Reilly: So *we* say. Anyway, my mother and sister were somewhat stunned that I actually took the plunge. I think they both thought that my life would be lived in the basement of the house, and they counted the days until I took my vows, wondering if I would change my mind. During my regency—where I was sent to live among a Jesuit community—I was directed to Santiago, Chile, so that I could minister to and teach the community. It was a wonderful time in a beautiful country; I was particularly drawn to the community of cloistered monks who spent contemplative hours away from modern civilization, praying in their locked monastic cells with only a small bed, a wooden altar, and a kneeler. In Chile, I felt satisfied and happy with my new life. When my mother visited me, she seemed pleasantly surprised at my work ethic and this new lifestyle.

Interviewer: That's lovely but let's not get off track. How did you make it up the ranks?

Father Reilly: In my free time, I learned Excel and used it to reorganize finances and administrative duties, which caught the eye of many supervisors, including cardinals, who tended to avoid administration as if it were sacrilegious. There was a definite need in the Catholic Church for a priest who could make the trains run on time, and I developed a reputation as a sharp and capable administrator. When you combine that with my complete disregard for tact when confronting someone with inefficiency, I was the point man for many a crisis.

I was assigned to the State Council, a significant part of the Vatican organization, which was considered an underrated promotion. After a period of time at the council, I was moved to the Department of Health. The spectacle of Rome and Italy was wonderful, especially for a young man who wanted to avoid personal interactions. I could always retreat to the Vatican gardens or the many secluded prayer rooms hidden in the vast structures on the grounds.

Around the same time, my mother was diagnosed with breast cancer, and after she collapsed in front of her car leaving her first chemotherapy treatment, I knew it was time to go back home. So I was in the U.S. when the evil was unearthed. That sounds so melodramatic and discriminatory but it is the truth.

My mom always wanted me to watch Dancing with the Stars with her on the couch, and although I despised television in all forms, I knew she looked forward to this time with me so she could tell me her critiques of the dancers' abilities and their garish outfits. Then we always turned to the news, and we were watching one night when the CDC made the announcement about the new virus—they called it a virus at first. I know people want to forget that, but it's not a condition that simply appeared by happy magic.

Interviewer: So by now the NOBI virus was becoming more well known.

Father Reilly: True. Amongst this backdrop of a new species appearing, my mom's condition stabilized. She needed my help less and less. I began to think of where my next assignment might take me when I saw on BuzzFeed a long-form article about a string of deaths and disappearances linked to a woman named Liza Sole. After that, the New York Times broke an exclusive story about a new virus carried by the same Liza Sole, and I realized this new virus had mutated into something distinctly more sinister.

The rest of the media picked up the story of the virus as some sort of new Ebola. But soon it became a story about how many more people had contracted this virus. The press was calling it the Nogales organic blood illness [NOBI]— and then Twitter and Facebook took over. NOBI became an avalanche of fear and hysteria. Many fake news stories filled Twitter and Facebook, proclaiming this disease would turn people into bloodsucking zombies or large human bats. In those early days, it was ridiculous how many people called 911 to report a feeding vampire. I would visit a local Chipotle every so often and I overheard people exchanging conspiracy theories about the NOBI virus.

Every day that I cared for my mother and her cancer was another day the doctors released more information about Liza Sole. Every day it became clear this virus was not killing her but making her stronger—and different. Something—some part human or not human at all. And when she disappeared, other people came forward as carriers of this virus. A few "normal" people at first, then the 1 percent: celebrities who wanted that long life and those enhanced abilities. TMZ first published the files of a doctor attesting to their enhanced physical capacity, and various YouTube videos emerged showing various re-created persons breaking the one-hundred-meter world record of 9.58 seconds. Another showed a mildly muscular fifty-year-old NOBI-infected man breaking the raw-bench-press record by lifting over 780 pounds.

I think when Taylor Swift re-created, that's when it truly hit everyone. The *New York Times* reported that she was re-created by the only known child carrying the virus, a white-haired ten-year-old hermit named Herjólfur Vilhjalmsson, at the lava fields which fed into a lagoon in Grindavík, Iceland. Herjólfur never conducted an unsuccessful re-creation; however, he was extremely selective as to whom he would choose.

Interviewer: Oh, I know you and the order have been after Herjólfur for a long time now.

Father Reilly: Let's stay on track, shall we?

Interviewer laughs.

Father Reilly: NOBI became something *desirable*. A cultural earthquake hit the Internet and soon everyone wanted to be "re-created"—a term I sincerely disliked. Why should we be re-created? They were no different from all of us—they sought the gratification of two- or three-hundred-year lives. They became the top of the social status. Every hedge fund manager and tech billionaire wanted to become re-created and join that status and secret society where you could live for over two hundred to three hundred years. This facet of NOBI pathology was discovered when a body was found in a shallow grave near the Nogales, Arizona, field where Liza Sole was found. An examination determined that the corpse shared the identical NOBI virus DNA and that the body was between two hundred and three hundred years old. Not forever, but long enough to live many lifetimes. And to have the physical and mental prowess of a god—I'm certain it was beguiling to have that opportunity.

I mean, look: at the beginning we were all amazed and mystified. Even I was fascinated by this novel disorder—there were so many articles and blogs and news stories about these different people. They would show up at all the major sports events: the Super Bowl, the NBA championship, the World Series, and the World Cup. I remember being in Europe for the European Society for Catholic Theology, and taking a trip to the Premier League soccer championship at Holloway borough in London to see the evening match between Arsenal and Chelsea, and there were a group of Gloamings, although the term had not been used yet, wearing the distinctive red-and-white-striped scarves of the Arsenal colors. They were mobbed like movie stars.

Many writers began to call them a new species of human, if that made any sense. I was certainly willing to give them the benefit of the doubt as afflicted people. There was an international wave of interest and optimism with the introduction of these modern people. Intellectuals and commentators wondered how they would integrate into society—would they be allowed to participate in amateur or professional sports given their enhanced physical attributes? Given their attributes and the length of their lives, would they be the perfect space explorers? Would these people lead to even more advances for our continuously changing society?

My first thought was that God had created something incredible from a harmful virus. Reading about the physically enhanced, I could think of Lazarus of Bethany, who was raised from the dead. Or Moses parting the Red Sea. Was this another miracle humanity was privileged to witness?

Interviewer: So let's get to the part where you started to...feel yourself a bit. Taste the shadow aspect of your personality, if I may get all Jungian on you.

Father Reilly: About the same time the Liza Sole situation was unfolding and she was once again on the run, I received an email from one of my fellow priests—Father Mark Rogers; we were assigned to the same department in Chile—asking me if I was interested in joining him in Rome for a new position: custodian of the Vatican Library. My mother was in remission and encouraged me to consider the job. So I accepted.

The day I arrived at the main plaza of the Vatican was exhilarating. Isn't it always the return trip where you see everything so much more clearly? Everything so richly hued—like an overexposed photograph. To walk through the acres of arches and granite lined with frescoes of scenes from the Bible. Cobbled roads and sidewalks from another time slanted and skewed with every step. Each corner might bring a different smell: from lilacs to gardenias to incense to candles. The beautiful frescoes on the walls closest to the gardens spread across the thirty-foot-high walls that depicted the shipwreck of Saint Paul in Malta. The massive piers that extended from the dome like arms of a spider that became stone. I could find myself deep in prayer staring at the floor in the atrium of the Vatican Library, where painted into the floor were circles with the names of the winds: tramontane, sirocco, ostro. The miles of naves and hallways covered in murals which always caught my eye. I always seemed to find something different in each scene every time I studied them. The library—the *Biblioteca Apostolica Vaticana*—sat inside the Vatican Palace. The entrance was through the Belvedere Courtyard, with its fifth-century triumphal arch and view of the other side of the Tiber River. Amazingly, the library had over twenty-five miles of shelving, both modern and antique, wood and iron. The wonderful smell of paper and parchment wafted through every corridor.

The head of the library was the cardinal librarian and archivist of the Holy Roman Church with two prelates below him: the prefect of the Vatican Apostolic Library and the prefect of the Vatican Secret Archives. Below them were two vice prefects, who assisted in their duties. And below them were the custodians. I should have done a bit more research into the actual job, I realized, as my excitement turned secretly to despair, upon realizing I had accepted a job that was essentially on the lowest rung of the library: an assistant to the assistant to the curator.

But I was in Rome! And by the time I arrived back at the Vatican, people were congratulating me for making it out of America before catching the NOBI virus. Guess it's all a matter of perspective. If you'd care to loan me some perspective that would be nice.

Anyway, little did we know, NOBI had already hopped over to Europe and Asia well before I returned.

People magazine, March 29

**A father's search for a cure to his daughter's cancer
leads him to a Gloaming—and lifesaving blood.**

Robert Allen had watched his eight-year-old daughter, Jennifer—a
precocious girl with a toothy smile—suffer with multiple myeloma,
a cancer of her plasma cells. He held her as her bones ached
from an unimaginable pain and fractures caused by the marrow
weakening. Her shortage of red blood cells caused Jennifer to lose
breath from even the smallest activity.

"It was day after day of despair and stress for her," Robert told
PEOPLE in March. "She was always outside playing in nature and
discovering plants and insects. But when her condition worsened,
she was bedridden. You could see the longing to be outside when
all she could do was stare out a window. And even that took
immense effort."

Robert took his daughter to Dr. Travis McCauly of the newly
constructed Rio Grande Institute in Albuquerque—a medical
research facility primarily dedicated to the particular health issues
of Gloamings. The Institute had made great strides in blood
research as a result of the NOBI virus and its side effects. Dr.
McCauly had recently modified certain blood cells infected with
the NOBI virus but had rendered it inert. In other words, it kept all
of the properties that encompass the NOBI virus except it wouldn't
turn a person into a Gloaming.

"I always felt that this discovery had the capacity to save lives,"
Dr. McCauly said. "It was just a matter of finding the right fit."

Numerous Gloamings donated blood to help with Jennifer's
condition, going so far as to organize nighttime blood drives at the

underground Madras House center for Gloamings to find a match for Jennifer's specific blood type. These parties even included a performance from *Spring Awakening,* performed by Cian Clery!

Dr. McCauly constructed a proprietary inoculation of the NOBI blood and administered it into Jennifer's bone marrow and blood. Within five months Jennifer's cancer had gone into remission. Now she spends all of her days outside, studying and discovering nature and living like a normal eight-year-old should. "I'm going to be a scientist for nature and also run an animal shelter," Jennifer told PEOPLE in between bites of ice cream—a dessert she wasn't able to enjoy when sick.

"The Gloamings saved her life," Robert told PEOPLE as he held his daughter in his arms. "I'll never forget that. And neither will she."

CHAPTER 3

FEBRUARY 10
NINE MONTHS AFTER THE NOBI DISCOVERY

Dr. Lauren Scott
Research Physician, Centers for Disease Control

I heard a faint tap on the APR window seal and my earpiece buzzed, which let me know someone had entered the lab extension. I placed the containers back into the biosafety case and unhooked myself from the positive pressure suit. I sprayed my gloved hands with disinfectant before walking into the chemical shower container, which sprayed the suit and then automatically air-dried the exterior. I had been viewing the few slides of old NOBI blood samples that had not degraded, comparing them to computer models associated with degradation and differential, and platelet count with coagulation testing, specifically prothrombin time. Normally these samples would have been sent to and reviewed solely at the Integrated Research Facility at Fort Detrick in Maryland, or at the National Institutes of Health in Bethesda, but I received permission to conduct my research here at the CDC headquarters. I removed the suit and disinfected the inside of the face shield before hanging it up on the hooks outside the shower area. I put on my pants and T-shirt before stepping into the buffer area.

After being prompted by the mainframe computer, the air-locked door opened and I stepped into the buffer corridor, where the pre-filtered air supply swept past my entire body. The computer system green light signaled I was cleared to leave the buffer area. The CDC headquarters in Atlanta was freezing as usual, and I had forgotten my sweater in the car, so I could feel the chills run down my spine.

Michael Spence, the CDC's congressional liaison, stood against a bookshelf with his ever-present bow tie and happy demeanor. I already knew this couldn't be good.

"Hey, Lauren," Michael said. He was rocking back and forth, as usual.

"Michael. I suppose you're here for a good reason. I know you haven't liked this floor ever since the time you thought you caught botulism from sitting on a chair."

Michael scrunched up his face. "Not a memory I want to revisit, thank you. I still maintain I have some latent botulism cells in my blood, but the CDC refuses to test me for it."

I turned away from the screen to glance at him. "You never know…"

Michael smiled. "Trying to give me more nightmares, I see. Well, I *am* here for a pretty good reason. A congressional committee has requested that a CDC representative appear before a hearing about the NOBI virus."

I nodded and stretched my torso after being hunched over for what could have been hours. "Okay. Who's giving the testimony? I'll brief them on all pertinent matters regarding the virus."

Michael stared at me for a moment before breaking into another smile. "Want to know who the director has chosen?"

"Sure."

He stood taller, as if preparing to recite: "Lauren Scott will be testifying before the U.S. House of Representatives Committee on Homeland Security."

My face flushed. "Oh no. That's not possible. I'm certainly not qualified or experienced enough to—"

Michael took a seat next to me, though judging by the look on his face, he instantly regretted it, given his previous botulism scare. "Sorry, Miss Scott, but the director requested you. I mean, you know more about this than anyone. It'll be a good experience."

I could only nod as my stomach burbled. I dreaded any kind of public speaking, especially when there was a strong possibility of cameras and media involved. The hearing was scheduled for this Thursday— so much for any time to prepare.

Representatives from the majority and minority committee contacted me and were helpful in advising as to what questions the members would want answered. The CDC liaison staff also prepped me for what I could expect.

I called my dad every single night before leaving Atlanta. He tried to lend me some comforting words but I felt like I was intruding on his college basketball binge. When I reminded him the testimony was in Washington, DC, he said, "If you can make it there you can make it anywhere."

"Dad, I'm pretty sure that's New York."

"Uh-huh. That's right," he said.

In DC, I spent a restless night in a ridiculously fancy hotel room—paid for by the government. I woke up early, paced the room, and tried to calm myself. "*Fuck!*" I rose up on my toes and took a deep breath. My attempt at meditation lasted about ten seconds before my mind was assaulted by an army of nervous thoughts. It was nearly time to leave. Running late, as usual, I was gathering my papers, knowing the taxi would be at the hotel entrance within minutes, when I heard a knock. *Why are they early?* I thought as I opened the door.

My sister stood there with a big smile.

"Oh my God—Jenny! What are you doing here? I mean, I'm glad you're here." I stepped aside, flustered, so she could come inside. I grabbed her in a hug. It had been nearly a year since I had seen my family. I just wanted to sit her down, ask her about her life and school and boyfriends, but I didn't have the time. Just like her to pop up at the most inopportune moment. I was struck with an intense sadness.

"Daddy told me you were here to talk to Congress—Congress!— and I was in Philadelphia for the weekend to visit Hannah and Eleanor—they're on an acoustic tour of the Northeast. So I thought I would come see you."

We sat down on the bed. "I have a few minutes before the driver gets here," I said. "So what are—"

"Why do you hate the Gloamings?" She couldn't look at me for a moment but then raised her face with a pained expression.

My mind went blank for a second. Jenny leaned forward. Her face looked grave and taut.

"What…Why would you ask me that?" I replied.

"Because it's distressing. You're prejudiced against a whole segment of our population."

I stood up. "Why are you bringing this up now? We haven't seen each other in months."

"It's just been on my mind for a while. I've seen all these articles about you. It all seems so hateful. I've met some Gloamings and they're great people." Jenny's face softened a bit.

Something in her words struck me as odd. "Did someone put you up to this?" I asked. "Did they get to you?"

I had practically raised Jenny. I could spot her every lie and anxious facial tic. Now, her face betrayed her. "No," she replied, "I…A few of them, friends, asked me to only see why you hated them so much. That's all. I know you're not really like that."

I grabbed her in another hug. Now wasn't the time to get angry. "Jenny, you have to be careful. They're dangerous. I've seen their violence up close. You haven't. They only have their own interests at heart. They will use you—"

"No they won't, Lauren! They deserve to have a life just like anyone else—like any other human." She broke away and walked over to the window, pointing at the Capitol dome in the distance. "Those people should be protecting them, not trying to tear them down. That's not what we're about. You know that."

She was hurt, racked. I had to back off. I placed my hand on her arm. "I know. Just be careful."

I kissed her goodbye. We left each other in a cordial truce, and as I sat in the taxi I tried to concentrate on my testimony. But all I wanted to do was go back, find my sister, and never let her go.

I left still stressed from my encounter with Jenny and arrived at the Capitol at about nine in the morning. One of the majority staff members greeted me at the entrance and walked me to the ornate but small waiting room for the committee. "Make yourself comfortable," he said, and vanished.

The room was well stocked with refreshments and snacks. I nursed a cup of coffee but couldn't bring myself to take more than a sip. What if I had to pee during the hearing? All I needed was one more thing to worry about. I tried to console myself by thinking this couldn't be as difficult or dangerous as chasing homicidal Gloamings across the Southwest. It didn't work.

After a couple of minutes, the door opened. A tall, distinguished-looking man with a head of close-cropped gray hair walked in. Something about his manner told me he had walked these halls many times before. I straightened my jacket as I extended my hand—

I was struck by his powdery scent. It assaulted my nostrils—familiar, but my mind was incapable of summoning the exact memory. Strangely, I felt as if I were a flower waiting to be pollinated by this man standing before me.

"Hi," I said. "I'm Dr. Lauren Scott."

The man did not shake my hand. He pointed at a chair and sat in the one opposite. His eyes were green, as if carved from a perfect stone. Was everyone on the congressional staff this rude?

I sat and took a deep breath, but that only made my head swim more.

"Can I speak to you for a moment, Dr. Scott?"

"Yes," I answered. "May I ask who you are?"

He ignored my question. "I want to talk about your testimony today."

"What about it?"

"I would like you to reconsider some of your conclusions. I've read your report and your testimony notes and—"

I rose up from my seat. "I'm sorry. How did you get ahold of my testimony notes?"

The man put a hand up as if that would keep me quiet. He also ignored my question. "I represent a few entities with an interest in seeing that the NOBI virus and those that carry the virus aren't slandered or subjected to undue suspicion. It's a reasonable request, I believe." He placed a folder on the empty chair. "We made some corrections to your testimony notes and we would like you to use them when answering any questions."

I could not believe what was happening. Was this man out of his mind? "Are you out of your mind? Who do you represent?"

The man stood up and smoothed out his expensive tie. "It's for the best. Just take the folder."

The man opened the door as one of the congressional aides entered the room. "Oh, good morning, Senator," the aide said with a practiced smile on his face. "Great to see you again."

The senator said nothing but nodded and left.

The aide turned to me with a smile and clapped his hands. "So! Five-minute warning. Ready?"

"I am," I answered, though I was feeling shaky. "Who was that man that left the room?"

"Oh, that's Senator Guy Bale—he was a senator from Wisconsin for a couple of terms. He's a big-time lobbyist now."

I could only nod, and soon I walked out of the room and was led toward the hearing area. With only minutes to go before the hearing began, I knew my testimony would not change, but it still worried me.

That was my second encounter with a Gloaming.

CHAPTER 4

Father John Reilly
Ordained Catholic Priest and Jesuit

The interviewer, a larger man wearing a bucket cap and a five-pocket vest, sits on a creaky metal folding chair in the center of a cramped office. He shifts position but appears unable to find comfort.

Interviewer: Are you ready, Father Reilly?

Father Reilly: Are we in Montana? Did you just come from a fishing trip?

Interviewer: How original. Hadn't heard that one before, although most of my subjects would contend I only have a passing familiarity with humor.

Father Reilly: Do you believe that?

Interviewer: My last subject recommended that I read *Naked Lunch*. I recommended that he read de Lautréamont.

Father Reilly: I'll say a prayer for the morning after.

Interviewer: You were telling us about your new job at the Vatican.

Father Reilly: Well, unfortunately, my new position at the Vatican Library was not the most exciting. Even academics who thrilled to be among these historic books and literature might grow bored with the tedious monotony of cataloging books or combing through stacks for those materials that needed repairs. Our crew was the front line on the enormous—some say futile—task of digitizing the extensive collection, though how long it would still take to make twenty-five miles of shelving available online was beyond me.

We used state-of-the-art scanners—the Better Light Super 8K-HS scanning back, a large scanner used exclusively by museums for exceptional detail and clarity—built to minimize any harm to the manuscripts. If the manuscript was too fragile, we used large-format cameras to photograph and digitize. It was a painfully slow, monotonous process that frequently took more than one scan to ensure a correct image.

Every day felt the same as the last, and I searched for an outlet to break the monotony. Which led me to the Vatican

Secret Archives. We all knew the archive wasn't a real secret. Of course, conspiracy theories all over the Internet speculated as to what was hidden in these archives. But in truth, the archive was open to scholars with approval for the course of their particular research. Most of the documents in the archive had not been cataloged in ages, and records were quite incomplete and unorganized.

I became interested in the assorted correspondence and investigation reports of various sightings of the Virgin Mary. In our church, the Virgin Mary has appeared before the faithful at various times to deliver a message or prophecy about the coming times and what must be done to save the people from despair. The archives included records of a few sightings approved by the church, in addition to those many, many more sightings not approved.

The apparition that interested me the most was the famous encounter of the Virgin Mary in Fátima, Portugal. The Holy Mother appeared to three girls "brighter than the sun, shedding rays of light clearer and stronger than a crystal goblet filled with the most sparkling water and pierced by the burning rays of the sun." This was detailed in one of the children's memoirs. The children encountered a total of six apparitions of the blessed Virgin Mary between the thirteenth of May and the thirteenth of October 1917, and the Holy Mother gave them three secrets over the course of these months.

The first secret was a vision of hell that all three girls experienced.

The second secret regarded a devotion to the Immaculate Heart of Mary as a way to save souls and bring peace.

The third secret was transcribed by a local administrator of the parish, where the children lived. The children would not allow anyone else to accomplish that act. The letter was then given to a local parish priest, who gave a copy to Pope Benedict XV, who then declared, "The secret will remain, forever, under absolute seal."

Interviewer: Ah, Father, you are definitely the last of the true believers.

Father Reilly: I will take that as a compliment.

In the century since then, there has been much speculation as to the contents of the third secret and why the church would not allow the secret to be released. And as I scanned and photographed page after page of far less interesting works, this third secret grew into a minor obsession. I spent months pondering: What could the message be? I even dreamt about it at night, sometimes awakened in the dark, imagining the destruction that would follow. I became convinced I needed to find the letter that contained the third secret.

Interviewer: Wait. Are you hungry? **[Pause.]** Let the record show subject has shaken his head in dissent. Okay, hope you don't mind if I eat this sandwich while you're talking. Pause. Let the record show subject has nodded in agreement. I thought you wouldn't mind. Keep going.

Father Reilly: Anyway, the new carriers of the NOBI virus, as their status increased, began calling themselves

Gloamings. The term was first used in a *New York Times* article discussing a new group organized in New York City, Berlin, and London for people living with NOBI. Bobbi Smithson, a NOBI carrier, organized the New York group and told the reporter that the group had decided to use the term "Gloaming"—a benign term and, in her words, "a proud image," as opposed to constantly having to refer to themselves as by-products of any "virus."

The transition to "Gloamings" in other countries did not go as smoothly. The German translation was roughly *Zwielicht*, a clunky reference for most German speakers; in Italian it was *crepuscolo*—dusk. However, due to constant use by the American media, and cemented by Taylor Swift's reinforcing the term on all her social media, the term stuck.

I suppose we were all familiar with the concept of a vampire from popular culture and literature and film and folklore. Every culture has some ancient belief in a monster that feeds on the blood of an innocent—take your pick. It's hard for me to pin down exactly when the European and American mood towards this new word, "Gloaming," began to adapt—living in the Vatican, I was a bit removed—but the Gloamings started to assert their rights to define their own identity by shaming people who used the word "vampire" or "leech." They claimed that those words were unambiguously pejorative, although one Gloaming philosopher declared that Gloamings should reappropriate the word "vampire" amongst themselves. The state of California symbolically banned, with a formal resolution, the use of the word "vampire." When Nick

Bindon Claremont said, during his campaign for governor of New Mexico, "In the past thirty days, I've been called a vampire more than any time since I re-created," opponents accused him of "playing the vampire card" to save his political life.

Many people began to have certain romantic notions about the Gloamings and their resemblance to the vampires of literature and film, leading them to seek out Gloamings for amorous relationships. These relationships did not succeed, as these men and women realized the substantial differences between Gloamings and humans. The Gloaming personality—as far as it could be studied by experts—generally leaned towards narcissistic personality disorder or psychopathic tendencies. I know that this has been refuted by certain organizations, without research to back their claims. Other research seemed to indicate that these Gloamings were not necessarily born with those character traits. However, the re-creation process seemed to alter certain biological processes in the brain. The nature-versus-nurture debate was constant. Anecdotally, it quickly became clear that the Gloamings, both men and women, shared certain traits: high IQ, contempt of others, cruelty to others, amoral, secretive, grandiose, and authoritarian. Unlike humans with similar traits, Gloamings did not have significant feelings of inferiority.

Interviewer: So you were already obsessed with the Gloamings before your archival research began.

Father Reilly: My sister called me every week, and

always wanted to discuss the latest Gloaming news. She was particularly fascinated by the men and women who attempted romantic relationships with the Gloamings. She emailed me a famous morning show interview with Becky Bennett—a morning anchor for the local CBS television station in Los Angeles—detailing the challenges in these relationships. Becky had met a Gloaming named Zachary Howard, a well-known British realist painter, at a premiere for the latest Marvel superhero movie. He was a late arriver given that he needed the sun to completely go down before he stepped outside, and Becky was waiting outside after all the other movie stars had slipped past the red carpet and into the premiere. Seeing Howard wander in, she struck up a conversation with him because there wasn't anyone else outside. Becky and Zach's relationship began normally enough, with Becky admitting she was the initial pursuer given the reticent nature of the Gloamings. They met for their first real date at a late-night coffee bar where they talked mostly about Zach's art, how he unlocked even more of his subconscious to fully explore the limits of the human and Gloaming experience. Becky noticed the lack of questions about her occupation—she offered up information about herself without prompting from Zachary. "I found it all rather crass and self-important," she told the reporter. "All he wanted to talk about was himself. And then he would disappear for days without any communication. I've never felt so lonely in my life while in a relationship. It was impossible to make a personal connection with this man."

The reporter asked her why she stayed with him.

"Because he was impossible to resist!" Becky replied.

"I began to question my sanity because I couldn't stop thinking about him. Look, I've lived in L.A. my entire life and I've dated them all. I hope this doesn't sound weird, but he reminded me of the many drug addicts I've loved. Addictive personality, odd self-esteem, and an infinite capacity for denial. But I'm not trying to put down L.A. because it's as perfect a place as can be with people."

She had no regrets? the reporter asked.

"I suppose I'm pretty lucky that I didn't, you know, disappear," she responded coldly.

At that point, the reporter quickly changed the subject. Becky was referring to the reports of missing women and men who disappeared after dating or going out on a date with a Gloaming—including a significant number of women in Britain, where Zachary Howard was born and kept three homes. Some of the bodies were found to be devoid of blood, which initially began the speculation that Gloamings could not safely interact with humans over a certain period of time without needing to feed on them. But the Gloamings considered such questions offensive.

As scientists began to study the Gloamings more carefully—their increased strength and durability, their inability to be in sunlight—they determined that their bodies decayed at a slow, almost imperceptible rate, making their life span, scientists predicted, a possible two hundred to three hundred years. This determination was further supported by excavating one of the bodies from the mass grave at the Nogales, Arizona, border. Eight bodies were recovered but seven were stolen by unknown thieves at the morgue. However, one was already en route to the

University of Arizona and was saved from the theft. An analysis using radiometric dating methods determined that the body was between two hundred and fifty and three hundred years old at the time of death, of which the conclusion was death by natural causes. That allowed the scientists to approximate the life span of Gloamings.

But various scientists also established that the entire Gloaming DNA was constantly being altered because of this virus. I don't pretend to be a scientist but that seemed pretty amazing. Then there were the stories about their ability to disappear and hypnotize with their eyes and voice—who really knew about all of those rumors? That was never proven and I did not believe any of those theories. It was such a crazy period of time.

Interviewer: What was the clergy's position on these new creatures? Surely you were a part of that at the church.

Father Reilly: The church had yet to take a position, only reiterating its support for all living beings. But there was one man from the Catholic Church who sounded the alarm about the new species. Bishop Lawrence Thomas.

Interviewer: Let's focus on him for a moment. When did you first become aware of Bishop Thomas?

Father Reilly: When he spoke at the Confraternity of Catholic Clergy conference in Zurich. Most of the speakers spoke in general terms about the state of the clergy, but when Bishop Thomas took to the lectern, he spoke of a "great awakening" of the flock. In order to stand against the wickedness of man, he said, the church must conduct a great revival. He stood there, basically lecturing the clergy, including many high-ranking cardinals. It did not endear him to many at the conference.

Interviewer: And you?

Father Reilly: Oh, I was... **[Pause.]** Enthralled.

Interviewer: You know, of course, that Bishop Thomas is from Alabama. That he suffered from symptomatic partial epilepsy, caused by congenital brain scarring. All of this was public knowledge. It's even meticulously noted in his journals. What he and his followers viewed as visions— weren't they just seizures? I mean, look at his actions: the man was called the Cave Bishop. He took solitary hikes into the Arizona mountains to pray in silence for days at a time. Did you not consider that instead of a prophet, the man might just be... **[Pause.]** With respect, Father, but just a goddamn eccentric?

Father Reilly: With respect, what you call an eccentric, others saw as an anchorite for a new era.

Interviewer: How so?

Father Reilly: Yes, his somewhat overbearing manner and his frequent tirades against the wealthy made him a lightning rod for complaints against the church, by patrons and politicians alike. Many laypeople winced at his dire warnings to change their ways or prepare for purgatory and hell. He spoke of the intention of God eternally to cast off and destroy sinners and the stubbornness of man's sinfulness. "So that sin against God, being a violation of infinite obligations, must be a crime infinitely heinous, and so deserving of infinite punishment!"

But he had a more empathetic side too. He frequently ministered to the homeless at the day camps in various cities. He organized food drives. He did cause a minor scandal with his call for more redemptive suffering: taking one's suffering as punishment for sins. He implied that many victims of disease should look at their ailments—including the Gloamings.

Bishop Thomas was the first in our clergy to openly question this new species and demand an inquisition into their true intentions. And this was even before their leader emerged from the ground.

Interviewer: How did you come to be in possession of the letter?

Father Reilly: Of course, knowing where the letter was located and taking it was easier said than done. I had access to the secret archives, but I was just a custodian. The Marian Archives themselves were housed in a small room adjacent to the larger archives, and although most of the room was not reinforced—that would disrupt the architecture of the original building—the room was protected by a photoelectric beam system to detect the presence of an intruder. In addition, they incorporated electromagnetic locks, although not reinforced, but with cameras and lasers. Glassbreak acoustic detectors lined certain windows and walls with vibration and inertia sensors.

I turned to my friend Father Mark Rogers, who had originally brought me to the Vatican Library. A grizzled Irishman, he had been working there for many years longer than me. I was assigned to work with him at the Council of the Bishops' Conferences of Europe as an administrator; he had spent most of his time as the director drinking in various pubs. Father Mark took note of my Excel migration, thought I had just turned water into wine, and demanded that I go out with him and his friends to a pub. It was the first time I had ever been drunk. I suppose we've been friends ever since. He knew all about where hidden treasures in the Vatican might be found.

I broached the subject over dinner in a small restaurant in the Jewish ghetto. The cramped dining room held tables close enough that you couldn't avoid touching the one next to you, with walls covered in old photographs. Old waiters in white dinner jackets and black bow ties still roamed and bent beneath the low ceilings. We had just started a small carafe of bitter red wine.

"Are you serious?" Mark asked me as his red cheeks crinkled mischievously. "You crazy bastard."

I nodded and picked at the bread on the table. "I only want to look at it. That's it. I need to know. Look, it's not like I'm going to steal it."

Mark shook his head and polished off another glass of

red. "Spare me the reasons," he said to me. "Look, I can dig around to see where it's located but after that you are on your own. I know for a fact it's not at the Marian Archives."

"It's not?"

"No. The cardinals don't want anyone snooping around those letters. There's nothing in the Marian Archives that's of real value." He stared at his empty glass, thinking. "They must have put it somewhere else. But I can't imagine it's lying in some desk for anyone to go grab a peek."

"Yes. God always makes a way."

The good father rolled his eyes and signaled to the waiter for another bottle. "I need another one of these bastards before you start talking about God."

Over the next few weeks, Father Mark made inquiries of several custodians as to where different materials were located. He was clever, keeping his probing to generalities without mentioning the third secret. Of course, given the age of the structure and the bureaucracy, some of the important documents were kept in different depositories and secure structures; others were haphazardly kept in desk drawers and cabinets. Differing degrees of security in different buildings and rooms—this ended up being a good thing for me. For us, I mean. Sorry.

At last we determined the letters were housed in the upper floor of the cardinal's office who oversaw the Vatican Judicial Office. Apparently, they were placed in that location after a Vatican scholar had inspected the other two letters quite some time ago. The third letter was placed in a lockbox with the key residing within the realm of the Pope and his current secretary.

The good news was that the letter was not housed within the Pope's official residence—an unmanageable location to get inside. But the bad news was that getting the key was next to impossible.

Father Mark checked with the Pope's secretary's assistant and found the papal secretary was scheduled to be in Spain for a week. With a skeleton crew on that third-story office, it seemed like the perfect time to at least explore the possibility of trying to find the key to the lockbox in his office.

At this point, Mark was invested. He readily agreed to help me in this quest and we formulated a quick plan.

Interviewer: Take me through the robbery.

Father Reilly: Well, the Vatican is a series of buildings connected by entryways and courtyards. Most of the buildings face Saint Peter's Square, so once you're inside the complex, it's easy to sit on a bench and conduct surveillance given that you can view all of the buildings from most locations. We picked a Wednesday night when the building we needed to access was empty for the Lenten adoration—a twelve-hour nightly prayer during the Easter season.

I was nursing a cup of coffee, watching the third floor of the building adjacent to the Academy of Sciences, and shivering. An unseasonable cold front was passing through Rome, and the open frescoed hallways of granite and marble seemed to direct the cold air to my location. I wore my cotton cassock but now wished that I had opted for the wool one. I stared at the large order of Corinthian columns from the Palace of the Governorate that were topped by thirteen statues hit by the orange glow of the departing sun. After about an hour, no lights were visible in the building. The closest building was the Mater Ecclesiae convent, which was closed down.

I opened my psalmbook every now and then, in case someone was watching. I would simply be another priest reading the good book. A bit after midnight, I texted Father Mark: "GO." Fifteen minutes later, he took a hard seat next to me.

"What took so long?" I asked.

"I made a perimeter around the building," he said, "to make sure there weren't any people near. To make sure no one was watching." He pulled out a flask from his pocket and unscrewed the cap to take a long drag. He offered it to me.

I raised my eyebrows in surprise. "That's pretty smart. Other than the crippling alcoholism, you could be a Special Forces operative," I said.

He chuckled. "Liquid courage, amigo. I'm about to go Jason Bourne on these bloody fools. We need to do this the right way." He looked around and put the flask away. "Okay, so I have a key that will get us into the building. But then we're on our own."

"We have a key? What could go wrong?" I told him with a sad smile.

Interviewer: Let's get into some specifics here.

Father Reilly: We walked over to the front door of the

building with the decorative arcading of scenes from the Old Testament. Father Mark pulled a key out of his pocket and opened the front door—pretty easy so far, I thought. We took out our flashlights and walked down the long hallway of oval rectangular groin vaults and clustered piers made of granite. I instinctively looked up for cameras, but there weren't any—or they were well hidden. Either way, we would find out pretty soon.

We found the staircase and sprinted up to the third floor. I glanced at Father Mark before I gripped the door handle. It opened smoothly. I could barely conceal a smile as we walked down the dark hallway with my flashlight, searching for room 3C. The oak from the walls glistened from the lights. The ceiling bore a fresco of Italian maps from the tenth century painted by a cleric who occupied the building hundreds of years ago. Each doorway was a curved arch with crafted angels on each segment. The light blinked off the marker and we were standing in front of the office. I clenched the door's handle and it didn't budge.

"Your move," Father Mark whispered.

I took out a thin piece of metal I had borrowed from the book repair room and slipped it through the flush bolt and the frame. I swiped the metal up and down until the lock pulled back and the handle turned to open.

I grinned at Father Mark. He shook his head and motioned inside. We stood in the ornate reception area, full of cabinets encrusted with gold figures of saints. The faint smell of incense wafted through my nose. I shined the flashlight over the other part of the room—a desk and some chairs on that side.

Father Mark pushed my arm down. "Try not to shine the light near the windows."

"Good idea," I said as I walked over to the door to the main office. Luckily it was open and we walked inside. This couldn't have turned out better. The hard wooden floor creaked as I stepped along the walls looking for a safe or lockbox—anything that looked like it might contain the documents.

Strangely enough, we found the safe inside a cabinet behind the large gold-decorated desk. Even at this point it hadn't occurred to me that I would be unsuccessful. The safe was locked but I turned and saw Father Mark rifling through the desk, looking for the password. The papal secretary at the time was of the age where remembering passwords was sometimes a chore. We believed the safe code was written on something inside his desk.

After a few minutes, I saw Father Mark's head pop up; he was waving a small notepad. Hard to believe, but I would learn in the coming years this is the way most of the world's companies get hacked—passwords are useless if they are easy to find. I shined the light on the password list and found the one for the safe written in scratchy Italian. I punched in the numbers. I took a deep breath as the handle turned and the large safe creaked open.

The inside was a mess. Items accumulated for hundreds of years, and I wondered how long it would take to sift through the scattered contents. Father Mark visibly relaxed after another tug of his flask, peering over my shoulder. He shook his head. "We can't be here more than an hour. Every minute that goes by increases the odds of us spending quality time in a jail cell."

"Yes," I told him.

"Well, let's get on it, then."

We took out the items one by one, inspecting them closely and then placing them on the floor. About thirty minutes later I pulled out a wooden box of about two feet in diameter. I sat back on my heels and opened the lid. Inside were three smaller metal boxes with locks. Each was labeled with the papal seal in wax. I knew this was what we were looking for: Fátima.

Father Mark knelt beside me with his strong scent of bourbon. Under the seal of each lockbox was written in Latin: "Letter One," "Letter Two," and "Letter Three."

I was shaking and I took deep breaths. I grabbed the "Letter Three" box—

There was a crashing or slamming sound. It seemed to jump inside my ears. I almost dropped the box. Where in the building had the sound come from?

Father Mark cut off his flashlight and I did the same. I whispered, "Let's clean this up!"

We placed the items back in the safe except for the third lockbox, which I placed on the desk chair. I very gently closed the safe as Father Mark pointed to the closet on the other side of the desk. Nodding, I turned my thumb and index finger, as if turning a lock. He seemed to understand. I sprinted back to the office door and gently turned the lock from the inside.

Footsteps and voices could be heard, down the hallway, just as I moved quickly to the closet. It was a tight fit as Father Mark and I peered through the slats of the door.

The office door clicked open. Two voices were speaking

in Italian with fervor. My Italian was passable, but they were speaking too quickly. I could only make out a few phrases here and there. They seemed to be wondering why they saw lights inside the building when no one should have been on the third floor. And now there were no lights on inside. I could make out a sliver of them, looking from the window to the desk and back.

I was sure they could hear my heart beating. Father Mark placed a hand on my arm, as if to calm me.

The men moved closer to the closet, and one of the men's arms reached out to the door handle. Then the other one said something and his arm pulled back.

We waited another half hour after they left the room. Then we stepped out, muscle-cramped and tired. My hands were sweaty as I held the lockbox. Father Mark and I rushed back downstairs, avoiding the front door. We left through a second exit intended for large deliveries and, with a quick nod to each other in the silence, sprinted off in different directions.

Interviewer: Some skill and a lot of luck. I've been on missions like that. What happened next?

Father Reilly: It was three in the morning by the time I got back to my apartment. I placed the lockbox on my bed. My hands were shaking. I took a deep breath and stuck a screwdriver into the primitive lock. I pushed with all my strength and it popped off with a clatter against the wall.

Inside was a folded letter, consisting of three sheets of brittle paper. I spread them on my bed. One page was in

English and the other was the original in Portuguese.

The blood of the lamb was rained upon the living souls to carry on the battle now being waged on behalf of the Church of God and the salvation of souls. The sad sight has presented itself to Us of the evils of the creatures of despair and sin begotten from the arid ground where no such thing should be living. The slaughtered souls that lie in the shadow of these creatures of the absence of light that continue to take the blood from the lamb must be eradicated. These creatures bare their teeth as they spew contempt for all that is good and holy with their perverse words and deeds and they shall shake the foundation of our holy Catholic Church. Baring their teeth to suck the glorious blood from the holy lamb shall wash away the sins of these creatures so that we may renew our lives in the embrace of our God.

My mind raced: the warning about teeth. The taking of the souls. I felt my heart pounding. It was a warning from the blessed mother about these people—the Gloamings— leading us to the end of civilization.

Interviewer: I see. Is this verbatim?

Father Reilly: Absolutely.

Interviewer: But one ancient text does not a terrorist make—

Father Reilly: I disagree with that term.

Interviewer: Okay. Explain. Then surely there had to have been more.

Father Reilly: When the former president of the United States re-created himself, my world truly began to fall apart.

The event was the game changer. When he re-created himself it was on the news all day and night. Politicians, commentators, and academics all espoused their theories on why and what it meant for society. Everyone was wondering who was the Gloaming that re-created him—as if that was what mattered! Every gossip site went down the list of famous Gloamings who might have done it.

For me, it all came to a head when I was sent to the annual Catholic stewardship conference, that year in Dallas, Texas. It was an annual gathering to coordinate religion, education, and social policy impacting Catholics for the coming year. It was attended by all upper-level bishops and other senior clergy. The conference also consisted of many laypeople and their children, with family events designed to get everyone involved.

The plane had a two-hour layover in Chicago and I saw many attendees waiting alongside myself for the plane to board. A group of college students praying and sharing laughter, a few young couples with their toddlers spending time together, some random clergy resting from the long trip.

I felt even more anticipation rising in my chest after seeing this—it had been a long time since I had been to a communal event where the essence would be fellowship among the faithful.

The beautiful Dallas Hilton and its glorious atrium provided a calming backdrop against which the attendees could gather. I spent the first day of the conference giving a few presentations on the Vatican Library and the project to digitize many of the manuscripts and books. Afterwards I would sit myself at the hotel café and have discussions with various clergy about spiritual issues facing the church in the near future.

When the organizers added an evening social the next night, I was expecting it to be a social gathering of the attendees because there was no description of it in the program and it wasn't publicized. I walked down to one of the conference rooms and I could sense discomfort or excitement in the air.

I was shocked to see the event was actually a night to meet Catholic Gloamings.

And not just any Catholic Gloamings. They were clergy.

I was appalled. I had seen Gloamings from afar but never met one in person. These appointments and re-creations had been accomplished without any publicity by the church. There were two of them: both tall and fit, with immaculately groomed silver hair and beautifully tailored garments. Immediately, I felt a negative energy that came from their entire being, yet I seemed to be the only person who felt this reaction.

The others lined up to greet the Gloamings with smiles plastered on their faces. The Gloamings were extolling the virtues of re-creation as if it were some type of biblical raising of the dead. I heard one of them refer to John 11:25, in matching re-creation with "resurrection." And another talked of Matthew 10:8 and "raising the dead."

Shameful comparisons, yet they seemed to hypnotize the attendees.

I watched all this unfold in one evening, terrified. I wondered what my father would have thought of these creatures. The man who climbed stairs, who saw belief as a way towards peace, not glory. This could not be the true way of my church.

I stayed for maybe fifteen minutes before I found myself physically unable to be in the same room as these Gloamings. My unfamiliarity with the Dallas area did not stop me from walking from the downtown hotel to a strip of clubs and restaurants in the Deep Ellum area. Groups of young people laughing and talking loudly walked up and down the block. I seemed to be the only person alone in this entire area. I sat on the curb and watched all of these beautiful carefree people and wondered about the future of a population that could be bartered for blood and transmuted in the blink of an eye. I didn't sleep that night and wandered into darker blocks and alleyways. I sat among the homeless people digging through trash cans and sleeping on cardboard. I thought of them too and how they could be used as legal tender for a hungry population.

How could I just go back to the Vatican and copy papers?

Interviewer: How was this affecting your work in Rome?

Father Reilly: When I returned to Rome, new rumors began. I refused to believe them, of course. It was absurd.

Out of the question. These reports violated every principle we held true.

But the rumors persisted.

The Vatican press office parried and deflected. It drove me to insanity. Deny it! Tell them no!

I remember waking up on that Thursday with my phone ringing off the hook. The Vatican announced Pope Victor II would make an announcement that evening.

The Internet descended into madness that day. And the rumors began to take on the aura of fact, and they were definitive that the Pope was going to announce that he had been re-created. It was covered over the Internet like a poisonous vine. Vatican City was in a state of panic and anticipation. No one could muster up the courage to work that day, and everywhere in Vatican City, small groups of workers and clergy spoke in hushed tones about the impending announcement. Many others were in the various chapels, praying.

I spent the day in a constant state of nervousness. I knew in my heart that the Holy Father could not have re-created.

He would not.

Would he?

At the appointed hour that evening, the Pope called an audience in the Vatican papal sitting room, instead of the balcony. And he did not allow television cameras inside. That worried me because of the common knowledge that the Gloamings gave off a particular and not yet understood electromagnetic radiation that invariably interfered with the audio or video recording of them. A type of radio-frequency interference that rendered it impossible for them to be filmed or recorded in any manner or by any type of equipment.

Crowds had gathered outside and in the square all day, but I decided to stay in my room. The news came in swiftly: Pope Victor II announced that Cardinal Alexander Naro, the prefect of the Congregation for the Doctrine of the Faith, the most powerful and influential office at the Vatican, had been re-created.

I felt tears run down my face—I am unashamed to say it. I didn't know if it was from relief that it wasn't the Pope who had been re-created, or from despair that Cardinal Naro had. Naro's explanation left me hollow: he wanted to minister to the new species; he wanted to welcome them into the church; he wanted to show that we are all the same species; he wanted to foster an openness among all peoples; he wanted to have many more years to complete his goals for the church.

I could only grieve, mourn, and fast. After a period of mourning came confusion.

And then rage.

This cardinal was much too close to the Pope. The level of influence he had on the church was unrivaled. This is exactly what the third letter had warned.

I needed the help of someone of high rank in the church—someone who would be willing to fight for his beliefs. So I packed my minimal belongings with the letter—which, to my surprise, had still not been reported missing—and booked a plane ticket.

Interviewer: Where to?

Father Reilly: Back to the U.S. When I landed, I took an Uber and all the driver could talk about was the leeches—the Gloamings. Now the NBA and NFL were considering whether to admit this new species into their leagues and how to accommodate their medical condition in spite of the fact that it would be difficult to televise those games if the camera couldn't record them. People were still buying into this farce like a shared madness.

I arrived at my destination close to midnight. I considered renting a hotel room for the night but I felt such a sense of urgency, and I couldn't conceive of a delay. I knocked on the caretaker's door and a woman answered with a less than inviting look on her face.

"My name is Father John Reilly," I told her. "I am a Jesuit assigned to the Vatican Archives. I am here on a matter of great importance and I need to see Bishop Lawrence Thomas immediately."

Interviewer: I'm sure it won't surprise you, but we are extremely interested in how this first meeting with Bishop Thomas went.

Father Reilly: The woman directed me out into the desert where Bishop Thomas was praying. The desert air was cool before the sun came up. I studied the map with my flashlight and it seemed like I was starting at the correct trail—I whispered a prayer just in case. I trudged up the path and flashed the light everywhere at once, trying to spot any snakes or animals in my path. Every once in a while I heard something rustling in the bushes but I kept my concentration on the trail.

After a couple of hours, I was covered in sweat and puffing loudly. The sky was beginning to lighten just a bit. But then...this was strange. I looked up and caught a faint light on the side of the mountain. I wondered if it was my mind playing tricks.

Another hour and I was closer to the light. My legs began to cramp at the calf and I haltingly paced up the trail. My back was bent over and my head hung down to the ground. I could see the spit and sweat fall to the ground with every shuffle of my feet and every labored intake of breath. I finally could experience what my father felt climbing the steps up to the shrine. But I could find no satisfaction in this, let alone deliverance. Another half hour of my legs moving as if of their own volition, and I reached the flickered glow and saw a large candle in the dirt at the front of a cave. I stepped inside the cave. At the back I saw a man in a monk's habit kneeling on a makeshift rest of burlap and wood. He sat with his back to me in front of a scattered altar of rosaries, scapulars, and pictures of saints. I heard a murmur of prayers.

I began to pray myself until his voice cut through the cave. "I suppose you're not here to rob me."

I paused to compose myself before I answered. "Bishop Thomas, I'm so sorry. My name is Father John Reilly. I am a Jesuit assigned to the Vatican Archives and I need to speak to you about a matter of great importance."

Bishop Thomas rose and turned around to face me. His angular features were more pronounced in the dim light of the shadows, and his thin body looked almost as if it would blow away with any wind. "It's about those bloodsuckers, isn't it?"

CHAPTER 5

FEBRUARY 10

NINE MONTHS AFTER THE NOBI DISCOVERY

U.S. HOUSE OF REPRESENTATIVES COMMITTEE ON HOMELAND SECURITY
One Hundred and Seventeenth Congress
First Session
Serial No. 117–20

The subcommittee met, pursuant to call, at 9:00 a.m., in room 225, Canon House Office Building, Hon. James Kerr (chairman of the committee) presiding.

Present: Representatives Duncan, Gervin, Gilmore, Martin, Gonzalez, Brady, Johnson, Washington, and Leslie.

MR. KERR:

The Committee on Homeland and Security will come to order. Our first witness is Dr. Lauren Scott, assistant researcher of the research division at the Centers for Disease Control. Welcome, Dr. Scott.

DR. SCOTT:

Thank you. Thank you. Um, yes. Thank you—

MR. KERR:

The committee meets today to examine critically important issues related to the NOBI virus and its effect on the health and security and economy of the country. This hearing will help us determine whether we are appropriately prepared for any possible NOBI virus spread, especially within the next year, and identify public health responses for future deadly infectious disease outbreaks. Our witnesses will help inform this committee's future oversight and legislative efforts.

NOBI is of urgent concern to Americans for a number of reasons: because it is presently untreatable and its means of transmission are not fully known, because it appears to have potential for rapid international spread in this interconnected globe, and because its effects on our society are still unknown. If this disease were to become something on par with AIDS and Ebola, the results could be catastrophic for our citizens and our critical infrastructure.

Fortunately, there is evidence that NOBI is not as easily transmissible as Ebola or SARS, and that apparatuses of public health are working well to contain it. On the other hand, there is much we do not know if NOBI continues to spread: How would we handle large infection rates or isolate and treat infected people? Is our hospitalization infrastructure prepared? Do our public health professionals have the facts and tools to combat this disease? And what about gaps in international and local surveillance? Will we be able to develop vaccines and other treatments? Do we have the financial resources? What are the consequences of having NOBI-infected people in our general population?

Luckily, the NOBI virus is, as far as our information reveals, limited to the United States.

Hopefully this hearing will dispel many of the disturbing

myths that surround this new disease.

The committee, in an effort to provide a balanced commentary, attempted to extend an invitation to a Gloaming citizen to testify today, but we were unable to find a willing participant. I do want to thank the witnesses who are present today.

Dr. Scott?

DR. SCOTT:

Thank you again. It is...It is great to be here...with this distinguished committee.

You have been a great friend of the CDC's and public health, and we respect and appreciate that you are taking time to focus in on NOBI, especially at the local level, where so much of our efforts really have to come to fruition on the research end. Although we do have much work to accomplish, I want to give you a brief recap of where we are right now with the virus. And I am hoping to dispel many of the myths surrounding this illness that have been widely circulated throughout the media and especially the Internet.

I won't go into the origin of the discovery of the disease, as we are all well familiar with the discovery of Liza Sole by myself and the Nogales police department.

Unlike other diseases such as SARS and bird flu, NOBI is by all indicators deliberately spread to others as an intentional act. Therefore, travel advisories are of little to no impact in regard to this disease. We have recorded no instances where the disease has been passively spread. Although reported cases have spiked during certain days of certain months, we have yet to determine the significance of these instances. Interestingly, we have yet to find any evidence that this virus is zoonotic, the result of crossing species from animal to human. The University of Texas at Austin has been at the forefront in developing methods for detecting NOBI using a proprietary cell culture approach, but we have not made significant progress in developing diagnostic tests for NOBI. Additionally, the university has curtailed their DNA and recombinant vector vaccine research due to ethical concerns expressed by numerous private entities.

Another issue that the public health sector has had to confront is the numerous cases of the disease that go unreported. We surmise that there are certain societal pressures that would make a person not be inclined to report an infection. Therefore, there have been no reports of any variant forms of NOBI, unlike other communicable diseases which do report a certain percentage of variant forms. We still do not know about the effect that a particular genetic profile has on the infected person. It may establish why certain people are successful in "re-creating" as opposed to others who are not successful.

As a side note, as a medical professional, I prefer the term "infection" when referring to the point when an individual's bloodstream has been introduced to the biological mechanism which becomes NOBI. I dislike the term "re-creation" as it implies a positive result, when we have definitive evidence that the instances which would define a so-called re-creation are at approximately 50 percent. It is imperative that health professionals gain access to the bodies of the unsuccessful re-creations to better understand the intricacies of the disease.

In other words, when a Gloaming infects a non-NOBI, there is only a 50 percent chance of the infected person surviving and becoming an actual Gloaming. Re-creation is a myth I have no interest in glamorizing.

Today, we estimate that close to one thousand probable cases of NOBI have been reported. We cannot estimate the amount of people carrying the virus, as we have not found an acceptable means of conducting a census of persons who identify as Gloamings. One of the more troubling aspects of the virus has been the simultaneous reports by law enforcement of the mysterious deaths of individuals closest to the Gloaming.

As far as the mechanics of the disease are concerned, we still have little information. We know that the virus infects dendritic cells which kill off the body's T lymphocyte cells but with no appreciable effect on the body. The virus then manufactures never-before-found proteins which block immune cells from signaling to the antibodies to attack the virus. At this point, the virus begins to replicate and change the internal structure of the body. Many viruses work in part by inhibiting interferon, but NOBI actually structurally changes the interferon of the person. This is the limit of our knowledge of the disease. I realize that Congress has expressed concerns about our ability to map the complete genomes of the virus similar to what has been done to other viruses.[3] The NOBI virus [NOBI]—although hampered by a lack of full-length viral genomes—genome substitution rate in the Nogales/Sole strain has been estimated at between 1.5 times three to ten mutations per nucleotide, per genomic replication. This is equivalent to

---

[3] "Genome sequencing in viral outbreaks is desirable to characterize the infectious agent and determine its evolutionary rate. Genome sequencing also allows the identification of signatures of host adaptation, identification and monitoring of diagnostic targets, and characterization of responses to vaccines and treatments." Quick J, Loman NJ, Duraffour S, Simpson JT, Severi E, Cowley L, Bore JA, Koundouno R, Dudas G, Mikhail A, Ouedraogo N, Afrough B, Bah A, Baum JH, Becker-Ziaja B, Boettcher JP, Cabeza-Cabrerizo M, Camino-Sanchez A, Carter LL, Doerrbecker J, Enkirch T, Garcia-Dorival I, Hetzelt N, Hinzmann J, Holm T, Kafetzopoulou LE, Koropogui M, Kosgey A, Kuisma E, Logue CH, Mazzarelli A, Meisel S, Mertens M, Michel J, Ngabo D, Nitzsche K, Pallasch E, Patrono LV, Portmann J, Repits JG, Rickett NY, Sachse A, Singethan K, Vitoriano I, Yemanaberhan RL, Zekeng EG, Racine T, Bello A, Sall AA, Faye O, et al. 2016. Real-time, portable genome sequencing for Ebola surveillance. *Nature* 530:228–232. 10.1038/nature16996.

fifteen to thirty-five mutations in each genome, meaning that sequences diverge rapidly enough to identify distinct sublineages during the epidemic. NOBI appears to evolve moderately at the epidemiological level but also at the within-host level. Our current class of machines and sequencers is not yet fully capable of analyzing the virus in its current state.

At this moment, public health authorities, doctors, nurses, scientists, and law enforcement and laboratory staff around the country are struggling to cope with NOBI at a time when some hope remains that the disease might still be contained. Economists and market analysts are simultaneously struggling to calculate the present and future costs. Another, less publicized aspect of the disease is the reluctance of major pharmaceutical companies to begin research on any aspect of the virus. Numerous institutions of higher education are avoiding conducting any research on NOBI even when offered substantial grants from the federal government. This has left our medical community severely shorthanded regarding research and forced to conduct its own research on a smaller scale without the equipment and resources that are available to the major participants in medical research.

One of the other aspects of the virus which hampers our ability to adequately analyze the disease is that most microscopes are unable to evaluate the particles. The inherent radioactive ingredients cause interference with the equipment.

The NOBI disease has no vaccine and no treatment. It is forcing health authorities to resort to control tools dating back to the earliest days of empirical microbiology: isolation and quarantine. At the same time, we are combating certain media organizations glamorizing the disease. Neither of which have been successful due to our limited aspects of our current laws in dealing with such diseases. Attempts by certain media organizations to glamorize the disease have hampered our efforts to learn more about it; in addition, the provincial and clannish behavior of the Gloamings has left many of our health authorities in the dark when it comes to analyzing the virus.

Our greatest fear when it comes to diseases such as NOBI is the tendency of the disease to mutate into forms which could be substantially more detrimental to our health system and society. The nature of the infected to disperse radiation is another concern that should be studied from a long-term impact assessment. The novel nature of the NOBI virus has created an extra step in the containment response—many wish to be infected. This desire to become a Gloaming leaves many citizens at risk of a failed re-creation or, in the alternative, the risk of the long-term effect on the body of a successful re-creation.

Another aspect of the virus is the desire or requirement of the NOBI-infected people to ingest blood for their survival. However, without the cooperation of the Gloamings, any evidence we obtain will only be in theory. Must the Gloamings feed on human blood, or can they ingest other types of blood? This is imperative to determine in order to know whether the Gloamings can be safely integrated into general society.

The CDC will continue working with our partners to monitor NOBI. This is simply a snapshot of where the country stands today.

I hope this hearing will illuminate the issues and successes of our health system in combating this and other diseases.

Thank you, Mr. Chairman, and committee.

MR. KERR:
Thank you, Dr. Scott. My office will continue to provide oversight

of CDC programs through a combination of proactive audits, inspections, and administrative investigations.

We shall now hear from Dr. Chad Kelly from Northwest Memorial Hospital of Chicago, Illinois, to discuss the treatment of NOBI patients within their hospital system...

Rolling Stone magazine
November

Each month Rolling Stone *features first-person accounts from individuals on the front lines of conflicts that are given limited exposure through the mainstream media. This month we feature an account from a doctor stationed with a refugee camp in South Sudan, Africa, after it was attacked by a neighboring militia.*

Dr. Keith Miller—Doctors Without Borders:

When I arrived at the Girba refugee camp, Drs. Henry and Bradford—the two Gloamings out of the ten aid workers—showed me around the camp, which was in dire shape. Tarps fitted with salvaged wood pieces created a makeshift tent, and a three-foot trench winding through the camp was a provisional sewage system.

The Gloamings were incredible in transforming the refugee camp. Although they were confined to their pods during the daylight, they made the most of the night hours. They coordinated a clinic and immunization room, and helped dig a pit for trash disposal, which cut down on disease. Dr. Henry researched and found safe chemicals for placement in the trench for human waste treatment. They worked harder than any of us—immune to fatigue.

We were caught off guard when a United Nations ambassador for Chad called our supervisor in South Africa: a peacekeeping unit in North Sudan detected a column—estimated at two thousand troops—of National Liberation militias moving toward the refugee camp. The troops would arrive in about two days. Doctors Without Borders contacted the United Nations peacekeeping forces in neighboring nations, but the UN indicated it needed Security Council approval. That process could take months.

Dr. Henry contacted the Gloaming Council and in twenty-four hours they had assembled a private mercenary force which stopped the militias' advance for a month, until United States and French forces dispersed the militias from attacking the refugees. The Gloaming Council and the Gloamings on our staff saved thousands of lives.

When people ask me what I think about the Gloamings, I tell them this story and hope that they can see the hope and promise of a future where the Gloamings are involved in all aspects of our lives.

CHAPTER 6

Hugo Zumthor
FBI Agent

It's not easy chasing ghosts. Especially ones bigger, stronger, and faster than you. But that's what I've been doing for a long time now. Hey: how does a ghost say goodbye to a vampire? So long, sucker!

By chance, I was actually on the FBI's original extraction team investigating the Liza Sole incident. I worked closely with Dr. Lauren Scott of the CDC to understand the NOBI virus and how it affected the bodies of the carriers. The agency needed to know the risks involved in confronting this virus. As I learned more from Lauren, I advocated for a large team to guard Liza Sole at the hospital, but my superiors denied it—and then, of course, she escaped.

Even so, at the start of the Gloaming presence, we never had a dedicated Gloaming unit in the FBI. It really wasn't until the art heist incident that the FBI determined there should exist a dedicated unit for crimes suspected of involving Gloamings.

After the Liza Sole case and the accompanying investigations, I was considered the closest thing to a Gloaming crime expert.[4] So when the alert came in about a theft at the University of Texas campus's Blanton Museum of Art, I was sent to Austin to help the investigation.

An alert came into the office of the special agent in charge about a theft on the campus, specifically at the Blanton Museum of Art. Now, normally this wouldn't cause much of a blip on the screen of our crime roster, but one of the local FBI agents had taken a Geiger counter to the scene and the radioactive traces were off the charts, which caused the local office to suspect a Gloaming angle.

The Jack S. Blanton Museum of Art was located on the campus of the University of Texas at Austin. It's a beautiful campus among the hills and green grass of central Texas. It was also one of the largest university art museums, with a pretty substantial permanent collection and endowment. The museum was an imposing and modern building constructed of granite and limestone surrounded by a well-manicured lawn and shaded with rows of pecan trees.

During the time of the robbery, the Blanton museum was hosting an exhibit entitled *Haring, Warhol, and the Beginning of the Media Street Art Generation*. It was an exhibition of works of art primarily from the 1980s focusing on the abstract political illustration of that time period—with its garish colors and outlandish messages.

There were several valuable paintings among the collection, but the thief, or thieves, only took one particular painting: *Untitled (Madonna, I'm Not Ashamed)*, a 1985 piece by Andy Warhol and Keith Haring. The painting consisted of synthetic polymer, Day-Glo, and acrylic paint on a canvas measuring twenty by sixteen inches.

At the time, the FBI didn't really have a theory as to why that

---

[4]   Please see Appendix Three.

particular painting was stolen. Arguably, the Lichtenstein and Basquiat artworks were more valuable, and the thieves had ample time to take any number of works from the collection, but they took only the Madonna painting.

When I arrived, the museum was teeming with cops and museum staff, all in a state of nervous panic. No doubt the respective Warhol and Haring trust representatives—not to mention the insurance investigators crawling the museum floors—had everyone on edge. It was a sweltering July day, and I felt sweat roll down my legs when I was dropped off near the yellow crime scene tape at the museum's entrance. Campus security appeared overextended: the news crews were spilling over into the fifteen-story dormitory and other classroom buildings.

Special Agent Dana Webb of the Austin field office led me to the exhibition hall. "This is where the exhibition was being held," she said. "It takes up all three of the large first-floor halls." A posse of technicians pored over every inch of a blank square on a pale wall between a Basquiat and a Rauschenberg. "This is where it was hung," she continued, pointing at the empty space with almost a shrug.

I suppose my face said it all.

"You don't like modern art," Webb said.

I winced as if I felt bad about it—I didn't. "I have a distinct love-hate relationship with fine art. All that money trading pictures that could be drawn by a child. It's like a middle finger to the poor."

"Well, this blank space is like a middle finger to us," Webb replied.

I nodded. I could already tell they weren't going to find much of anything on that wall. "Before we get into the actual theft, explain to me the security system in place." Webb and I first reviewed the museum's security apparatus—they had a central station for security personnel at a secure location in the basement. I quickly learned that for a university museum, their standards were actually quite rigorous, based on the requirements forwarded to me by the Museum Association Security Committee of the American Association of Museums.[5]

By all accounts, the thief or thieves entered through the single service entrance door at the northwest corner of the museum—the back of the building. The metal door was opened from the outside with a duplicate key apparently stolen the night before but not found until after the theft.

I was then taken to the security headquarters located in the museum's basement. Entrance was limited to members of the security detail, the museum director, and her two direct assistants. The security room was lit with banks of fluorescent lights and rows of closed-circuit feeds on numerous screens and monitors. I sat

---

[5]   The secure station was equipped with a secure panic button for any intrusions into the area. The secure communication lines met requirements of the Standard Line Security as defined by Underwriters Laboratories 827, Standard for Central Station Alarm Service. Magnetic switches could be found on every door in the museum to alert security when any door was opened that should be closed. All windows—none were capable of being opened—were fitted with electromagnetic switches to detect any outward motion. They also contained interior volumetric motion detection devices to sense intrusion. All of the alarm systems were hardwired per acceptable industry standards. They included a system in which attempts to cut the wires, damage or remove the detection device, ground the system, or short out the circuit would send a signal to the monitoring station and to law enforcement.

Every ten to twenty square feet of space contained a motion detector activated at the closure of the museum. Duct entrances were also equipped with motion detecting implements. The exhibition hall itself had locked doors with intrusion detection monitors on the doors.

Unfortunately, unlike many of the most prestigious pieces of art in the permanent collection of the museum, the individual paintings in the exhibition were not alarmed. There was card access but no biometric access on all the doors on all floors except the basement. A bank of closed-circuit cameras lined most corners of every room and on the outside as well, providing coverage for every square foot of the museum exhibition spaces.

at the table as an assistant cued up the replay, and as we studied footage from the outdoor cameras around the university at the time of the robbery, the pattern of the static and warped reception correlated approximately with the effect of a Gloaming being recorded, based on my experience. A further analysis from the FBI lab would later confirm this suspicion.

The cameras that covered the road leading to the back entrance showed no vehicles from an hour before to an hour after the burglary. So I requested any cameras at the university that encompassed coverage for half a square mile from the museum. The university police provided us with access to the full bank of surveillance videos for a square mile around the museum. An hour of further scrolling later, I spotted a car in an empty lot near the philosophy building—a late model black Mercedes with heavily tinted windows. A specially fitted Gloaming-safe automobile.

The plates on the Mercedes were removed, and a physical inspection of the trail, using a portable electronic dosimeter to check for radiation, led us back to the first-floor exhibition room and the empty square on the wall.

Honestly, this crime scene told me nothing—well, nothing except that the crime was committed by a Gloaming. But hey, that was a start. I could feel Agent Webb's eyes on me as I stared again at the empty square on the wall.

"Any ideas?" she asked as she put her business suit coat back on—truth be known, they kept the temperature in the museum at winter levels. She leaned over and her mouth smelled like domestic beer and clove cigarettes. This girl was more me than myself.

"We're not going to get anything from this damn crime scene," I said.

"Any way to salvage the videos?" Webb asked.

I shook my head. "We've tried many times, but our technicians, and other outside consultants, have failed to make anything usable out of them. The radiation they give out completely ruins the video." To be honest, I wasn't feeling much confidence in getting any closer to solving this crime. I had been here before with other Gloaming-suspected crimes, mostly high-end burglaries of upper-income estates, but hitting a museum was a first. The only thing the crimes had in common was a 0 percent clearance rate by the authorities.

"We should follow the Mercedes," Webb said. So we then turned to plotting out every possible path of the Mercedes. As I suspected, after a canvas of local police, most of the cameras located at different commercial establishments in the area had been disabled by laser or gunshot.

However, detailed canvassing by the Austin PD and Agent Webb found a residence off Lamar Avenue which contained several cameras outside the structure, in front and on the fence line. Apparently the Gloamings missed these on their rampage. I had to give Webb credit: she had found this clue by walking miles from the museum in the oppressive heat, searching for any angle.

The home surveillance video did indeed show a black Mercedes traveling down Lamar Avenue past Thirty-Fifth Street within the approximate time after the robbery, being 2:30 a.m. But Austin was still a pretty big city encompassing many square miles, so we had hit another dead end.

At this point, I decided to change our search. The University of Texas provided me with a list of all events and meetings scheduled on the same day as the theft. One meeting immediately jumped out at me: Drone Club. The thieves picked the same date that the Drone Club was filming a meteor shower falling through the sky. Lucky coincidences like this have broken open many cases. We needed the drone footage, if any, before it was erased.

The Drone Club address led us to a shabby west campus house with two shaggy-haired college dudes in band T-shirts and cutoff shorts. The living room was cluttered with strewn papers and dirty plates and I wondered how many students actually resided here. Keith and Tom, the leaseholders and current occupants of the couch, in addition to being the president and vice president of the Drone Club, fidgeted throughout the interview. The blond, mop-headed one—Keith—rambled, "We weren't spying on anyone! Dude, seriously: we were only flying them over the city, and that's legal. I mean, why would the NSA trip on that—"

Webb raised her hand. "Look: you haven't done anything illegal. And we're with the FBI, not the NSA. We're just here because we need your help."

Webb's sympathetic blue eyes and pretty face warmed the room, but I had a feeling if this didn't work, she could turn on a hard-ass persona that would make these kids pee their pants.

"Sure, man—uh, Miss…Officer. Whatever you need," Keith said.

As I suspected, the kids had thrown a "nighttime drone party" and still had all the footage. Webb and I stepped behind them as they booted up the videos on their laptops. I viewed Keith's footage as Webb checked out Tom's computer. A few minutes later, Agent Webb shouted me over. Tom's computer showed a black sedan rolling down Lamar Avenue. Our Mercedes.

"Looks like either Forty-Ninth Street or Kerbey Lane," Keith said as he leaned closer to the monitor.

Tom joined him, nodding. "Definitely Kerbey Lane."

*   *   *

The next morning, after three coffees each from Starbucks, Webb and I headed to Kerbey Lane. As we drove, I asked her why she'd joined the FBI.

"To hold a gun, of course." She laughed.

"There are easier ways," I replied.

"I know." She paused for a moment. "I've heard about you. I know you're trying to get the bureau to concentrate on these Gloamings. I feel the same way. I'm hoping to learn something from you."

"Well, you learn something from everyone—even if it's what *not* to do."

She smiled. "To answer your question, I was a total nerd in high school and I thought I wanted to become a chef after college. And then my mom was robbed. The robber beat her pretty bad. She was in a coma, and it just made me so afraid. So angry. I mean, look at me: I'm, like, five foot five and a hundred and five pounds. I started taking karate, and one of my instructors was retired FBI. It had never even entered my mind but he saw something in me. And here I am, fifteen years later."

I suppose the surprise was all over my face. "Really? You look like you're all of eighteen as it is, to be honest."

She laughed. "Thankfully, no. I have a seven-year-old kid too." She looked at me. "You?"

"Just me," I said. I wasn't sure why I didn't mention my erstwhile wife. Probably because she would never come up in any future conversation. I was going to ask about her kid—boy? girl?—when she said she was turning onto Kerbey Lane and slowed her car to a crawl.

"What do you think we're going to find here?" Webb asked as she squinted at the houses on the odd-numbered side of the block. "I don't see any Mercedes."

I scanned the even-numbered side of the block and wished we could walk this instead of driving. I needed to see each house individually. "I don't think they would have taken a chance on driving the Mercedes much further; it might be spotted by another camera somewhere. Probably dumped the car and switched."

Webb nodded. "Worth a shot, I suppose." She drove slowly down the block and onto another street. I saw nothing out of the ordinary. Then, something just barely out of place in the corner of my eye...

I grabbed Webb's arm on the steering wheel. "Slow down but don't stop. Stop at the far corner," I said.

Webb pulled the car over at the corner. "What are we looking at?" she asked as she turned to look out the back window.

I pointed. "Third house on the odd side of the street. The one with the brown garage."

Webb squinted at the house. "What about it?"

"It's hard to explain. The windows don't look right. Like the window's covered with something. The house just doesn't look real for some reason. The light is kind of reflecting off the window... weirdly. The house looks like a display or something. Like it's trying too hard to be a normal house in suburbia..."

Webb cocked her head to one side. "You might be right. I mean, the more I look at it..." She looked over at me and her eyes narrowed. "So now what?"

"I need to get inside that house," I said almost to myself.

"We don't have a warrant," Webb replied. I detected a hint of apology in her tone, and I ignored the comment, as she probably suspected I would.

"We need to wait until the sun comes up," I said. "Then we can get a closer look."

* * *

The next few hours before sunrise were spent alternating naps, sweating in the Texas summer heat, and watching the house between us. Obviously it wasn't the perfect situation, but it would have to do. The sun rose like a slow yawn, throwing its warmth around my knotted shoulders. I could not remember the last time I had a decent night's sleep. Webb was leaning her head on the steering wheel, sound asleep. I felt bad about waking her up but we needed to move. I pushed her arm and she startled awake.

"What? I was having a great dream where I was in my own bed asleep."

"The sun is up. I'm going to take a look at the house," I said.

"You need me to back you up," Webb said as she stretched and yawned. "I could do that at the Starbucks, you know."

"You wish. No, stay here and scan the area. I'll be right back." I stepped out of the car and walked up the block to the dark house. No need to scurry under the cover of daylight.

I stopped in the driveway of the house and scanned the entire area. The daylight hours were the most vulnerable for the Gloamings, as they required an undetermined period of rest inside a pod filled with soil, so I was confident that they were not watching me at this point. They would be locked inside, though. It did not mean there weren't any aspiring Gloaming apprentices who could be conducting surveillance during their rest period. They would do anything for their Gloaming masters, and I could handle those types.

I walked along the hedges up the side of the house, the branches lightly brushing my face. There were no visible cameras. I stepped closer to the window by the front door. I had been right: it appeared that the glass had been removed and replaced with concrete, and covered with a dull reflective surface to simulate glass.

This was a Gloaming safe house.

The dirt near the foundation of the house had been tilled or moved. I didn't know what this meant—maybe a construction within the house which might include a basement for the Gloamings to sleep in? It certainly added to my suspicions. The backyard was surrounded by an eight-foot cinder block fence. I advanced over to the garage and pulled on the handle but it was locked tight. I squatted down to peer through the cracks but I could see nothing inside—not enough light. I stepped back and walked the perimeter of the house. The fake window structure and shabby construction covered the entirety. From there I moved to the cinder block fence guarding the backyard, where I searched for a divot, gap, or outcropping, in order to secure a foot and climb over. I was attempting to pull myself up when I heard a noise behind me.

"Come down and turn slowly with your hands in the air," the voice said.

I recognized the police officer cadence and got down—I could feel the pistol pointing at me before I even turned around. And there it was: an Austin police department officer looking hard at me, pointing a gun at my face.

"Officer, I am an FBI agent," I said. "My credentials are in my left-hand coat pocket."

The cop said nothing, just continued to stare at me. I wondered if this idiot ticket writer was going to put a few in my chest. "You know," I continued, "there's an actual medical condition where you're too stupid to know how stupid you are. I think you might have that—"

"FBI. Put that fucking gun down," Agent Webb commanded as I saw her step from behind the hedge and around the cop. "Put it down," she repeated. "FBI. Drop it now or I blow your fucking head off."

The only thing more surprising than the gun pointed at me was the language coming from Agent Webb's mouth. And she looked like she wasn't even looking for a reason to pull that trigger.

The skinny cop scowled before he knelt down and placed his gun on the ground. I walked over and picked it up and stuffed it in my waistband as I took out my FBI badge and slapped him in the face with it a few times. My heart was flapping like it was having a goddamn heart attack. "I should have told her to blow your head off for pointing a gun at a federal officer."

The cop glared at me with numb eyes as Webb holstered her gun.

"I saw you on the fence and thought you were a thief," the police officer said in a monotone.

"Who called in the incident?" Webb asked.

This question perplexed the young cop and the blond mustache above his thin lip quivered with the wind. I could see the flicker of a lie forming in his eyes.

"If I call the dispatch supervisor, will I find an incident report?" I asked him. The cop looked away and said nothing. I pointed to the house. "Did they call you? Are you on the Gloaming payroll? Did they promise to re-create you one day? It'll never happen."

The officer paused before answering in a soft voice. "I was on patrol and—"

"Bullshit," Webb said.

The officer stared at the sky for a moment. "I—I received a call from a number that indicated a burglary was in progress." The officer stopped at that point and seemed satisfied with that lie.

I glanced over at Webb and smiled. "I totally believe you," I said as Webb wrinkled her face, looking at me like I had completely lost my mind. Even the officer seemed confused. I pointed at Webb. "I think we have a possible criminal event in progress, Agent Webb. According to this police officer. Extenuating circumstances dictate that we enter the residence to make a protective sweep to ensure the safety of any possible residents in the house."

The cop sputtered "No!" as Webb grinned. She again unholstered her weapon.

I pointed to the officer. "You stay here." And to Webb: "We'll go through the front door."

I kicked open the front door with little resistance. Inside was a makeshift booth-like area with another thick door that was also open. I assumed it was a safeguard against any sunlight entering, especially when the front door was open: they'd close the front door before opening the second door.

I startled a moment when Webb kicked each door back open. She shrugged. "We might need the sunlight," she said.

The den was completely dark and I assumed it was because that would make it easier to determine any stray leaks of light. I flipped the switch on the wall and illuminated an empty living room with a white floor. It was stark and somewhat jarring. Jagged graffiti was sprayed on the wall: "ANOESIS."

I took a picture with my cell phone.

Webb stepped over to clear the kitchen. I heard her breath catch: "Fuck." Empty bags were piled on top of each other on every inch of the kitchen. The bags were splattered with dried blood. It looked like the scene of a bloody civil war battle. Yet the room smelled like a doctor's office: antiseptic and sharp.

"Looks like my aunt's house," I said to no one in particular. "I bet there are carpeted toilet lid covers in the bathroom."

In the closest bedroom, we found a skinny naked man on a cot with a needle stuck in his arm. I pushed his face with my gun, although I could tell by his bluish pallor that he was probably gone. "Wake up, asshole," I said.

Agent Webb leaned over and checked his pulse. She shook her head. "I don't get it," she said. "I didn't think Gloamings would be so sloppy about the people they hire."

"They treat these idiots like apprentices, offering them a chance to be re-created," I told her. I had seen this a few times before. "They ply them with drugs or alcohol—if these apprentices readily accept it, then the Gloamings know they don't have the real discipline. And eventually they allow them to OD when their usefulness is over. Like this poor bastard here. Gloamings only take the best and brightest—someone that adds to, not subtracts from, the whole."

Webb opened the closet and whistled. "What do we have here?" she said as she kicked on a steel plate built into the floor.

Exactly what I was looking for—there was one in every Gloaming house. "Jackpot! It's the entrance to the real Gloaming residence," I said. "It'll be locked from the inside. They don't like to be bothered."

I waved Webb back and her grin told me she knew exactly where this was going.

I raised my gun and sighted the lock with the barrel before I pulled the trigger. *Bang. Bang. Bang. Bang.* Smoke filled the closet. Briefly, I wondered what the idiot cop outside was thinking. The lock split and Webb lifted the cover as I stood above her with my gun pointed down. I wished I had checked out some of the experimental new ammunition specific for Gloaming threats. I had been harping about Gloaming-specific weapons, specifically the depleted uranium bullets, to my colleagues for a while but my requests went up the chain of command with jack shit coming back down.

I went down the stairs first. Webb shined her flashlight for me. The air smelled metallic and foreign, yet as I stepped farther down, a dry, flowery scent began to filter into my nose. I clicked on my flashlight and swept the light across the room as I took the last step to the floor of the basement. My eyes went straight to the light switch on the wall and I flipped it up to see the entire room illuminated.

The size of the room and extensiveness of the renovations were shocking. Behind me, I heard Webb's breath catch. The walls were pristine, cold, clean, and steely, like a hospital. In the middle of the room were two rows of the foil sleeping bag pods which serve as the rest mechanisms for the Gloamings. They're usually filled with a particular mixture of proprietary dirt combination and chemicals. I counted quickly: two rows of five.

Potentially ten Gloamings, fast asleep.

Normally they would use what I would call a space pod of high-grade machined aluminum. Apparently, these sleeping bags served as a temporary resting place for Gloamings in transit.

"Are those…what I think they are?" Webb hissed. "I've only seen pictures of this kind of stuff."

"You bet," I said. "No need to whisper."

I resisted the temptation to empty my new clip into every bag. Then again, like my mom used to tell me, only an idiot goes around kicking hornet's nests. Webb walked over to one of the pods and leaned over to study it closer. I stepped along to the other side of the room and scanned the shelves, looking for anything useful regarding the theft. I opened a few cabinets but found no blood or anything of note.

I can still recall that sweet smell of blood and iron and perfume or incense. I had read about that smell so many times, but smelling it firsthand…It intoxicated me for several seconds and that was all that was needed.

I turned around at the faint sound behind me. I saw a Gloaming man. More monster than man, with tree trunk legs, long fingers and nails, and a shock of wavy red hair—and those hands around Agent Dana Webb's neck.

He snapped her neck and left it hanging by the sinew and skin.

I moved through instinct and emotion all at once. I clearly recall emptying my clip into the Gloaming as I rushed toward the staircase. The bullets would only buy me so many seconds, given the Gloaming resistance to conventional weapons, so I sprinted and lunged for the stairs as I popped another clip into my pistol. By the time I reached the first step, I saw many Gloamings exiting their pods. *Why would they leave the safety of their pod during daylight hours?* I wondered.

I tripped on a middle step and a hand scraped my leg as my pants ripped and my skin burned along with it. I kept scrambling up the stairs. As I reached the living room, I was finally knocked to the ground. I felt a rush of air from my lungs. I barely held on to my gun, and my eyes lifted to see that the front door was closed.

I felt hands reaching for my neck.

I could smell the burning aroma of something more than flesh, almost like rotting flowers, coupled with a scream that rang inside my head.

The weight lifted off my back as my gun erupted toward the front door—and bursts of sunlight shined into the room through the bullet holes. I rolled onto my back and lay there for a moment to catch my breath, bathed in the light from outside. I was still in a haze seconds later, when an FBI tactical team stormed the safe house.

Upon closer inspection, we later found a hidden tunnel behind a cabinet that led to another safe house on a parallel street. Three Gloamings were arrested and convicted of conspiracy to capital murder and sent to the recently constructed Gloaming wing of a supermax prison in Colorado. Ultimately, the three Gloamings escaped from a holding cell while awaiting transfer. They are currently at large and on the FBI's ten-most-wanted list.

The missing Madonna painting was never recovered.

Agent Dana Webb's funeral was held in Austin two days after the raid. I attended and stood in the back. It was a small graveside service. Her kid, the seven-year-old, was a boy.

Several weeks after this art heist incident, the FBI formally announced the formation of a dedicated Gloaming Crimes Unit— light-years in normal government speed. Three full-time agents were assigned initially—myself being the special agent in charge.

CHAPTER 7

American Bar Association Law Journal
Fall/Winter Issue

"Gloaming and NOBI Virus Litigation as a Precursor to Legislation"
by
Kenneth Holm, University of Virginia School of Law
Endowed Professor of Civil Rights and Public Policy

At the time I was contacted by the Human Rights Campaign and the Equal People foundation—and later the Gloaming Council—I was an associate counsel with the law firm Curran, Forest, and Rogers, a New York firm that specialized in civil law, particularly employment issues.

I was drawn initially to the case involving Whitney Talbot, an architect who lived in the East Village in Manhattan. After graduating from Boston College, Talbot accepted a position at Taylor and Wilson Architects in New York City.

Whitney met Ben Oates at a secret late-night EDM party organized by a well-known DJ. Ben was a former physician and now researcher who re-created a year before from an unknown donor.

Whitney was entranced by the man, who, in her recollection, seemed to move with every beat of the music "like a solitary gust of wind." She loved to say things like that. Ben seemed to perceive her interest in him and walked over to her with a smile, and that night they danced for over two hours and never left the floor.

They swiftly began a relationship and spent every night together for months, in spite of Whitney's demanding day job. Ben Oates lived in the basement of an old tenement in the Bowery that had been renovated to ensure that no sunlight would ever reach the interior living areas. Whitney would leave work and catch a few hours of sleep at home before heading to Ben's place as the sun went down. From there they attended any number of parties and meetings and openings. As with other Gloamings, New York society embraced Ben; there was always a place to go.

Whitney accompanied Ben to Britain for London Fashion Week. Ben, himself a DJ, among other ventures which marked him as a Gloaming dilettante without peer, would be playing for the Mercedes-Benz Fashion Week–sponsored Topshop Unique party, curated by British *Vogue*. The nighttime party was held at Winfield House—the Regent's Park residence of Oscar Lampley, the United States ambassador to the United Kingdom, and his wife, Felicity. The party was the premier event of Fashion Week. Whitney almost felt like an afterthought as Ben interacted with a multitude of admirers. An informal receiving line even grew, as if Ben were a head of state.

Ben was the type of person to make rash decisions (this was before the Gloamings put self-imposed restrictions on the type of people to be re-created) and totally immersed himself in his relationship with Whitney. When he impetuously offered to re-create her so that they could be joined as one, Whitney (rather impulsive and

RAYMOND A. VILLAREAL

passionate herself) readily agreed. It was a successful re-creation and she moved in with Ben soon thereafter. Unfortunately, and surprisingly, the relationship did not last. They went their separate ways: Ben to London and Whitney back to her life in New York. Her employer was perfectly happy to accommodate her new status, as it was a progressive firm.

Talbot applied to purchase a unit in the high-end cooperative building the Barclay, on West Seventy-Fifth Street. After her offer on the property was accepted, Whitney completed the application (presenting a stellar credit score, three years' worth of tax returns, reference letters, and a 2 percent debt-to-income ratio). She then conducted an interview with the five-person co-op board, which lasted about twenty minutes. One of the board members asked what kind of modifications Whitney would make so that the apartment would be Gloaming-friendly.

Whitney informed them that any modifications would be temporary and that nothing in the physical structure of the apartment would be changed.

The next day, Whitney Talbot's broker was informed that the board had rejected her application.

Talbot sued under the Fair Housing Act in New York State Court, alleging that the rejection was based on a discriminatory reason and violated various state and federal civil rights laws. Obviously, it was illegal for the board to reject an application based on race, ethnicity, or religion. However, status as a Gloaming was not immediately considered one of the protected classes.

The case was sent to mediation, where no agreement could be reached.

The case went to trial and the court found that Whitney Talbot's status as a Gloaming was considered to be a protected class and that the board discriminated against Talbot by denying her application.

As the Gloaming population increased in those few months, many of the re-created began to push for more rights to accommodate their unique position in this country. Many of the Gloamings were being terminated from their jobs because many employers had no use for an employee that could not work during traditional nine-to-five working hours. The Gloamings attempted to assert that their condition was covered by either the Family and Medical Leave Act (FMLA) or the Americans with Disabilities Act (ADA). Many courts upheld the rights of employers to terminate them for the material change in circumstances; federal courts were also unwilling[6] to extend the protections of FMLA or ADA to cover the Gloamings and their new condition.

However, the Supreme Court soon took up the first case involving Gloamings in *Kurt Jennings, Petitioner v. Allen and Jacobs, LLC.* On writ of certiorari to the United States Court of Appeals for the Ninth Circuit. Let's look at the relevant portions of the opinion (see Appendix One for the full opinion by the court):

Justice Kagan delivered the opinion of the court:

---

[6]   For example, in *Andrew Davis v. Grant-Johnson Advertising*, the plaintiff, Andrew Davis, re-created and immediately requested from his employer a reasonable accommodation of his position as a creative advertising executive at Grant-Johnson Advertising. The employer asserted that the collaborative nature of the work and the normal daytime working hours of the other members on the staff precluded them from making a reasonable accommodation—such as telecommuting—for Davis. The Ninth Circuit Court of Appeals upheld the district court's ruling against the plaintiff; the court went even further by holding that the "reasonable accommodation" requested by the Gloaming would result in an undue hardship to the employer.

We address in this case the application of the Americans with Disabilities Act of 1990 (ADA), 104 Stat. 327, 42 U.S.C. § 12101 et seq., to persons infected with the Nogales organic blood illness (NOBI). We granted certiorari to review, first, whether NOBI is a disability under the ADA when the infected person has willingly taken affirmative steps to become infected.

Petitioner Kurt Jennings has been infected with NOBI since 2019. He admits that he sought out the NOBI illness over a certain number of months in order to be re-created as a Gloaming.[7] Jennings did not inform senior partners at the law firm of Allen and Jacobs, where he was employed as an associate counsel. After taking two weeks of accrued vacation leave, petitioner informed senior partners of the firm that he had re-created and become a Gloaming. After which he used another two months of sick and vacation time. He then asked the partners at the law firm if he would be able to continue his work for the firm but with hours solely during the nighttime, as he could not safely be out during the daytime. Respondent informed Jennings that if he was unable to conduct his job duties during the assigned daytime hours, his employment would be terminated. Thereafter, petitioner's employment was terminated.

Petitioner filed a charge of disability discrimination under the ADA with the Equal Employment Opportunity Commission (EEOC). After receiving a right to sue letter, petitioner filed suit in the United States District Court for the District of Arizona, alleging that respondent had discriminated against him "on the basis of his disability, or because [respondent] regarded [petitioner] as having a disability" in violation of the ADA. App. 26.

---

[7]   The preferred nomenclature of humans who have been infected by the virus and are currently alive with a radiation level of 20 mSv (millisieverts).

Specifically, petitioner alleged that due to his acquiring the NOBI he actually has a substantially limiting impairment or is regarded as having such an impairment, *see id.*, at 23–26, and he is thus disabled under the Act.

Petitioner sued respondent under state law and § 302 of the ADA, 104 Stat. 355, 42 U.S.C. § 12182 alleging discrimination on the basis of his disability. The District Court dismissed petitioner's complaint for failure to state a claim upon which relief could be granted. *See* Civ. A. No. 18-5-115 (Mar. 13, 2018). App. to Pet. for Cert. A-27. Because petitioner willingly acquired his impairment, the court held that he was not actually substantially limited in any major life activity and if he was then such limitation was self-imposed and thus had not stated a claim that he was disabled within the meaning of the ADA. *Id.*, at A-32 to A-36.

The court also determined that petitioner had not made allegations sufficient to support his claim that he was "regarded" by respondent as having an impairment that substantially limits a major life activity. *Id.*, at A-36 to A-37.

The Americans with Disabilities Act of 1990 prohibits discrimination by covered entities, including private employers, against qualified individuals with a disability. A "qualified individual with a disability" is identified as "an individual with a disability who, with or without reasonable accommodation, can perform the essential functions of the employment position that such individual holds or desires." § 12111(8).

We first review the ruling that petitioner's NOBI infection does not constitute a disability under the ADA. We hold petitioner's NOBI infection was not a disability under subsection (A)[8] of the

---

[8]   A physical or mental impairment that substantially limits one or more of the major life activities of such individual.

definitional section of the statute. In light of this conclusion, we need not consider the applicability of subsections (B)[9] or (C)[10].

Our consideration of subsection (A) of the definition proceeds in three steps.

First, subsection (A) requires us to determine whether respondent's condition constituted a physical impairment.

NOBI is not included in the list of specific disorders constituting physical impairments, in part because NOBI was not identified as a known virus until 2018. *See Cartwright.* NOBI infection does at first glance fall within the general definition set forth by the regulations, however.

The disease follows a predictable and, as of today, an unalterable course. However, all research into NOBI has, as of yet, failed to determine specifically how the virus changes the structure of the human body or if it changes every carrier in the identical manner.[11]

A person is regarded as having NOBI when his or her internal and blood ionizing radiation measures 20.0 millisieverts (mSv). U.S. Dept. of Health and Human Services, Public Health

---

[9]   A record of such an impairment.

[10]   Being regarded as having such impairment.

[11]   Once a person is infected with NOBI, the virus invades different cells in the blood and in body tissues. NOBI causes molecular changes in the DNA and cells in a rapid period of time. NOBI is a quasi-retrovirus, which means it uses an enzyme to convert its own genetic material into a form indistinguishable from the genetic material of the target cell. The virus's genetic material migrates to the cell's nucleus and becomes integrated with the cell's chromosomes. Once integrated, the virus can use the cell's own genetic machinery to replicate itself. Additional copies of the virus are released into the body and infect other cells in turn. At this point, neurons in the brain release a chemical called GnRH. Normally, this chemical is used in puberty and causes the pituitary gland to release reproductive hormones, but in a person infected with the NOBI virus, the hormones create physical changes inside and outside the body, creating a new type of almost every organ and material inside the body. Billy Wilder, *The Replication Cycle of NOBI* (Frederich Salka and Terry Oats, eds., 2d ed. 2018).

Service, CDC, 2018 *Revised Classification System for NOBI Infection and Expanded Surveillance Case Definition for NOBI Among Adolescents and Adults*. Such molecular changes in the person afflicted with the NOBI virus cause the person to have an absolute inability to be exposed to direct or indirect sunlight. Any exposure to the sun in even an indirect manner (although research is incomplete regarding how indirect the exposure can be to qualify as physically safe) will cause a form of spontaneous combustion within the body of the Gloaming and if the exposure covers a substantial portion of the body can cause death. Watt and Collins, *NOBI Principles,* 7.1–8, 8.1–20.[12]

The Rehabilitation Act of 1973, 29 U.S.C. § 706(8)(B) (1988 ed.) and the definition of "handicap" contained in the Fair Housing Amendments Act of 1988, 42 U.S.C. § 3602(h)(1) (1988 ed.), are not operative, and the definition not satisfied, unless the impairment affects a major life activity. Petitioner's claim

---

[12]   The initial stage of NOBI infection is known as acute or primary NOBI infection. In a typical case, this stage lasts forty-eight to one hundred and twenty hours. The virus concentrates in the blood. From there, the immune system is overwhelmed and the virus enters the brain. The person suffers from a sudden and serious decline into shock. There is no latency period. All known evidence, although incomplete, concludes that convulsions occur and a coma-like period occurs when the body undergoes its transformation. The prions that have been injected within the virus begin to fold and mutate inside the bloodstream and fold into the DNA and RNA to increase the transformation. Usually these symptoms abate within twenty-four to forty-eight hours, although there is speculation that other latent symptoms last for thirty to seventy days based on the known "disappearance period" of newly re-created Gloamings. Romo and Ambrose, *Primary NOBI Infection, in Medical Issues* in *Infection* 22–45.

After the symptoms associated with the initial stage subside, the virus enters what is referred to sometimes as its post-creation phase. Although it varies with each individual, in most instances this stage lasts from two hundred to two hundred and fifty years according to scientific and computer models and statements from the Gloamings themselves. Watt and Collins, *NOBI Principles* 7.1–8, 8.1–20.

throughout this case has been that the NOBI infection placed a substantial limitation on his ability to spend any time outside during daylight hours. App. 18; 1015 F. Supp., at 587; 200 F. 4th, at 515. Given the pervasive and incurable course of the disease, its effect on major life activities of many sorts might have been relevant to our inquiry. Petitioner and a number of amici make arguments about NOBI's profound impact on almost every phase of the infected person's life. *See* Brief for Petitioner 35–45; Brief for Gloaming Medical Association as Amicus Curiae 20; Brief for Infectious Diseases Society of America et al. as Amici Curiae 8–15. In light of these submissions, it may seem legalistic to circumscribe our discussion to the activity of sunlight. The ability to be exposed to sunlight falls well within the phrase "major life activity." A person's ability to be in sunlight and the activities that accompany such an ability are central to the life process itself.

While respondent concedes the importance of petitioner having the ability to be safely outdoors during daylight hours, they claim that Congress intended the ADA only to cover those aspects of a person's life which have occurred through no fault of their own. Brief for Petitioner 18, 32, 44, 77; *see also id.,* at 55–57 (citing *Flack v. Roberts Construction,* 22 F. 5th 574, 225 (CA8 2018)). The argument centers on the definition of disability in the ADA which defines a person with a disability as a person who has a physical or mental impairment that substantially limits one or more major life activities.

These regulations are contrary to petitioner's attempt to expand the meaning of the term "disability" to disregard the intent of the disabled person. Petitioner attempts to note no difference between a person who engages in risky behavior such as skydiving, working with hazardous chemicals, and operating in a war zone as a soldier and the manner in which he acquired his disability. People in the occupations that petitioner listed accept the chance that they may acquire a disability in their chosen profession but they realize that it is not a certainty that they will be disabled. In contrast, petitioner knew with absolute certainty that when he became a Gloaming he would lose the ability to be in direct or indirect sunlight for the rest of his natural life. Petitioner advances no credible basis for having one's own detrimental actions lead to coverage under the ADA.

In the end, the disability definition does not turn on personal choice. When significant limitations result from the impairment, the definition is met even if the difficulties are not insurmountable. However, when a person willingly brings changes of a harmful physical nature which are an absolute certainty then the Act should not afford the person the same protections afforded those who have acquired the limitations through no fault of their own. Testimony from the petitioner that his NOBI infection was entirely his choice is unchallenged. App. 22; 721 F. Supp., at 412; 107 F. 5th, at 524. In the context of reviewing summary judgment, we must take it to be true. Fed. Rule Civ. Proc. 56(e). We agree with the District Court and the Court of Appeals that no triable issue of fact impedes a ruling on the question of statutory coverage.

In conclusion, petitioner's NOBI infection is a physical impairment which substantially limits a major life activity, as the ADA defines it; however, his impairment is not covered by the ADA because he willingly and with absolute certainty acquired the infection through his own actions.

The determination of the Court of Appeals that petitioner's NOBI infection was not a disability under the ADA is affirmed.

The judgment is vacated, and the case is remanded for further proceedings consistent with this opinion.

From that point, the Gloaming hierarchy, without the court system available to address their issues, decided to concentrate on legislative changes to correct the civil rights deficiencies in the current laws. They began operating a civil rights organization called Equal People—which was staffed with investigators and attorneys. Surprisingly or not, the majority of them were non-Gloamings. These were people derisively described as hangers-on or groupies of the Gloamings—or more likely those who aspired to be re-created.

The organization began to receive reports of private businesses and state government entities that refused to accommodate the night dwellers: by not having courts open during nighttime hours, by not accommodating inmates in jails who were Gloamings, or by not having driver's license offices and other essential state offices open during night hours. Other issues dealt mostly with private business discrimination against the Gloamings: landlords who wouldn't rent to Gloamings, or hospitals that refused to equip instruments or medications to assist ailing Gloamings.

And then, according to many Gloamings and Gloaming historians, one of the most important events in the Gloaming equal rights movement occurred: the killing of Guy Brady.

Brady was a forty-year-old Gloaming who had been re-created a year before. The circumstances of his re-creation are unclear, but Brady was a highly successful and wealthy attorney who made his money litigating medical malpractice suits in numerous states.

It was a Thursday night in Dallas, and Brady had been socializing with friends at an upscale bar on Greenville Avenue, a well-known nightlife strip of bars and restaurants catering to an upper- and upper-middle-class crowd. He was with a group of non-Gloamings the entire night, until he left his friends at about 1:30 a.m.

At this point, details become scarce. There is no accounting for the following hours until about five thirty in the morning.

Around thirty minutes before the sun was about to rise, a loud series of knocks was heard by the barista at the Coffee Chick coffeehouse on Greenville. The coffeehouse was about half an hour from opening to the morning crowd.

The barista looked up and saw Guy Brady banging on the door, yelling to be let inside.

The barista stated later that she really couldn't understand everything he was saying, but she obviously would not open the front door, as it was against policy and she did not feel safe. She called 911.

Shortly after, police officers arrived as Brady kicked open the door. The officers exited their vehicle with guns drawn. They ordered Brady to raise his hands and get on the ground. He apparently told them he couldn't be out in the sun—at this point, the sun was about a minute from rising into dusk.

One officer approached, but Brady threw the cop aside like he weighed nothing.

He moved to run into the coffeehouse, but the other officer immediately discharged his sidearm five times.

Normally a human would hit the ground like a rock, but we are all aware that Gloamings are built differently, and they are able to sustain great trauma to their bodies in addition to harboring their incredible strength. Brady hit the ground but rose up and sprinted down the street as the sun came up over the horizon. The cop unloaded more bullets as Brady ran away, but it was the sunlight that killed him as he continued to run down the block.

The controversy of this event, even in the aftermath, was the top news story for months. It was amplified by the differing accounts from the police and the witnesses.

The police officers on the scene contended that they had no choice in their actions based on the erratic nature of Guy Brady and the threat they felt from his increasingly violent actions. The officers were adamant that they were never aware that Brady was a Gloaming.

But a witness from across the street states that Brady begged to be let inside because he was a Gloaming. Of course, given the nature of the Gloamings, the video bodycam was not usable, nor was the audio.

The police officers were never charged.

Immediately following the incident, Equal People organized a series of night demonstrations with Gloamings and friends of Gloamings which brought out thousands of people to the streets on one night in various cities including New York and Los Angeles. The Gloamings were a wealthy assortment for such a small subgroup. They used their prosperity to keep the protests going for quite a few weeks. In addition, the Gloamings were fighting a disinformation campaign of conspiracy theories bred on the Internet with such accusations as, they were behind the recent thefts from blood banks; they were behind a series of unsolved murders and disappearances where the heads of the bodies were cut off (the decapitation is significant because apparently it precludes a person from being re-created when a Gloaming sucks the blood from their artery, thereby passing the

NOBI virus); they were looking to use the population as a living blood bank to feed themselves.[13]

The Gloamings and their supporters started a civil disobedience campaign aimed at keeping the spotlight on the inequalities they felt in everyday life.

You might wonder who these fellow non-Gloaming protesters were—and what their motivation was. Most were people aspiring to be re-created; others were simple adherents seduced by the allure of the mysterious Gloamings. It certainly was not that hard for the Gloamings of the Equal People organization to find people sympathetic to their cause and willing to help with their protests. And if that failed, the Gloamings were more than willing to pay people to join their protests.

The civil disobedience campaign began with a sit-in at various government offices in Phoenix and Tucson, Arizona.

The Gloamings, especially the wealthier ones, had been drawn to the Arizona and New Mexico areas, going so far as to move there or buy second homes in the region. Many speculated that it was to be closer to Nogales, where Liza Sole was re-created.

The other major incidents of civil disobedience were the picket

---

[13]   In Albuquerque, New Mexico, on November 1, four bodies were found under Highway 85 near Central Avenue: a husband and wife and their twin fifteen-year-old male children. Their bodies were found in a row with all their blood completely drained from them. The presence of radioactive elements from the two teeth marks at the carotid artery clearly pointed to the murderer being a Gloaming. News programs and the Internet stoked Gloaming fears once again, and we were forced to conduct our work on the defensive.

The case remained pending as with all Gloaming-suspected crimes, since their latent radiation renders most DNA tests invalid and their transient nature leaves few clues. But once the two senators were placated regarding the costs and assurances were given that private business would not be impacted, then at that point they began to waver again after the Albuquerque incident. We decided to add money for Gloaming research so as to better find new methods to trace DNA from them.

lines and disruption of various businesses (including grocery stores, banks, fast-food restaurants, gas stations, pharmacies, and colleges and community colleges) that would not accommodate Gloamings with nighttime hours and technology. The protests culminated in police using force to break up the protests at the various locations. Many of the protesters were injured, and this only increased the publicity from the protests. One protest in Phoenix resulted in forty-five injuries and seventy-five arrests.

However, no state legislature was willing to afford the Gloamings any more protections than those of other citizens. This led them to begin more intense efforts to find recourse through the federal government and legislature. By the end of the second year of the NOBI virus, the Gloamings took it upon themselves to attempt passage of a civil rights bill in the U.S. Congress.

The Equal People foundation began an advertising and social media offensive showing Gloamings in natural social situations and with their families.[14] [15]

The Gloamings began a publicity push, granting interviews to news organizations and blogs. The notoriously shy group appeared at rallies and meetings, before government organizations and congressional committees. Equal People also began the process of hiring Kurtz and Long, a high-powered team of lobbyists, to help craft their proposed legislative push.

At this point, a wealthy hedge fund manager named John Dory became involved in the movement. For a brief time, he became the face of the movement. A thin and energetic fifty-eight-year-old, he built his career on a sharp mathematical mind that took advantage

---

[14] They were Photoshopped pictures, of course, given the inherent difficulty of taking an acceptable photograph or video of a Gloaming.

[15] As an aside, during this time, Google and Microsoft were collaborating on a camera that could take an actual photograph of a Gloaming.

of the commodities market in particular. A participant in the New York City social scene, he was never shy about attending gala events and fund-raisers for prominent causes, but he disappeared for about a year, which caused great speculation among certain members of the media and others in the philanthropic class.[16]

Then, one evening, John Dory showed up at the annual Red Ball for the Columbia Hospital Cancer Fund. As soon as he entered the Waldorf ballroom, most people in the audience could tell he had been re-created. The almost imperceptible slightly goldish hue on his beaming face. The sparkling eyes and catlike movements as he walked inside, as if he moved in concert with the wind. He was quite open about it when asked. In fact, the blogs and gossip columns couldn't publish the information fast enough, and Dory began a media blitz to discuss his re-creation, going from the *New York Times* to the *Today* show (although that television appearance consisted of a blurred and fuzzed image with a dubbed voice).

Dory's team of lawyers and lobbyists crafted early drafts of the proposed Gloaming Rights Act, while Dory confronted the bill's most pressing issue: how many senators and congresspeople could he sway to support it? Dory had a lot of work to do, and he decided early on to concentrate on Montana's senior senator, Tommy Ward.

---

[16]   Dory had attended the opening night of the Tribeca Film Festival and then the invitation-only after-party for the sponsors held at Mission Chinese Food on East Broadway. There were several Gloamings in attendance but that wasn't anything unusual for a high-profile event in NYC. Dory then left the party—although there were no witnesses—and was not seen for another year. During this time his business interests went into a court-ordered receivership but his only heir—Dory was single and had no children—his sister, refused to initiate proceedings to declare him deceased. Although no one filed a missing persons report, the FBI did initiate a preliminary investigation given Dory's stature and the vast sums of wealth he controlled. Seven months after his disappearance, Dory released a statement through his attorneys that he was fine and that he would return to public life in an undetermined amount of time.

TMZ.com: Celebrity Gossip | Entertainment News | Celebrity News

Justin Bieber and Kanye West together *GASP* at a concert for Quebec Rights in Canada?!

Well, those Gloamings seem to have an almost uncanny ability to find a subculture to exploit for their own aims. Now it's recently re-created Canadian grocery store magnate billionaire George-Étienne Bouchard—you remember him. Looks like your slightly creepy, drunk uncle—if said uncle had enough Botox injected in his face to resemble a wax figure. Bouchard is spending untold millions (how dare he?) to conduct a referendum—yes, look it up!—on Quebec sovereignty.

Now, Billionaire Bouchard is hosting a benefit concert (maybe he's not crazy-crazy, but FUN) with Justin Bieber and Kanye West headlining: "Québec Solidaire!" Were Drake and Alanis Morissette busy?

Bieber cut his performance short after audio issues surfaced—or more likely issues with his prerecorded voice tracks. Afterward, as if the weekend couldn't get any stranger, Bieber was robbed at gunpoint outside his hotel with the thieves stealing his cell phone and jewelry estimated to be in the amount of $10 million. Of course his hysterical (drug-fueled?) crying fit afterward on Instagram didn't make things any better.

Check out the comments—ouch!! "Should have happened a long time ago" or "Damn shame they didn't pull the trigger."

CHAPTER 8

OCTOBER 12
SEVENTEEN MONTHS AFTER THE NOBI DISCOVERY

Marcy Noll
Counsel for the House Committee on Homeland Security

I spoke extensively to various participants in the following meetings between John Dory and Senator Thomas Ward. My conversations were part of a House investigation into allegations that various congressional staffers and elected officials were part of a vote-peddling operation to pass Gloaming legislation. The charges were never proven and the investigation was terminated after seven months.

It took John Dory months to get a meeting with Senator Thomas Ward, who, born and raised in Gardiner, Montana, had once traveled the entire state, shaking hands and bending ears, in an off-year election with an unpopular president, winning his first run for office three decades ago with 51 percent of the vote. And so commenced his storied career in the U.S. Senate. Ward took to the Senate as he took to selling computer equipment, his photographic memory learning all the intricacies and movements of the institutions in order to influence people and policy.[17]

But Dory knew of the senator's apparent indifference to the plight of the Gloamings. Their meeting would finally come on a full moon evening in Helena, Montana, at a twenty-four-hour upscale diner in the block-long hipster enclave. Senator Ward had spent Labor Day weekend catching up with constituent services and attending local parades and parties.

Senator Ward and one aide sat at the table. Ward drummed his fingers on the table.

The sun was deep on the other side of the earth as a custom limousine with no side windows took a slow roll to the front of the restaurant. Almost as soon as it stopped, John Dory opened the side door and stepped out of the car. A younger man in a dark suit followed Dory into the bright diner. The crowd had mostly thinned out; the late eaters would arrive about midnight.

Senator Ward waved Dory over with the fork he had been using to eat a mountainous piece of apple pie à la mode. Dory's assistant walked over to the counter, and Ward's aide followed to the counter. Ward rose to grip Dory's hand in a lingering shake.

"Thank you for meeting me," Dory said.

"Take a seat," Senator Ward said as he pointed to the pie on the table. "Would you like some pie? Or something else? My treat."

John Dory paused a bit, probably considering whether Senator Ward was attempting to make a point by offering him food, knowing full

---

[17] His photographic memory became a well of knowledge of parliamentary procedure and Senate rules. Most senators could not be bothered to learn the intricate and mind-numbing rules of order, so Tommy became a body of proficiency to lean on when in need of parliamentary help. After a couple of unopposed terms, he became the indispensable majority whip and retained significant influence given his knowledge of the legislative rules and his inherent charm.

well that Gloamings do not eat proper food for nutrition. Only blood.

Dory ignored any kind of malicious intent and began his pitch. "I want to discuss our proposed Gloaming Rights Act with you, Senator. My understanding is that you have read the proposal in its current form. I want to know what you need from us to support it and any concerns that you may have about the contents of the proposed bill."

Senator Ward took a bite of apple pie and chewed it in silence. "I understand the need of the Gloamings to establish their rights consistent with those of other Americans. My concerns are those regarding the cost of such arrangements and, frankly, the necessity, given the number of them in contrast to the general population and the preferred lifestyle a majority of the Gloamings enjoy."

Dory nodded. This might have been more difficult than he had imagined. "Fair enough. But with all accommodations—for example, those regarding the ADA—there is always a cost involved. Wheelchair ramps, crosswalk changes for blind and deaf persons—those cost money, but our society felt that it was sufficiently important that afflicted persons have a measure of equality and safety in order to pursue a full life. Most of these people are not asking for something more than others have: simply equality."

Senator Ward let out a long sigh. "I understand that, but I don't think we can compare those groups with Gloamings. The Gloamings are new and occupy a distinct minority of the population. A quite insular type of community, you must admit. Not given to participating in any other culture but their own."

John Dory stared straight ahead.

Senator Ward placed his fork down on the table. The restaurant was clearing out the few patrons that had finished their meals. It had suddenly become very quiet. "The Gloamings chose their way of life and continue to choose that way of life. I'm not judging your choice either. Many Gloamings have used their re-creation for noble purposes, I'm certain. But the others you mention who have disabilities would choose another way if they could. We would be forcing local counties and cities to open all government functions basically twenty-four hours a day. Buses would have to make the same accommodation. Perhaps legislatures would need to have night sessions. Voting booths, elementary and high schools, colleges—where does it all lead?"

Dory nodded. "I understand your concerns—entirely valid. This is merely a starting point for the discussions to follow."

With somewhat of a sigh, Senator Ward took a drink of his wine. "Then we will leave this to another discussion and I will assure you that I can keep an open mind in the interim." And with that the meeting concluded, and Dory knew he still had a long road ahead of him.

When Senator Ward ended up cosponsoring the Gloaming Rights Act three months later, naturally there was an abundance of speculation: had Senator Ward re-created as a Gloaming himself? What other reason could there be? But that was totally inaccurate. No one could ever know Ward's true reasons, but I suspect his conversion to the Gloaming cause was due to Dory's money. Representative Ruben Drew of Louisiana, the father of a Gloaming, introduced the Gloaming Rights Act in the House, as Senator Ward introduced the identical bill in the Senate.

The evolution and construction of the bill as it progresses through stops and starts over a period of eight months is a fascinating process of logic, emotion, and political grandstanding, which many historians have captured in more rigorous detail.[18]

The bill that we eventually constructed proposed the following elements:

1 Educational institutions that receive federal funds must accommodate the Gloaming population with night classes at least two days a week during each semester. Elementary, middle, and high schools shall not be required to make accommodations to the Gloaming populations. The Department of Education shall study the viability and economic impact of Gloaming accommodations for children's schooling when the Gloaming population reaches a yet to be determined percentage of the population. Gloaming parents of Gloaming children shall be eligible for an educational tax deduction of 50 percent for any tutoring or homeschooling expenses incurred.

2 States and municipalities shall be required to provide early nighttime voting for Gloamings in every election. Every state shall comply whether the state has an early voting period or not.

3 Essential government services consisting of driver's license renewals and exams shall accommodate the Gloamings with nighttime hours at least three nights per month, and Gloamings shall be exempt from certain licensing restrictions—such as a picture required on a license—based on their physical characteristics.

4 The bill prohibits discrimination against Gloamings by covered employers. This applies to an employer who has fifty or more employees for each working day in each of twenty or more calendar weeks in the current or preceding calendar year. The bill

---

[18]   See Appendix Three.

would also prohibit discrimination against an individual because of his or her association with another individual classified as a Gloaming, such as by intermarriage with a Gloaming.[19]

With the context of the bill intact, advisers to the president indicated that the president would support the bill in its current form. However, even with that important endorsement—although not public—the bill was on decidedly shaky ground. With lobbyists working overtime, the head count in the Senate was still fifty-two to forty-eight against passage. And this didn't even take into account the group of five or so hard-line senators that vowed to filibuster any Gloaming Rights Act. At the time, surviving a filibuster was thought to be the biggest challenge to the bill.

The head count in the House was passage by two votes, so if our side could hold on to those votes then we could spend our time concentrating on the Senate and attempt to persuade the two most likely converts to the bill: Senator Colin Peterson of Minnesota and Senator Matt Kelley of Illinois. Both senators were wavering on the merits of the bill, more concerned about the costs associated with the act as opposed to any misgivings about the Gloamings.

The two senators wanted to ensure that private business would not be affected by the act and any costs associated. Equal People determined that passage of the first Gloaming Rights Act was more important as a first step than a bill that met every one of their wishes. It was enough to have the government accommodate the

---

[19] However, an employer is permitted to discriminate on the basis of a protected trait where the trait is a bona fide occupational qualification (BFOQ) reasonably necessary to the normal operation of that particular business or enterprise. The BFOQ exception is a narrow exception to the general prohibition of discrimination based on being classified as a Gloaming.

Gloamings; Equal People figured subsequent bills could add more protections and include private businesses. So they approved of the bill that we constructed.[20]

The bill was reported out of the House Judiciary Committee by a vote of thirty-one to twenty-nine, which was a bit closer than we expected at the time. The bill was opposed by many members of the committee on the merits; however, other members who were inclined to support the measure voted against the bill in committee because of the expedited consideration of the bill and the absolute dictate from the chairman that he would not entertain any amendments to the bill. The deliberations during the closed committee meetings were stressful and the atmosphere toxic. Shouting could be heard down hallways, and there were even a few pushing and shoving matches between staff members. Threats were commonplace and were made every hour of meeting until no one could be bothered to remember what particular type of retribution was coming their way, if any. A broken iPad Pro 3-D that belonged to the ranking minority member was left in a hallway and no one took responsibility for the act, but the assistant chief took to wearing it around his neck like a re-created Flavor Flav of the future to every staff meeting as a sign of disapproval. The bill was thought to be dead in the water when the Congressional Black Caucus and the Congressional Hispanic Caucus decided to

---

[20] A week of massaging by the White House chief of staff, who assured the senators that the president would actively support the bill, brought them back into the fold, although with a decided air of uncertainty. On July 10, Representative Ruben Drew of Louisiana introduced H.R. 4287, the Gloaming Rights Act. Representative Drew, whose daughter Wendy had re-created the previous year, was soon thrust into the media as the new face of the Gloaming rights movement. Although not a Gloaming himself, Representative Drew could articulate their positions from the point of view of a loving father and, more importantly, could appear on camera.

withhold any endorsement of it. Reports from the Internet and the news said that the Gloamings were composed of less than 5 percent people of color; other sources stated that it was even less than that. The Gloamings protested that the figure was grossly overstated and that a complete census of the Gloamings was an impossible task given their tendency to live off the grid and their secretive nature. However, the Gloaming leaders in Equal People assured the congressional critics that their racial makeup compared favorably with that of the actual demographic racial composition of America. After much discussion and assurances from the Gloamings that they would conduct a census of their people within a ten-year period of time, the black and Hispanic caucuses came out in favor of the bill.

The president then did an interview on *Good Morning America* where she wholeheartedly endorsed the Gloaming Rights Act and discussed why the bill was needed at this point in time. It was an important event in the history of Gloaming rights. Of course, commentators parsed her language and wanted to know why she used the words "only bill" and "final bill" when discussing the act when many Gloaming advocates considered this bill to be the first in a series of measures giving Gloamings equal rights.

The interview became more pointed when the president was asked about her reaction to the recent re-creation of the previous president and why he wasn't present at any of her appearances given his stature and importance to the Gloaming community. She deftly avoided the implication and question by saying that she was confident they would be making appearances together and that his support for the bill was crucial. However, many off-the-record statements from aides to the president indicated that she was extremely angry that the former president did not inform her of his impending re-creation and that this swiftly pushed the Gloaming rights issue when she had intended to proceed with a more measured approach.

After the initial period of media attention and the president making a strong case for this limited bill, sixty senators came out to support the vote to deny a filibuster of the bill. It didn't mean that the bill had sixty votes in favor, but it did mean that a large majority supported a clean up or down vote on the bill in the Senate. This was probably the most important hurdle that was jumped, and now the members in favor of the bill could discuss the merits without having to argue against a filibuster.

On October 12, in the House of Representatives, 140 Democrats and 80 Republicans voted for the Gloaming Rights Act—newly renamed the Equal Rights for All Act—and 95 Democrats and 120 Republicans voted against it.

The Senate Judiciary Committee then passed the newly renamed Equal Rights for All Act.

Gloaming opponents could see that the act was very close to passage, so they upped their opposition to the bill. They ran commercials contending that being a Gloaming meant having the NOBI virus and that it should be considered an illness, not a segment of the population. They argued that people were not born Gloamings through no fault of their own, but that they actively sought out this virus that limited the freedom of their full lives by making them avoid sunlight. It didn't help that many of the more outspoken and radical Gloamings began to refer to themselves as "bloodsuckers" or "blooddrinkers." Of course, the Gloaming opponents seized upon this and advertised it at every chance as proof that the Gloamings were a threat and never intended to fully assimilate into proper society.

However, on November 7, in the Senate, forty Democrats and twenty Republicans voted for the Senate's version of the bill, called the Equal Rights for All Act, whose lead author was Senator Robert Logan from New York. Twenty-five Republicans and fifteen Democrats voted against the bill.[21]

---

[21]   On November 28, after experiencing a broad backlash from his constituents regarding his support of the Equal Rights for All Act, and after a news report came out that he had received free plane rides from a wealthy Gloaming and his daughter had received a job from a wealthy Wall Street Gloaming, Senator Graham McCoy of Ohio reversed his position and stated that he would not vote for the bill nor would he vote for cloture, effectively a vote supporting the filibuster of the bill.

Supporters of the bill now realized that the sixtieth vote needed to pass the bill was not there anymore. Senate supporters of the bill, both Republicans and Democrats, decided to use budget reconciliation in order to get to one bill approved by the House and the Senate. The use of budget reconciliation only required fifty-one senators to vote in favor of the bill in order for it to be approved and sent to the president for a formal signature which then enacts the bill.

The Senate began to deliberate H.R. 2212, a bill dealing with tax breaks for companies whose inventory has been damaged and determined unusable due to a stage four natural disaster. As the United States Constitution required all revenue-related bills to originate in the House, the Senate took up this bill since it was first passed by the House as a revenue-related modification to the Internal Revenue Code. The bill was then used as the Senate's vehicle for its Gloaming Rights Act, completely revising the content of the bill. The bill as amended would ultimately incorporate all elements of the House and Senate bills, which were almost identical as passed by the respective committees. With the anti-Gloaming minority in the Senate vowing to filibuster any bill they did not support, requiring a cloture vote to end debate, sixty votes would be necessary to get passage in the Senate. When Senator McCoy changed his position, supporters of the bill only had fifty-nine votes for cloture.

The supporters then drafted the Gloaming Rights Reconciliation Act, which could be passed by the reconciliation process. Once again, Senator McCoy changed his position for reasons that would not be clear until years later, when it was confirmed that he had re-created. Shortly after he resigned his seat, he went to work for a Gloaming hedge fund.

The president signed the Gloaming Rights Act into law on February 10.

Many people would point to that day as the last time the human majority felt any sympathy with the Gloaming minority.

Dagens Nyheter (Stockholm)—October 11—Daily Edition[22]

The Swedish Ministry of Justice and the Swedish Police Authority announced this morning that, in what seem like separate incidents, two bodies were found decapitated and two car explosions occurred—both on the same evening that wealthy housing manufacturer Nils Karlsson was the victim of a robbery. The Ministry believes all three events are connected. The theft occurred at Karlsson's downtown Italianate brownstone with its distinctive gold-bracketed cornice and towers, located in the affluent Östermalm district, among the eclectic shops, art galleries, coffeehouses, and restaurants. The thieves took approximately 182,922,000.00 Swedish krona ($20 million) worth of 400-troy-ounce (438.9 ounces) Good Delivery gold bars from the secure basement safe of the house. The safe also contained a large amount of precious stones which the robbers ignored. The elaborate security system was triggered, and as three police officers were two blocks from the scene, two car explosions on the main street caused them to delay their arrival by thirty minutes. Two decapitated bodies, possibly witnesses, were found in an Audi parked across the street from Karlsson's house. Sources close to the Ministry said that elevated radiation levels indicated that the perpetrators were Gloamings.

---

[22] Translated into English from Swedish.

Comments Section 1:23 a.m. [written in English]

Profile: Anonymous

Text: I was there that night when the robbery occurred. I'm a bike messenger for food deliveries. I had just dropped off an order at some condos when I stopped by the street where the robbery occurred. I was resting and texting when I saw this Mercedes van—all blacked out—park in front of the brownstone. About ten people clothed in black coveralls with masks piled out of the van with this weird precision. It was unnerving so I kind of hid behind a truck and watched. The men or women then came out in pairs, carrying something covered by a blanket. While this was happening, one of the figures walked over to a car parked three car lengths from the truck. There was a couple sitting in the car. The figure opened the door and bit the woman as he or she punched the man. The figure then bit the man and I could see the figure using hands or an implement to cut the heads off. I was shaking and sobbing. I crawled under the truck and stayed there. I don't know how long it took or when they left. I will not go to the police. I fear who these people are and if they are Gloamings I fear them even more.

CHAPTER 9

Hugo Zumthor
Special Agent in Charge of Gloaming Crimes Unit, FBI

You want to hear something really funny? And I mean laugh-out-loud funny. Where did the vampire open a savings account? At the blood bank!

Okay, for real: the Gloamings love gold. I mean, we all love gold, but their infatuation with gold was something extraordinary, bordering on obsessive. I was convinced the Gloamings sought gold because of the metal's excellent ability to conduct heat and electricity, and its ability to reflect infrared radiation—given the Gloamings' physical ability to emit radiation themselves, it could be a soothing element for their system. But just the vision of a Gloaming rifling through a pile of gold like some fairy tale or *Lord of the Rings* character—I don't know why, but this always makes me chuckle.

Other investigators and scientists have suspected that Gloamings somehow coat their clothing and skin, perhaps, in gold to reflect their radiation back into themselves. But the physical purpose of this has yet to be determined.

At the time the Gloaming Crimes Unit was formed, the FBI had not established a Gloaming connection to the reports of gold theft—until an ambitious new agent who, studying the evidence for many months like a reclusive scientist, found that each theft of gold coincided with a performance of the opera *Nixon in China* traveling the country. It seemed a tenuous connection, yet it fit together like a puzzle.

This all-Gloaming opera production that was touring the country—I still trip on how, instead of being an accomplice to the boredom of America, an opera actually helped catch a Gloaming— was a high point in Gloaming history because it brought the Gloaming people and culture to many who might not ever have come in contact with a Gloaming, given their reclusive nature and inability to appear on video or audio. This connection soon brought me into the orbit of Cian Clery.

Cian was purportedly born in New Orleans one night during a Category 4 hurricane. His mother gave birth in their crumbling garage apartment on Saint Charles Avenue, with a midwife and a gardener providing support. When Cian was five, he and his mother moved to Ames, Iowa. Following that, records about him are scarce, as Cian was never enrolled in any formal school—he was apparently homeschooled by his single mother until he entered Yale School of Drama on a full scholarship.

Even as an undergrad, he spellbound his professors and fellow students with his Teutonic good looks and exceptional capability to truly become another person while playing a part. His classroom exercises brought fellow students to tears; other students audited his classes if they thought he might be performing even a one-minute exercise. Devoted to his craft, Cian soon adopted an ascetic lifestyle, staying in his dorm room to study and abstaining from extracurricular activities and socializing. He simply meditated on his craft, performing scenes from his favorite plays alone in his dorm room. His roommate had long since moved to a different room. All this only added to Cian Clery's mystique, and classmates honored his lifestyle by leaving him to his own devices.

As a freshman he was awarded the lead in Yale School of Drama's fall season production of Lanford Wilson's *Burn This*. An article in the university newspaper noted that Cian Clery, as Pale, the combustible lead character, "held the audience in a hypnotic spell" for the entirety of the play.

From that point on, he was the lead in practically all of the productions, from *Spring Awakening* to *Desire Under the Elms*. Each staging was dubbed a classic, with ticket prices skyrocketing and a thriving New Haven black market of students scalping tickets to dedicated theater fans from Boston and New York. In fact, the school had to hire extra security to stop people from attempting to sneak into the auditorium to see Cian. Hollywood came calling during his sophomore year, but Cian rebuffed every offer. He simply wanted to study.

Summer after junior year was the seminal period in his life. From what we could discover—albeit via sometimes unreliable sources—Cian hitchhiked to Austin, Texas, to try out for a role at an independent theater called the Ultimate. They operated as a low-budget co-op producing operas—as opposed to the usual small theater's one-act plays. He auditioned and sang flawless Italian—although the original was in Russian—and took the lead of Robert, Duke of Burgundy, in the Ultimate's production of *Iolanta*. Many patrons in the audience who were interviewed for an article in the *New York Times* still remember his presence completely overshadowing the other actors onstage. They could recall tears running down the faces of the patrons and others sobbing from the emotions involved in his performance. It still affected them to that day.

Maybe in the same way I'm still affected by the Dallas Cowboys losing to the New York Giants every year. I'm misting up just thinking about it.

After five performances, and with no notice, Cian left Austin and proceeded to hitchhike back to Yale. Yet somewhere between Austin and New Haven, Connecticut, Cian was re-created.

The exact circumstances of his re-creation are not known—though many journalists have tried to investigate the mysterious circumstances—but what is known is that upon arriving at Yale, Cian went straight to the house of the dean of the drama school at two in the morning. Cian informed the dean of his new status as a Gloaming and said he wanted to be accommodated in order to finish his degree. This was before the passage of the Equal Rights for All Act, but the dean readily agreed, and Cian received his bachelor's degree within the year. However, strangely enough, during his senior year he refused to participate in any more productions at Yale, preferring to study his craft in isolation and plan for his next venture.

Cian was a shoo-in to become a Hollywood heartthrob, but his new Gloaming status made film and television work impossible. By all accounts, however, he would not have it any other way—he felt more comfortable connecting with a live audience than in front of cameras. After graduation, his first starring role—greatly anticipated in the theater world—was soon announced. Thanks to Gloaming investors, Cian formed his own production company, and he would personally star in the company's debut, a ten-city tour of *Nixon in China,* an opera based on President Nixon's groundbreaking—given his status as an anti-communist leader—visit to China in 1972.

It was a decidedly strange idea to stage this opera—or any opera—especially as the first production of Cian's company. The subject matter seemed incredibly dry and not sexy enough to attract a mass audience. Cian would be taking the title role of Richard Nixon, looking nothing like him but somehow feeling that such a difficult transformation would be a challenge worth undertaking. He had been working on the performance in private throughout his senior year, until he felt it had finally come to him and was ready to be seen by the public.

But Cian's next coup was securing the original director, Peter Sellars, to direct this revival. The opera premiered in New York City and was an immediate success. Cian's voice and presence exploded throughout the concert hall; people claimed he could be heard outside, where a crowd waited for any glimpse of Cian. By the end of the performance, many audience members would describe themselves as exhausted and exhilarated by the portrayal, considering it more of a communal event than an opera.

The show's front-page *New York Times* rave led to two more sold-out shows and tickets being scalped for thousands of dollars. The Internet only increased the hype after an article in BuzzFeed raved about the production and about Cian in particular. The site used accurate drawings to show scenes from the opera and backstage, including outside the stage door, where hundreds, even thousands, of fans mobbed Cian for autographs and an opportunity to see or touch him. The city had to assign over fifty officers to crowd control, including their mounted units. The mayor threatened for weeks to shut down the production unless the producers contributed to the cost of security and crowd control. Lawsuits were threatened but eventually the city decided to provide security for the limited run of the production.

The media and the Internet would publish stories about the energy of the show, and various patrons would go to great lengths to describe how Cian's eyes were a deep shade of yellow that seemed to sparkle and see every face at once.

Every scheduled performance was sold out, and during its run, no movie or concert was a hotter ticket than *Nixon in China*.

The first gold theft occurred during the third performance in New York City, at the home of John Hatcher, a wealthy trial attorney who'd amassed a small fortune suing asbestos manufacturers. As a person given to unorthodox views, ranging from government conspiracies to advocating doomsday prepping, he kept a portion of his holdings in gold to inoculate himself from the next economic collapse. He built a private gold depository in the basement of his Manhattan brownstone. The depository was constructed out of the gutted former washer-and-dryer room; it didn't meet the specifications of a bank vault, but it was solidly built with reinforced concrete and Kevlar, with a one-foot-thick steel door with a retinal scan lock. On the night in question, John Hatcher attended a performance of *Nixon in China* and ate a late sushi dinner with friends at Masa, which lasted for three hours. He departed for his brownstone with only his bodyguard. When he arrived, the first thing he did was go down to the basement, where he kept a bar, and he saw the safe open and all of his gold missing.

The FBI was called in two weeks after the burglary, the length of time due to Hatcher's reluctance to disclose how much of his money was kept in gold. Wealthy people know how such admissions can lead to the IRS taking an interest in their finances, and most have something to hide when it concerns income. Immediately after the theft, Hatcher hired a team of confidential private investigators, but they failed to turn up any solid leads. That's when he called the FBI—two weeks later. The regional New York City FBI office took on the case, but between terrorist alert investigations and counterespionage, it languished.

The next theft occurred in Boston, during the opera's run of three nights in that city.

This one occurred at an independent gold distributor, the Ellison Corporation, located on the first floor of an old bank building in downtown Boston. On the night of the second performance of *Nixon in China,* someone, or a group of people, disabled the cameras; broke into the building's basement, where only gold was stored, without sounding the alarm; incapacitated the guards by an unknown means; and emptied the vaults of $5 million worth of gold. Unlike Hatcher, the Ellison Corporation reported the theft immediately to the FBI, although as with Hatcher's case, this one languished. There were simply no clues.

The third theft occurred during the opera's next series of performances, in Houston, Texas. At this point, the young FBI agent Calvin James, who was based in Los Angeles and assigned to the recent theft, sent me his theories regarding possible Gloaming involvement. It was a week before I read the email and considered his theories, but I was deeply impressed by Calvin's meticulous evidence.

There had to be a connection. Of course, others in the FBI assumed it was my suspicion of all things Gloaming that made me draw this conclusion, but it was hard to dismiss the elaborate coincidences related to the thefts and the opera. They say you live and learn, but I had long since dismissed that advice. I'll live from not learning and be fine with it.

So I booked a ticket to Houston, only to find out that the opera was already moving on to its next destination: a weeklong residency in Los Angeles.

"Tip the world over on its side and everything loose will land in Los Angeles." I think it was Frank Lloyd Wright who said that. It was my first thought stepping off the plane and being accosted by all the Botoxed faces. It looked like a remake of Vincent Price's *House of Wax*.

I met Agent Calvin James at LAX. He was a tall, built, ex–college football player with caramel skin and model good looks. He had joined the FBI after a two-year stint as an accountant for HP computers. He had already established himself as a thorough agent, someone you could count on to have your back.

To plan our next steps, we had dinner at the Lucky Grill, a crowded old-school diner that smelled like breakfast day and night. Old counters and faded leather booths packed with new suits and tight faces. Also hipsters. The buzz of conversations bounced off the walls with the sizzle of grilling food and the clanging of pots and pans.

"How can you live here?" I asked James.

He smiled and took a bite of his avocado toast hamburger. "Other than the urban blight, vapid idiots, endless traffic, pollution, how people couldn't care less about you unless you can do something for them or advance their careers, a psychotic indifference to anything resembling empathy, and lack of soul? I fucking love it here! It's perfect."

After a few minutes of reviewing the evidence, we both were convinced the Gloamings were behind the gold thefts and that the opera played an integral, yet unknown, part in the operation. I felt we had a few days to find the means of the upcoming—or so we thought—theft before it occurred. Agent James proposed some plans.

Our first objective was to research and find any possible targets, which would include private gold depositories run by companies and private investors who held their gold at their residences. Obviously not an easy task considering the time constraints. However, the FBI assigned us a staff for two days to help us narrow down our list to the most likely targets. We established three possible targets: a four-story 1950s-era commercial building in Boyle Heights housing the Inland Valley LLC, a private metals holding facility; another precious metals dealer handling heavy quantities of diamonds and gold, located in a nondescript one-story building in Westwood and known as Millennial Corp.; and a ten-thousand-square-foot residence in Bel Air owned by dot-com billionaire Sasha Bowie, who held a substantial amount of gold at her residence.

We concluded that the Bel Air residence was most likely, since it arguably held the most gold and had the lightest comparable security. We scheduled an immediate meeting with Sasha Bowie, which was one of the more difficult things the FBI has ever attempted—I've had an easier time scheduling a meeting with the Speaker of the House or the secretary of Homeland Security.

Of course, as we all knew, Sasha Bowie was pretty busy Instagramming, Snapchatting, and tweeting her glorious life and numerous parties and premieres. Her fortune was made as one of the original Facebook employees—she was an engineer by training—who had cashed out her billions in stock and invested in other tech supernovas, only multiplying her wealth. She also had millions of followers on every social media app you could imagine.

We met at her house in Bel Air, which sat on a gated 2.5-acre lot—all post and beam, steel and marble. If you need any more evidence that the top 1 percent need to be taxed to within an inch of their lives and that the inheritance tax should be 99 percent, look no further than this estate. We sat in a large banquette in her kitchen the size of a Denny's. It was only myself, Calvin, and Sasha—no lawyers or advisers or publicists. She spoke on the phone near the refrigerator as we waited. I leaned over to Calvin. "She's thirty-five and looks like she's had more Botox than Madonna or Meg Ryan."

"Thirty-five?" Calvin snorted. "She's been thirty-five for more than a decade."

Sasha strolled over and sat across from us. "So where did you get this information that I—if I do have gold here, that is—might be at risk for theft?" she asked.

I sighed. We had already told her, and her lawyers, that the FBI couldn't reveal our means of acquiring such information. "I'm sorry about that, but we do feel that our information is correct and conclusive."

Sasha stared at me for a moment and scrolled on her iPhone as she continued. "Let's say for the sake of argument that I do have a large amount of gold stored here. It would be beyond the capabilities of any so-called burglars to come in and take it. It would be virtually impossible to penetrate the security measures I have installed here at my house."

I leaned over toward her and opened my palms. "You have to understand that the other thefts were from safes that were guarded by some of the most secure systems ever built. As secure as yours, I assure you."

"What exactly do you want from me?"

"Let us have surveillance on and around your property for the next three days. If nothing happens then I can safely assume your gold is okay. No harm in that."

Sasha went through the charade of actually considering all this, even though I knew her lawyers had determined the answer days earlier. She finally grinned. "Oh sure, why not? It's only three days and I'm going to be in Colorado for some work stuff. Heck, my people will probably leak it to the press after it's been done for some publicity later too. Be my guest."

I wanted to do a slow clap but that would be pushing my luck.

We thanked her profusely. In the car, when we finally exited her property, Calvin and I looked at each other—and just burst out laughing.

"I don't think you realize how sensitive this matter has become." Cian's publicist, one William Gascoigne who oddly kept referring to himself by his full name, stood in front of us wringing his hands and twitching as if someone were poking him with a cattle prod.

Calvin and I arrived at the Standard hotel—purportedly now Gloaming-owned—at nine in the evening. This was the hotel closest to Disney Hall, where *Nixon in China* was being performed. William Gascoigne met us in the dim lobby, hands mincing at his chest in nervous energy. His silk shirt stood out like a neon sign in the dark space. He was not a Gloaming. I could tell. I wondered why, given that he was a powerful Hollywood publicist, he hadn't been re-created yet like most of his colleagues. It must have been somewhat humiliating for him. Maybe he needed that carrot dangled a while longer. He seemed to have a nervous tic of rolling his eyes after every sentence.

Getting access to Cian was even harder than scheduling our interview with Sasha. William Gascoigne was quite stubborn in his attempts to delay or refuse any interview, to the point of calling in Cian's high-powered law firm to issue threats of litigation and to our job security. But I had threats of my own to offer: I could leak details of the investigation to the media about the Gloamings', and the opera production's, involvement. William Gascoigne finally offered a quick interview before rehearsals for the Los Angeles premiere.

"You do realize the sensitivity of this?" William Gascoigne shouted. "Am I talking to myself?" He shook his head as if done with us.

Behind Gascoigne stood a few large European-looking bodyguards in black suits, shaved heads, and scowls. William flattened the front of his black trousers with his twitching hands before he took my own hand in a limp shake and moved over to Calvin's.

He finally nodded and pointed at the elevator behind us. "This way, please," he said, and we followed him into the elevator. I caught Calvin glancing at me with a face that said "I'm ready for anything to go down."

We found ourselves on the penthouse floor. William Gascoigne stopped in front of the room door. "Please remember to be respectful of Mr. Clery. He requires a highly meditative state of mind before each performance, and that state must not be altered in any negative manner. You are being afforded a great opportunity, so please make sure this interview is entirely confidential."

Then William Gascoigne abruptly stopped talking.

He stared at each of us, as if to confirm we understood this valuable information.

I glanced over at Calvin, who suppressed a slight grin. "Yes sir, William Gascoigne," he said. "You have our word."

I wasn't surprised to find the large suite in almost total darkness, as most Gloamings could see in the dark easily. I rested my hand on my sidearm out of habit; by now the FBI kept us in ready supply of depleted uranium bullets.

My eyes were drawn to the light in the far bedroom, and I followed William in that direction. I was somewhat disoriented by the peculiar scent—that flowery yet metallic smell I knew to expect around some Gloamings by now, yet I could never get used to it. I wanted to completely expel it from my nose but was unable to, just like that day in Austin. I could feel a mix of anxiety and anger brewing in my mind.

We stepped into the suite's bedroom and one bright light—a lamp—illuminated a small table next to a figure reclining on a red velvet chaise. There was no other furniture in the room. *A nice touch,* I thought. No place for us to sit, so as not to prolong our interrogation.

I strode over to the lounge chair and Calvin followed suit with a cough, the flowering stench seeming to reach its peak as we approached the chaise lounge. The figure in the chair leaned forward and closer to the light, and I was struck—I must admit at that moment I saw everything that had entranced every person who attended the opera and every person who ever came into contact with Cian. What led them to post messages about the encounter on every Internet outlet imaginable. Every single person who met Cian had a story about seeing him the first time, and here was mine. I'd only viewed drawings and read descriptions before, and now here he was—a captivating, angelic face that seemed to radiate and reflect light at the same time. The famous yellowish-gold eyes appeared to look through and inside me. I found myself leaning in toward him.

Cian seemed used to this reaction, and he waited. As if his whole presence emitted a pull similar to gravity, dragging planets into his orbit. I knew that this display was only a fraction of his capability.

I wasn't sure how much time had passed when Calvin sighed

audibly next to me. I snapped out of it—reminding myself, *This thing is a Gloaming,* and actively resisting his assertion of power over my mind.

"Why are you here?" Cian asked in his deep melodious voice. His voice sounded like a favorite song that you wanted to play on repeat over and over again.

"We need to talk to you about a series of gold thefts that have occurred in different cities that correspond to the dates of your tour," I said, meeting his eyes.

The light seemed to sparkle off his skin and eyes, but now that I was focused on our agenda, I felt less transfixed.

"And you suspect me in these thefts," he said carefully. "Because they occurred when I was in that particular town with my opera?"

"It's not that simple," I replied. "No one is accusing you of any participation in or knowledge of the thefts. Our investigation, through individual radiation-marking testing, shows conclusively that the crimes were committed by one or more Gloamings. These tests are infallible, as you know."

"Infallible," Cian said, as he drew out the pronunciation. "That is an interesting word. Free of blame or error. 'Every word of God is flawless.' Isn't that what you believe, Agent Zumthor? You must know that we are the closest to that ideal among living, sentient beings—save for a saint, if you believe in such concepts."

I breathed through my mouth to avoid the sickly-sweet smell in the air.

Calvin found his voice. "You have many Gloamings on your staff. That's a fact. And the thefts were committed by Gloamings. Another fact. We simply want to know if you have any information. Any strange behavior you might have seen."

Cian stared and once again I struggled to push back against

those eyes. "I can't imagine," he stated. "No, I absolutely am certain that no one on my staff has participated in or facilitated any theft of gold. Gloaming or not."

I forced a smile but I wasn't sure he bought it. I'm not sure I did either. I probably looked pale and sweaty. "Be that as it may, I would like to talk specifically about each Gloaming on your staff—"

A cough behind us. William Gascoigne was back. He stepped forward with a raised hand. "Agent Zumthor, I believe that should be enough for now. We've clearly fulfilled the obligations that were discussed with your superiors."

"We only just started—"

William Gascoigne waved both of his hands. "We had an agreement. Mr. Clery is on a strict schedule. And any further questioning should be in the presence of Mr. Clery's attorney—"

"Fine," I said, not wanting to hear any more from this spittle-talking maniac. Plus, the FBI brass would have my ass if I interfered with tonight's performance. The governor of California and other elected officials and dignitaries were slated to attend. "But I'm not done with this. I'll want to schedule another interview." Sooner than later. I wanted to talk to Cian about all the dead bodies drained of blood every time he visited a city.

"You will have another interview, Agent Zumthor," Cian said. "And you as well, Agent James. You could ask a hundred and eighty-three questions, my friends, and I would answer them all. Such an obsession with blood you have, Agent. For the life of the flesh is in the blood, and I have given it to you upon the altar to make an atonement for your souls. For it is the blood that maketh an atonement for the soul." He stared at me for a moment longer than I wanted. "William Gascoigne, please give the agents a list of all the members of our staff and crew, and specifically note those who are Gloamings. Agents, you may make of it what you will."

I nodded and met his eyes for a moment longer. I felt myself on the edge of the zone of ignoring the scent and sights and focusing on the interrogation and what I could get from this slick Gloaming. Who I knew was lying. I couldn't wait to step outside and take a deep breath of clean air. "Whatsoever soul it be that eateth any manner of blood, even that soul shall be cut off from his people," I said with a long glance. "Thanks. We'll be talking again soon."

"You are welcome, Agent," Cian replied. "I'm so sorry about your partner in that incident in Austin. I find it hard to believe those criminals were true Gloamings."

I felt my breath coming in waves and my hands flexing in anger. My fingers brushed the gun in its holster as I stared. How dare he even mention the incident at Kerbey Lane? I wondered if I could even get the gun out of the holster with his Gloaming twitch muscles always at the ready.

Calvin's hand on my arm scattered my thoughts.

William Gascoigne handed us a piece of paper—he had already prepared a list for us—and turned around and proceeded with steps and stomps that I followed. The steps took me halfway to the door before I stopped. I twisted back to look at Cian. "You know," I said, "I'm glad we met, and the thing is, I'm pretty sure that I've made my point here. We all know the Gloamings never take chances. They cut and run. As if they're always being chased by a thousand suns."

With that we left the penthouse suite.

I am not sure whose ego is bigger: a Gloaming's or an actor's. I had accomplished what I needed to, though: I disparaged Cian's talent as a thief. And if I knew the psychology of the Gloaming—which I had been studying for a few months now—they never missed an opportunity to correct a doubter. They would make that attempt on Sasha's gold. But I was always one step ahead and if I wasn't then I'd get there soon enough.

At Sasha's property, we were met by a team of three more agents and two Los Angeles police officers on loan to us as they were setting up the surveillance. I had requested three five-man teams with outside perimeter surveillance and backup but had been quickly rejected by my superiors. The estate was surrounded by a high fence with cameras and laser detection, but those would be useless in a Gloaming attack. Just ask the director of the Blanton Museum.

We needed eyes on the ground.

The first two nights at Sasha's house—the first being opening night of *Nixon in China* at Walt Disney Hall—were quiet. But I knew the Gloamings wouldn't back off on this one. Too much pride.

The third night started strangely enough, with a full moon and rain. Though they say it never rains in Southern California, it only pours. Calvin and I took up our post in the large living room with wall-to-wall windows that seemed to cover half of the house. I wasn't sure whether to feel better or distressed that we could see pretty far out yet also be seen by anyone out there. The entrance to the vault was located under a stainless steel floating staircase in the middle of the room which led up to a small loft area. The bottom of the staircase moved to reveal the vault when you pressed a button located under a latch at the third step or when you cranked a large iron handle hidden inside the second step. You could access the handle by lifting up the second step with the press of a small button underneath the step.

A press of the button or a crank of the handle and half of the staircase moved to the side to reveal an entrance in the ground covered by the vault door. The vault door, made of reinforced steel and concrete two inches thick, could only be opened with a biometric password. Only three people had the requisite password: Sasha Bowie, her attorney, and her father.

At 2:30 a.m.—after my fifth cup of cold Blue Bottle coffee—I needed another bathroom break. I called one of the police officers to cover the living room area for me. Calvin also took a break, to make another one of his protein shakes. He said it would take less than five minutes.

Sasha's bathroom was an elaborate space pod of mirrors and steel, as if Apple had decided to make a restroom instead of a phone, although I noticed some mold growing among the tiles. I had an immediate urge to regrout the bathroom. Alas, I took a deep breath and had begun to urinate when the lights flickered and went out.

I unholstered my pistol and waited for the backup generator to kick in. But after half a minute still in the dark, I took out my cell phone and clicked the flashlight app on. With my gun leading the way, I jogged a few paces out of the bathroom. I hit my earpiece. "Zumthor here. James, what's up?"

Silence.

I pinged all the other agents. Nothing.

"Calvin," I tried again. "You there?"

"I'm here." A whisper. "Gun out."

I sighed deeply. I couldn't afford to lose another new agent. "You see anything?" I asked.

"No. I'm going into the den."

"Wait for me. I'll be there in a second."

After gliding along the wall with my light in front of me, I stepped around the corner and down another hallway. While dodging sculptures and paintings I jogged the carpeted hallway. I stepped into the kitchen and froze. The barrel of a gun. Then it lowered, and I saw it was Calvin.

"What's going on here?" he asked.

"I'm not sure. The generator should have kicked in by now."

Calvin looked at his cell phone. "I tried to call in backup but something is blocking our cell signal."

"Mine too. But I prepared for that. I left instructions with Gibbs at the field office that I will text him every ten minutes and that if I haven't texted him back, and he can't reach me, then he will send backup immediately."

Calvin nodded. "Let's hope they're on it. I'm kind of wondering how long we can hold off a gang of Gloamings."

"In about five minutes, they'll be expecting my next message," I replied. "But we can't wait for it. We need to go to the living room to check on the gold."

Calvin looked deathly serious.

"Hey, Calvin," I said.

"Yeah?"

"What's it like being kissed by a vampire?"

He rolled his eyes. "What?"

"It's a pain in the neck. Come on. Watch the back and I'll take the front."

I walked forward and Calvin stuck close, taking his steps backward. I decided not to use the flashlight so as not to highlight our position, although the Gloamings were adept at seeing in the dark. A few shards of moonlight gave us precious little light to see the way back to the living room. I cursed these megamansions, with half a football field from the kitchen to the living room. We tripped down some steps that led to a lower part of the expanse and I was surprised neither of our guns went off at that moment. As soon as we reached the floor, I heard a mechanical sound, as if gears were turning or grinding. I knew that couldn't be a good thing. I could practically sense Calvin gripping his gun tightly. We stepped farther down the long length of carpet and I knew we were coming close to the living room and the staircase.

A shot rang out.

We both hit the floor, slipping behind some kind of sculpture of the Milky Way galaxy—at least that was my interpretation. Calvin leaned over to me. "Bang out those windows," he said. "I don't want any reflection—and they need to know we're here."

"On three."

So on three, we shot. As the glass shattered, we heard shouts and equipment dropping. I was suddenly thankful for California homes and their ridiculous floor-to-ceiling windows. The sound of breaking and falling glass filled the room, and I thought it odd that there was no return fire.

The fractured gaze of the large-faced moon showed through most of the living room. And in the moonlight, I could now make out a few figures near the staircase and a peculiar mechanical object—like a Segway with arms.

I heard a couple of deep shots that sounded almost like shotgun blasts as something whizzed by my head.

Calvin and I returned fire and one of the figures lifted what looked like a small bazooka-type weapon mounted on his shoulder. He pointed it directly at us.

"Move!" I yelled as I heard a hollow popping sound. Calvin and I ran back as a few canisters hit the ground next to us. The canisters hissed and emitted smoke. Tear gas? I had just lifted my free arm to cover my face when everything went black...

* * *

I woke to bright lights and my head a mess of disorientation. I started coughing. Someone placed a cup to my mouth and I swallowed cold water.

A young man in blue scrubs leaned over me. I realized I must be in an emergency room.

"How are you feeling?" the young man said.

"Like shit," I answered. "Tell whatever asshole did this to me they just made my list of things to do." I looked at myself in the reflection of the iPad on the table. Cracked teeth, a smile, and blood. And I wear it well...

"You may have a residual irregular heartbeat, restlessness, body aches. That's from the Narcan."

Even in my fog I recognized the name of the medication used to reverse a drug overdose. Must not have been plain tear gas in those canisters. Subsequent tests confirmed it to have been an aerosol advanced chemical weapon filled with a fentanyl derivative.

Luckily, my backup signal was caught and the FBI and local police had brought EMS with them, who recognized the overdose symptoms in the entire team and administered the Narcan immediately. I was hospitalized for two days so they could monitor my health—a nightmare for a workaholic. By day two I was anxious to get reports on the status of the robbery and conclusions about what happened that night.

Calvin came to visit me on the second day, and though I was delighted to see him, I have to admit I was jealous. I suppose it didn't take him as long to recuperate because of his age and physical condition.

"You back on the job already?" I asked.

Calvin smiled and shook his head. "Not really. I was released yesterday and technically I'm not allowed to be back on official duty, but I couldn't wait to see the evidence they recovered from the scene."

"So, what did they find?" I asked as I sat up in the hospital bed.

Calvin sighed. "Half the gold was gone. Apparently they used a modified Segway to get it up and out of there so quickly. Needless to say, Sasha Bowie is not happy."

I shook my head. "She loves the fucking publicity. This is the best thing to happen to her in years."

Calvin nodded and moved closer to the bed. "She's already done an interview with BuzzFeed and Facebook news. It'll be released in a day." He leaned closer to me with a big grin. "But I haven't told you the best part."

I leaned forward.

"One of the bullets from your gun was collected and it had Gloaming radioactive blood on it."

I could barely contain my glee. "I hit one of the bastards."

"Even better," Calvin stated. He was sitting on a gurney beside me. "One of our sources at the Standard said that Cian Clery was rushed inside the hotel through the back kitchen entrance with his face bandaged. All performances of *Nixon in China* have been canceled until further notice, and Cian is nowhere to be found."

I couldn't stop smiling. "That smug fucker. I knew it. I bet that face ain't so pretty no more."

"You bet," Calvin replied. "Hey, Zumthor?"

"Yeah?"

"Why are vampires such good actors?"

I thought about this. "Who knows? They're such complicated—"

Calvin grinned. "It's in their blood."

The medication was clearly still messing with me. It took me a second. Then I laughed out loud—and gasped. Fuck, it hurt to laugh. "Good one," I groaned.

Then Calvin was all business again. "Not sure we'll ever find the gold, but I don't think Cian will be back anytime soon. The Internet is already going nuts."

"It's not over yet," I told him, but even I knew it would be next to impossible to find Cian if he didn't want to be found.

True enough, Cian Clery was never seen again.

Harvard Theological Review
Spring Semester

Edited by Jonathan Newton

Despite the many articles and verbal pronouncements regarding current major religious institutions and the integration of Gloamings, there has been a decided dearth of scholarship concerning the doctrine of each denomination and how it guided its views on the Gloamings. In his new treatise entitled "Phänomenologie der Religion auf die Gloaming" (*Tübingen*, 2022, Mohr, xii–670), Gerard van der Leeuw considered how many major religious bodies confronted the Gloaming appearance.

Many people are aware of certain members of the Catholic Church being opposed to Gloamings and everything they represent. However, there are other religious institutions which have issued opinions on the Gloamings and their newfound presence in society. The Church of Jesus Christ of Latter-day Saints (generally known as Mormons), under the doctrine of continuing revelation, and through the church president, considered a modern-day "prophet," in consultation with the Church's quorum of the twelve apostles, stated that they believe that the Gloamings could be considered a type of angel, yet they are still awaiting further instructions from God in order to fully determine how the Gloamings are to be represented in the land of God. Mormons believe that there are three types of "angels" that might be sent to minister to people. Therefore, the Church of Jesus Christ of Latter-day Saints has counseled to their members that they are prohibited from re-creating until guided by God through Apostolic Revelation.

The few Gloaming Mormons that exist were all summarily considered by a disciplinary council and subsequently informed that they had been excommunicated from the church. However, if church doctrine were to change, they would thereafter be allowed to return to full fellowship at a later date.

In Israel, the office of Chief Rabbi and the *Moetzes Gedolei HaTorah* (Council of [great] Torah Sages), the supreme rabbinical policy-making council, in stating that "G-d has commanded that certain species must be pure to their nature," announced that under Torah law the Gloamings would be considered Unnatural in relation to non-Gloaming humankind in accordance with verse 2:7, which describes how Man was created through "the dust of the earth." The Council prohibited the act of re-creation as defiling one's G-d-given body given that the Gloaming is created by a transfer of infected blood. The second part of verse 2:7 describes the spiritual nature of Man ("He [G-d] blew the soul of life into his nostrils"). The Council thus objected to the fact that Gloamings were re-created by other Gloamings because only G-d could create another true being. However, the Council also prohibited the wanton killing of peaceful Gloamings due to the obligation to save and preserve life (*pikuach nefesh*) as decreed in Leviticus 18:5: "You shall keep My laws and My rules, by the pursuit of which man shall live: I am the Lord."

Many intellectual Buddhist monks wrote certain treatises that Gloamings possess Buddha nature and therefore the potential for enlightenment. In fact, on many occasions the

Bodhisattva (the past-life Buddha) appeared as an animal. The first of the five precepts bans the taking of life, and thus this applies to the Gloamings as well. The Buddhist concept of compassion for all beings certainly led to their ready acceptance of the Gloamings.

Professor van der Leeuw conducts a critical analysis and critique of each major religion and their views on the Gloamings and how they correspond with their religious texts and evolved issues, and how these views have impacted those of their followers and the cultural issues that ensued.

CHAPTER 10

Joseph Barrera
Political Operative

Do I blame myself? Did I have a hand in starting all this crap? Maybe. Who knows? The historians may tarnish my memory, but I have no desire to do so.

So let's go back. At the time I had been a political strategist, or I'd been employed by political and consulting firms, ever since graduating from the University of Pennsylvania. I ran my roommate's campaign for class president. He was a drunk slacker who only wanted to win for his résumé. I made bumper stickers of just his name and posted them everywhere on campus—especially in the bathrooms. By the time the election came along, every student recognized his name. It was a landslide win. He was the laziest student body president ever and is now the Speaker of the Pennsylvania House of Representatives, biding his time until he can become a lobbyist.

Over the years, I worked for various candidates running for local, state, and national office. I wasn't above the occasional sleight of hand—though some might call it "dirty tricks." You know: recruiting and paying filing fees for homeless people to run in various primaries to dilute the vote and ensure a runoff. Or publishing rumors that certain candidates were having affairs. Whispers of illegitimate children or serious mental health issues. Stuff like that.

But it worked. I had great luck with unknown candidates in Democratic primary races, helping them leap to victory, especially against incumbent Republicans, some with multiple terms and decades behind them. I think this was because I loved a challenge. I also probably had more in line with progressive Democrats than with any other political affiliation. I always wanted to see how far you could push the line before it pushed back. Higher taxes, more regulation, more marijuana—how far could I go imposing my values on these beleaguered candidates who hired me?

About five months after the latest victory—Lisa Manning, Salt Lake City—and after five months of clinical boredom taking meetings with prospective private business clients in Chicago, I received a phone call from a senior partner at one of the largest law firms in Illinois and California. Her name was Judy Green and we'd met at several fund-raisers, as her firm was a big contributor to both Republican and Democratic candidates. She didn't want to discuss her proposal on the phone; she asked to meet in person, and quickly.

We met the next day for lunch at a food truck caravan in Logan Square. There was a beautiful view of Lake Michigan. We sat at one of those refurbished picnic tables that looked like props from *Game of Thrones*—made of hollowed-out oak and then adorned inexplicably with old concert posters from the 1970s. I ordered a brisket sandwich with curly fries and Judy had the mixed greens salad. Two craft beers topped the meal for both of us.

After small talk about our recent trips to Europe, Judy placed her fork down. "I suppose you're dying with anticipation," she said with a half grin.

I answered with a mouthful of chopped brisket. "You wouldn't be wrong."

Judy pointed her fork at me. "You don't need me to tell you that you've had an incredible run of electoral success. I—and a lot of other, more knowledgeable people—would say you're in the top five of campaign strategists in the country right now. But with an incumbent president running for reelection, it's going to be a while before you can catch on with a presidential campaign that has a chance."

"True," I replied. "But I'll be fine. Some time left alone."

Judy leaned forward with a smile. "A competitive guy like you? If you keep lying this badly you're going to give all political consultants a bad name."

She was right, but I hated to show my cards so early. I just shrugged.

"I know you have only worked with Democratic candidates," she said while watching the birds pick over crumbs on the ground.

"Because I am a Democrat," I said, probably a little louder than I wanted to. Now I was really wondering where all this was headed. Did she want to sign me up with a corporate gig? "Tell me what you're looking for, Judy."

Judy took a deep breath. "Okay. I am not in a position to give too many details, if any. But I do want to gauge your interest in running a political campaign. You would be paid more than you ever have been before. Let's get that out of the way immediately. I can tell you the candidate is a wealthy businessman. He's a political newcomer, so you will certainly have a greater impact not only on strategy but on policy. And you'd have all the money you need to run a top-of-the-line campaign."

I took another gulp of IPA. I specialized in challenging campaigns, but never with someone who had not held public office before. "I don't need the money. I live beyond my means, only in the sense of bars, hookers, strippers, and recreational drugs."

Judy scrunched up her face with a slight smile.

"I assume there's a catch," I continued.

Judy shrugged her thin shoulders. "A few catches, actually. First, he's a Republican."

I placed my beer down with a bang. "Come on, Judy. I'm a true believer. You know that."

Judy grabbed my arm. "I know, Joseph," she said. "But this race is going to be historic. I—This candidate is not your typical Republican."

"You need a better reason than that."

Judy rose and walked over to the beer trailer to pick out a new import. I glanced around at the dwindling lunch crowd. Long lunches were becoming the norm and that wasn't a good thing for me. I needed the juice of competition and drama and stress—and not many things fit that bill more than a political campaign.

Judy returned with a new bottle. "Think of the reaction if you ran the winning campaign for a Republican after doing it with Democrats. You would be a legend. And if you got him a high percentage of Democratic voters, you could argue you ran a true bipartisan campaign. Then comes a book deal. And your pick of other candidates and campaigns."

Judy paused, picking at her salad in silence. I watched pigeons poking at stray chunks of bread, bobbing their heads. I tried to quickly run through a possible Rolodex of outrageously wealthy businessmen who were rumored to have ambitions for public office, but I came up with nothing. Half the states in the union were going to have upcoming gubernatorial elections, so that didn't narrow it down much.

"Okay," I said. "I'm officially interested. But that's not a yes. I don't know who the candidate is and I don't know what state this race will happen in and that's pretty important—"

"You will," Judy replied. "I only need to know that we can move on to the next stage."

"Which is?"

"A meeting." Judy smiled again and wiped her mouth with a napkin. She seemed inordinately happy. "Just a meeting."

By the end of the week, I was restless. Judy finally called on Friday. She apologized profusely for all the intrigue, but it was per her client's instructions—"You'll understand completely once you meet him, I promise." I would be picked up by a hired car and taken to O'Hare, where a private jet would be awaiting my arrival. My phone would be confiscated. I would not be informed of my destination until we were in the air.

In the cabin of an extremely luxurious Bombardier BD-700 personal jet, I was waited on by the accommodating crew. The plane had an Xbox One X and a few books, but I kept myself busy with doodles and note-taking in my binder. Definitely no Internet access. One of the pilots came out from the cockpit and leaned over with a smile. "We'll be landing in Las Cruces, New Mexico, in about an hour," he said. He returned to the cockpit. I was left to ponder that destination: New Mexico.

I mulled over the many issues that a businessman or businesswoman would encounter in a run for governor or senator or Congress—although most businesspeople I knew would never begin a political career at a lesser office. It's senator or governor—of that much I was certain. But money can only resolve so many issues.

It was well into nightfall when the plane finally touched the ground. I didn't notice another plane in the sky or on the ground— we had flown near the airport and circled for an extra hour until the sun went down. Was I going to be put up in a hotel for an early morning meeting? On the runway, I was led into a limousine where Judy Green waited for me, in her smart business suit and with a bright iPad.

I must have looked surprised. "I know what you're thinking," she said.

"I'm not so sure you do."

She laughed. "You're thinking, *Why didn't she come with me on the plane?*"

"That's not even in the top ten," I replied. "But yes, it would have made the trip a lot less boring."

"I completely understand, but I had a lot of arrangements to make for your visit. We're going to a bar in Las Cruces called the Lonely Armadillo. It's pretty much a dive bar, but we're trying to keep this as discreet as possible."

I stared out the window at the deserted road and star-filled sky. "No way this can get any weirder."

Judy looked away. "Don't be too sure."

When the limousine pulled into a gravel parking lot, I saw that Judy had not been kidding: this was a true shit dive bar, like something out of a bad movie where the main character walks in and the music stops as everyone in the bar turns around to stare.

Judy and I walked inside to the smell of cigarettes and the sound of "London Homesick Blues" on the jukebox. It was an old Calloway jukebox like my dad used to own. He'd bought ours at a run-down junkyard in Chicago from an old Mexican with a glass eye. Used to walk up and down the block with an old cane hollowed out and filled with Johnnie Red and a cork stopper. Fucking dude was crazed.

A few patrons sat around nursing beers and not talking. Judy led me to an office in the back. Strangely enough, the old Marlboro man bartender barely looked up.

I noticed that a multitude of cameras lined the ceiling, with more concentrated above the door to the office. I heard the familiar *whoosh* of a remote electronic lock opening the door as Judy stood in front of it. I had seen and heard these particular types of locks in secure buildings on Capitol Hill, when I served on staff for the various intelligence committees. Definitely top-of-the-line security measures. Where the hell was I?

Inside, four mountainous men in black suits—obviously private bodyguards—stood by an elevator door at the back of the office.

"Seriously?" I said, glancing at Judy.

"Oh, it gets better," she replied as the elevator door opened without the push of a button. We got in, and soon enough we were headed down what seemed like two or three floors. The door slid open to a short, well-lit hallway. More cameras, watching every square inch. Judy walked to the door at the end of the hallway.

We stood in front of the door for a moment, presumably to be scanned by some camera, before the door opened electronically and we stepped into an impossibly enormous, opulent office with shelves lined with books. All the furnishings were aged leather and oak, although the room was so poorly lit I could barely see

what was in front of me. I could feel my adrenaline maxing out, only matched by my blood pressure. As we approached the desk, a man stood up from behind it. His face was vaguely familiar, but I caught my breath and stepped back when I realized this was the person I had been brought all this way to meet.

This man was a Gloaming.

I had only had scant interactions with the Gloamings before then. I had encountered some at certain political functions and fund-raisers and art openings, but they were few and far between. Their presence or aura—in addition to their physical appearance—unnerved me.

The man stuck his hand out. My first thought was of the long-standing rumor that Gloamings did not enjoy shaking hands with non-Gloamings. But he gripped my hand in what felt like a loose pocket of warm velvet. It was so soft and…bizarre. Neglecting to shake Judy's hand, he pointed at the chair in front of the desk.

"Please," he said. Then he glanced at Judy. "Thank you, Judy."

She winked at me and left. Strangely enough, it hit me only then that this man was the candidate running for political office. As I sat, I was struck by how enormous this news would be: the biggest story of the year, and in a year of life-changing stories, no less. I continued to process this information as the man watched me. He pushed a sheet of paper across the desk.

"This is a nondisclosure agreement," he said. "It's pretty standard."

I signed the form without even reading it. I pushed the paper back and leaned into my chair.

"I am Nick Bindon Claremont."

I knew the name. Nick Bindon Claremont, early fifties, wealthy industrialist who made his fortune in the fuel sector: fracking, coal, refineries, and even nuclear power plants. He was a billionaire several times over. I remembered some controversy when he disappeared and the rumors came heavy that he had re-created, until his press office issued a statement confirming that he had re-created but that the core businesses that encompassed the Claremont Corporation would not be affected. From that point on he maintained a low profile. He'd ignored all interview requests. I wasn't aware that he was a resident of New Mexico.

"Pleased to meet you," I said as he placed the nondisclosure in an accordion envelope on the desk.

"I'd like to be the next governor of New Mexico," he said. He let it sink in. "What do you think about that, Joseph?"

I released a deep sigh and spoke. "Well, from what I remember, currently the sitting governor of New Mexico is term-limited from running again. And she's a Democrat, so people may be looking for a change. The climate might be right for a nonpolitician candidate from another party. But…"

"The elephant in the room," he said in his vibrating baritone voice. "That I am a Gloaming."

"That you are a Gloaming," I repeated. "I mean, people are just now coming to terms with having Gloamings in society. But look." I felt adrenaline kicking in, my mind buzzing. "You start off with so many more advantages. The novelty and publicity of this election. The amount of money you can invest into your race. All that helps, obviously."

"But the disadvantages?"

"Well…you are limited to campaigning during nighttime hours. There is a prevalent natural distrust many voters have of Gloamings and their goals. And what really hurts you is the inability to have your face in commercials or pictures or any other print media. I mean, we can't even record your true voice in advertisements."

"So how do we solve these—"

"Well, off the top of my head, because a campaign is an organic process that you adapt and attempt to mold to your benefit during changing circumstances, such as falling poll numbers and adverse publicity, I'm of the opinion that in situations such as yours, your campaign must include a heavy amount of individual campaigning. Meeting voters face-to-face. Lots of hand-shaking. It's the only way to make up for the lack of individual presence in conventional media."

Claremont leaned back to consider this. His gaze extended beyond me. I heard his breath move like a brush of wind. "You make it all sound so simple," he said. "Like a good salesman."

"It's not—it's not going to be easy," I protested. "But you do have some inherent advantages. The wealth. Your age. You look like a damn governor—aristocratic face and perfect gray hair. It certainly won't be easy, but if you're willing to take the hits, then you have—I think—better-than-even odds of being elected. And you'll make history either way."

Nick looked to his right toward a darker area of the office—it was the third time he had looked in that direction. I wondered if it was a physical tic. "What I want to know is why you are the right man for this job," he said.

"What job is that? Getting you elected? I can get you elected. It's what I do—I win tough races. My record speaks for itself." In the hypercompetitive arena of politics, I found that extreme confidence worked more often than not with politicians who sought out challenges.

"Damn, you talk a good game." A different voice had suddenly sprung up. I nearly jumped out of my seat. "I'd almost welcome seeing you fall flat on your face," the voice said. The most beautiful woman I had ever seen materialized next to the desk. Later, because real details about her would be hard to track down for years to come, I would hear her described as the type of woman nations go to war over. A real-life Helen of Troy.

"I can only hope you execute your plan as well as you talk it."

I was speechless for more than a moment—I can only imagine how long—and my thoughts were difficult to gather in her presence. "I—I believe my—uh—background of successful races can be translated to any political race." I wiped my mouth with the cuff of my jacket and I found my hand shaking.

The woman glared at me with clear gray eyes. Her skin glistened like sand in the morning sun. She wore a black business suit and white shirt that gripped her toned body like a second skin. Nick flashed a quick crocodile smile, and even in my distraction, I made a mental note to fix that. He needed a far more approachable smile to win the electorate.

"I'm Leslie Claremont," the woman said, keeping her arms crossed at her chest. "The wife."

Early on, I decided we needed to keep this campaign under wraps until a surprise official announcement could be made at a public, outdoor venue with a lot of pomp and circumstance: the remodeling of the Santa Fe Opera House, a beautiful jewel of Santa Fe culture, bankrolled by the Claremont Corporation. It was soon to culminate in a large weekend celebration open to everyone, with a huge fireworks show at the ribbon cutting. Especially perfect for families—most of whose adult members were regular voters.

But that was only two weeks away, so I would have to organize the event on my own—from the building of a main stage, to hanging flags and lighting, to writing the media invites, which needed to be intriguing but vague. Everything seemed to be proceeding relatively smoothly—I hadn't even gone back to cigarettes and Scotch yet—when, a week before the announcement, a clusterfuck dropped in my lap.

I received a call—actually a message—from Wade Ashley.

Wade was an accomplished reporter for the *Washington Post* who split his time between the political beat and Gloaming issues. He had broken many important stories, including the attempted suicide of Senator Barnes during his candidacy for the Democratic nomination for the presidency, which Barnes then tried to cover up in order to continue to run in the primary. Wade also broke the story about the recent re-creation of several hedge fund billionaires and what that meant for the finance industry. Wade was smart. A message from him could only bring bad tidings. He must have caught a whisper or a piece out of place on his political chessboard and it jarred something in that inquisitive sense; he knew there was something underneath all the clouds and camouflaged trails. It wouldn't do to brush him off, or try to con him with misinformation—he was too smart for that and it would only spur his curiosity. That left me with the only strategy to employ when dealing with an overrunning journalist: bargaining.

After consulting with Nick and Leslie—who seemed willing to let me take the lead—I called Wade. He answered on the first ring. "Joseph, my man! How's it going?" he asked in his ever-hyper cadence.

It was unlike him to not get to the point immediately. "What can I do for you, Wade?"

"Well…I've been hearing things and I'm putting two and two

together and…I just want to run them by you."

The hairs on the back of my neck stood up.

"Well," Wade continued, "I was researching an article on the new crop of elite political strategists—of course I was considering your name. But you've been gone for a while. I finally traced you to New Mexico."

"Not much there," I replied. "Actually pretty boring. I'm doing some corporate PR work for the Claremont Corporation."

"True that. But then I tried calling people to see if they knew what you were doing in New Mexico. Came up blank. So I did more digging. It's what I do! And I found your name on the listing with the New Mexico Ethics Commission for a newly created political action committee."

I almost threw my phone against the wall. Shit. I gripped the arm of my seat instead. In compliance with state ethics laws, I was required to file the requisite paperwork in order to legally spend funds to organize the announcement event. The good thing was that I would not be required to audit where the funds came from for another month—well after the announcement, when the secrecy wouldn't matter. Unfortunately, I was required to place my name on the form as the temporary treasurer of the political action committee. I had hoped to keep this information undercover for at least another week, given that no one actually reads ethics filings. I guess the gamble didn't work.

"Well," I replied, "I keep my fingers in many things."

"Uh-huh. And the Santa Fe Opera redesign, with Claremont Corporation funding, is coming up, and they're inviting a lot of statewide media to the event. Maybe some national media? And I thought to myself, *Why would big-time Joseph Barrera waste his time on some bullshit corporate gig in New Mexico?* So I look into

Nick Bindon Claremont and—"

I had heard enough. He knew what was up. Time for damage control. "Okay—okay, Wade. You should fly down here and let's see if we can work something out. Something exclusive."

Wade wanted that exclusive story, so I wasn't too worried about the news getting out before the official announcement, but Nick and Leslie were not of the same opinion when I informed them of this new wrinkle. They were distressed, to say the least. In fact, they seemed truly angry, but I was used to extreme control freaks, Gloaming and human, and convinced them to let me play this out.

I met Wade the next day at a run-down Mexican restaurant near the airport. I nibbled distractedly on a rubbery chalupa as Wade dove into a plate of red enchiladas and two beers. I wanted to get this over with but Wade preferred to ease into it after a full stomach and a light buzz. I suppose the life of a reporter wasn't much different from that of a strategist, except for more beer and illicit drugs.

"You know I burned out on the game and quit reporting for a while," Wade said with his mouth open and full of beans.

"Really? What did you do?"

"I did what we used to do in college: waiter."

"No way," I said with a surprised expression.

"I used to love it, bro. The atmosphere of a kitchen and dining room. The drama. The crazy-ass love lives of the staff and bartenders. The infinite string of alcoholic and uncommunicative cooks and dishwashers that waft through the kitchen, the coke fiend bartenders that fuck a customer a night, the incompetent hostess, the trivial conflicts, the stolen tips—I could go on and on. If this is my misspent youth again then so be it."

"But?"

Wade threw his hands in the air, as if trying to catch the wind. "I missed the grind of being a reporter. This means something, man. You used to want to do this shit too, when we were coming up."

"So you'd rather be back to hanging out with politicians? You realize they are the worst thing about living in DC. And I include the smog, homeless, traffic, and crime in that list."

Wade pursed his lips in a wry grin. "Well, I would include lawyers myself, but I guess we're confining this to human beings."

There it was. "So, shall we get into it?" I said.

Wade grinned and waved his empty bottle at the bored waitress leaning against the cash register. "Might as well."

"Before we talk about anything of substance, let's get this out of the way. I'll get you exclusive but limited backstage access to the event in return for total secrecy until day of," I offered, as the waitress slapped down another Miller Lite.

"I want an interview."

I shook my head. "You'll get a few comments backstage, but that's it. You can write a great story with all your access. But no interview. Can't happen. You know that has to be with a New Mexico media outlet."

"I got you," Wade said.

"And nothing for your editor, Wade. Not Ving Rhodes *or* Terry Phillips. Bezos can't know about this before we announce."

He leaned forward. "So Claremont is really running—for governor, I'm assuming?"

Though the room was mostly empty, I was thankful the jukebox was playing loudly. I nodded. "Yes."

Wade smacked the table with a crack. "Fuck. A Gloaming! Out of the shadows and running for office. This is going to be amazing! A guy who can't be photographed. Or use a microphone."

"We know it's not going to be easy," I replied. Understatement of the year. "He's prepared to rely on face-to-face contact."

"Human contact, huh?" Wade grinned.

I ignored the joke. "It can be done, and he's the man to do it."

Wade drained his beer. "If you can pull this off..." He took a deep breath and pointed at me. "I need to hit the can." He rose and walked to the bathroom. A few minutes later, he walked over to the window near the front door before returning to the table. His face was creased with worry lines. "You're going to think I'm fucking crazy—"

"That ship sailed long ago..."

"I'm serious. And it's not the alcohol, but since I left DC I think I've been followed. I saw another Escalade following my cab. And it's still out there in the parking lot."

I wondered if all the rumored drug abuse had finally gone to his head. I shrugged. "I think you're seeing things."

Wade sat down and looked around the restaurant a few times while tapping his fingers on the table. "I hate this kind of shit. These Gloamings, man—fuck it. They're bad news. Do you have much contact with them?"

"I've had some," I replied. "I mean, it's only been a week or so. Mr. Claremont and his wife prefer emails or texts."

"Oh, I bet," Wade said as he waved for a new beer. "That's how they are, my man. Listen to me: they will do anything to avoid us, unless it's to steal our blood. They just stay within their own groups and clubs doing DXM all the time—"

"Wait. What? DXM?"

"Holy shit—you don't know about DXM? It's an over-the-counter cough suppressant, like Robitussin. People have used it to get high for years. It's the dextromethorphan that gives you the high, and for the Gloamings it's like LSD. You hit plateaus depending on how much you trip on. You see inside your mind and go traveling through your subconscious and other consciousness. You get visions and memories from the past and the future. It alters the thought processes, inducing visions, emotions, euphoria—a detachment from our present reality."

"I would think they're above that kind of thing."

"They're trying to find their origins. Where they came from. How to proceed in the future. They believe that if they can reach back into their own consciousness and unlock whatever is inside, they can—I don't know—multiply their powers. Mind control shit. God control shit." Wade's hands were going wild now. "Immortality, my brother!"

"That's crazy," I replied. "Are you sure about that?"

"Fucking positive. They have plans for the future of their species. They're trying to take over and all this might be the start of it. And you—" Now he jabbed me in the chest. "You, my man. You're helping."

"Cut that shit out, Wade." I grabbed his arm to keep him from taking another drink. He seemed truly unhinged. "You're starting to make me wonder if I made the right decision with you. I want a great article, with this access I'm giving you. None of this conspiracy crap."

Wade nodded. "Don't worry. I know how the game works. You'll get a nice sweet piece to kick off the campaign. But don't come crying to me when you're a fucking Gloaming slave after they take this bitch over."

I gave him a big smile. The smile of a winner. "Well, don't blame me when I'm dancing on election night. I'm going to make Nick Bindon Claremont the next governor of New Mexico."

* * *

204

The announcement went off even better than I expected.[23] The flags flying in the gentle wind, the band playing on point, the fireworks spectacular in the lovely weather. The crowd was entranced—perhaps because they were seeing a Gloaming in the

---

[23] Here's the full text of Claremont's historic announcement:

"I am sorry. I suppose not many political speeches start with an apology—but this one will. About three months ago, I was inside my office and I happened to look outside my window from the eighty-fifth floor of my building. And I realized that I couldn't see the street below. Only clouds and a constellation of stars. I could not see what was going on in the streets below me. I couldn't look out the window. My view of the world—of humanity—was not one based on reality. I knew there was a lot going on outside that window that I didn't know about.

"On that day I resolved to look at the world outside my confines. You have to look. A city that is set on a hill cannot be hid. And what did I see? I saw people—my people—the American people struggling in hunger with a thirst for righteousness. But what keeps them moving? A sense that our country—our individualism yet also our collective traits—can bring us forward together. We are not a people that look backward. I could list the problems which cause people to feel cynical, angry, frustrated, but what good is that without a solution for each and every one of them?

"There are no Gloaming problems and there are no human problems. There are only New Mexico problems. And those we can solve together. New Mexico has a 20 percent unemployment rate and a 30 percent dropout rate for high school students. When did we start to believe that was acceptable? When did we believe that this cannot be fixed? When did we stop fighting for something better? I believe we can find a collective destiny which surpasses the glories of the present and the past. That we are led by 'the shining light that shineth more and more unto the perfect day.'

"I know there are many people who hate me and do not trust my intentions. But I will work for them too. Someone once said to love your enemies, bless them that curse you, do good to them that hate you, and pray for them which spitefully use you and persecute you. Every single person deserves a piece of the American dream and a seat at the table. I will ensure that we all have a place at the starting line of prosperity.

"There are times when history and fate meet at a single time in a single place. And I believe this is one of those times. I pledge to you every resource of mind and strength that I possess to change the direction of this state into that place we all yearn for and struggle to reach. And together we can look out every window and see the problems that we must face and the solutions we will find. I hope that we can meet again in every town and village in New Mexico."

flesh for the first time. Regardless, it made for great stories and photos that set the Internet on fire. We even got the advanced bioshield capsule microphone—something scientists had been working on with uneven success—to work by splicing it with a human voice in the background, supplementing Nick's speech, and it sounded better than expected.

The crowd loved it.

I watched the festivities backstage, with Claremont's main enforcer, Toshi Machita, at my side. Toshi—technically Nick's personal assistant—was not a Gloaming, but it was only a matter of time. He started as an attorney for the Claremont Corporation, though details were murky as to how he ended up working for the couple on a personal basis. The rumor was he came from a legendary yakuza family in Japan before his parents moved to the United States. The most infamous Toshi story I heard was when Nick—pre re-creation—took some junior staffers to a bar for a few late-night drinks, where they encountered some rowdy bikers. Nick attempted to intervene, the bikers tried to take Nick's head off, and next thing you knew, Toshi was beating down four bikers by himself, putting two of them in the hospital, until the police arrived to shut the party down. Even then, Toshi's smooth talking kept the cops from arresting the lot of them.

In the weeks after our announcement, no other Republican challenged Nick for the nomination. In hindsight I suppose I was rather naive about this advantage. I told myself it was the unusual nature of his campaign: no one wanted to run against a Gloaming who was also a billionaire. Unfortunately, I did not know until much later that this was due to Toshi bribing, threatening, and blackmailing the other individuals considering a run for governor on the Republican ticket. In this way, it wasn't that Nick Bindon

Claremont was a Gloaming, but rather that he was already like other politicians or their financial backers: they used their wealth and power to move obstacles out of their way.

Our first goal was to consolidate Republican support so that these voters would not stay home on Election Day because of some dissatisfaction with the nominee. The campaign began a voter registration drive using analytics to identify college students and other young voters who might be receptive or more open-minded toward a Gloaming candidate with Libertarian leanings. Even then there was a feeling that younger voters would be a key constituency.

It always helps to have someone from one's own community support a candidate, as opposed to having an outsider promote him. So I decided to recruit "campaign captains" in each county of New Mexico who—funded by Nick's millions—hosted parties, barbecues, and cookouts to raise interest within the community. I thought having all the events at night might require an adjustment period, but there was little to no negative feedback.

Our Democratic opponent in the general election would be Duncan Caplin, the current New Mexico attorney general—a dry and charisma-challenged longtime officeholder. Gray-haired and lean, Caplin occupied the somewhat dour persona of an accountant or bill collector. He had been elected to various state offices, from state auditor to state treasurer, and then to attorney general. As impressive as this trajectory was, his problem was that even after a quarter century as a state official, Caplin was still unknown to the electorate. In other words: he was the perfect candidate to run against.

Sometimes I don't have a good track record when leaning on my instincts with regard to toxic people. So I shouldn't have been surprised when Wade Ashley's gratitude proved to be short-lived. Wade began to obsess over the failure of any challenger to appear in Nick's path to the Republican nomination. The two potential Republican candidates that had been preparing to run before Nick announced his intentions were John Sawyer, a state senator, and Amanda Allen, a well-respected attorney who served as state treasurer. Sawyer dropped out of the race in perfunctory fashion. But Amanda Allen's situation was, admittedly even to me, a bit stranger. Youthful in her appearance and demeanor, Amanda had for years held consistent press conferences to promote her agenda as state treasurer. She was not demure or camera-shy about her ambitions. So, two weeks after Nick announced his campaign, when Amanda released a written statement that she would not be running for governor—declining all interview requests—there was a considerable amount of speculation around her decision. The speculation lasted about a week, when the state media lost interest and soon latched on to all things Nick Bindon Claremont. Just as I had hoped.

But not Wade Ashley. He could smell something out of the ordinary and made it his mission to find out the real story of why Amanda Allen had dropped out of the race.

He'd never before shied from illegal or unscrupulous means to find his path to a story. This was no different. He hired a hacker to go into her computer and scan her account statements and email to determine where she was located. He concluded that she was probably based at the home of a wealthy friend in Albuquerque—and that is where he went, not caring that a front door was slammed in his face every day for two weeks in a row. He finally left Albuquerque empty-handed.

After one meeting at Nick and Leslie's house in Santa Fe, Leslie asked to speak to me alone. The house was located about ten miles from downtown Santa Fe, near a small mountain range. The home looked like it was used to house modernist art. Granite covered the floor like a white sheet of fine rice paper that, halfway across the room, shifted into a gray limestone. By the room's center was a silver table fashioned from one mold without a cut. Not a sliver of glass to be seen, nor any flower or plant. They even dispensed with the fiction of a kitchen: many other Gloamings kept a kitchen to advance the illusion that they were similar to humans in their eating habits, although if one looked closely enough, one would see a modified refrigerator for storing blood at the requisite temperatures and maybe a few polyolefin plastic bags for storage. Light-bronze anodized aluminum covered the walls without any decoration save for an original painting of Judith beheading Holofernes by Caravaggio. It seemed to compete with the Gloamings in dominating the large living room.

Two servants—one female and one male, both non-Gloamings—stood at attention, one at each end of the room, each staring intently at Leslie for any hint of an order. With a wave of her hand, everyone else in the living room left, and I was stuck in my chair with a gut like a basket of snakes. "Is anything wrong?" I asked. I sat on the couch, which seemed to swallow me whole.

"Yes," Leslie replied. "We need to discuss Wade Ashley. He's causing problems again."

"How?"

Leslie sat down in the seat across from me. "He is attempting to interview Amanda Allen."

I was confused for a moment as to what this had to do with anything. "The state treasurer? She got out of the race."

"Yes, I know," Leslie continued. "But Joseph: he's still trying to make a story out of the reasons why she declined to run."

I shook my head. "There's nothing. Zero story. He'll give up, and it'll go away."

Leslie stared at me. A Gloaming's stare—even after all these months, it was still a disquieting experience. Equally frightening and glorious, or…something. You wanted them to stare at you, but at the same time you hated it. I wish I could impart the feelings of anticipation and curiosity—kind of like trying coke for the first time. You feel lighter, and words and awareness feel repetitive. A weird combination of commotion and clarity. You feel trapped because all you want to do is leave and be alone to reflect on all of this. "Unless…I'm guessing there's a story?" I asked.

"Yes."

There are certain periods in a political campaign when issues like this arise. You spend so much time with the candidate and their family that you learn things: the candidate is having an affair, the candidate was seen doing hard drugs at a party, the candidate engaged in unethical business practices. You get the picture. I tend to subscribe to the philosophy that, as campaign manager, I just don't want to know. Unless the information gets out publicly, I'm not there to judge. I was there to run a campaign, not put out personal fires. For a campaign manager, ignorance can be bliss.

This felt like one of those quandaries. I wanted to ask her not to tell me. To simply handle it on her own. "Do I need to know this?" was all that came out of my mouth.

"You do," she said.

I gulped and sat there like an idiot.

"I wanted to clear the field for Nick. So I got rid of the candidates. We paid off the other guy, but Amanda Allen would not be swayed so easily. So my team did some investigating and we found out that the recently divorced Miss Allen had quite the reputation at the capital. Various affairs with different lobbyists who conducted business with state government. We installed cameras and took photographs of these sexual encounters. Toshi met with her—"

"Oh no," I groaned. "Not Toshi."

Leslie went on, as if I hadn't said anything. "Toshi confronted her with all the evidence and offered to find her a nice landing spot to get out of the race. She refused. So we had to get tough. We threatened to kill her if she stayed in the race. Simple as that. And now..." She trailed off. She looked uncharacteristically uncomfortable.

"And now Wade Ashley is getting closer to finding out," I said.

She didn't reply.

I found myself with my head in my hands. This was a disaster beyond anything I could have imagined. These types of circumstances landed people in prison for many years. "I wish you hadn't told me," I said. "I can't know all this."

Leslie sat next to me.

"What are you going to do?" I asked.

"Well," Leslie replied, "I'm already monitoring Mr. Ashley's movements."

"Maybe you should let me handle Wade—"

"You need to concentrate on the election," Leslie said. "I will handle Wade Ashley in my own way."

Then she patted my leg.

As if the information she just told me didn't scare me enough, her reaching out to comfort me with physical contact was even more terrifying.

"Joseph," she said, "don't think of going soft on us now. I think you know you're in this with us the entire way. We're going to win this."

In my defense, over the next few weeks, I tried to warn Wade Ashley. I knew I couldn't call or text him—that could be traced back to me. I found out where he was staying and, disguising myself as a janitor, snuck into the hotel and knocked on his door. Wade answered in his typical state of raggedness—he was clearly on some kind of bender. He didn't even recognize me. I held up my hands, as if in silent apology for disturbing him, and walked away. I would have to leave him to his own devices—after years of covering the Gloamings for the newspaper, he knew the risks. Perhaps he knew the risks even better than I did.

Leslie had been right, of course. Nick was going to win, and I was part of all this now. It was like the Mafia: once you were in, you couldn't leave until you were smoked.

Blood in, blood out.

CHAPTER 11

Father John Reilly
Operative, the Order of Bruder Klaus

Subject stands in front of a window, watching the glittering light below. His hands and feet are shackled but his face betrays a slight smile.

Interviewer: See anything interesting?

Father Reilly: Well, first of all, I can't believe we're in New York City, and secondly, I can't believe there's a window in this room. It's been a while.

Interviewer: It's the only room we have available and it has a window. What can we do? Anyway, I've been told that the odds of you escaping our current location are under 40 percent.

Father Reilly: Seems kind of high to me.

Interviewer: We're pretty far up. I like our chances.

Subject points at the window.

Father Reilly: We must be at least seventy floors up. I see the Central Park Zoo, Rockefeller Center, and that might be the Apple store right below...Holy shit, we're in 432 Park Avenue! Billionaire's row!

Interviewer: I'm impressed. You have acute geographic sensing skills.

Father Reilly: So, what billionaire is letting you use his luxury home?

Interviewer: Why don't we get to the questions? Did the rise of Governor Claremont affect you and the order?

Father Reilly: When I first heard about Nick Bindon Claremont running for governor of New Mexico, I was shocked at how swiftly the Gloamings were transitioning from a mysterious elite to more palatable fellow members of human society. They already had infiltrated pop culture; now they were going a dangerous step further.

Surprisingly, the Order of Bruder Klaus decided as a whole to not pursue any sabotage against Claremont's campaign—we had too many operations in progress to have any real success in undermining a gubernatorial election. Although they did agree to begin surveillance on Nick Bindon Claremont. I disagreed vehemently, and thought I might try my hand at stopping a Gloaming from becoming a state governor.

I shadowed the campaign manager, Joseph Barrera, for a couple of weeks. I had done my research: Barrera was a lifelong Democrat who seemed committed to progressive causes. It made me wonder why such an enlightened person could suddenly support a Republican Gloaming for high office. He also seemed to be under considerable stress, with his constant smoking, his shaky hands and rumpled appearance.

Interviewer: Hmm. I've never heard this one before. Go on.

Father Reilly: I needed to approach Joseph, but he was surrounded by campaign staff and other contractors day and night. He stayed at a Holiday Inn next door to the rented office space that served as the campaign headquarters. On many nights, too, he entertained various females at the hotel, adding another wrinkle to finding a window where he was entirely alone.

I spent some time watching him and seeing if I could find a night when he seemed to be in a solitary mood. Then one night I sat on a bench close to the storefront type of building where the campaign headquarters was located. The bench was somewhat angled off from the front of the large window of the campaign office. One night, I saw Barrera leave the campaign office at about four in the morning—alone. I rose from the bench where I sat, but noticed a black van with darkened windows nearby. I walked the opposite way from Barrera, and sure enough, the black van began to trail me. I was being followed. Probably since I landed in Albuquerque, if not earlier—and this made me angry for neglecting my preparation. I walked another block, then doubled back to the previous block, and jumped inside a large metal Dumpster. I spent the next two hours stuck in a greasy and stinky mess of garbage before I figured it was safe enough for me to get out—or before a dump truck arrived.

I walked back to my La Quinta in a cloud of garbage. I resolved to be much smarter about tracking Barrera. Two days later, I rented a room at his Holiday Inn, one floor below his fifth-floor double.

I made a point to ensure that there was no surveillance on myself as I watched the comings and goings of the guests and staff at the hotel. I hacked into the Holiday Inn server, so I could monitor the security cameras inside and outside the hotel. Three nights later, on the outside camera, I saw Barrera make the walk from the headquarters across the street—he was alone.

I switched to a view of the lobby. It was empty. This would be my chance.

I rushed out of my room and took the stairs to the fifth floor, where I stood in front of the elevator. I said another quick prayer that he was alone. When the elevator door opened, Joseph stood there sucking on a straw in a McDonald's drink. I stepped aside and he glanced at me while walking out.

"Joseph Barrera," I said.

He froze. "Yes. Can I help you?"

His eyes seemed wary but his exhaustion seemed to override any self-defense mechanisms he thought of putting up.

"Do you have a minute? I'd like to talk to you."

"Look, I'd like to, but I'm beat and I have to be up early again tomorrow. Call my office. Let's make an appointment for this week sometime."

I stepped closer. We needed to get inside before someone saw me in this hallway. "I'm not a reporter but I do have something very important to talk to you about," I said as I glanced at the elevator, expecting its door to open at any time. "It's about Nick Bindon Claremont and the campaign."

I could see Joseph's tired eyes glow awake. I said, "I am a member of the Order of Bruder Klaus—I think you know who we are." I told him straight-out: "You can't let him win."

I saw Joseph relax. Not the reaction I anticipated. "Look," he said. "I get your type approaching me every week. No offense, but—"

This was my only chance. I had to convince him. "I don't think you understand who I am. I am a member of an organization that has infiltrated the upper reaches of Gloaming society. If you give them this foothold, they will run over this country without regard and..."

Joseph stared at me for a moment. "I'm in for good. You need to understand that. Your words aren't enough to make me go back. I may have had some doubts but those are gone, and I couldn't leave even if I wanted to. And after all this shit I'm not sure I would want to." He cut me off. He straightened his shoulders and pointed to the elevator. "Please leave."

I had badly misjudged myself and this man. "I'll leave, but I will be back with evidence," I stated. "Then you will know."

Joseph nodded as if he had heard this all before. "Have

a good night." Then he watched until I called the elevator and got in. He even slipped in, pressed "Lobby," and slipped out as the door closed.

The elevator stopped on the next floor. I barely had time to look up before the first fist hit me on the side of the head. I stumbled back to see two men in dark joggers and jackets step towards me as I bounced off the wall. My self-defense training kicked in along with a headache as I pushed my foot out and struck the blond guy directly on the nose. The blood poured out in an instant but it didn't slow him by a second. I knew that I couldn't take these guys by myself and I needed to get out of there, so I bolted towards the stairwell exit. The bad part was that that's exactly where they wanted me to go and they grabbed me as I opened the door.

One of the guys punched me in the back near my kidneys and I dropped in agony to the ground. They each grabbed me and dragged me into the stairwell. My body shook as I dropped to the ground—

One of the men's heads rolled back, off his shoulders—I saw blond hair flowing with the head—and thumped down the stairs like a flat basketball.

I wondered if I might be hallucinating as I looked up to see a young female with scattered black curly hair laying a whip kick on the other guy. He fell back into the wall. I wanted to help her but my right leg felt numb and my head was a mess of sparkles and pinwheels.

I watched the woman slap both of her palms against the man's ears and the guy dropped to the ground just as she released the curved blade in her hand and swung it faster than I thought possible. His head, too, rolled cleanly off his body.

The woman looked at me with some exasperation, which confused me. "Get up. We need to go," she said. "You've been causing a lot of trouble, and I don't know how many more of these guys are out there."

That's how I met Sara Mesley.

Interviewer: Ah, yes. Sara Mesley. We've been after her for a while.

Father Reilly: So had I. When we were back on the road, speeding down the highway towards the airport, I was finally able to gasp out, "I'm a little bit at a loss for words. Sara Mesley: you're like a ghost or something. I confess, I didn't expect you to look so young. I mean, you really took care of those dudes like—"

"Don't think for a second that this is it—that we won," Sara said. "You're lucky that the order isn't angrier with you. You really put some of our plans out of sequence. I had to drop what I was doing just to come out here and save your ass. I'm still shocked you're the same guy that did the Vatican job. You were way out of your depth back there."

I ignored the snipe. "We need to stop him from being elected governor. Am I the only one who sees that?"

Sara looked in the rearview mirror for maybe the hundredth time. "You might be, Father. The order has decided that Nick Bindon Claremont should be elected governor."

"Why?"

"We're not getting anywhere with our current

operations. Sure, we can pick off a high-ranking Gloaming when we want—but even that is becoming harder. The advances we make are incremental. We need the greater society to see what the Gloamings are about and what their goals entail. Hearing us speak about it is not enough. We're losing the war for people's minds. Let the Gloamings win the governorship and they won't be able to help themselves. And then people will have concrete proof of their intentions. And we win."

Hawkeye Mom
31-year-old mother from Des Moines, Iowa

I know I'll probably get flamed for this but it has to be said: I don't trust these Gloamings! And before the Moderators come in and ban me—I'm not advocating violence. I'm just saying that they can't be trusted. Is that American? They only come out at night?? What is that about? And they're supposed to be so loving. What did I miss? You and I both know they are responsible for all those unsolved murders. I suppose it's all a matter of opinion but...

Everyone wants to be one. It's that whole "I want one too" syndrome all of our kids have. Missy and Wayne begged me to take them to see that boy band Hit This sign autographs at the mall—you know one of them is a Gloaming. Okay, so we went and it was creepy. He looks plastic—like a real-life Ken doll. Everyone in my PTA says that they don't trust them either. Go to a grocery store or a state fair and you'll hear the same things. *10:28 p.m.*

DitmasParkmom—

"Is that American?" ???? Who says that? I bet you're really fun at parties. I bet your Facebook feed is the symbol of tolerance and filled with pictures of our "Duh!"-faced relatives. *10:31 p.m.*

Hawkeye Mom—

That's what I'm talking about! Any difference of opinion gets slandered with hate. Does this make me a bad person? I forgive you, though. *10:33 p.m.*

DitmasParkmom—

Thanks. I'll sleep better knowing you forgive me. I happen to think that the Gloamings will bring about a measure of diversity to our population. Maybe its evolution or something. I've seen some here in New York and they seem so civil and polite. And they do shake people's hands while being patient and willing to answer all questions no matter how absurd. And they do really good things— the Gloaming Council's food and toy drive helps thousands of children in the Greater New York area. They're not just taking— they're giving back. *10:40 p.m.*

Hawkeye Mom—

They never come to this part of the country and I think that's a shame. Maybe if they came to my state more I would find them acceptable. The only thing we hear about them are rumors. And sometimes rumors turn out to be true. Put some effort into it. *10:41 p.m.*

DitmasParkmom—

That's kind of clueless. *10:42 p.m.*

Hawkeye Mom—

Fuck off! You're the type of mom who feeds their kids artisanal baby food quiche. When they're sucking all the blood from your babies don't come crying to me! *10:44 p.m.*

[Moderator ended thread]

CHAPTER 12

FALL

TWENTY-EIGHT MONTHS AFTER THE NOBI DISCOVERY

Joseph Barrera
Political Operative

The next time someone tells you there is no such thing as karma, tell them the story about the liberal political operative who went to work for a Republican candidate for governor. It'll make their day.

We called Nick's campaign tour leading up to Election Day "New Mexico Forward!" and it was a surprising success—perhaps not so much in the attendance, but in the accompanying publicity.

We encountered a few logistical issues regarding Nick's inability to be in sunlight. But the Gloamings started turning out in droves. They had their own official Web page which posted the exact times for every area in the world when it was safe to exit their homes—usually thirty to forty minutes after sunset. The Gloamings also had developed modified Apple watches to provide an alarm that alerted them when it was safe to venture outside. They were particularly adept at using technology to better their quality of life and health given their numerous physical requirements. Their personal Gloaming pages, which provided all essential Gloaming services from the nonprofit Gloaming Foundation, were private and housed on a confidential server in a restricted portion of the dark Web; therefore, not much was known about what services were offered to the Gloamings on this page, but it was well known that the "outside alarm" was a part of the services. Attempts were made almost daily, but the website was notable for being impervious to hacking from private or government sources. Interestingly enough, it was rumored that the server farm was located somewhere in New Mexico or Arizona. Also interesting, at least to me, was that there was a growing movement in the Gloaming community that eschewed most technological devices, even going so far as to construct elaborate Rube Goldberg–ish pinhole sundial systems within an enclosed box that let them know when it was safe to venture outside.

Meanwhile, the campaign rolled smoothly along; each day, I received an email informing me what time Nick would be available to the campaign for public events. I was still concerned about events scheduled after eight in the evening. The challenge was that people—non-Gloamings—tended to be winding down then. I always made sure that there was plenty of coffee for the audience. Leslie even suggested—at first I thought jokingly—that they develop an aerosol mixture to stimulate people's senses, which could be piped into the crowd. Needless to say, I nixed that idea quickly. But all this kind of endeared the Gloamings to me. In some ways, we were cut from the same cloth: face a challenge, craft a solution, and implement it, no matter what the circumstances.

With money being no object, I became obsessed with polling the race on an almost daily basis. By the Labor Day mark, the most recent poll had the race Duncan Caplin, 51 percent, to Nick

Bindon Claremont, 49 percent. Nick and Leslie panicked in their own slow-burn Gloaming way, but statistically this was nearly a tie, and we still had months until people went to the polls.

We were at a Labor Day picnic rally—at night, of course—listening to various union leaders who had surprisingly decided to endorse Nick Bindon Claremont. I could only imagine what kind of threats or payoffs were involved to get these unions to endorse a Republican over a Democrat, let alone a plutocrat billionaire who'd likely worked to obliterate unions in his business pursuits. But I was happy for the good publicity that night, given the fact that every time there was an instance of Gloaming behavior that was deemed detrimental to humans, the press always decided to ask for Nick's opinion on it. Dead bodies found in a ditch, drained of human blood? The press would ask Nick to comment on it. So for once, the publicity would be about Nick's views on policy, not his Gloaming status.

I was scanning my iPhone, attempting to pretend I was listening to this union leader go on about the minimum wage, when my phone went nuts. Ten messages popped up on my screen simultaneously.

They were all about the same thing: Wade Ashley was dead.

I jumped out of my seat and shoved my way through the bodyguards into the cool night air. I clicked the link attached to one text: the *Washington Post* site announcing Wade's passing. He had been found in his apartment, hanging from a homemade noose made from a leather belt and lashed to a door. Certain conspiracy theory websites disputed the suicide theory since the autopsy report stated that Wade had suffered a cervical fracture from the hanging. Quite a few contended that while the belt around his neck was sufficient to cause death, it was not enough to actually break the neck.

I heard a step behind me, and I whirled around.

Leslie.

She must have seen the look on my face and understood that the news was out.

"We need to talk," I said.

Leslie cocked her head toward her SUV and walked over as one of her men opened the door. I stepped inside with her.

I knew that their cars were soundproof and covered with what is euphemistically known as a "ring of electronic waves" designed to thwart any attempt to eavesdrop on communications inside the vehicle. The car was covered in a tent of material designed to keep sound in and detection out, similar to the Sensitive Compartmented Information Facility that travels with the president of the United States. The bottom line was that I was free to speak freely and on any subject while in one of these secure portable facilities, whether in a car or in the portable tent ones they carried with them.

"You didn't have to kill him!" I yelled.

Leslie simply stared at me as if she were waiting for me to expend all of this negative energy so we could get back to business.

"I could have handled it," I continued. "I would have done whatever it took, short of—"

"It had to be done, Joseph. Do you realize how close he had come to blowing this whole campaign for good? He subverted our surveillance on himself and Amanda Allen. He convinced her to tell him the whole story. Obviously he had little except for her word, but that would have been enough. You know how the press is with…" She trailed off. "With us. I was not going to let that happen."

She paused. Then calmly, as if reciting, she said, "Joseph. Listen to me. When I was a little girl my dad would read me books about the great Roman generals. He was obsessed with them. My favorite general was Scipio Africanus. He conquered Hannibal in the Punic Wars. He was outnumbered two to one but he used guile and intelligence to best the greatest army known to man. Hannibal's elephants charged forward but Scipio arranged his columns in a manner easiest for killing the elephants and the soldiers. And in that way he defeated a larger adversary. Afterwards, Scipio said this: 'Go, therefore, to meet the foe with two objects before you: either victory or death. For men animated by such a spirit must always overcome their adversaries, since they go into battle ready to throw away their lives.'"

Leslie pointed a finger at my chest. "Wade knew—we warned him. I have little sympathy for a reckless man who knew the consequences of his actions." Her gaze narrowed as if she were already weary of this conversation. "Do your job, Joseph. This probably would have happened whether or not you were here. In fact, it probably would have happened a lot sooner, if not for your sense of morality and guidance. Nick respects it."

I nodded, still too stunned to realize she had, in her own way, paid me a compliment.

We sat in silence. I wondered if I would ever forgive myself or if I simply did not care anymore. Even today I couldn't tell you.

"Okay," I said as I tossed my soul and everything with it. "Time to get back to work."

From that point we prepared for our bulk of campaign advertising to focus on specific issues of concern to the voters of New Mexico. We had spent the summer focusing on biographical advertising given that Nick was not well known among the electorate. We emphasized his middle-class upbringing in Las Cruces, where he excelled on the football field and in the classroom. We concentrated on Nick's extended family being longtime residents of New Mexico.[24]

The main challenge we encountered in our advertising was the inability to show a current photograph of Nick Bindon Claremont. We could show older pictures from before he was a Gloaming, but that only got us so far. The campaign needed something that *felt* current for the voters; our focus groups specifically mentioned this issue—that voters felt disconnected from Nick personally. I decided it would be elegant and unique if we had different portraits painted of Nick. Just like iconic presidential candidate photographs: Nick in shirtsleeves reaching out and grabbing the hands of supporters. Nick deep in thought alongside distressed voters. Nick smiling with union supporters and families. It took a bit of experimenting to find the best results, which came from portraits done in oil on canvas, but Nick and Leslie were impressed and satisfied with the execution.

The one painting that really seemed to resonate with the public was of an introspective Nick with his arms crossed, an identical pose to the painting of John F. Kennedy in his official White House portrait by Aaron Shikler. Apparently, the "contemplative nature" appealed to voters, according to our focus groups, so we used that painting in numerous mailers, from large posters to lawn signs to stamp-size stickers.

For the first televised debate, I insisted that Nick's voice be dubbed on a small tape delay, to ensure that the voice-over actor could get the inflection correct. I wanted Nick to appear at once forceful and empathetic.

---

[24] Nick's paternal great-grandfather moved to New Mexico from Pennsylvania to seek his fortune in the minerals trade. This was important because Nick and his family left New Mexico while he was in high school and Nick didn't return until about five years ago to become a full-time resident. Even that was a stretch, however, given the amount of time he spent at his other homes in California, New York, and Paris.

The throng of reporters covering Nick seemed to grow every day, and they flew in from all over the country. I expected this to happen at first but naively thought most would lose interest in the larger campaign until Election Day itself. I was wrong. It was a mess trying to navigate and handle each separate reporter. I endured on Red Bull and five-hour energy for days on end because I stayed up very late with the Gloamings, then needed to be up early in the morning to accommodate the human staff and reporters throughout the regular day.

For months, I fended off sleazy Gloaming attacks from the Caplin campaign and their super PAC. Of course, it didn't help that there were a few more bodies found drained of blood in various cities in New Mexico, but we ended up working with the particular police departments to keep the news under the radar until after the election. I don't even want to speculate about how Leslie and Toshi accomplished this maneuver. For every billboard that warned that Gloaming policies were bad for New Mexico's children, we bought three billboards showing Nick volunteering at soup kitchens. For every commercial that questioned Nick Bindon Claremont's ability to understand the "true humanity" of New Mexico, we bombarded the airways and Internet with warm, colorful Nick Bindon Claremont advertisements: "I'm Nick Bindon Claremont, and I approve this message."

On the morning of Election Day, I woke up after two hours of sleep, with three Red Bulls and a cigarette. The day was a blur.

I was a nervous wreck when the returns came through, and it was still light outside, so I went to the basement to watch them with Nick and Leslie. I tried to stay away from the booze but I was too nervous to manage it straight. We took the lead through the early returns and never let go, and Governor Nick Bindon Claremont won the election by a bigger margin than even I thought he could get: 57 percent to 43 percent. An electoral blowout. We were ecstatic. Nick and Leslie seemed oddly restrained, but I wrote it off to being Gloamings. Needless to say, my entire staff partied until the wee hours of the morning, when Toshi appeared and asked to have a word with me.

We walked over to a dark corner of the hotel bar, near the bathrooms. He said Nick and Leslie were pleased with my job performance and would add a hefty bonus to my fee, but they would not need my services any longer. As if I were simply a worker being laid off with a severance. Then he shook my hand and walked away.

It was an odd and disconcerting end to the campaign.

Impersonal and demeaning.

It did not surprise me one bit.

The New York Times

Demetrius "Quick" Johnson, undefeated welterweight professional boxer and number one on the *Ring* magazine pound-for-pound best boxers, died yesterday in New York City from massive organ failure due to an unsuccessful re-creation.

Johnson was born in Mobile, Alabama, the second son of two middle school teachers. After being picked on by classmates because of his missing front tooth, Johnson was enrolled by his father in the Southside Boxing Academy. Johnson took to the spartan nature of training—the repetitive shadowboxing in front of the mirror, jumping rope for hours—and soon entered various tournaments to become Southern Golden Gloves champion for three years in his weight class. Chosen for the United States Olympic team, he surprised everyone by making it to the medal final round and beating the favored Russian boxer Ruslan Aleksandrov to win the gold. The next year, Johnson defeated Roman Martinez in the most-watched pay-per-view bout in history.

The most famous contemporary boxer in the world, Johnson soon came under the influence of Ivan Kozlov, an American of Russian descent who made his fortune in automobile sales. Kozlov loved combat sports—he met Johnson at a boxing match where they reportedly struck up a friendship.

No one knows the exact circumstances of Johnson's attempted re-creation, but a few of Kozlov's associates indicated that it was a spur-of-the-moment decision. After the attempt was made, Johnson lapsed into a coma. His associates waited five hours before taking him to a hospital, where he died two days later.

The deceased is survived by his wife and two children.

CHAPTER 13

LABOR DAY
TWENTY-EIGHT MONTHS AFTER THE NOBI DISCOVERY

Dr. Lauren Scott
Research Physician, Centers for Disease Control

Cancer, AIDS, swine flu, bird flu, SARS, MRSA, Ebola…Who am I to think that anyone should really care about this NOBI virus? "If you could see the faces of the mothers, fathers, or children afflicted with those diseases, you'd be working on a cure for those and ignoring anything dealing with those bloodsuckers." That was my previous director, moments after I demanded more resources and personnel for my research. It became so bad that I almost felt like he had a point. What would we all gain if I found a cure? I probably should have listened to him, but I truly felt that my work might save our population as much as Ebola or cancer research could, although I'm certain it was hard for other people to envision that same concept.

However, there were still many people in the CDC besides the director who refused to support my research. The slights that only used to seem like normal workplace personality conflicts now felt more personal and sinister. Birthday parties for coworkers that once involved everyone were now cordoned off like a Berlin Wall checkpoint, depending upon "whose side" you represented. Expenses that were once granted freely were suddenly rationed and reserved for those now favored. I was subjected to three audits within two months, involving me attesting under penalty of perjury that my expenses were correct. It took me hours of my own time to comb through reports to make sure they had not been tampered with before I signed off. The CDC then began installing cameras at various points in the building. In fact, the assistant director attempted to institute a policy of installing cameras in each individual office. I fought back against this as a violation of reasonable expectation of privacy: I was sometimes required to change clothes in my office before going to the lab. I won that battle and the cameras were removed. But that didn't stop the CDC from instituting a program that retrieved and scanned all emails and phone calls originating from within the building.

The Gloamings were powerful in their desire to cease all government research into the virus. It didn't help my research that many in the CDC thought any research into the virus was a waste of time given that it was something permissively taken by humans to change themselves. It wasn't a disease that we were trying to prevent. But that's exactly how I viewed it. The battle lines were drawn and I was almost alone in this big bureaucracy where a memo or directive could kill your funding in an instant. It didn't help my cause that my efforts were riddled with failures and miscalculations in the early months.

Obviously, the first action I took was to sequence the NOBI virus—specifically, complete viral RNA genome sequencing of at least 50 percent of the available samples. Easier said than done, though, with this virus. After months and months of stops and starts, I finished a partial sequence and submitted my findings, but then I was horrified to find—after running another computer sequencing check—that the samples I had used had been degraded by partial exposure to the sun, which altered the specimen in a way that would not yield an accurate RNA of the stable virus.

I could already see the CDC's official narrative taking shape: Dr. Scott's research has reached its logical conclusion and there is no cure to be found. It's time to allocate our money elsewhere…

After reprimanding myself, the first thought in my head was *How could I have been so irresponsible?* Maybe I was becoming too obsessed and didn't have the patience. Maybe I just couldn't see the finer details while haunting myself with finding something to destroy this virus. But I knew, with certainty, that I was never that irresponsible or haphazard with my studies. It had to have been some effort at sabotage. A simple exposure of the sample to a full spectrum bulb would have accomplished it. But sabotage by whom? Someone inside the agency was my only guess at this point in time. But I was playing the long game and this wasn't going to stop me from complete understanding of the NOBI virus. And finding a cure.

Of course, I could hear my sister's voice in my head the entire time: "This will end in tears…" Yes, fair enough. Especially when work issues take a back seat to family matters. And that always meant my sister. Jennifer was pretty consistent about communicating with me, at least every other day. Of course, this was always on her terms. With great embarrassment, I was forced to sign up for every social media site you could think of: Snapchat, Facebook, Instagram…Jennifer demanded this, as she preferred to communicate through these means as opposed to a simple phone call. Not that I was the talking type to begin with, which fed into my sister's argument that I was more intelligent than emotional.

At least she was consistent in sending me messages every few days, using Snapchat as her latest method of communication. But I hadn't heard from her in a week. This was after I'd sent her numerous messages on every social media site she subscribed to. I was always looking for one more thing to worry about, and this was next up on the menu. Then, following one more argument with my research director, already near tears, I finally received a Snap from her directing me to a YouTube page URL. Okay...I clicked Play and on the screen was Jennifer grooving to the beat at the Tomorrowland EDM festival in Boom, Belgium. Blue skies and green grass completed the picture. She looked peaceful, happy, swaying her body to the beats with her eyes half closed.

I remember being that free—all so long ago; maybe the last time was in college? Summers on a beach in Wisconsin, dancing and beats and brats with friends, never a worry about the next day.

But there Jenny was, on the video, and I knew what was coming next before she even said it. It was all over her smiling, hopeful face. "Hey, Lauren! Guess what? That's right! I met the most incredible man! He's a filmmaker and I'm helping him with his next documentary film, which is going to be so..."

Switch the names and the occupations, and I'd heard this same story many times before.

This would be the first time I heard this particular name, though: Mael Roux.

Roux was born in Sainte-Féréole, located in central France, to middle-class socialist schoolteacher parents, although the exact year is under dispute, as Roux has been known to give different dates of birth to different interviewers. After college, he worked as a freelance journalist for *Le Monde,* scouring for assignments in various war zones, from Iraq to Afghanistan to Darfur, where he gained a reputation as someone willing to dive into dangerous environments to cover a story—and also someone willing to tell anyone who listened about how dangerous it was but how deeply he felt about the risk.

Mael soon acquired an interest in video documentation. He took a video camera with him wherever he went and self-published these reports on different visual outlets, including PBS and Vice. A half year and only three recordings in, Mael announced his need to "break free" from the constriction of normal documentaries. He decided to try his hand at fiction filmmaking, soon establishing a filmmaking co-op he dubbed the French Resistance. It consisted of a group of renegade filmmakers dedicated to withholding the use of any special effects or "elaborate maneuvers," in order to purify filmmaking. In a sense, what was put on the screen was actually felt and experienced by the actors. The co-op was disbanded after an actor on a production was recorded being stabbed with a knife and hospitalized. Another acquired an STD from filming a sex scene in an Ohio State University frat house. Unsurprisingly, the clip of the stabbing went viral.

Mael left the movement, dropping his friends and now-tainted collaborators in order to concentrate on documentaries, where he felt the intent and the images were "of value." His ethos—which appeared to change with the circumstances or day of the week—was that the documentary director should act as an educational arbiter instead of hiding in the background. His ego seemed quite absurd.

Mael's new venture was documenting and attempting to capture the emotional, agnostic spirituality—that was the exact quote—and physical sensations involved in attending EDM music festivals. I'm not usually one to dismiss things out of hand, but I might make an exception in this case. I mean, who says there are no more worthy causes? Roux also told Jennifer that he wanted to be a "social media influencer." That bounced around in my head for a few days without a resolution.

Every other day, Jennifer would post a new video on her page, and with every passing day, I couldn't wait to see what she posted next. It seemed exciting, surprising, and alive. Her life was something that I could never have, though I'm not sure it would've been enough for me.

Jennifer looked so different at this point in her life. Her hair was more natural—long, curly, and windblown—as if she hadn't had a haircut in weeks. Every new video revealed another part of my sister that I hadn't seen in such a long time. She seemed more optimistic and positive. Her smile was wide and her voice was strong, and those smile lines crowding her eyes seemed to glow in the sunlight.

"Okay, Lauren," she said, pointing at me through the camera with her eyes squinting mischievously, "we've hooked up over five hundred—yes, five hundred—8K Oculus Rift cameras all over the festival and even on many of the participants. There will be no dialogue or narration—only images and sound. No soundtrack— natural sounds from the festivals. It will be mind-blowing."

With every new video, even I got caught up in her excitement for the project. Maybe it would be something sensational. Yet as my work inevitably found its way in, this excitement was short-lived. Two weeks into Jennifer's return to social media, I entered the lab, as I did about three days out of the week, and was processed through the decontamination and disinfectant spray process. I walked into the adjacent changing room, and as I lifted the positive pressure suit from its rack, I decided to inspect it for a moment. I don't really know why I did that; the transition from distraction to focus can trigger things.

As I smoothed my hands over the suit, my eyes immediately focused on a rip in the seam near the faceplate. It was a shocking sight, staring at me there, almost hidden. Like a mole or wrinkle on your face that hasn't been there previously or you may not have noticed until something in it draws your attention. The suits were inspected on a biweekly basis by our support staff, who were trained in procedures related to maintaining level four suits. It could not have been an accidental symptom of erosion or overuse—that would have been caught in even the most cursory exam. This was unthinkable within the context of our procedures. The results and consequences could have been devastating to my health. My mind instantly crawled toward sabotage, and that idea built a home in my brain and it wasn't leaving anytime soon. From then on, my safety procedures in the lab veered toward an extreme form of OCD.

I didn't have long to consider my options when Jennifer sent me a message saying that she was going to be in New York City at the same time as me: she wanted to meet up. Finally, a pleasant distraction to get my mind into! Unfortunately, Hector was on call that week and wouldn't be able to make it. I really did want him to come, but at least it would give Jennifer and me some alone time, which we hadn't had in years. I could barely wait to see her and I rushed through my presentation at the UN Committee on Infectious Diseases. This sounds grandiose but the conference was actually a smaller gathering of scientists, mostly focusing on the sharing of data within a new database being implemented for our shared servers—nothing too substantial.

With my report finished, I sprinted out of the UN building without attending the after-meeting social that usually made its way from the East River to the Hilton bar, across the street. I took a Lyft to the address Jennifer had given me. I was in front of a pawnshop that looked stuck in time, all faded neon and pastel shades. I double-checked the address and texted Jennifer, and she assured me the restaurant was inside. At least the name was correct: Beauty and Essex.

I walked into the barely lit room, so elegant and different from the outside. Tables and banquettes lined the floor, and I saw Jenny sprinting toward me. We fell into each other with hugs and kisses. Jennifer was positively glowing. She was winning at life, finally. We talked through the past half year of our lives before we even sat down at a table. Jennifer and I ordered identical tomato soup dumplings and were rewinding the last few months with laughter and rapid conversation when her phone buzzed. She smiled as her eyes scanned the screen and I knew it had to be her new man—those types of smiles are reserved for very few. She placed the phone back on the table and turned to me. "He's coming," she said; her voice went higher as she spoke. She didn't need to tell me—anyone could have figured that one out. I thought she might float into the air with happiness.

"That's great—" Before I could say another word, Jennifer jumped up and into the arms of who I could only assume was Mael Roux. He was handsome, rough, and thin, with messy hair, in a journalist-filmmaker type of way. The expensive clothing was just rumpled enough to lend an air of faux apathy. After a few minutes of kissing and outwardly massaging each other's tongues, they finally flopped down in the chair across from me, with Jennifer sitting on his lap.

"It is my pleasure to meet you, Dr. Scott," Mael said with his French-accented English as he shook my hand.

"Please call me Lauren."

From that point, we ate poke tacos and gulped strong drinks, all as Mael and Jennifer talked eagerly about their work. It would be transmitted to Oculus Rift systems everywhere, creating one giant collective rave. I tried to keep an open mind. It seemed different, at least.

"There's only one thing keeping it from being truly comprehensive," Mael said as he shook his empty drink, as if more Scotch would magically appear.

"What is that?" I asked.

He raised his hands. "We don't have the technical capabilities to involve the Gloamings in this project."

I shrugged. "That's not surprising. It's the holy grail for every tech company and camera manufacturer. Soon, though. Every major tech company is working on it, and spending billions to do so."

"Maybe when this project is done I would do a documentary, or at least an interview, with you about your research," Mael said as he rubbed Jennifer's hand.

I didn't expect this, and he wasn't going to like my answer, but maybe the alcohol would soften the blow. "Well, you'll have to clear it with our media affairs department, but it's probably not so likely. They're pretty strict on those kinds of things."

"Maybe later this year," Jennifer added, with a look into my eyes that told me she wanted to impart some hope of it happening.

Before I could answer, Mael asked another question. "How do you feel about the research that you do?"

I felt a tingle ripple down my back. "What do you mean?"

"It seems to me as though you're looking for a cure for the

NOBI virus. That would be very close to a form of, how do you say, eugenics, would it not?" Mael sat back with his arm around Jennifer and his eyes focused on mine.

"It seems that way to me also," Jennifer interjected with a stern look on her face.

I was taken aback by the sudden change of tone in the conversation, and my sputtering only made me feel more uncertain. It felt so planned and I felt so unprepared. "Well, I mean, to me it's more that we can use our technological advances to enrich other research, including preventative medicines."

Mael leaned forward, his brow creased in concentration. "But you're trying to prevent a segment of this society from, say, reproducing. One that is to be normal and productive by any measure. It would be like you are trying to change an embryo to prevent a certain race or sexual orientation. Eugenics. Controlled breeding of the humans."

"Now wait a minute," I replied, arching my back and answering probably too loudly even for this boisterous restaurant. "My research is nothing like that. I'm trying to learn about a particular virus. And the Gloamings are hardly a marginalized segment of the population."

Jennifer stared at me with a confused look on her face. "Well, what happens if sometime down the line NOBI can be passed through normal selection such as procreation? Will the research continue? Will you still be looking for a so-called cure?"

I felt ambushed and angry and I lashed out before even thinking. "Absolutely."

Everything was silent for a moment amid the chaos around us. The conversation then continued, somewhat less hostilely, about the new cell phones coming out, and would the Warriors win a fifth title in a row, and we left with hugs and kisses that felt more perfunctory than endearing. I tried not to think about it and concentrated on how good it was to see Jennifer again. But two days later, I felt slapped in the face by a repeat of the evening: a new article in *Wired,* with my picture front and center, entitled "The New Era of Eugenics at the CDC."

What followed was an article debating the merits of my research into the NOBI virus; it seemed in essence like a rehash of previous articles, which didn't bother me. What did bother me was the accompanying video: Mael had recorded our entire dinner conversation in New York City. It made me look like a complete fool, without concern for the ethical considerations of my research. I never really had the most television-friendly mannerisms, and I knew it was my anger that had pushed me in that direction, in spite of my true moral considerations. It certainly wouldn't be long before my supervisors heard about the video from the directors, and it would then come back down to me. I couldn't blame this one on some treachery in the CDC, but I felt ambushed and betrayed nonetheless.

I barely had time to process the article and video before the CDC, among other agencies and businesses, was hit by the "This Town Needs an Enema" ransomware attack—complete with a picture of "The Joker" wearing a huge smile. This DDoS barrage on the CDC servers only affected them minimally, as they were somewhat protected against such attacks. However, some idiot tech placed a few of my research files on a temporary unsecured server while he or she ran "tests." The files were erased. So much for "protected."

After that incident, I couldn't shake the notion that my work was being undermined by forces inside and outside the CDC. As a result, I began to upload copies of my research to a private Dropbox account, knowing full well that this was specifically prohibited by agency regulations as well as federal law. I couldn't take a chance on losing any more of my research, though, or having my findings altered in some way. I couldn't say much for certain, but I could say that this was only the beginning and I had to prepare for more.

The research itself divided people to a certain extent: loyalties ranging from appreciating aspects of the research to personal familiarity simmered underneath the genteel behavior of the public health governmental agencies. I had already grown tired navigating the Montagues and Capulets of the CDC. But it was an interagency directive for a proposed memorandum of action that ignited the dynamite and floated the opinions and beliefs to the surface. In association with the National Institutes of Health [NIH], the CDC issued a proposed comprehensive program for the prevention of the NOBI virus. Among the more controversial suggestions were understanding safety among Gloamings you are not familiar with in relation to relative feeding habits and determining the self-control tendencies of certain Gloamings.

A discarded previous draft that was simultaneously leaked to various news organizations had a section considering the effectiveness of requiring registration for carriers of the NOBI virus, which would then be placed in a national registry. In addition, the draft discussed behavioral guidelines for Gloamings that, if not adhered to, could result in a temporary quarantine for health reasons. As per current statutes, of course.

Each CDC and NIH member felt different, no doubt. I simply wanted to find a cure because I believed that this virus was a social threat. They hadn't seen what I witnessed those early months in the Southwest.

Regardless, the directive and memo caused more controversy

than the director envisioned. Many attorneys found the directives to be contrary to current statutes and case law. Even academics and politicians, who were skeptical of all things Gloaming, found the memo an affront to the sacred civil liberties enshrined in the Constitution for all citizens.

It led the nightly news for a few days—doesn't everyone want to hate on the government when given the chance?—with the president and the administration absolving themselves of any knowledge of or participation in the construction of the memorandum and thereafter disavowing every aspect of it. The secretary of the Department of Health and Human Services, our boss, slammed hard on the agencies' executives, and the drama quietly filtered down with the instructions that we would desist from all Gloaming research.

Of course, my name appeared on the masthead of the memo and directive, even though I had *zero* input into the contents. I was a convenient target given my notoriety and media exposure. I tried to tell people in the days of the fallout that I was a scientist, not an administrator or a policy maker, but no one seemed to have a desire to listen intelligently to an opinion other than their own. What was contagious, I thought, was all these people choosing to only hear what they wanted to hear.

But that memo did accomplish something my research never had: illuminating the battle trenches at the CDC. There was no more hiding behind whispers or pleasantries, behind funding allocations or personnel requests. It was a defining moment for me in determining who supported my research and who was actively working against it.

I'm not a big believer in coincidences, and the specter of construction at the CDC headquarters, on my particular office floor, came as a surprise in that we were normally given months of notice, considering the nature of our research. It took the agency a day to mobilize and carry my belongings to the basement.

I accepted it without grievance—heck, I even loved it after a couple of days. It felt safe down there. Fewer visitors. In reality, I really only saw other people during sessions at the lab. The new office was like my own personal cave. I blasted *Revolver, Pet Sounds, …And Out Come the Wolves, Milo Goes to College,* and *Walk Among Us* without anyone complaining or banging on the walls. I had my own personal mosh pit and no one could do a damn thing about it. I transformed back into that black-hearted girl I used to be in medical school.

I was only thirty, but I had the rage from years of putting up with other people's shit.

Amid all this turmoil, though, and adhering to the concept that when it rains it pours, I hit a breakthrough in my research.

My use of the most sophisticated microscopes—specifically, high-input electron microscopes—was limited by the radiation emitted by the NOBI blood. I was in the basement and with limited funding, forced to use more primitive techniques: modified light microscopes.

It was beneath these old-fashioned lenses that I stumbled upon an unidentifiable prion hidden within the sample. It appeared to be in the formative stages, and I wondered how long the incubation period would be, what it would bring. Would the core attributes modify into something stronger? How would these changes manifest? It was an unusual four single-stranded, negative-sense RNA segment that appeared and disappeared in my microscope. It appeared to be refolding the protein and, instead of degrading it, making it more substantial. Most prions did not contain RNA, but this one seemed to have hidden folds of the prion within its body. I was making great strides in understanding the process of re-creation, and the processes involved which changed the human body.

The lurking problem was that I had used up most of the samples that were in my possession. I needed new samples of NOBI blood, even if it was a microscopic amount—anything to replace the degrading specimens.

Needless to say, this put me in a deep funk. I prayed that I wouldn't have to rely on computer simulation models to supplement my research. It would be like someone telling you what's in your subconscious and pointing you in that direction. My funk had reached its apex when I went home that evening. I think Hector could tell when I was depressed. I talked a mile a minute when not guzzling our dinner wine.

Hector was camped out at my place with suitcases still open as if it were temporary—like he would leave at any moment. As if. I let him be—I was long past the point of telling someone else how to live their life. In fact, this dusty Arizona cowboy had taken to the more cosmopolitan life in Atlanta quite well: wine, sushi, organic vegetables, and beef without recombinant bovine growth hormones. He even got to the point of inquiring as to whether my condo was LEED certified.

Though this living situation had gone on for months, it was on this day that I found a used sleeping bag on the floor.

Hector threw me an eye shrug. "Got it off Craigslist. Never know when it might come in handy." Of course, you could say that about many things.

"I should probably start researching the life span of the common bedbug," I told him with a smirk.

"It would probably lead to a cure for NOBI. God seems to have a sense of humor about these things," Hector replied. "Hard day at work?" He sheepishly kicked the sleeping bag behind the couch.

I nodded my head and threw my backpack on the floor, bedbugs be damned.

"Wanna bounce some ideas off me?"

I shook my head and snatched the glass of wine from his hands. "It's not so much a science thing as much as a...The samples are degrading and we're running out of viable specimens."

His downbeat look told me that even he knew replenishing the samples was a futile aspiration.

It was. Even during this period of time, it was virtually impossible to acquire any type of blood or tissue sample from a Gloaming. Reportedly, there were a few research clinics in France, Russia, and China that had procured—by various means—viable specimens of Gloaming blood, but their research was never shared with the public. The Gloamings were obsessed with only having contact with their own private clinics. Human hospitals were off-limits even during an emergency.

The Gloamings became adept at establishing their own private medical network, with speakeasy emergency rooms for any illness or injury that could occur. The methods used were never revealed but they were effective in providing medical care for any Gloaming that needed it. I needed to analyze Liza Sole's samples against those of other Gloamings to determine if they shared the identical powerful and enhanced physical characteristics or if they degraded with each new re-creation.

I even dared to consider the most extreme schemes. Hector had informed me that in the months and years since the emergence of the NOBI virus, rumors had circulated of a subgroup of Gloamings without homes, wandering throughout the United States and

European countries. The various blogs and news organizations dubbed them Wanderers. They seemed to take on the mythology of Bigfoot or Slenderman, minus the hazy photographs and fake footprints.

Reports from the people who claimed to witness one described a human creature quite distinct from the standard Gloaming: disheveled and sickly yet still with those flashes of substantial strength and the enslaving taste for blood. They were running the streets at night like a rabid dog looking for food in overturned trash cans. If these creatures did indeed exist, they must have had a genetic mutation after re-creation that kept them from attaining physical and mental perfection. They occupied that space in between an unsuccessful and successful re-creation. Between life and death. If only I could get a sample of their blood or tissue and compare it to the analysis of Liza Sole, I could then begin to find the best way to distinguish this virus, perhaps attack it using its own RNA.

We tracked and documented every known Wanderer sighting, however ridiculous they sounded, on an elaborate flowchart, and then tried to predict where the next appearance would be. Hector took it upon himself to sort through most of the obviously bogus sightings in contrast with the ones that seemed somewhat relevant. We had yet to stumble upon a lead that was solid enough, although we did take an impromptu trip to Córdoba, Argentina, to chase a reliable sighting of a Wanderer, from a retired university professor and his wife. It turned out to be a case of a mutated rabies exposure contracted by a vagrant.

A month after that particular excursion, I received a call from a journalist named Jerome Liu, with whom I had established an offhand working relationship by providing him with anonymous quotes and information about the governmental response to the NOBI virus and the incidents that had followed its detection.

Liu called me on the phone and basically screamed his excitement about a credible sighting of a possible Wanderer outside Melbourne, Australia. The details were somewhat weak in contrast with his elation, but several facts held my interest. A press release from the Australian Federal Police stated that authorities were searching for a white male—perhaps fifty years old—who had resisted arrest on a suspected burglary and trespassing and caused substantial injuries to two policemen while they were facilitating the detention.

Hector and I pored over the report like it was a microscope on a virus. The officers had sustained fractures to the ribs, sternum, radius, and clavicle—in addition to various internal injuries. All of which could only be described as inflicted by hand. There was no indication that a weapon was used.

It seemed auspicious, but Hector and I had promised each other that we wouldn't chase every half-baked lead that came across our computer. This one sang, though. It seemed legit.

"No human could do this kind of damage," Hector said with an inscrutable look on his face.

"I agree." And I really did. This had to be a Wanderer.

Hector stretched his arms above his head. "Then again, if it's another rabbit hole then I think—"

"Then so what?" I replied, fake punching his stomach as his arms swept down to protect himself. "At least we get another trip."

I had been implicated in tending to my own paranoia ever since I was a child. Every trip outside my house was an opportunity for me to be kidnapped or assaulted—or so I claimed. Therapy helped, but I knew the paranoia was only hibernating until the next opportunity. And the Gloamings sure woke it up. I was fine now but close to the border of mania. I knew when this trip to Australia began that my growing neurosis would be nurtured by every odd gesture or face or circumstance I encountered. We were being followed—I could sense it and see it in the faces of the men and women in different places and vehicles who stared until I caught them, at which point they looked away.

Cars following us to and from the airport and on the plane— was that the same guy I saw glancing toward me at the Starbucks? It had to be him, and now he's on our flight? Hector could only shake his head but I knew he felt it as well.

As we walked to our terminal, I grabbed Hector by the arm and pulled. "Wha—"

"Let's grab a quick coffee," I said.

He was getting used to my myriad of eccentricities and only nodded his head as I pulled him to the coffee kiosk. He looked at me expectantly with a face that said, "This should be good."

"Don't make it obvious," I ordered, "but the guy with the purple carry-on is the same guy at the gas station this morning, at the Starbucks afterward, and at the CVS when we bought Advil."

Hector turned his head in segments like a stuttering movie reel— his way of being cautious but curious. "Maybe? I don't know."

"I hate when you do that," I spit out.

"Do what?" we both said at the same time, although mine was more sarcastic. "You're going to make me fill in the blanks again?" I continued. "I hate when you dismiss things out of hand—not with words but with your attitude. Makes me think I'm crazy."

He shot me that half smirk and I knew when to let it go. The point had been made. Fair enough, I'd say.

I supposed that would have to do for now. I didn't know what I was expecting but I knew this trip would be one more land mine we would be skipping to avoid.

The sky was clear and blue when we arrived in Melbourne. As night fell, we wasted no time in arranging to meet with our contact: Jack King, a former police officer and now security consultant, journalist, and blogger. Interpret that as you will. I prayed he wasn't one of those crazy conspiracy theorists. Kind of like what many people claimed I had become.

We took a Lyft to the Bayswater district of Melbourne, where we would meet King at a fish-and-chips restaurant. Hector pulled me closer as we navigated a street on a block of broken-down row houses with shot-out streetlights and hands-in-pockets thugs manning the corners. I wasn't sure whether he was trying to protect me or himself.

"How about next time let's have the Lyft drop us off in front of the restaurant?" Hector said as he looked behind us for, like, the tenth time. "An ounce of prevention…"

"I thought it would be better to walk a few blocks to ensure there was no one tailing us," I replied, my steps faster, although I was questioning that plan in real time.

We walked inside the fish-and-chips place with the door off the hinges and a barking nonservice dog in the corner. It looked like there was a sheen of dirty oil on every square inch of the place. And the smell: a deep fragrance of rancid cooking oil mixed with the trash can of a fishing boat. Mismatched wooden tables and chairs covered the floor, and there was a crooked counter built into the wall. Various bearded guys leaned against it…watching…

A burly man in a cowboy hat and pressed jeans and shiny boots—with the attitude of a cowboy vagabond—nodded at me and stepped over. "Are you Dr. Lauren?"

I gripped his hand. "I'm Lauren Scott. You must be Jack King?"

"I sure am."

Jack glanced at Hector. "And you must be Dr. Hector—I've heard a lot about you."

Hector nodded as his shoulders fell—he could finally relax for a moment. "So what's the plan?"

Jack sat down on one of the metal chairs and pulled out a sheet of paper with a diagram printed on it. "This is the layout. The Wanderer has been spotted a couple more times still in this neighborhood since the incident with the police. So I'm thinking, why would he do that?"

"Why?" I repeated.

"Well, I looked at some of the architectural plans of these old buildings along these blocks, and guess what I found?" He pointed at a spot on the paper.

"A blood bank?" Hector said with a smile.

Jack returned the smile with a crooked grin. "Two buildings down from here. Old abandoned three-story that used to be a social services building. Best part about it: has a bomb shelter in the basement."

I glanced at Jack and then at Hector, who had a smirk on his face as he got up from his chair and clapped his hands. That was our cue to get it on.

We walked a block before Jack stepped in front of us in the middle of the sidewalk.

"I have a question, say," Jack said.

"Sure," I replied.

"I'm wondering what we do if we find him."

I glanced up at the top of one of the buildings and could feel Jack's and Hector's eyes burning into me. I knew how difficult it would be to get a tissue sample from a Gloaming. Almost impossible. Every obstacle was planned for, but it all seemed like a war game scenario, trying to find all the moves and countermoves.

All of my planning ended with blood being shed. Back at home everything seemed so conceptual, but here in the rain it was so damn real. There was no way to truly plan for all of this.

"I brought a gun," Jack stated with a hesitation that made it almost sound like a question, as if that were the answer to all of our problems.

Again I was stumped. What can one reply when it's suggested that you use a gun?

"A gun could get us a viable sample," Hector said with a look that seemed to wonder if I was going to get mad at him for the suggestion.

I elbowed him in the side and he shrugged, but he was right. We might need the gun. It might end up being that way. "Let's go in," I ordered, pretty much ignoring the gun option and leaving it to chance.

We walked the two blocks as my anger built up inside me even more. I wanted to call this off and start again tomorrow, when we had an actual plan, but my stubborn mind refused to consider it.

The rain was beginning to fall, and we stepped inside the former social services building. Try to imagine the three of us gingerly stepping through from a side entrance, the door pried off its rusty hinges. A few hunched figures startled and took off running as we walked into the dark, large foyer. Rain splattered our jackets, dripping from the rotted ceiling and decayed walls.

On the far side of the room, Jack led us through the open doorway to the basement and the bomb shelter. Our flashlights swept the crumbling walls of the staircase like comets streaking through the sky. The walls seemed to envelop us like a dark blanket or the night sky I had feared for the past eighteen months. We stepped down three flights of stairs, where the ground met with thrashed flooring and cold silence. We had reached the bottom. I couldn't hear the rainfall anymore. My light skimmed the room and found nothing but decomposing walls and trash.

"This is a lot larger than it seemed in the diagrams," Jack said as he skipped over a pile of rotted wood. "I'll go down this way," he continued with an expectant look, as if he wanted someone to disagree with him.

"Sounds good," Hector replied while trying to look everywhere at once with his light.

"Go down the opposite way, Hector, and I'll take this side with the office," I told him.

He looked at me with a fixed gaze. "Are you sure? I really don't think that's a good idea."

"You'll be in the other room," I countered. "If I need you it would take all of ten seconds for you to be here. And if you need me, the same." He nodded and walked across the room with his eyes on me until the darkness took his face from me.

I took each step deliberately with my flashlight in front of me like a sacred staff of invulnerability. I shined the light from end to end but it was only trash and furniture. Ducking under a fallen beam, I slipped inside the office and saw a torn-up old couch and a desk tilted from a missing leg. Nothing that indicated there was anyone else but vagrants in this area.

I knew that I should go back and find Hector and Jack, but I wanted to check out the corner area of the floor first. My feet could barely keep up with the light shining on the ground as I stepped over bottles and needles strewn every few feet. A large doorway was located at the end of the wall and I couldn't make out exactly where it would lead, given its proximity to the walls.

A freight elevator. I should have guessed. I lifted the gated door and the metal accordion scissor gate and stepped inside. The wood reeked of rotting water damage and that should have been a clue to step out, but I went one foot too far and—

Snap!

I wasn't sure if it was the wood or my ankle that made the sound, but the pain made me scream from anger and not fear. This would bring Hector and Jack running this way, for better or worse. I pulled my foot out from the splintered wooden floor and leaned against the wall.

I heard Hector's and Jack's loud voices calling my name.

As my eyes scanned the room, my nose twitched with that familiar sweet smell, and my instincts kicked in as my knees buckled. I rose up with pain and turned to sprint—

A figure stepped in front of me from I don't know where and I tried to lift my other leg but it wouldn't move with me and I slipped again, stumbling back against the wall, and the figure slammed the metal gate down and closed the elevator door. Banging sounds rang through the elevator as Hector and Jack attempted to force their way inside. No hope of that happening.

The elevator ascended and I was surprised there was even any electricity in this building to power it. But up we went and it seemed I had too much time to think about it. It's weird what thoughts we have in times like this. My old German grad school boyfriend came to mind. So eccentric. People would ask where he was from and he would always answer, "I am from the Free State of Thuringia." He was a nervous bundle of energy, always lamenting the many things that could go wrong in any situation, however benign—"We shouldn't eat there. We could get sick or not find parking or get mugged or…" He hated the situations I would find myself in. Every time I involved him in something, he would mutter the German word *durchwurschteln*. It was one of those untranslatable foreign words. He said it meant literally to "sausage" through a situation by winging it, usually compounding the problem somewhat. I took to muttering *"Durchwurschteln"* to myself in certain sticky situations. Like this one. I was going to sausage myself out of this one, one way or another.

"Why are you here?" the voice asked in a cultivated Australian accent.

I couldn't even bring myself to shine the flashlight on his face then, so I gradually moved it up with care as if it weren't even my own hand. His face was a mess, covered with curly black hair, open scabs, and an angry red tint. His hunched body was thin, as if it were merely skin covering bones without any muscles in between.

The elevator stopped with a shake. The man opened the metal screen and pulled up the door with a rattle. Another door stood about five feet away. He then reached out his hand to me and I could only stare at it for a moment before grabbing it and rising up. I stumbled on one leg and placed a hand on his shoulder as he walked and I hopped to the door, scanning for any escape routes.

He opened the door and a rush of wind and rain slapped my face. We were on the roof.

The Wanderer led me to the edge of the building, with the lights below blinking and the sound of the chaos below filtering up ever so slightly. My hands and legs shook and the pain in my ankle seemed to disappear for a moment, taken over by the nerves firing off shots throughout my body.

"Why are you here?" he asked again.

"I'm—I'm a doctor with the Centers for Disease Control in the United States." My breath came out fast and I was talking too quickly. "I'm looking for a sample of your blood or tissue for my research into the NOBI virus."

The Wanderer laughed and it sounded like two rocks scraping together. His lips were cracked and swollen. "I'm not well. I'm not like the others."

"I know that," I replied. "That is exactly why I want a sample."

He looked me directly in the eyes and it made me feel the fear of Liza Sole all over again. "Is that why you brought the man with the gun?" he spit out.

"Well, that's one of the reasons," I answered, my hand shaky on the flashlight.

He laughed again and a chill went up my neck like a cold hand around it. "Points for honesty, Doctor. But you're still in the negative, my dear. I used to be a doctor myself, you know."

For some reason that statement made me move closer to him for a better look, as if I could see the doctor inside him. "What did you practice?"

"I was an oncologist. A pediatric oncologist, if you must know."

"That's a tough one."

"Tell me about it," he continued. "I can tell you the name of every child that died under my care. Every time it happened I thought about joining them. I would think of different ways to do it. If there even is a heaven, I thought they might be at the gates waiting for me. Either to welcome me or throw things at me."

"I would say the former."

"You will never be able to know or understand what we feel," he stated.

I wasn't sure what he meant by that but I felt offended in some way. "Maybe so," I finally answered as I rubbed my ankle.

"We feel everything. It's like being attacked by parasites every second of the day. Our minds are compartmentalized: there is madness, truth, love, hope…But nothing compels us more than our own survival. You can look in your microscopes all day but we will always be here."

His eyes left my face and looked out over the skyline. "What kind of blueprint or design could have made people like us? What do you see in your microscopes so casually to think you can see what is inside? Our fecundity is not measured in eggs or seeds or environment! And you're going to find a so-called cure with your microscopes! 'The eye with which I see God is the same eye with which God sees me.' Isn't that what they say?"

"I'm not—"

He coughed and stepped back a bit. "Fuck. I've never been good at being the villain. Why would you want my blood? I'm a mess. I have pain every minute of the day, like my body is trying to burn whatever is inside of me. Every second of the day. They say we live two hundred or more years. I can't imagine being in purgatory for so long."

"I don't mean to—"

"Yes you do!" He looked back at me with a fatigue of a hundred years. "The sun will be up soon. I can feel the tingling in my spine. Some dormant fear response, I imagine. I do miss the daylight for whatever reason. I miss it all. The brightness of it all."

"I would miss it all," I replied, not sure what I was thinking or saying. "It's where things come to life. Nothing is hidden."

"Everything is hidden."

A loud *bang* on the rooftop door rang through the rain-splattered night and I jerked my head with the sound.

"Your friends are here," he said.

"They're probably angry," I replied, as if he needed a warning.

I almost screamed for help when he held up his hand. "Look,

259

I'm still a doctor. I still have my oaths. Take it. Take the blood and tissue. Take it all."

I opened my bag and pulled out my blood draw tubes and a knife. He held out his arm for me. "This shouldn't take long," I told him.

"What's time to me?" he asked, with the hint of a smile, but with the rain in my face I wasn't so sure. He put his arm under my shoulders to hold me up. I pulled up the sleeve of his dirty white shirt and saw a tattoo sleeve of faces.

I looked up at him and he could sense my questions. "They're just people. Cut them out. Take the flesh and blood, if you must."

My knife sliced his skin and a smell hit my nose like an odd fragrance—unlike the metallic scent from our own blood. The chunk of skin peeled off and I placed it in a secure metal container. The Wanderer tilted his head back as the blood flowed out into the vial, but then he tilted it forward, close to my face, and I wondered if he was becoming ill. Or if I was in danger...

A loud *bang* and *crack* behind the lone door jerked my head up as I capped the last vial of blood. I didn't even feel him step away from me as I heard the shouts of Hector and Jack, and I flexed my leg to rise and call off the dogs when bullets whizzed by and the Wanderer pushed me to the ground, and he stood up on the ledge, the flapping lights skewed from the rain and his body windblown like a tattered scarecrow. He stepped off the ledge and I screamed in silence as the sunlight rose above the darkness and through the angry clouds.

My mind was a mess. The boxes where I compartmentalized everything were spilling over and thoughts pushed aside each other like maniacs bum-rushing a stage. Our bags were packed on the hotel bed, and Hector sat next to me on the couch, staring at the samples sitting snug inside the medical case. "This is more valuable than we know."

I nodded my head. "Look, we need to get out of this hotel and back to the lab before my paranoia hits harder."

"This is totally going to change your research."

"I hope so," I said with a sour look on my face. But I wondered if this would really make a difference in my research, or if it would only lead me down another mad search inside the maze of the NOBI virus that seemed to change with every re-creation. "I still need blood from Liza Sole—I need to see the origins—and that's about as likely as winning the lottery."

Hector ran his hand through his hair and sighed. "If only I had done a true, substantial autopsy we would have had all kinds of specimens to choose from." He pointed to the specimen in the container. "What is that? Why is it so dark?"

"The guy had a tattoo sleeve. By the way, what kind of autopsy *did* you do?" I was suddenly looking for a fight to calm my nerves.

Hector shrugged with an impatient look on his face. "A cursory examination. I had to wait for you to arrive. Didn't want the Feds to get mad at me. I only took—" He slammed his hand on the table and his phone bounced off the glass.

"What?" I screamed.

Hector jumped up from his chair. "Liza Sole. She had a tattoo near her waist. I took a picture—"

"Okay, so?"

"So, I was worried that it might degrade, so I cut it out!"

I hopped up and held him still. "The tattoo? You kept it?"

"Yes!"

"You kept it!"

"Yes! I put it in a specimen jar and put it in the alarmed refrigerator." Hector looked up at the ceiling as if to thank whoever might be up there.

"My God, I wonder if it's still there," I said, cursing the fact that I was in a Melbourne, Australia, hotel room and not in Nogales, Arizona. "We need to get back there now!"

I could go crazy with the moon so bright…Hector drove the rental Prius down the dusty road, as I watched each crooked cactus on the highway from Phoenix to Nogales. It was monsoon season and dark clouds fought with the blue sky as I was a witness to it all. It looked so different from those early days, when we scoured the West like miners seeking the gold rush. Was the road always this long? Did the brush always sweep across the horizon with the sand? Back then the chase seemed so erratic and exciting—so intense and yet satisfying. I wasn't so tired back then.

I turned again to look out the back window. "That Escalade is still behind us," I said with a smug look across my face.

Hector checked the rearview. "Are you sure? There are a few cars behind us."

I rolled my eyes. "We've got the Wanderer sample and we might have another Liza Sole specimen soon. To say I'm pretty unnerved to have those samples in my possession would be an understatement. We need to get back to the lab."

He nodded at me. "No argument here." He stole a glance at me. "But less paranoia, please."

I popped him in the arm.

* * *

We pulled into the Nogales Department of Health; in it was the medical examiner's office. I had waited until we were about twenty minutes away before I called Sheriff Wilson, in order to keep it low profile in case someone was listening to our phone calls and beat us to it. More paranoia, thank you. I was intentionally vague, but Wilson agreed to meet us. As our car pulled into the parking lot, the sheriff was waiting in front of the entrance with a worried look on his face.

We stepped out of the car and shook hands. Hector grabbed him into a hug. "Good to see you, Sheriff," he said.

"Thank you so much for meeting us," I added.

Wilson shot us a wry smile, which wrinkled his face even more, before he gave us the slow drawl. "Good to see you two again. Gotta be honest. I'm concerned as to why you're here all of a sudden."

As we walked inside, each of us talked over the others about the past year of our lives and how much the NOBI virus and all of the accompanying chaos had changed us in so many ways. Hector got to the point after a few moments. "I'm looking for a sample from the Liza Sole examination that might still be here, unless it was discarded," he said as we made our way to the medical examiner's rooms.

"Do you have a new coroner?" I asked.

Sheriff Wilson shook his head as he pulled off his cowboy hat and wiped the line between his tanned face and pale head with a handkerchief. "We've been sharing an ME with Tucson. She comes down as needed. I used the money saved to hire a few more deputies. God knows we need them more than ever with all the bloodsucker groupie tourists coming here to see the so-called birthplace."

"Seriously?" Hector asked.

"Oh sure. They come into town looking for something that ain't here. There are no Gloamings in this town, far as I know. And I would know. These tourists come in, cause trouble, then leave."

We stepped inside the autopsy room. Hector moved over to the big refrigerator. He scanned the large shelves filled with various samples, and if I'd been religious I might have said a prayer, but I could only hope that the give-and-take of the universe would allow us something good after such a long time.

"Yes!" Hector shouted as he raised his hand, holding a large jar like a championship trophy. And inside the jar were the blood and tissue from the body of Liza Sole. Cue the confetti and the marching band...

Hector shifted and grimaced on the lumpy bed as a squeak spilled out inside our cramped motel room. "We just had to stay in the same busted motel room, didn't we?" he said.

I shrugged and smiled. "Don't we all miss the good old days?"

"I totally miss being beat down by crazy Gloamings."

I threw up my hands and moaned. "Shit."

"What?" Hector said, sitting up.

"The cooler needs more ice. I want those samples ice-cold."

Hector waved a hand at the refrigerator. "Why do you have to scream it? Use the fridge."

"I don't trust it," I answered. "Just when I was getting ready to relax." There was no way I was going to safeguard the integrity of the specimens in some old broken-down motel refrigerator. I wouldn't be able to sleep, worrying over whether they were cold enough. I grabbed a couple of the ice buckets from the top of the desk.

"Need help?" Hector asked.

I smirked. "I think I got this." I stepped out of the room and into the warm Arizona breeze. I walked down the outside breezeway, past the other rooms, and into the laundry room, where the ice machine sat against the back wall. I knelt down and slid the bucket under the dispenser opening, and as I raised my hand to push the button I felt something hard and metal press against my head.

"Mind if I look up to see who's pointing a gun at my head?" I asked.

"Put the ice in both buckets and get up," a male voice told me.

I complied and stood up, holding both buckets of ice.

"We only want the samples," the man, who was wearing a blue bomber jacket, said, still holding the gun on me. "Then you two can go on your way."

"Just like that?" I asked. I rolled my eyes, but inside my guts were churning like a pot of boiling water.

"If you want it to be easy, then yes."

We walked back to the motel room and I cursed myself for staying at this shithole again. They say you should trust your instincts, but looking back now it seems I don't have a great track record on that. I stopped in front of the room door.

"Open the door, Doctor," the man said.

"I didn't bring the key."

The man didn't say anything for a moment and then nudged me with the point of the pistol as he stepped to the other side of the doorframe.

I knocked on the door.

Nothing.

"Again," the man whispered.

I raised my hand to knock again when the door opened and Hector stood in front of me with an irritated look on his face. If we got out of this I promised to knock that look off with the back of my hand. His eyes scrunched up, his hands on his hips. "Next time take the key," he said as he stepped aside and pulled my arm and body to the other side of the doorway. My eyes opened wide as I saw Sheriff Wilson on the other side of the door holding a gun, which he immediately slammed against the side of the head of the man in the blue bomber.

Tires screeched in the parking lot as two deputies in their cruisers boxed in a black Escalade. I had to laugh to myself: Hector wasn't so oblivious and inside his own mind after all. Things might actually work themselves out.

Sheriff Wilson grinned and shook his head. "I knew you two couldn't stay out of trouble in my county. Hope you don't mind that I followed you."

All I could do was grin like an idiot.

I ended up taking part of the samples to a fertility clinic in Atlanta, where I told them I wanted to store my eggs. They had no idea it was the sample, but I needed an anonymous place to keep the specimen safe.

Now it was time to finish my research.

CHAPTER 14

WINTER
THIRTY-TWO MONTHS AFTER THE NOBI DISCOVERY

Marcy Noll
National Security Adviser to the President

I was the first national security adviser to the president when the National Security Council was merged with the Department of Homeland Security after the terrorist attacks in New York and Los Angeles. The congressional act combining the two departments came together relatively quickly. My promotion came quickly after that, when the two more senior advisers in line abruptly resigned; they were found to have leaked classified information to a reporter. I had nothing to do with that, contrary to unsourced gossip on various blogs.

People warned me not to work on Capitol Hill. It's a cesspool of sexism, glass ceilings, and harassment. I guess they didn't realize I used to love kicking over a hornet's nest. Once you bitch-slap an offender when no one else is around and dare them to say something, once you learn the subtle art of blackmail, once you sabotage a rival and then let them know about it, once people fear making your list of things to do today—this makes the ride much smoother. It's these kinds of milestones that expose our true character in Washington, DC.

After years grinding away on various budget committees, I had recently landed a plum assignment: the Homeland Security Committee. When not strategizing new legislation, it was my duty to keep members informed of current events affecting Homeland Security, many of which were classified. As chief counsel, I had top secret clearance and the constant thrill of being privy to our most closely held secrets…It was intoxicating! This was all in spite of the soul-sucking atmosphere of this town. Once I told an acquaintance I just couldn't trust anyone in DC. The response was "Yeah, but once you get past that…"

I also was promoted over my fool of a boss. I can still remember the dumb look on his face—a weird painted-on fake smile, like the Joker's permanent grin—when the news came down. I fully deserved the promotion, but that idiot didn't even realize how he'd hijacked his own prospects—a sexist to the very end. He always tried to interject "personal" topics into everyday conversations. His go-to phrase was "Sorry, I'm just a very sexual person"—I must have missed that part of his personality—as he ran his tongue along his teeth with a weird smacking sound. He'd gotten away with it for years, but luckily the White House wasn't about to take a chance on that kind of press relations time bomb with so much else at stake. So I got the nod, and without having to resort to any dirty tricks.

The year from hell began with the hacking of the Spring Meadow Power Plant, which served power to the Greater Philadelphia area; the hacking knocked out power for a week for over two million people. Over 70 percent of the 112 power substations were inoperable. It was a devastating economic and physical hardship and the first incident which led to a reassessment of how to better coordinate our agencies to protect the American people.

That was only the beginning of a summer of hacks on different prime structures in the United States, Europe, and Asia. Both agencies were running blind—how do you stop an army of code attacking something you cannot see?—and Congress thought it was time to try a unified front. I was appointed as the new head of the combined departments.

But two more power plants on the East Coast were attacked by a malicious code before Congress finally empowered us by approving funding for more vigilant tracking and secure additions to the computer code used by most of the nation's power grids.

Then came the operations-specific hacks: firmware updates that caused failures in systems providing crucial niche services, such as hospital monitoring and medication dispensing equipment, traffic lights in major cities and populated thoroughfares, and aircraft control systems.[25]

---

[25] The Seattle-Tacoma International Airport incident highlighted the damage that these hackers could inflict on United States civil aviation and the economy as a whole. The hackers were able to change the computer-generated flight progress strip for all flights in the control tower. The plane's transponder broadcasts an encoded radio signal that provides the controller with the aircraft's flight number, altitude, airspeed, and destination. An electronic figure representing the airplane appears on the controller's radar screen with all relevant flight information next to it.

US Airways flight 1231 and Aer Lingus flight 277 were both entering the airspace for Seattle-Tacoma International Airport when their respective flight patterns were altered by the hackers. US Airways flight 1231 flew over the airport's traffic pattern traveling south-southeastward. At the same time, Aer Lingus flight 277 was climbing through the traffic pattern at twenty-five thousand feet and collided with the US Airways aircraft, killing all passengers on board both planes.

Other planes were forced to divert to other airports, and other aircraft were left circling while awaiting permission to land after the controllers ordered visual flight rules. The result was the worst domestic aviation premeditated crime in U.S. history.

[26] These types of essential functions left no room for error, and their disruption caused billions of dollars in damage and the significant loss of lives.

This resulted in a greater emphasis on server and computer security led by private corporations and governmental agencies. It was after these events that the NSA was merged into the new Homeland Security Department. The head of the new agency was the National Security Council, and as the president's national security adviser, I was appointed as the new head of the combined departments.

As the new national security adviser, most of my time was consumed by the long war against various terrorist groups and the deteriorating Russian governmental structures. My personal life was in shambles during this time due to my workaholic ways. My first divorce was years behind me, and I was eager to get back out there, but I couldn't keep a date for anything. And then the various Internet attacks came to the forefront and we had to confront the policies that would dictate our responses to these attacks. Given the obtuse nature of Internet

---

[26]   Hackers based in Brazil but working on the orders of various countries engaged in state-sponsored terrorism, attacking the servers of Hong Kong Sanatorium and Hospital, a private hospital established in 1922 and generally accepted as one of the best hospitals in Asia. The group entered the hospital computer network through an SQL injection exploit. Once inside the network, the group modified several active medical devices, including insulin pumps, heart defibrillators, and CT scan machines. The heart defibrillators were modified to deliver an excess amount of electricity, which killed the relevant patients. The insulin pumps were made to deliver an inordinate amount of insulin to the patients, resulting in five deaths and three patients in comas.

The hackers modified various medical charts and courses of treatments thereby assigning the incorrect medication to various patients, resulting in numerous deaths and significant bodily harm. They interrupted several remote access surgeries done by computer, causing several deaths. The hackers also altered work orders on all patients within the hospital system. The work of the hackers ultimately resulted in the deaths of seventy-five patients and significant medical harm to three hundred others.

disruptions, it was imperative that these be investigated thoroughly to determine if these attacks were state supported. Some of these attacks did have links to state entities, and thus began an Internet cold war with retaliatory hacking strikes by the U.S. against other countries, including China, Russia, and North Korea, and vice versa. Although it was never made explicit, such attacks became commonplace over the summer. Though the media implied that the disruptions were the work of criminal elements seeking monetary gain, the reality was a covert war waged by coders and hackers backed by state governments.

The Gloaming issue just wasn't a priority with the administration—well, let me take that back. The Gloamings weren't a *national security* priority for the administration in the beginning. Obviously, they were a health-care concern at first, but after the initial hysteria regarding the unknown aspects of the condition abated, and the Gloaming Equal Rights for All Act passed, the Gloamings simply became another segment of the population at large, although a segment not yet entirely understood. The president put the Gloamings back on the shelf as a public interest story.

We had some concerns when the reports came out that the Chinese were doing experiments on a kidnapped Gloaming, trying to replicate a serum to create an army of Gloamings. Given their physical abilities of strength and camouflage, it was a given that scientists would attempt to weaponize them. But we all know now that those experiments failed miserably—it's a scientific fact that a Gloaming can only be re-created through the bite of another Gloaming. Re-creation certainly cannot happen through a test tube.

And even then, re-creation often failed. Nearly half died during the process—so many people in thrall to the glamour of the Gloamings seemed to conveniently forget this difficult fact. It brought a certain somberness to the idealized perception of re-creation.

Our informal biweekly council meetings were normally held in a secure conference room at the Central Intelligence Agency headquarters, where we would discuss the recent occurrences that might make our list of "inclusion events" for the president's daily briefing. At this particular meeting, attended by Richard Crawford, deputy director of the CIA, Lauren Scott, from the CDC, and myself, the subject was whether the Gloamings should be considered a threat. There was a sizable amount of friction among various CIA analysts as to whether more effort should be made to consider treating the Gloamings as a possible threat and adjust our intelligence efforts accordingly.

"Can we just stick to the basics right now?" Richard asked as he poured himself another cup of coffee. "Can they not acquire the necessary nutrition from a source other than blood?"

Lauren put her hands up and shrugged. "They say they can. Our research is somewhat limited but it indicates that they can only survive by consuming blood. They have a certain enzyme that inhibits microbial decay of the blood they have consumed in their system, so the blood in their stomach can stay there like solid food. It's generally accepted that they can survive on animal blood. But for how long, who knows? They need human blood."

Richard glared at her. "Great. Like a tick."

"How do they view non-Gloamings?" I asked.

"What do you mean?" Lauren replied.

I rubbed my temples; my head was throbbing. "Are we simply a vessel for food or are we partner species who coexist through a system of ethics that binds all knowledgeable species? Reasoning. Values. Religion. Any of these—are they moral persons that value the life of others?" I was trying to determine how to even begin assessing the threat of the Gloamings. Did they *want* our blood—or did they *need* it?

Richard poured himself yet another cup of coffee and rubbed his eyes. "Those murders. We know they're Gloaming-related. Why cut off the heads?"

"The Gloamings, when they feed through a bite, will re-create the person unless the head is cut off," Lauren stated. "The Gloamings have become quite discriminating when it comes to who is re-created. Hence the research for devices that attach to a person's neck to facilitate feeding without the re-creation."

Richard didn't even attempt to hide his disgust. We ended the meeting with no clear answers.

Of course the re-creation of the Pope caught most intelligence agencies off guard. German and British intelligence agencies were especially disturbed by this occurrence. After the Pope re-created, Chinese leaders passed various laws prohibiting any re-creation of their citizens, barring Gloamings from entering the country. It was rather shortsighted in that many upper-level government officials and many wealthy Chinese desired to become Gloamings. But this was somewhat mitigated by the terrorist attacks on the U.S. embassy in Buenos Aires and the thirty-five-day war between Israel and Iran, which spilled over into Lebanon. The president and the secretary of state were busy trying to broker a cease-fire and prevent World War III. A pope becoming a Gloaming just wasn't as pressing.

Only the FBI, as an agency, was involved in any threat posed by the Gloamings, as a result of the Gloaming Crimes Unit. But that was essentially a local law enforcement issue, not national security, until the FBI began an investigation into the disappearance of several top in vitro fertilization physicians around the world. Though others point to the National Guard issue as the spark, I'd mark IVF as the beginning of the recent troubles.

* * *

In vitro fertilization, or IVF, is a scientific process where an egg is fertilized by sperm outside the body. For women under thirty-five years of age in America, the success rate of IVF is about 50 percent. Doctors take ova from a woman's ovaries and let the sperm fertilize them in a container with liquid. It's cultured for about a week and then implanted in the same or another woman's uterus— essentially, an egg is fertilized by sperm outside the body in order to establish a successful pregnancy.

The original unincorporated Gloaming Council began secret discussions about starting a reproduction program to find a way for Gloamings to reproduce as humans do: within a natural pregnancy. The first doctor hired by the Gloamings was Dr. Larry Cranston, one of the world's foremost IVF experts. He moved from New York City to Las Cruces, New Mexico, and took a position at New Mexico State University, as well as at a private clinic, the Casablanca Lily Clinic. The clinic was built with a one-story ground floor and a five-story complex below the ground.

Dr. Cranston authored a confidential report that my security council intercepted during the National Guard crises. The report detailed a reproduction failure of 100 percent within the studied Gloamings. The study also found that in 40 percent of the women studied, unprotected sex with a Gloaming male caused irreversible damage to the uterus. In addition, Cranston found that he needed to rely on more speculative and primitive invasive procedures to do his testing, because modern imaging tests, such as ultrasound, hysteroscopy, and laparoscopy, could not be performed on Gloamings due to their radioactive nature.[27]

---

[27] Relevant portions of the report concluded, "While we had no means to test for actual 'egg quality,' with our proprietary anti-Mullerian hormone testing of the ovaries we were somewhat able to ensure the viability of the eggs used in our processes. Most of the women in our test group were between the ages of

Any ethical doctor would have terminated the study there, or at least paused to investigate a less invasive path, especially given the dangers in the first place of allowing Gloamings to enter into consensual sexual encounters. But not Cranston: he kept going, in spite of the larger percentage of female participants who ended up with irreversible medical conditions ranging from pelvic inflammatory disease to uterine fibroids. His research further showed that while the female Gloaming's estrogen and progesterone levels were as low as those of a human female beginning menstruation, and while female Gloamings went through a similar ovulatory and luteal phase in which ovulation occurs, a key difference was that the female Gloaming did not engage in menstrual bleeding.[28] Dr. Cranston's study diagnosed the issue as a hybrid polycystic ovarian syndrome [PCOS], in which follicles are unable to produce a mature egg.

---

twenty-one and thirty-five, given that as women age past thirty-five years, the probability of embryo transfers and pregnancy with live birth drops more than 70 percent. Unfortunately, the percentage of Gloaming assisted reproductive technology (ART) cycles that resulted in a pregnancy were zero, although the percentage of eggs successfully fertilized was 10 percent. More specifically, regarding fertilization, the results were:

—Gloaming Man to Human Woman = 2
—Human Man to Gloaming Woman = 3
—Gloaming Man to Gloaming Woman = 5

"Given our relative success in fertilization with one party having Gloaming traits, we believe that future advancements will lead to a probable and successful pregnancy resulting in a live birth of a baby that shares at least 50 percent Gloaming DNA.

[28] Cranston's research further indicated that the hormones estrogen, progesterone, and testosterone were secreted naturally and did not seem to have an impact on the female Gloaming's inability to engage in reproduction. The main point the study considered was that female Gloamings lost the ability to have a defined menstrual cycle after they were re-created. However, the female Gloaming did have certain physical characteristics that seemed to mirror a menstrual cycle, such as the follicular phase.

Cranston also found that all of the female participants had blocked fallopian tubes which prevented the sperm from reaching the egg. In some of the subjects, the tubes prevented a fertilized egg from reaching the uterus. Apparently, these conditions in Gloaming females were attributed to the elevated blood levels, enlarged organs, and decrease in the amount of water in a Gloaming body. The forming of never-before-encountered hormones in the Gloaming body was also a cause of these infertility conditions.

Ironically, as some cultural commentators pointed out years later, the Gloamings then followed a distinctly "human" path. In other words, after this study failed and they were forced to abandon the idea of procreation through natural means, they turned their interest to the next option: in vitro fertilization.

Construction began in secret for a laboratory engineered about seven hundred feet into and under the side of a mountain in the San Andres mountain range, between the cities of Caballo and Tularosa, New Mexico. The unnamed facility consisted of four large underground buildings and one aboveground facility, with state-of-the-art environmentally controlled rooms. Our surveillance indicated that the combined structures consisted of four seventy-five-thousand-square-foot halls and research labs and over twenty-five administrative structures designed with concrete walls at minimum seven feet thick, to withstand the blast of a nuclear device. The walls were protected by a concrete wall seven feet thick, itself protected by another concrete wall of undetermined thickness. The roof was hardened with reinforced concrete and covered with fifty-five feet of earth.

Additionally, the facility contained a two-year supply of fuel, a deepwater well, NBC filtration systems, and geothermal heating and cooling. The laboratory was designed for wartime use and included manually operated ventilators in case supplies of electricity or gas became scarce. Ventilation openings that lined the structure were protected by titanium blast valves. A blast valve is closed by a shock wave but otherwise remains open, which ensures the viability of the structure and the occupants.

The Gloamings kept the construction of this facility secret for a surprisingly long period of time. A week after Nick Bindon Claremont was elected governor of New Mexico, a solo hiker working an off trail in the San Andres Mountains spotted the construction of the laboratory. He snapped a few photographs with his cell phone before he was chased off by private security. He posted the photos on a couple of Reddit subreddits dealing with hiking and the Greater New Mexico area, and discussions as to what was being built in the area quickly made the front page.

From that point, the Internet erupted.

At first, Governor Claremont refused to comment on the reports.

Then, when building permits to a newly formed LLC called the Rio Grande Institute were linked to a company Nick Bindon Claremont owned, he issued a statement saying that he indeed was the guiding force behind the laboratory, and emphasized that the complex was for medical advancements for humans and Gloamings alike, with the main focus on cancer research. But this did little to contain the conspiracy theories sprouting up—namely, that the complex would be an enormous blood bank to feed Gloamings on the blood of various persons reported missing throughout the country. Or that the laboratory would be used to study the enhancement of the already powerful Gloaming physical characteristics.

Several months prior, various in vitro doctors and researchers began to disappear. After the fifth disappearance and an article in the *Wall Street Journal,* the FBI began an initial investigation.

Evidence had been previously nonexistent until the case of Dr. Maggie Fitzpatrick.

Dr. Fitzpatrick was last seen leaving a bar called the One-Eyed Cat, where she had met coworkers for a drink and left when she complained of being tired. The cameras inside the bar recorded Maggie leaving alone.

The parking lot was behind the bar, but you had to walk behind the building to enter the lot. This was downtown, so most people tended to either walk down the sidewalk or through the alley. There were no cameras in the alley but there was one at a restaurant across from the One-Eyed Cat. A review of the tape from the relevant time period showed that no one resembling Dr. Maggie Fitzpatrick used the sidewalk to reach the parking lot.

Therefore, she had to have used the alley to get to her car. The parking lot had several cameras which showed Maggie never made it to her car. The FBI narrowed her abduction to the alley beside the bar—and the camera from the restaurant across the street showed a van driving into the alley at the exact time Maggie left the bar. An alarming number of other security cameras in the area had suddenly been broken that night, but one secreted inside a nearby antique shop showed the same van about an hour before Maggie entered the bar. The passenger door to the van was open but the footage was full of static—consistent with feedback caused by Gloaming presence.

The FBI then turned the investigation over to the Gloaming Crimes Unit, which chased various dead ends until the publicity about the New Mexico laboratory hit. The FBI—specifically Agent Calvin James—made the connection quickly, and verified that several companies had transacted sales to the laboratory for the following equipment: storage tanks, embryo freezers, inverted microscopes, incubators, fertilizer workstations, culture dishes, and embryo dishes.

Frustratingly, though we now had hard evidence about the secret use of Governor Claremont's laboratories, and we had evidence that Dr. Maggie Fitzpatrick had been allegedly kidnapped by a Gloaming, we could only connect the two facts in theory. And the FBI's Gloaming Crimes Unit had to bend over backward to avoid unimpeachable evidence—which might smack of conspiracy theory—or the unit would lose weeks, sometimes months, dealing with the ACLU's Gloaming defense league.

So the FBI's investigation stalled until Dr. Maggie Fitzpatrick escaped from the laboratory and confirmed that she and four other doctors had been kidnapped and forced to conduct research on accomplishing procreation for the Gloaming community. Their efforts had proved unsuccessful until a female Gloaming named Leslie Claremont became the first to naturally give birth to a Gloaming baby.

But by then other troubles had begun and the FBI didn't have the resources to investigate the laboratory.

The first bombing on a Gloaming residence occurred in Portland, Oregon. Initially it was thought to be an explosion resulting from a gas leak or some other similar occurrence. But when it was determined to have been a bomb that made the explosion, the ATF and the FBI became involved. During the investigation, the FBI found radiation traces that indicated the house had been occupied by Gloamings for a significant period of time. And strangely enough, a check of the house ownership found that the house had been bought two years earlier from an LLC. Finding the actual buyer of this property would entail combing through a maze of paperwork and shell companies designed to hide the true ownership of the house.

At first the FBI thought it might be a recurrence of the ISIS terrorist attacks from the past summer, but those three attacks were centered on commercial or government buildings and none of the evidence recovered from the cell indicated that they ever considered residential targets. With the Gloaming community so closed off, we knew that any number of possible theories could account for someone wanting to hurt the Gloamings.

The second bombing occurred in Tempe, Arizona, at another residence in a quiet upper-class community close to the mountains. Device fragments found at this scene had identifiers inscribed in Italian, which the FBI and Interpol traced to a construction supplier in Naples. Interpol was already investigating two other bombings in Italy and Germany under similar circumstances— both Gloaming houses too.

No Gloamings or humans were harmed during the explosions, but the Gloaming residents vanished and refused to be interviewed. Therefore, any hope of finding a motive seemed very distant, until Agent Zumthor, the lead FBI investigator, found a damaged hard drive in the Tempe, Arizona, rubble. They recovered data showing different shipments of dextromethorphan to different locations in the United States. DXM is a psychoactive cough suppressant found in many over-the-counter and prescription medicines and can cause delusions and hallucinations, depending on the dosage. The Gloamings frequently acquired and ingested DXM, although this hard drive was the first evidence we had showing they were actively trafficking in the drug.

The other documents on the hard drive addressed certain members of the Catholic clergy in North and South America who were sympathetic to the Gloaming cause and open to re-creation.

The Gloaming Council had never publicly addressed the Pope's re-creation and the schism it had caused within the Catholic Church. But it seemed the Gloamings were far more interested in that situation than they let on.

The Order of Bruder Klaus and its leader, Bishop Lawrence Thomas, were out in front as the strongest opponents of the Gloaming interest in the Catholic Church. They were never positively confirmed to be involved in the murder of the cardinals at the Vatican or of the Pope—if he was indeed actually murdered—but most intelligence agencies in America and in Europe regarded the order as the organization behind the assassinations.

The United States government never took formal legal action against the order, but the FBI did keep a close eye on them with infrequent surveillance. And they did scrutinize the order on the few occasions when some of the monks went abroad for various activities. However, the FBI never found any evidence of wrongdoing as the monks and clergy were extremely careful to disguise any criminal activities or the true purpose of their trips.

The investigation into the bombings certainly helped lend our intelligence community further context regarding Gloaming goals and beliefs, but we were still no closer to finding a motive for the attacks. Agent Zumthor—who, it should be noted, was in the minority at the time—believed these attacks were more than a Gloaming family squabble, and that greater forces were at play that reached into the upper ranks of the Gloamings and the Catholic Church.

Those greater forces finally made their presence known with the appearance of a single fingerprint. Italian authorities, at the request of the FBI and Interpol to investigate a potential lead, found a strip of metal at their attack site—which they surmised to be from whatever box had housed the explosive device—with a single fingerprint.

Interpol and our own FBI databases both came up with the same match. I still remember the phone call from Agent Zumthor when he delivered the news about the fingerprint hit.

"Who the hell is Bernard Kieslowki?" I asked.

If it was possible to be both exhausted and excited at the same time, that's how Zumthor sounded. He sighed. "The Order of Bruder Klaus, ma'am. Here we go again."

CHAPTER 15

IN-BETWEEN DAYS

The Seeker

I miss my mother and father. I miss my sister. But I can't go back. I'm not even certain we share the same blood.

Instead I seek out the sounds and sights of the night skies, shadowed horizons, darkened homes. On some nights when my mind empties, I can hear the silence, apart from others, maybe in the desert or a forest. All of my preceding lives leaking from my mind. The daughter, the student, the sister, the friend—all of them walking into the trees or the scrubland. Their faces turned against me as they drift away.

These days it is my senses that have replaced them, no me, no others, each feeling a new chorus of the world. Those drugs I used to do—alcohol or cocaine, H or Molly—are ghosts compared to this. Instead, the sound and light—I feel my nerves move up and down my body floating above it all. I seek out music in a roadside bar, people at the pool tables, lonesome bartenders, the lights and noise. I could have stayed out all night—for weeks if my body didn't crave the cold dirt in the ground. Or more friends, if I didn't view them as the bird sees the worm before it's plucked from the leaf. The hawk, the hare. The panther. The—

People look different now. I see their faces and their facial cues of emotion: disgust, anger, fear, sadness, happiness, surprise, and contempt, surrender. Even before they show it. A muscle twitch that maybe even they didn't know happened. A stride, a limp— every step taken tells me something about what they are thinking in that moment.

I can smell their fear and happiness. Everything about them fascinates me. Was I ever so easy to unlock…

It's clear I am not myself anymore. That even these memories, these words, these stories, are a kind of liability. But desire pulls me back just as it pulls me forward, and all of these thoughts that must have been forgotten come back now and again when I'm listening to an old cowboy strum a tune, or Vivaldi on a car stereo, or just a tune of the wind in the trees. I'll just have to search for the joy in experiences and love…the joy of this place—raising the dead when it suits us…

What remains is the slow, pulsing experience of tomorrow, the next night, the one after that. The song of the sad musician dying in my mouth, or the deer I follow through the field, or the evening owl who, like me, feels both defined and released by his prey. Someone once told me that if you see the sun rise once, a child being born, a deer taking its last breath, you'll always want to see it again. What more can they do to me? There's no question or questioning of this world—just what is next.

CHAPTER 16

SPRING

THIRTY-FOUR MONTHS AFTER THE NOBI DISCOVERY

Hugo Zumthor
Special Agent in Charge of Gloaming Crimes Unit, FBI

Washington, DC, is my town and it's beautiful on the outside—where it counts, I thought to myself as I looked out my office window. I tend to idle with my thoughts sometimes, which I was doing the afternoon Interpol reached out to the Gloaming Crimes Unit as the revelation of Bernard Kieslowki, radical and terrorist, came across my radar with a series of *pings* in my inbox, one after another, before I could even open the first.

The intra-agency sharing of intel was still somewhat new, so it came as a shock to hear that the Drug Enforcement Administration and Interpol were closely tracking Miguel Velazquez Trevino, head of the Gulf Coast cartel, the largest and most profitable drug cartel in the world. Trevino was known as El Gusano—the worm—for smuggling wares into the United States via sophisticated, hard-to-trace tunnels constructed of reinforced steel beams and wired with electricity, proprietary tunnel ventilation, and even a primitive rail system. A crime king like Trevino re-creating? This was one of our greatest governmental fears come true.

I couldn't wait to sink my teeth into it—in a manner of speaking.[29]

I was sent to Naples to coordinate efforts with Interpol. We had received information that Trevino was attempting to enter Europe, where he would be re-created by an elusive Sicilian crime lord named Abramo Moretti.[30] This all happened rapidly, though once I got to Rome it took me a while to get used to their languid pace of investigation: so much sitting around, talking, waiting for things to "pop up." Case in point: the afternoon I sat at an outdoor table in a Rome coffee bar with Interpol's Agent Emanuela Baresi, watching the crowds make their way along the busy streets.

"How can you live here?" I asked. "I've had my damn pocket almost picked twice."

Emanuela shook her shiny black hair and smiled. "I used to live in New York City," she said, as if that alone answered my question.

I tapped the table with my espresso cup. "What's good about living in Rome?"

"It's not New York."

---

[29] Miguel Velazquez Trevino was the head of the Gulf Coast cartel (GCC), the largest and most profitable drug cartel in the world. The GFC started out as poppy and marijuana farmers, but years later they imported marijuana, methamphetamine, cocaine, and heroin to the United States and Europe. With a net worth estimated to be $10 billion, Trevino was annually listed by *Forbes* as one of the richest men in the world. He also happened to be on another well-known list: the FBI's ten most wanted.

[30] Moretti was re-created at the age of eighty by an unknown creator in an abandoned castle in Sicily. He then became known in Gloaming circles as a creator without failure. For Moretti, money was not a concern when considering a re-creation. He simply chose—by all reports, very selectively—whom he wanted.

I had to grin. "Funny. What's bad about Rome?"

"It's not New York." Emanuela threw her head back and laughed.

We were watching a four-story eighteenth-century apartment building, about half a block from our table. Trevino was reported to be hiding inside, a suspicion that was confirmed when—as I lifted my hand to order another espresso—an explosion threw me from my seat.

An hour later, Emanuela and I and her tactical team stood in the burned-out cavern of a third-floor apartment. Money of all different denominations and countries was scattered along the floor. We found the partly charred body of Miguel Velazquez Trevino, who it seemed had not re-created after all. "Better call Mexico," Emanuela muttered.

And, as if on cue, one of Emanuela's officers handed her a composite picture of two faces. "Who are they?" I asked.

"Two men seen leaving the adjacent apartment before the explosion," she said.

I studied the photo. "Do you know who they are?"

"Oh, without a doubt," she said. "They would be Bernard Kieslowki and Kamel Paquet. The Order of Bruder Klaus."

A French citizen, the son of a Polish émigré and a French mother, Bernard Kieslowki was raised in various towns in France due to his father's tuberculosis, which led Kristof Kieslowki to a number of doctors around the country. Bernard's mother, Juliette, was an engineer by training and, to her agnostic husband's dismay, homeschooled their son and only child, Bernard, to ensure his strict Catholic education.

Young Bernard fell gravely ill at age sixteen. His mother found him incoherent one morning, in the throes of a high-grade fever. In the evening, Bernard suddenly screamed out, "Do not fear my condition for I bear on my body the marks of our Lord," then fell back into a coma. When Juliette rushed in, Bernard's hands displayed the wounds of Jesus Christ on the cross: the stigmata.

The coma and stigmata lasted for days. Juliette insisted, once again to the dismay of her husband, Kristof, that Bernard did not need to be transported to the hospital. He would recover with prayer. So she prayed, next to his bed, day and night. On the seventh day, as Kristof was almost to the point of forcibly removing his son and taking him to the hospital—his wife be damned—Bernard displayed wounds on his forehead similar to those caused by the crown of thorns. This is the story, at least, and at the end of the seventh day, late in the night, Bernard woke up from his coma with a loud cry.

The doctors had no answer for his recovery. This drove Juliette into an even stricter religious life, and she moved into a separate bedroom from her husband to spend more time in prayer, reciting the rosary for hours a day.

Later that year, Bernard entered Bellebranche Abbey, to Juliette's delight. Even Kristof was supportive—he could see his son truly wanted a religious life. At the seminary, Bernard befriended a fellow seminarian, Kamel Paquet. Kamel was born in a mountain village in Algeria, near an ancient French-Algerian monastery named the Abbey of Our Lady of Perpetual Help. Orphaned when a band of extremists slaughtered most of the villagers, Kamel was left at the monastery gates and then transported to Bellebranche Abbey, where he and Bernard met and, being of identical age, quickly became friends. After their ordination they spent a few years working the farm on the abbey grounds, tending to the blueberry plants, avocado trees, and apple orchard.

Bernard, like most priests, took notice of the Gloamings' inroads into the Catholic hierarchy, but the abbey felt cocooned, far away from the noise in Rome and the rest of the world. Until one day, when Bernard was working on a broken pipe in the kitchen, the steward informed him he had received permission to accept an urgent phone call from his mother.

Bernard suspected it couldn't be good news—it was forbidden for the monks to communicate with people outside the abbey. Indeed, when Bernard picked up the phone and heard the sobbing, he knew: his father was dead.

Bernard received permission from the abbot general to attend the funeral, and when he arrived at his mother's home in the town of Alençon, he greeted her, then walked to the cathedral to pray before the mourners arrived.

He had been praying before the altar of Saint Joseph for about an hour when he heard a slight commotion. A group of four men entered the main hall of the altar in an animated conversation.

Bernard smelled an odd, sweet scent that overpowered even the strong fragrance of the incense and candles.

The four men in conversation stopped as they noticed Bernard at the side altar. One—a tall man with silver hair—approached Bernard. He wore a dark suit with a light sweater. Bernard, already overtired and in mourning, was angry that this man would interrupt his prayer. It seemed more than bad form, especially given that the man was in the company of two priests.

Bernard halted his prayer and looked up.

The man's appearance up close—gold eyes and an almost shimmering skin—was shocking. He emitted a tactile energy. "How are you?" he said. "I am Monsignor Arnaud Laurent and I administer this region for the diocese."

It hit Bernard: this was one of the Gloamings so many people had been speaking of. He had never met one before, certainly not in the clergy.

"How are you, Monsignor?"

"Good. I see you're taken aback—is it the way I am dressed?"

Monsignor Laurent was playing with him, but Bernard did not want Laurent to know he was unsettled. "Absolutely the way you're dressed," Bernard said.

Laurent smiled, but it was not a friendly one. "I knew you would speak without much fear, Brother. Truthfully, I've actually heard much about you since your arrival at Bellebranche Abbey."

"Is that so?"

"It truly is, Bernard. I've seen the spirit that you and Kamel exhibit in your duties at the abbey. I believe that spirit could be channeled in other ways to move our church forward."

"The church always moves forward," Bernard replied, making eye contact although it was a struggle. His heart beat faster and his gaze seemed to swim with every movement of the monsignor.

"True, but not always with all people." He knelt down beside Bernard. "I am starting my own order of monks. I think there might be a place for someone like you. Someone open to re-creation."

The nerve of this so-called holy man! "With all due respect," Bernard said, "I have no interest in a new order."

Monsignor Laurent's smile turned cruel. Full of pity. "May your days be blessed, then, my friend."

It turned out Monsignor Laurent was the priest who conducted the rosary for Kristof's funeral. Bernard could only sit next to his weeping mother, seething as Laurent conducted the prayers. Every so often, he glanced at Bernard with a smile. Following the service, the mourners flocked to Laurent as if he were a rock star or mystic.

Even Juliette was bewitched by this arrogant and evil man. But Bernard could see the truth.

Less than a year later, Bernard Kieslowki and Kamel Paquet joined the Order of Bruder Klaus.

The details here are sketchy. Trained by members who were former Special Forces operatives in other countries, Bernard was present in Rome during the troubles of Pope Victor II, which led to the great schism in the Catholic Church: the College of Cardinals must call a conclave to elect a new pope, yet the dean of the college, a Cardinal Benelli, refused. He had recently been re-created and knew that the non-Gloaming cardinals outnumbered the Gloamings, which meant the next pope would most certainly be a non-Gloaming. There were even rumors that the Gloaming cardinals were prepared to call a Gloaming-only conclave, but even Cardinal Benelli must have realized the church would never support such a pope. The conclave was postponed—and postponed again—as Gloaming and non-Gloaming factions argued.

It became a standoff.

The Order of Bruder Klaus decided that for the church to continue, the most reasonable way to resolve the schism, and save the church, was to assassinate Cardinal Benelli. After the order presumably murdered three of the Gloaming cardinals within the walls of the Vatican, the security on Cardinal Benelli became even more strict. But the order was nothing if not patient. Cardinal Benelli enjoyed his newfound celebrity and could be found most nights attending some social event.

We know that Bernard and Kamel were appointed by the order to conduct surveillance on Cardinal Benelli for over a year. The order waited and watched.

Benelli's favorite restaurant, La Focaccia, was one of the oldest restaurants near the Piazza di San Pietro. Tucked between two large stores, it was a small restaurant. Gloamings don't eat food—they subsist on blood alone—but Bernard and Kamel surmised it had been Benelli's favorite restaurant before he re-created, and he enjoyed visiting the owner and basking in the ambience.

Bernard and Kamel continued to watch Benelli at night, and during the day they watched the restaurant. They even ate there more than a few times but couldn't figure out why Benelli loved La Focaccia so dearly: everything about it was ordinary. It was simply another Italian restaurant near Vatican City.

Rome contains vast, ancient underground tunnels and complexes that, even today, are hidden to most people. Although many are not connected to anyplace in particular, and they are not contiguous, Bernard and Kamel began to search various tunnels to find out if any reached La Focaccia. They reportedly hit literal dead ends until one afternoon, when Kamel was in the twelfth-century Basilica of San Clemente.

He had stopped there purely to admire the mosaics and frescoes, and to pray at the altar of Saint Joseph. As the candles burned bright and he felt comfort in the familiar smoldering scent, another feeling came over him—the presence of a Gloaming. Kamel kept his head down in prayer but cut his eyes to the side. He saw a figure exit a side door and walk toward the front entrance of the basilica. Strange. Where had the Gloaming come from?

Kamel looked up and glanced at the tourist sign next to the donation box. Although his Italian wasn't the best he could read that the basilica had three levels underneath that connected to various tunnels from old Rome. Another older basilica was on the second level and the tourist sign spoke of how it was used in previous centuries. Kamel thought to remind Bernard that here was another building with an ancient tunnel system, but first he had to see for himself where the Gloaming had emerged from.

Kamel reached the side door from which the Gloaming had exited. It was locked, of course, though poorly so. He pulled out a fine-edge blade and slipped it into the ancient keyhole. After a few twists, the lock's mechanism slipped back.

A long stairwell led down, lit by a few hanging candles on the wall. Kamel took the steps carefully until he reached a third belowground level. It was here that the rough stone floor opened into a sanctuary of an undetermined size. Kamel heard some movement and a few voices near a pedestal and altar. There were also several stone caskets of various lengths.

In the dim light, he noted another entranceway open, leading to a separate series of tunnels. He pulled out his compass and by candlelight directed himself to the tunnel that led east. In five hundred feet, he found a door locked with a biometric scanner. Clearly, this was no forgotten passageway and wouldn't make their job easier. Nevertheless, it was a breakthrough: after almost a year of surveillance around the city, Kamel had found their proof. He took out his phone and snapped a picture, texted it to Bernard.

A rusted placard was still fused to the door's stone casing: "La Focaccia: Established 1520 A.D."

On the appointed day, Bernard and Kamel armed themselves with various anti-Gloaming weapons, including explosives and a modified CPM 15G carbon scythe. They called the scythe—which could be used to cut the head off a Gloaming—the *Einig Wesen*. They dressed in expensive suits more befitting rich playboys or embassy employees out on the town. In case they were stopped by the authorities, they carried false identification listing them as employees of the French embassy.

Bernard and Kamel walked inside the basilica and made their way down the stone stairs, step by step and careful to stop every so often to listen for anything amiss. At the bottom, the ancient altar room was empty and quiet, unnerving them both. It couldn't be so easy. Kamel stopped before the series of sarcophagi along the wall. He shined his flashlight along the edges and noticed that the dust which was present previously had been cleaned up. The stone boxes also looked misaligned. Were they robbing graves now?

Bernard shined his light on Kamel's face as if to hurry him along. Kamel pointed to the stone caskets and gave Bernard a prearranged hand signal that meant "concern" or "danger." Bernard continued toward the east tunnel but stopped as he heard voices coming from inside the north passageway. He cupped his ear and pointed to the north tunnel.

When they reached the door to La Focaccia, Bernard pulled the cover off the biometric pad to disable the fingerprint scanner. The lock opened within five minutes. Bernard took a deep breath and pulled open the large oak door. Kamel pointed his gun and stepped inside.

The small room smelled musty. Kamel scanned the room with his flashlight: this appeared to be a storage space filled with an old desk, some overturned chairs, and boxes.

And another closed door.

Bernard assumed it led up to the kitchen, but he was unsure of how many people were working in the restaurant at the time. They'd assumed—correctly, as it turned out—that the kitchen employees would be uninterested in fighting two well-armed men. The employees stopped their activities when Bernard and Kamel entered the restaurant from a storeroom in the back.

Bernard looked over to the old swinging doors and to the dining room. There sat the man he believed was the owner with Cardinal Benelli and two other older men dressed in expensive suits. Every other table was empty.

Given the physical prowess of the Gloamings, Bernard and Kamel couldn't simply run in and expect to be successful in their task. They had planned for this. They changed into a set of kitchen uniforms and then stepped into the restaurant carrying dinner trays. Bernard went first. Gloamings were quite adept at catching any nonverbal cues to divine a person's true intention, so Bernard and Kamel both wanted to appear as though all of their attention was on the restaurant's owner and no one else.

Bernard glided across the dining room floor. Everything seemed to be moving in slow motion. The cardinal had not even looked up from his animated conversation. Could it really be this easy? As they took their last steps to the table, Bernard sensed Kamel twist and leap. He heard the tray clang before he understood that Kamel had deviated from the plan.

The Gloaming cardinal reacted to the attack as any Gloaming would—with fast, supple movements that had Kamel grabbed by the throat and pinned against the floor. The others at the table were in shock.

Benelli had his back to Bernard, and Kamel's eyes met Bernard's urgently.

At that moment, Bernard understood. Kamel had always planned it this way—to sacrifice himself.

Bernard dropped his tray and unleashed the scythe attached to his arm. He swung, with all the power mustered from weeks of practice for this very moment, and sliced Cardinal Benelli's head from his shoulders. It fell to the ground with a thud.

Bernard took a last look into Kamel's eyes, now devoid of life, before sprinting back into the kitchen in a spray of bullets from Benelli's security detail.

He jumped the stairs down to the basement in a tumble, his heart pounding, his weight still steady over his feet. Bernard reached the northern tunnel and ran the way he'd come, his heartbeat or his footsteps echoing off the walls. He knew they were chasing him; he just didn't know how many there were.

A few shots rang out but they seemed oddly distant. Another piece of luck: Benelli's people did not have any experience in the darkened tunnels below the city. Bernard reached the ancient altar room and stopped for a moment. One of the sarcophagus lids was fully removed from its base and leaning against the wall. He felt oddly transfixed, frozen before what he knew was waiting, but he raised his gun, knowing what was going to exit the box or was already out of it. He realized that he would have to deal with it or he would never make it upstairs to the main altar of the basilica. Running was not an option and he would have to make a stand here.

A figure stepped into the weak light, broad-shouldered and crooked, and then stepped closer. Bernard reached for and released what he later realized was one of the new anti-Gloaming grenades. Untested, it was a risky choice. Still, he leapt behind a large statue of a saint in combat. The blast moved the statue and threw Bernard back even with the cover. He heard a shriek and stood up. The figure was still before him but looked broken and in bad shape. *Maybe the grenade did work after all,* he thought. *Or maybe not.*

The figure was already aware of Bernard's presence so the scythe was out of the question—he would never wield it in time. He steadied his gun as the Gloaming approached him through the blast smoke. The body lurched over, Bernard released three quick shots, and then the beast was on him.

Even dazed, Bernard could feel the Gloaming lift him up

by his neck. He was ready to die.

As he felt his neck tighten, he looked at the gnarled face of the monster holding him.

In a flash, it was gone. He actually saw the face hit the ground as he did as well.

He looked up. Another figure in black, holding a scythe, just like his. The person—with curly black hair, tactical gear—came over and helped him up.

It was Sara Mesley. Once again, Bernard had been saved.

Benelli's death quashed the schism in the Catholic Church. Within a week, the College of Cardinals met at the Vatican and elected Pope Gregory XVII, a rather unremarkable and bookish cardinal from Denmark. Although the press hailed this event as the return of the traditional church, this was just a fine gloss over the turmoil still present in the Vatican: Pope Gregory XVII was, in truth, such a surprise and a begrudging choice that he was left with less power than the consensus of his cardinals. A considerable number of Gloaming cardinals still held high office in the church, and Pope Gregory did not have the will to excommunicate them. He actually felt there could be a truce with the Gloamings.

Once we—well, the Italian police, then Interpol, then the FBI—traced the fingerprints in La Focaccia to Bernard Kieslowki, we determined that the bombings were the work of the Order of Bruder Klaus. Soon enough, a pattern emerged as later bombings targeted legitimate shipments of the drug dextromethorphan [DXM] and/or shipments of its ingredients, and also illegal DXM labs.

The FBI then began a concerted effort to investigate the Order of Bruder Klaus and build a RICO [Racketeer Influenced and Corrupt

Organizations Act] case against them. In October, after a seven-month investigation, the FBI raided houses in several states tied to the order. The evidence recovered was not strong, but by then other forces were at play. The Gloamings had many friends in all branches of government, including supporters in the Justice Department, who wanted to take down the order by any means. To do this under the pretense of government legality would, for the Gloamings, be worth its weight in gold. In spite of the weak evidence, the U.S. attorney for the Western District of Texas charged the Order of Bruder Klaus with organized crime and terrorism.

Twenty members of the order were indicted, including Bishop Lawrence Thomas, the head and founder of the order. Legal observers assumed the cases would assuredly end up in jury trials; however, Bishop Thomas instructed his attorneys to seek a plea deal.

The government said it would drop all charges against the other defendants if Bishop Thomas would agree to plead guilty to the RICO allegations. Thomas agreed.[31]

---

[31] Federal sentencing guidelines mandated a prison sentence between twenty-five and fifty years in a federal penitentiary. On the appointed day of sentencing, Bishop Lawrence Thomas was brought to the federal courthouse in Los Angeles and sentenced to forty-five years in a federal prison. The crowd inside the courtroom ignored the judge's previous warnings against public displays—they burst into tears and shouts, as federal marshals forcibly ejected them from the courtroom and the building.

Two monks from a monastery in Spain, who had come to El Paso specifically for the trial, self-immolated on the steps of the courthouse, as a mortified crowd cried in prayer. One local couple later claimed they saw Christ in the flames, and videos of the incident were widely distributed on YouTube and other sites. Many people fell into tears and fits of ecstasy at the sights and claimed that the monks had attained a higher state of consciousness before setting themselves alight. The monks had left a sparsely worded suicide note with their bishop in Spain, which was then heavily redacted by the Vatican before it was released to the authorities and the public. Many websites claimed that the redacted portions of the note referred to a vision they shared, told in a dream about preparing for their "fire baptism" and the calamities that would follow if the Gloamings were to gain in power.

And what a spectacle that was, based on all the news reports. If I hadn't been so busy I would have shown up. With popcorn.

The Bureau of Prisons made a determination that Bishop Thomas would be sent to the minimum security prison[32] on Terminal Island, California. Located on an actual man-made island off the coast of Long Beach, California, the facility mostly held low-security male inmates serving white-collar crimes. Bishop Thomas acclimated himself well enough, even starting a prison ministry, and tended to his many visitors. The order had been effectively disbanded by court order but unofficially regrouped at their base in El Paso, Texas—and from the day of sentencing, we learned, the order's primary focus was extracting Bishop Thomas from the prison at Terminal Island.

Bernard Kieslowki would not be available, so they sought out the next experienced operative—though many claimed she was even better prepared for the task at hand than Bernard. Of course we all now know that operative's name.

---

[32]   Normally, a prisoner of such notoriety would be sent to the Supermax prison in Colorado. It's unclear why the federal judge removed Thomas to Terminal Island. Justice Department officials investigated, but an appeal to the appellate courts was dismissed by the Attorney General.

CHAPTER 17

MAY DAY
THIRTY-SIX MONTHS AFTER THE NOBI DISCOVERY

Sara Mesley
Nurse

I used to tell people the only way I'd go back to Baltimore was if I was born twice. Turns out I was sort of right.

My first tortured upbringing in Baltimore—doesn't that sound delightfully pretentious?—was by a single mother who worked three jobs. After high school, I enrolled in Johns Hopkins School of Nursing, and during my first year as a nurse, also at Johns Hopkins, I realized I was not cut out for the job. The suffering and ailments of everyday people weighed heavy on me; I became more despondent about the state of the world, bored by the monotony of my current position, and decided to enroll in the United States Army.

I was sent to Syria as first lieutenant assigned to the Forty-First Infantry Regiment to support Jordanian forces in the Battle of Sadad. It was somewhat uneventful as war zones go, but on October 5, I was part of a two-jeep convoy ambushed by forces aligned with the al-Nusra Front, ISIL, and the Free Syrian Army. I was riding in the back of a Humvee, rolling down a desert highway that could have been located in California or Arizona, when suddenly the world literally turned upside down.

I remember the flashing lights and the lack of sound. I always imagined I'd handle that type of situation well instead of temporarily losing my mind and good sense. But it took me far too long to get myself together after the blast. I found myself begging for help from whoever would listen as the smoke drifted out of the wreckage. I remembered my uncle teaching me the five rules of *Yijin Jing* and it was all I could do to remember it all: quietness, slowness, extension, pause, flexibility.

Five other soldiers were killed and I suffered a broken leg and arm as well as a gunshot wound to my shoulder. At first I wondered if we'd rolled over a stray roadside bomb, until bullets whizzed by my ear. I knew we were under attack.

Through waves of nausea, I maneuvered my way to the front of the overturned Humvee and grabbed an M16 lying on the upturned window. I spotted two Toyota trucks and an old armored vehicle about a hundred yards east. With the M16 cradled in my broken arm, I sighted one of the trucks—they always taught us to aim high from the sight—and pulled the trigger.

I wasn't sure if I hit anything, but the return fire drilled the engine block of the Humvee like a woodpecker on meth. We went back and forth, returning fire, until all my magazines were empty.

Though I called in my status and the vehicle was equipped with GPS, no reply came back.

So, like a little kid, I crossed my fingers.

I sat staring at the trucks for about an hour, until the sun made its descent and a large group of men exited the trucks, holding AKs.

I couldn't feel my leg anymore and certainly couldn't move—all I could do was wait for them to arrive. They took their sweet time slowly making their way to my Humvee, and it was agony. I almost wanted to yell at them, "Hurry this shit up! Get it over with!" They tramped around me, like zombies in turbans—I wondered if this was the walking dead or if my mind was already gone. Finally, they arrived and, without a word spoken, cleaned out the Humvee of essentials, like ants picking at a carcass, and left the corpses of my fellow soldiers. I was carried to their truck and we drove the highway for an hour to a recently shelled five-story building on the outskirts of Aleppo, a couple of miles from a cluster of refugee camps.

My ten days there were an odd mix of sheer terror and soul-crushing boredom. I was given primitive medical treatment from a "doctor." For meals, they fed me tahini, hummus, sumac, and flatbread. I got skinny and spent most of my time alone.

On October 15, after receiving reports of my whereabouts from a paid informant of the CIA, U.S. Marines from the fourth battalion—as well as members of the Navy SEALs and Army Rangers—staged a diversionary attack, while other members of the team infiltrated the building and found me on the third floor.

I had spent so much time sleeping that I was off dreaming when I heard a muffled explosion, screaming, and chaos. I had already been planning how I was going to make my last mark: I had constructed a makeshift knife from the wiring on my cot and had it hidden under a pillow. I was searching for my crude weapon when the cell door blew off its hinges.

I heard English. English! "We're here to take you home." I'm pretty sure I asked for a gun as they picked me up off the floor.

Two weeks later, I was back home in Baltimore.

*　*　*

The army didn't really know what to do with me afterward. I didn't want to participate in interviews about the capture and rescue. The thought of hand-shaking at the Capitol made my stomach turn. Admittedly, I was being rather difficult—when I look back on the entire ordeal now, I realize everything had to do with my anger: I hated my home, war, Syrians, Muslims, the U.S. Army, the U.S. government, the president, every fucking elected official I could think of, and yes, finally, myself. The army called my bluff with an honorable discharge—with a Bronze Star, Purple Heart, Prisoner of War Medal, and Army Commendation Medal. I accepted it through gritted teeth, though the prospect of going back to work in a hospital or doctor's office filled me with despair.

Reentry as a civilian was, for me, like trying to become a whole person, a new person, again. Maybe a less angry person, someone who didn't need the adrenaline rush of combat. I had learned about this in nursing school: a particular genetic variance that influenced my dopamine receptors to cause my subconscious to seek thrills. It sounds so mundane on paper, yet in real life, it was torture. I went mountain climbing, motorcycle racing, and became obsessed with amateur mixed martial arts. I craved remarkable success or remarkable failure. Nothing compared to the thrill of military combat.

I traveled to Portland, Oregon, for the wedding of an old classmate. I was in a pub killing time when I glanced over at the *New York Times* Sunday edition spread out on the table. Years later, I would tell a reporter I had felt almost supernaturally compelled to read that newspaper. My hands grabbed it as if they were not my own. I opened the Sunday magazine to one piece in a long-form five-part series by Maggie Haberman, on the Gloaming presence in

America and beyond. Obviously, I was aware of the Gloamings but I was incredulous to learn how they were attempting to take over the Catholic Church. I probably have some latent persecution complex or delusional disorder—as I've been accused of by certain weird outlets—but I read about this mysterious organization known as the Order of Bruder Klaus, and how the media theorized that the order was responsible for many assassinations and bombings targeted at the Gloamings.

Something in my mind—or my hearing—clicked.

This was righteous. This was true. *It was violence that made sense,* I thought.

No big surprise, the Order of Bruder Klaus's official office in Rome, Italy—like other male-dominated entities—first preferred to use me like a secretary. Obviously this did not sit well with me. I was a veteran. A fucking prisoner of war!

With pathological intensity, I badgered many of the high-ranking members of the armed operations section, including Bishop Thomas, to include me in any special projects that involved the armed missions; I argued, quite loudly, that my military experience made me a more valuable asset than others without that experience. They eventually relented but sent me on a few missions strictly as medical support.

Until the Gloaming safe house in Mexico City.

Our objective was to break in and confiscate all computer hard drives and documents. Surveillance showed that the house—located in a cramped row of old brownstones in an upper-class downtown neighborhood—was not currently occupied by any Gloamings. We rented two rooms via Airbnb in a brownstone next door and broke through the wall between the brownstones—the entrance and exits of the Gloaming house were covered with surveillance—with a handsaw to ensure maximum silence. Of course, I was tasked with waiting behind.

Everything appeared to be going better than expected—a classic red flag!—as the team collected three hard drives and other documentation from the one room where the computers were housed. After the team gathered the necessary data, one of the members found a locked door, and instead of checking for any irregularities—another red flag!—the team attempted to break down the door with brute force.

The door exploded off its hinges.

The explosion shook the house next door, where I waited. Chunks from the ceiling fell onto my head. I wasted no time crawling through our makeshift hole into the Gloaming house. I followed the smoke down a flight of stairs, to the smoldering mess on the first floor.

One of my team members was unrecognizable, just shredded body parts. The other two were covered in blood. I had to tamp down my nursing instinct. I needed to carry them to safety first—a seemingly impossible task.

There didn't appear to be any more people in the house. Unfortunately, there was something more concerning: two Gloamings, standing in the rubble and dust in front of me. One male and one female. Both were dressed in black and wore some very self-satisfied looks. It was as if they thought, *Is this the best that the Order of Bruder Klaus could send?*

I pointed my gun and pulled the trigger. I heard an empty *click*. Damn it.

Strangely, I kind of wanted them to laugh or make fun of my

empty gun, but the Gloamings just exchanged a blank glance.

I turned over my last card and pulled out a curved blade from my back holster. This brought the Gloamings to attention. The male Gloaming stepped back as the female stepped forward.

I smiled. I knew some things they didn't. I knew my self-preservation was matched only by my ambition. I knew I was about to put down the thirty-sixth chamber of Shaolin on their Gloaming asses. I knew I would never be as fast as them, but I could match their speed with my stillness.

I dropped into a qigong position on the floor, breathing measuredly as if in meditation, my curved blade held in front of my body. The female Gloaming seemed somewhat confused by my posture.

She jumped about ten feet in the air and, as if time had slowed beyond my perception, I felt closer to enlightenment than ever before.

I moved my blade a few degrees west with the wind.

It sliced cleanly through the woman's head, just below her ear and above her jaw.

The Gloaming man would be coming for blood, literally and figuratively, next. I took another deep breath and summoned memories of the five rules of *Yijin Jing*. The man pivoted until he was behind me, but I stayed seated with my blade before me. I felt the brush of wind from his hands and I swept the blade behind me.

I heard a sharp scream. I felt a tap on the floor.

I rose up and saw two hands on the floor. The male Gloaming, now handless, was running in the other direction.

I guess they didn't know what I knew.

Soon I was leading my own teams into operations. And with Bernard recovering from injuries suffered in a failed mission to find Liza Sole, it would be up to me to coordinate and implement the plan to rescue Bishop Thomas from prison.

* * *

The plan involved two helicopters: one as a diversion—I was always a believer in diversions, especially if Gloamings were involved; the more arbitrary the better, to deflect their infuriatingly precise senses—and the other to land on the roof of the prison where the administrative offices were located. All Bishop Thomas needed to do was make his way to the roof—specifically the nurse's office— at the appointed time.

A sympathetic janitor that subcontracted with the prison provided the bishop with a copy of the key to the nurse's office, but the bishop would still need to make his way there from the library. On the day of action, the bishop would forget his Bible and tell the guard he was going to borrow one from the food service secretary, who had an office next door to the nurse. He made it there without incident and, even with the cameras watching, he waited for a moment until he heard the large crash—which sounded closer and more explosive than he imagined it would.

Outside in the vacant rec yard, a large helicopter had crashed into the ground. It was a remote-controlled life-size helicopter. A diversion! The order's technician crew, in spite of their blue-collar name, was actually a highly sophisticated group of hackers and engineers. Unfortunately, the operation did not go as planned. The techs did not adequately account for the high Santa Ana winds that day and could not remotely allow for corrections to the path. The helicopter was meant to crash farther from the prison complex, but it crashed near the living quarters and caused four deaths: three prisoners and one guard. At the same time, the manned helicopter landed on the roof and I was there to guide the bishop inside. Even though we had the bishop and brought him to the safe house near

Joshua Tree National Park, I still felt the plan did not proceed exactly as conceived and that I had failed. Everything had been so much trouble and I was being ganged up on by fear, loneliness, and terror. I wasn't even sure I had learned anything from these experiences, but by God I would probably be forced to eventually because we never go to those places freely.

The prison escape shocked the nation. The federal government began a full-throttle effort to find Bishop Thomas and any other members of the order. In accordance with section 219 of the Immigration and Nationality Act [INA] of 1965, the secretary of state designated the Order of Bruder Klaus as a foreign terrorist organization [FTO].

This designation brought about a series of restrictions on all our offices, and our members were forced underground. The president went on television for a prime-time address from the Oval Office to discuss the order and the threats of domestic terrorism to emphasize how serious this issue was for the administration.

This event, of course, was a defining moment between the Order of Bruder Klaus and the federal government.

We had won the battle but brought on the war.

CHAPTER 18

JUNE 6

THIRTY-SEVEN MONTHS AFTER THE NOBI DISCOVERY

Jerome Liu
Reporter

"Is she a Gloaming?" Barbara asked.

"Well, I don't think so—"

"It is nighttime," she continued.

"True," I replied, "but she's holding two dogs, and dogs absolutely hate Gloamings, ergo…"

"That makes me feel so much better." But her glare told me the opposite. "What now? Outrunning her probably isn't an issue, but two pit bulls?"

I shrugged. "If we—"

The large woman holding the pit bulls laughed and looked me straight in the eyes. "You're going to die tonight, homeboy."

That was my first assignment with Barbara Budig, my new partner, who clearly was going to be an interesting highlight of my professional life. We were investigating reports of two degenerate

Gloamings taking down illegal gambling operations in Chicago. So we attempted to meet with a bookie in a South Side public housing complex. An open door, two reporters inviting themselves inside, and an unfortunate meeting with an obese woman and two pit bulls: all this soon led to a sprint down a staircase and three weeks of rabies vaccinations.

But we got the story.

I was hired by BuzzFeed after working for Facebook news and the Associated Press. They paired me with Barbara, a monster of a young reporter who had covered financial news for Bloomberg. On my first day at the office, Barbara took me to lunch, and by the time we'd finished she had made the waitress cry and had yelled at an older gentleman at the next table who hadn't realized his cell phone was beeping. I soon realized, however, that she had a knack for getting to the bottom of any story. No matter what.

I needed that kind of determined ally on my side. Our mandate from the start was to help put BuzzFeed on the map of more "serious" journalism, although it was hard to combat the clickbait BuzzFeed always generated with lists like "Hottest Gloaming" or "Funny Gloaming memes." Still, I knew there was something more out there, something less amusing and more disturbing. There had to be: their lifestyle was strange and perhaps illegal. And one day I found the lead I needed: an email from a man named Eric Holcombe, who wanted to speak to me about the mysterious Rio Grande Institute in New Mexico. Aha! I had always wanted to do a story about that place. The email had been sent through the secure ProtonMail system and encrypted prior to being sent through the Tor network.

No doubt Eric had reached out to several news sites, probably several a lot more hard-hitting than BuzzFeed. But this Eric Holcombe individual was an extremely paranoid sort of man, and I'm guessing no one at the *New York Times* or *The Guardian* had paid much attention, especially as it took many weeks of communication through email and private message boards on obscure role-playing video games before Eric would agree to a meeting. He would not meet me at the BuzzFeed offices, however, so we arranged to meet at an obscure San Francisco ramen bar—this particular one located upstairs from a craft brewing lounge.

I arrived and, with my love of ramen intact, ordered a big bowl of chicken, oyster, and spinach ramen. It was long past the dinner rush, so the restaurant was sparsely occupied. I kept one eye on the staircase and slurped my noodles from the large bowl. I really could have ordered another when I noticed a disheveled man in his midfifties coming up the staircase. He wore black pants and a black jacket—a sharp contrast with his treated blond hair and white skin. I knew this had to be my man.

I waved him over. He sat down hard. "Eric," I said. "Hi. I'm Jerome." I stuck my hand out but Eric refused to take it. Not a good start.

"We should have met during the day," Eric said, looking around the restaurant. "I don't know what I was thinking—I should have my head examined."

"I assure you I am not a Gloaming," I responded.

Eric stared out the window and seemed to think on this for a long while before he looked at me with a downcast gaze. "Let's make this quick, then. I was a lab technician for Dr. Robinson—yes, after the kidnapping. And yes, that Dr. Robinson who disappeared from Prestonwood Mall in Dallas after buying a new shirt at Macy's."

"Okay," I said.

Eric barreled on. "I knew Robinson had been kidnapped. I looked the other way because of the money and the allure of the Gloamings. I thought that one day they might re-create me. I admit it. Then I realized it would never happen. I'm not what they want in a Gloaming! It's all eugenics for them! The perfect being!"

As Eric had grown louder and louder, people were beginning to stare. I put a hand out. "I know this is stressful, but keep it down. We have to stay in the shadows here."

Eric nodded. "I know. I know." He took a long breath. "I couldn't take it anymore and I escaped from that place. Nothing is foolproof." He was breathing hard.

I had to coax him back to his story. "What do they do at the institute?"

"Everything. Anything to enhance their population. They've been trying to procreate naturally for years and then they tried in vitro—and none of it worked. We have been responsible for destroying completely healthy humans and Gloamings in the interest of science. And none of it has worked."

I moved my seat closer to Eric. "So they kidnapped all those doctors and scientists?"

"Of course they did!" Eric leaned forward. "They're obsessed with their food supply. We know scientists have been working on a synthetic blood supply for years. The Gloamings took that research and perfected it. Yet their bodies have not been able to adjust. They need human blood. They will never admit that—they can't. They need the human population to think that they're not a threat so they pay top dollar for human blood donated to blood banks, but they make it sound like some kind of luxury—like caviar. But make no mistake: it's a necessity. They need it to live. They have a blood bank at the institute filled by their captives."

"How is that even possible?" I asked, my own voice rising.

"You know how many people disappear in every country? It's fucking easy. Some humans come willingly. It's not hard at all."

"And these human captives…They just sit there and give blood?"

Eric laughed, a loud, scratchy cackle. "You know how foie gras is made? It's the same thing. They're strapped to a table and force-fed through a tube. I don't know what they feed them but it's been perfected by their scientists so that the humans' blood is rich in iron and nutrients. The recipe is a closely guarded secret and so is the optimal measure of nutrients in the plasma—they know exactly what they need in the blood to keep them at their ideal health. Proteins, glucose, minerals, iron, carbon dioxide, red and white cells and platelets." Eric stopped, out of breath. "Their bodies require an exemplary amount of each particular item. They have it all down to a science—to every microscopic particle. And only human blood can provide it. The humans they have are no more than a locked vessel for their pursuit."

Eric stopped. He looked around and lowered his voice, although at this point it was pretty much a stage whisper. "And I know what else they're working on."

"Yes?"

"They've been studying the effects of a nuclear winter on the population in general, especially Gloamings."

"Are you serious?" I asked. "What would be the point?"

Eric looked at me like I was a child. "What's their greatest weakness?" he asked slowly.

"Sunlight," I said.

"Correct." He nodded. "Remember the Kuwait war, when Iraq lit all of those oil wells on fire?"

I didn't want to point out that I had been in nursery school during that war, so I just kept silent.

"The soot and smoke blacked out the sky," Eric continued. "They want that. It would kill the ozone layer, of course, which would kill the humans even faster. But they don't care. They love radiation."

I realized I was holding my breath. I saw what he was saying. "So, you're saying…that they want to get rid of the sun."

Eric nodded. "Exactly. Imagine if there was never another sunrise. Permanent nighttime." He leaned forward. "And I have proof."

"Well, where's the proof?" Barbara yelled as we sat in my cramped modular office. She had her fists balled up. I could never tell where she kept all that nervous tension.

I felt the other reporters staring at us over the cubicle walls. "Keep your voice down," I told her. "He didn't actually give it to me. You know confidential sources aren't going to spill their guts on the first night."

"Not like the girls you date," she replied.

Classy, I thought.

Eric was jumpy as fuck, so I waited for him to reach out again. And waited. Then I dropped him a quick note. And then another. I must have emailed him ten times before it occurred to me that perhaps Eric wasn't who he portrayed himself to be. Was I being played?

A week later I received a call from a detective with the Seattle police department informing me that Eric had been found murdered in his apartment the night before. The shock lasted a couple of seconds. "How did you get my name?" I asked. Barbara was staring at me over the wall between our cubicles.

"I'd prefer to discuss it in person, if possible, Mr. Liu," the detective said.

I told him I would be on the next plane out.

"You bet your ass you'll be on the next plane out," Barbara said when I hung up. "With me next to you. And I want the goddamn aisle seat."

In Seattle, I met Detective Harold Moss at the precinct station. "Thank you for coming, Mr. Liu," Moss said, motioning for me to sit.

"Not a problem."

"Well, the reason I made contact with you was, we found Eric's body on the floor. There was a piece of paper. It had your name and number scribbled on it. There was blood on the paper too. As if it was written while he was being attacked."

"How could you know that?" I asked.

Moss glared. "Well, the paper was inside his mouth."

He tossed a file on the desk and a couple of photos slipped out. I picked them up and gasped at the scene: Eric Holcombe upside down, naked, and nailed to a wall in an X figure, his large body impossibly white. I had seen enough pictures of Gloaming kills to recognize the signs.

"The blood was drained from the body, correct?"

Moss's beady eyes cut to me. "Good catch. You've got experience with the Gloamings."

I nodded, but I was barely listening at this point. I couldn't wait to tell Barbara.

She was waiting for me at a Starbucks around the corner. "You want to break into what?" Barbara yelled.

I was waiting for her to punch me in the arm or chest—her common nonverbal reply to one of my crazy propositions. But it hadn't come. "Look, it's not really—" And there it was, a sharp punch on my forearm. I winced. "It's not really breaking in. Technically no one lives there anymore." I wasn't even sure I believed that reasoning, but it was worth a try.

"Okay," Barbara said. She dropped her cup of coffee, still half full and steaming hot, in the trash. "I'm not even arguing with that logic."

Within an hour we were standing across the street from Eric's Rainier district apartment building. A single officer guarded the front door, smoking a cigarette and walking back and forth to ward off the boredom.

"He's not letting us in there, I guarantee it," Barbara stated.

I wasn't about to give up at the first sign of police. Ah—I could see the solution right in front of my face. "Behind the building. We'll go up the fire escape." I cut my eyes to Barbara but she was busy looking the other way. "Come on." I brushed her arm and she followed me behind the building, where two cars were parked.

"There we go." I pointed to the drop ladder that began the fire escape that vined up the back of the building. "Watch my back," I whispered as I jumped up and pulled it down. It made a mechanical groan.

"Wake up the whole building, why don't you?" Barbara said. "Do you know which one is his apartment?"

"Third floor nearest to the end," I replied. "Look—the window is even cracked open."

"Have fun. I'll guard the bottom." Barbara looked at me with a poker face and hands on her hips.

"Both of us need to be up there so it doesn't take so long searching the place."

Barbara sighed. "Okay. I just hope that ancient ladder holds both of our weight. I don't have money for bail."

It took longer than I care to admit to climb to the third floor. Rung by rung, my arms burned, and I made a mental note to renew my lapsed gym membership. We had a close call on the second floor with a man cooking dinner in his kitchen, but luckily his ridiculously oversize potted plant hid us until he went into another room and we could sneak past.

Once inside Eric's apartment, I flicked on my phone's flashlight. Plastic coverings, labels, tarps, and bags were scattered in the living room, remnants of the recent police forensic crew and their search for DNA.

"Any idea what we're looking for?" Barbara asked as she threw pillows off the couch and looked on the shelves that lined the wall.

I could only stare at the marked outline on the wall where Eric's body had been nailed. Could I have done something to protect him? Probably not; his hysteria had kept any sane person at bay. But there was a reason he had my name in his mouth when he was killed. He knew I would come looking.

I stood in the middle of the living room, sweat rolling down my body. I stepped into the kitchen and looked through the cupboards: nothing. Barbara stood behind me, her mouth pursed. "There has to be something here," she said.

Where would Eric hide something he didn't want the Gloamings to find?

And then I saw a few packages of ramen noodles next to the knife rack. Ramen...

It couldn't be that simple.

Then again, sometimes the best hiding place is in plain sight.

I grabbed the packages. Hard ramen spilled all over the floor. One of the packages was already open, and inside, buried at the bottom, lay a flash drive.

Barbara and I looked at each other. "Motherfucker!" we both whispered.

On the plane ride back to New York, I plugged the thumb drive into my laptop. Eric had filled it with pictures of the institute.

The pictures were horrifying: modified stainless steel meat hooks suspended from the ceiling; bodies hung like pieces of meat; rows of functional oxygen saturation machines that measured arterial hemoglobin measurements; miles of polypropylene tubes attached to workstation racks; over three stories of low-temperature freezers, mix frozen epoxies, cryogenic detectors, blood bank refrigerated centrifuges and blood storage cabinets; human holding pods with chains and modified metal hog pens with head locks.

More disturbing were the pictures of hundreds of human bodies held in these hog pens and holding pods, faces numb from what could only be sedatives or pain.

For once, Barbara was speechless. "Unreal," I could only whisper.

We could only look at the pictures for so long on the plane. When we got back to the office in New York, we kept going through all the files obsessively. A few times, Barbara stood up and proclaimed, "Fuck this," and took the elevator downstairs to chain-smoke and stare at the Manhattan traffic. Asleep or awake, nightmares filled my head.

BuzzFeed hired forensic computer and photographic specialists, under strict nondisclosure agreements, to certify that the pictures had not been altered in any way, and then published our story a week after our return from Seattle. We called it "The Institute of Terror."

Every news organization on television, in print, and on the Internet took hold of the story and added to it.

> *Daily Mail* [United Kingdom]: "Gloaming Grocery Store of Humans!"
> *New York Times:* "Gloaming Abuses at Institute"
> *Times of India:* "Gloaming Terror Uncovered"
> *Sydney Morning Herald* [Australia]: "Feeding Gloamings Detailed in Report"
> *Asahi Shimbun* [Japan]: "Gloaming Terrors in America"

Politicians in different countries denounced the institute, if the facts were to bear out. They called for an investigation to ensure that the institute's subjects were treated fairly and voluntarily.

BuzzFeed had a field day with our scoop, working overtime to promote the story—and Barbara and me, the "Woodward and Bernstein of the digital era"—in the months following. We toured the morning talk shows, CNN, *The Rachel Maddow Show*, Sky News, and the BBC World News, ready and eager to discuss our story. More importantly, we had to refute the Gloamings' allegations that our evidence was falsified.

One Friday, I sat with Barbara on the sidewalk dining area of a Mexican restaurant off West Fourth Street, watching the early evening crowds. I couldn't feel any joy.

"What's wrong?" Barbara asked. "You own this town. At least for another fifteen minutes."

"You know Buzz Aldrin was the second man to step on the moon. He wrote a book when he left the astronaut program, about his clinical depression and alcoholism. And his whole point was, he said something like, 'What do you do when you realize your life's ambition at age thirty-nine?' I feel the same way."

"I feel great about it. I'm already looking for the next adventure." Barbara took a bite of her taco. "We're already hated by all the Gloamings. Fuck them! They don't run our lives."

Just that morning, the president had expressed feeling a "great disturbance" thanks to the details our article revealed. She promised a federal investigation into the institute to determine if it was following all relevant federal laws. And in the coming weeks, the FBI would open an investigation, which is where the first signs of the real conflict began.

Amazing that it all began in a messy apartment, in a bag of ramen noodles.

But thanks to my meeting with Eric, I knew even more. The Gloamings' "blood bank" was just the beginning. Their goals were more innovative and horrifying but there was no way I could publish these allegations without the requisite proof—and that was something I did not have at this point.

That Friday evening, before we could even know the changes that were nearly upon us, I already felt the nervousness of dusk as the sun retreated.

All I wanted to do was find a safe place to hide—to stop spending every night looking over my shoulder, praying for daylight.

CHAPTER 19

IN-BETWEEN DAYS

The Seeker

Museums are never open late at night. I miss the feeling of time crawling to a stop, of staring at a piece of art. On a snowbound Wednesday I broke into the National Gallery of Art in Washington, DC. A simple and satisfying activity. Inside, I spent hours staring at Andrew Wyeth's *Wind from the Sea*. As if I were actually looking out of that window and could feel the breeze that moved the curtains. This was feeling, and that feeling was loneliness.

I wept in front of *The Ghent Altarpiece,* its vivid re-creations and symbols. I wept standing next to the recently re-created Matthew Barney's Vaseline sculptures, which gave off an electric chill of reality.

Most of the time, though, I'm reduced to relying on my memory to realize how beautiful art tempted and amazed me. One night I found myself standing in the living room of one of the most wanted drug lords in Culiacán, Sinaloa, Mexico. I stared at his prized possession: Vermeer's *The Concert*. One of the most sought-after stolen works of art. I stood there for an hour, more, calm and centered, my body canted toward it. He indulged me because he thought he would fuck me, and that I would re-create him. It wasn't to be. I slipped out before his guards even knew I had left.

Instead, I walked to a bar in Sinaloa and watched an old man play a flamenco guitar and sing a feathery, halting corrido about a man who lost his wife to a wealthy landowner. The bar was like a painting of life in that moment: couples kissing, couples ignoring each other, someone alone with a beer for company. The loneliness of these broken people could devour your soul. So many puzzles in those I come across. The lure of searching for something that will show me my soul. The days of me indulging in pain to forget are over. From here on I resolved to step off the straight path and only follow detours.

CHAPTER 20

Dr. Lauren Scott
Research Physician, Centers for Disease Control

I finally agreed to marry Hector. We were in the car, on a weekend Target run. We had moved in together a few months after the whole Liza Sole fiasco—and I was rattling off my schedule for the next few months. After the whirlwind of media rounds and Congressional hearings, things were still quite hectic. My work at the CDC continued, and I found numerous colleagues outside the agency and around the country who shared my passion for finding a solution to the virus. I had a few trips coming up, and as I ran down the list of dates with Hector, he blurted out, "We should probably get married?"

This wasn't the first time he'd asked, but there was something in his voice that made me pause this time. It seemed right. Or maybe I was just getting soft and I let my guard down for a brief moment.

"Sure," I said.

The car was quiet. We continued down the freeway.

"Good," he said. "Okay, then." And just like that, we were engaged.

As the Gloamings assimilated around the world, my work on the NOBI virus was repeatedly challenged by Gloaming organizations who wanted all studies related to counteracting or curing the NOBI virus to cease. Even labeling it a "virus" had become politically charged. Many Gloaming activists resisted this label, arguing that it implied that people who had the NOBI virus were somehow socially disabled. They argued that Gloamings were normally functioning persons in society. Rumors abounded that the American Psychiatric Association was intending to classify Gloamings as uniformly afflicted with a mental illness or disorder. If that wasn't bad enough, I also continued to be hampered by my own coworkers. Research still went missing. Supplies never arrived. Test results "could not be located." I could never prove any of it.

Soon another event hijacked my focus and changed my life.

My sister, Jennifer, disappeared.

Jennifer went missing from the Electric Daisy Carnival in Las Vegas, the world's largest EDM festival and rave. She was always into the deep beats and hyped-up atmosphere of these raves: from the clothing to the drugs to the people, Jennifer loved everything about a good music festival. And given the nature of raves—late at night, filled with energy—they had become a favorite meeting place for Gloamings.

Jennifer used to tell me about her friendships with a few Gloamings. I didn't want to be that patronizing or nagging big sister, but I let her know, in no uncertain terms, that Gloamings were not to be trusted. She didn't want to hear it. I felt her tune me out when I talked about the Gloamings and their agendas. That weary *sigh*. The shut-down silence. After a while, I simply gave up trying to warn her.

And that's on me, and I'll never forgive myself.

When Jennifer's friend called me from the Vegas police station to let me know Jennifer had gone missing, I dropped everything and flew out there immediately. It was a full day before I could get my emotions together enough to call my dad. He was bedridden following two knee replacement surgeries, and it took threats of law enforcement intervention before he agreed not to leave the house and fly to Las Vegas too. That small victory of course led to a constant stream of calls and texts, with him demanding to be informed of all my movements and demanding updates on the search. Hector checked in a lot too, but he was a bit less insufferable about it. I think he already knew I didn't respond well to constant demands. He had offered to come to Vegas and was nice enough to understand when I declined.

The police had zero leads. Jennifer had stayed with her group of friends for most of Saturday night, but at some point she slipped away, and when they realized she'd been absent for a few hours, they started looking for her, texting, checking her Instagram. She never returned. Of course, there were numerous and different illegal substances consumed by all, including Jennifer. This didn't help us confirm a reasonable timeline—or keep the police interested.

I called a friend of mine at the FBI but he was now assigned to the Information and Technology Branch, no longer in the field. He did call a few agents he knew in Nevada and they promised to conduct some preliminary inquiries. I didn't have time for that. Already, the Las Vegas PD wasn't returning my calls. My father and I were frantic. I needed something to break soon. I had to get out.

The short flight from Atlanta to Las Vegas was an agony. My right eye twitched, my stomach turned, and I couldn't concentrate enough to read my reports. The claustrophobic feeling stayed with me until we landed, and then the fresh air wasn't enough to calm me down.

My first stop was meeting with the detectives investigating the disappearance. From what was explained to me, Jennifer and Mael attended the festival together, accompanied by three friends who separated from them after they entered the grounds. Cameras at the entrance captured their arrival in an Uber at about seven in the evening. Then they merged into the scattered crowd and bewildering lights, and disappeared from view.

It was an impossible task to determine her exact location inside the festival grounds, so we interviewed the persons providing security, as well as the workers who manned the food booths. This proved to be equally futile as Jennifer resembled all the other pretty blondes at the festival.

The following day I met with the FBI agent assigned to the case, Hugo Zumthor. He regarded me with some skepticism, with his hands on his hips. "You must have some stroke, Doctor," he remarked, reluctantly shaking my hand.

"Why would you say that?" I asked.

"I'm the head of a division at the FBI and I was pulled off by the director to investigate this disappearance. Seems like a weird allocation of resources." The arms now crossed at his chest told me he wasn't pleased by this.

"Well, thank you for your help," I replied.

The best lead to follow was Mael. Cameras at the front caught him walking out of the festival through the main entrance at 5:30 a.m. Alone. He caught an Uber and went back to the Airbnb condo off the strip. An interview with the driver indicated nothing unusual about the ride. Another camera showed Mael entering the condo. That was the last time he was seen alive.

Five laptops on the desk in my hotel room stared back at me, each one scrolling surveillance video from any camera within twenty square blocks of where the Electric Daisy Carnival was held: Amazon Stadium—the new home of the Las Vegas Raiders.

The stadium was located at the end of the Las Vegas Strip, close to the Treasure Island hotel and casino. Eight hours of footage from every camera in the immediate area. People walking in every direction like an excavation of an ant colony. So many people and so many faces that resembled Jennifer's. As my eyes scanned the flickering images I couldn't even keep my thoughts on the task, and my mind raced with a laundry list of what-ifs. What if I had gone with her? What if I had invited Jennifer to come visit me like I always insisted that I would?

With every face that passed the monitor, I wondered who they were, what their lives were like, and where they were going. What made them so different?

I could have sat there for years, staring at those screens with only my what-ifs for companionship.

Late that night, I nearly slipped off my seat at the image of a girl in a flowing yellow sundress among a crowd of people. That was Jennifer. Others were uncertain, but I knew it.

Each camera and each block traced her movements until the screen flashed to static. I followed the next series of cameras to confirm my suspicions: more static except for two other feeds that were devoid of people and clear as day.

I called over Zumthor to view my progress. He stared at the

screen of snow that snapped and stuttered over the monitor. Clear visual, then static over and over.

"I'm not sure," he said after what seemed like too long.

I must have misunderstood him. It was the last thing I thought I would hear him say, or wanted him to say. "Are you fucking serious?" I replied.

Hugo didn't seem surprised by my outburst as he continued to stare at the screen. "It's like someone is trying to make it seem like a Gloaming passed the camera when it never happened. I'll send it to our lab and see if it conforms to established norms of Gloaming interference. But I don't think you're going to like what they have to say." He sat down and leaned back in his chair as he cut his eyes at me. Probably wondering if my next outburst was on the way.

I tapped the side of the desk with my finger as if to release steam, like a battered valve attached to a bloated machine.

It wasn't working.

And sitting in a stuffy hotel room wasn't going to cut it. I dragged Hugo out with me to walk the path where the cameras began to static. We took off down the strip, starting at the stadium and down close to the MGM Grand, where the video stream had faded out. I flipped through my brain, trying to figure out why Jenny would walk this way when the Airbnb was in the opposite direction. Was she exhausted from the festival and not thinking clearly? She could have consulted the map on her phone to keep from getting lost. Was her intention to go this particular direction?

We took a right down a block of mixed condos and office buildings, nothing taller than four stories. "You sure she went this way?" Hugo asked.

"There's no other explanation. The cameras on the corresponding streets show nothing."

Hugo studied the buildings while I scanned the alleys in between. "I mean, there are cameras here," Hugo remarked, "but nothing seems to indicate—" He stopped in front of a two-story business building with no sign or markings. "Fuck!"

"What?" I grabbed his arm but immediately let go.

Hugo pointed at what looked to be another camera above the doorway.

"The camera?" I asked. It looked as though there were two cameras side by side at various points on the building.

"That's a camera," Hugo said, "but the thing next to it isn't another camera. It's a radiation portal monitor. It measures and alerts to high radiation readings in the vicinity. They are quite complex and expensive."

I glanced over at him. "Why would they have that there?"

"One to guard against humans and the other to guard against Gloamings," he answered as he texted someone on his phone. "I'm asking my office to check ownership on this address."

We walked around the building, into the alley, and saw more monitors and cameras. Hugo's phone buzzed and he scanned the messages with a shake of his head and his lips pursed.

"What is it?" I shouted.

"Have to say, I'm kind of surprised," he stated. "Believe it or not, this building is owned by a shell company for the Claremont Corporation."

"Gloaming-owned," I whispered, voicing my thoughts.

"Still doesn't explain why they're guarding against their own kind," Hugo said. "This could be something very interesting."

I wanted to break into the building and find out something about Jennifer, to drag Zumthor through the front door with his gun drawn, to call in the National Guard. None of these were an option.

* * *

Two weeks later, just after I had booked a ticket to return home, a man biking with his family found Jennifer's body when his dog ran off in search of the source of the scent. The remains were skeletal. The authorities confirmed her identity through dental records.

When the detective called me, I was in my rental car. I felt the tears running down my face before I knew I had started crying. I pulled the car over to the side of the road. I needed to call my parents. I needed to talk to Hector. But I couldn't do any of that yet.

One more sob and I turned the car off. I slumped over the wheel. I was still such a child in spite of everything. I wanted someone to tell me it was not true and that everything would be put back into place.

The Nevada heat boiled up into the car and was suffocating me as I stared out the window. I could feel my thoughts begin to jumble and the shapes in front of my eyes flutter before I turned on the ignition and the cool air slapped my face. I breathed the cold air deeply. Breathed deeply again. So many memories of her scattered through my mind and I couldn't seem to grab hold of even one to savor and love.

Okay, Jennifer, I thought.

I googled "Las Vegas morgue" and punched the address into the GPS.

For a moment, everything was put back in its place.

Already I wasn't the same person I was a week before. My heart was screaming for vengeance.

I pretty much forced my way into the autopsy.

Since there were only bones left, it was virtually impossible to determine anything substantive. I examined the anterior longitudinal ligament area and the cervical vertebra area close to the neck. I could not find anything that indicated a bite from a Gloaming. However, I'd snuck in my Geiger counter, and sure enough, the bones emitted residual radiation that could be attributed to a Gloaming. It wasn't a conclusive enough reaction for the coroner.

But it was enough for me.

Meanwhile, as my old man once told me, "You don't need a weatherman to tell you which way the wind is blowing." I knew my time at the CDC was running short. My supervisors had asked me to modify my research to focus less on eradicating certain elements of the virus to make it inert, and focus more on lessening the impact of the virus on the body. I pushed back hard on this: if that's all we did, I argued, then all my research would amount to nothing!

Soon enough, the assistant director called me into her office to announce that the CDC was terminating my employment.

I didn't even ask why. When I got home that night, I told Hector. He'd been telling me to leave the CDC for a long time, with all the resistance I had been encountering, but in that moment, he knew I didn't need to hear about that. He just wrapped me in a tight, silent hug.

Surprisingly—or actually not surprisingly, when dealing with the government—I was offered a new job the very next day. I was sitting in the Starbucks close to my apartment, nursing a large Frappuccino, when a woman in a smart suit walked in. She sat directly across from me.

"Can I help you?" I asked.

"You're Lauren Scott," she said, more of a statement than a question.

"So?" I thought she may have been a reporter looking for another interview about Liza Sole, but the interest in that period of time had waned to a point where no one cared about the beginning of the Gloamings. In fact, the Gloamings had done an excellent job of wiping out that part of their history, preferring to construct another "beginning" story, with the emergence of a Gloaming community in Santa Fe, New Mexico, as their origin fable. I suppose no one wants their fairy tale to begin with a murderous cannibal.

The woman leaned closer. "I'm Sally Lindsay. I work for a small pharmaceutical company called Atwater Corporation. We're currently focusing on expanding our research division."

"Okay," I replied. "What can I do for you?"

"Well, I know that you recently left your job at the CDC, and Atwater would like to offer you a very prestigious position."

I was shocked. "Well, it's kind of soon, given everything that's happened," I stated. "I hadn't really given much thought to my next move."

She left her card on the table. "Call me and let's coordinate a meeting. You need to get out of Atlanta, anyway. Come to California."

And with that she was gone. It took me about a week to call her up and arrange a meeting outside Stockton, California, where Atwater was located. It was a highly secured facility, and the meeting was interesting. The three executives and scientists that I met were young and seemed to have a lot of energy and a sense of fun.

"We want you to concentrate on the work you were doing at the CDC—specifically, the NOBI virus," said Terrence Davila, director of research.

I'm certain the surprise was all over my face. "Really? I didn't think many companies or universities were still willing to research the NOBI virus—especially with my focus."

"Well," Terrence continued, "we don't advertise it. In fact, we hide it quite well, but it is our primary focus right now. And that's not going to change, no matter the publicity."

I flew home to talk over this offer with Hector. I didn't want to admit it out loud, but the truth was, after the Liza Sole incident and my sister's murder, I still had it in for the Gloamings. I wanted to continue my research and fight the NOBI virus. Hector knew this. Plus, he was working part-time at a rural health clinic to supplement his income while writing his book about our experiences during those first few months in Arizona. He could do that in California as well as anywhere.

It wasn't until I'd been at Atwater for five months that I learned it was actually funded in large part by the CIA. My shock wore off pretty quickly. I'd worked for years in government. No matter how public opinion had turned, of course they would still have a vested interest in pursuing options in regard to the Gloamings. And with the abundant Atwater support, my research had progressed to the point where I had developed a working prototype for a postexposure prophylaxis for the NOBI virus infection if administered within forty-eight hours of the bite.

It helped that we were able to overcome many of the technical limitations we faced when studying the radioactive NOBI virus. For example, UC Berkeley had created a proprietary high-resolution electron microscope using the inherent radiation of the virus to reflect back to a beam of accelerated electrons. It was essentially an X-ray with high photon energies modified at a cellular level to reflect the NOBI radiation. But the energy created in the process tended to burn out the microscopes after about twenty viewings. At the CDC, obtaining funding for a disposable $50,000 microscope good for only twenty viewings had been a constant challenge.

At Atwater, my assistant easily took care of the paperwork, and new microscopes appeared as if by magic.

The day I successfully replicated the antiretroviral treatment, which would stop NOBI in its tracks, I remember viewing the enzymes and human DNA on a normal blood slide. As the NOBI cells began to bind to the receptors, I was in shock. My computer had recorded what had unfolded within the microscope, but I needed the verification of a real-life colleague.

I called over one of my team members, a Caltech grad student named Dylan, who was at her computer. I stepped away from the microscope. I pointed a finger at my chair. "Replicate my most recent experiment," I said.

Dylan performed the steps as she looked through the viewfinder. I watched her work by looking at the computer. Dr. Azoulay, my other researcher, stood next to me to view the monitor. "Oh my," Dylan said as her hands gripped the side of the table. "Holy shit!" she cried.

I called Terrence Davila. He was in a meeting, but I barked at his assistant to get him out.

When Terrence arrived, I asked him to do the same thing Dylan had done. A few moments later he looked up. He grabbed my shoulders and shook me like I was a Christmas present. "I'm getting drunk tonight!" he screamed, as if tonight would be any different from any other night.

Of course, without a live Gloaming to test the drug on, all this was theoretical. However, most of our computer models indicated that the drug would be an effective prophylaxis against the virus. The drug worked by inhibiting reverse transcriptase, the enzyme that copied Gloaming RNA into new moot viral DNA, which would bind to antithrombin and change the molecular composition of the blood to something closer to human. We named it Glomudine.

In addition, our computer models indicated that the chemical compound in Glomudine could be used to severely incapacitate Gloamings if administered in an aerosol form. Soon we began working with different manufacturers to compile a means to deliver an aerosol version of the drug during a conflict. However, similar to various other types of chemical weapons, Glomudine was fatal to humans if they were exposed to the drug in the amounts needed to incapacitate a Gloaming. I presumed our research was still purely theoretical or at least worth the risks.

Looking back on it now, I should have known the stakes of my research and the true costs of extensive Glomudine use. And at that point, security at the Atwater lab complex was stepped up, as the Gloaming tension in New Mexico was reaching a critical point. More and more military personnel were visiting the lab every week.

I should have urged greater caution. I should have been more vocal, more firm that we needed to get closer to 95 percent efficacy before moving to manufacturing the Glomudine.

But like Mike Tyson once said, "I got old too soon and smart too late."

Federal Bureau of Investigation—Department of Justice
Via Secure Email Congressional System

FROM: *Special Agent in Charge Hugo Zumthor*
TO: *House Committee on Homeland Security, Counsel; Office of the Attorney General*
SUBJECT: *Situational Information Report/Classified Law Enforcement*
MARKED: *Sensitive*
DATE: *August 13*

About three weeks after the BuzzFeed article was published, leading to formal Department of Justice and Congressional inquiries, I led a team of local FBI agents to the Rio Grande Institute to conduct a standard preliminary inquiry.

At the Institute's gated entrance, we were denied access by New Mexico National Guard troops stationed at the front. Thereafter, the FBI sought a search warrant from a Federal judge for Institute personnel and all records, including email, text, audio, and video records. After five days, Judge Koster granted the search warrant and again we went to the Institute, this time to serve the warrant.

Again, we were denied access to the Institute. I'm sure there is a logical explanation for these actions, though Lord knows we might not be here long enough to hear it. But this time, a significantly greater number of New Mexico National Guard troops were stationed along the main road which accessed the Institute's gated entrance.

Currently, we are awaiting further orders from the Director and the Attorney General as to how to proceed.

The Huffington Post

[Original post taken from the front page, Sunday edition, of *O Estado de S. Paulo*. Translated from the Portuguese.]

The annual Brazilian festival, known as Carnaval, which takes place a week before the Catholic celebration of Lent, has been the subject of much speculation after reports indicate that over seventy people went missing in the city of Ouro Prêto after the celebrations. For several months, details were scarce as multiple families reported missing loved ones and the Brazilian military opened a full-scale, but incredibly limited, investigation. Then, in late summer of this year, ten square blocks of the city were suspiciously declared a "forbidden zone" to all but certain credentialed personnel, indicating that some progress had finally been made.

Overcoming fear of persecution, witnesses finally emerged last month and told others that five Gloamings had attacked a group of revelers in the Jardim Botânico Bloco de Rua ("street block"). The street blocks of Ouro Prêto are famous for their own particular parties and themes led by the sounds of *frevo* and *maracatu* music, with brass and drums filling the air.

According to reports, the Gloamings were dressed in black silk pants with red trim and rumba shirts with wide red frilled sleeves and frilled calf covers. Their faces were painted white and they wore large top hats. They came out of the three-room apartment of a local grocer who was away with his family in Rio de Janeiro for Carnaval. The

Gloamings waited until after the parade, when there were no more floats but the streets were still crowded with revelers. Gloamings then began to dance with the people. This lasted a few minutes, until the Gloamings went into a frenzy and murdered the people on the entire block. In the commotion of the festivities, it took some time before people realized that friends and group members had suddenly disappeared. These events, thought to be just social disruption, went unreported for weeks.

After corroborating over thirty eyewitness statements, officers immediately called in the army, who then cordoned off ten square blocks surrounding the reported crime scene and refused access to any press or local government officials. Sources in the army indicated that after days of searching, all of the deceased were found exsanguinated and left in the sewer system under the street. The bodies were finally buried after an examination at an unknown mass grave site, which angered many of the families of the victims. Sources in intelligence agencies indicate that the government had prior knowledge of the event, but stalled a rigorous investigation because the government of Brazilian President Lucas Sousa does not want to antagonize the Gloamings he has become intertwined with through his business interests.

CHAPTER 21

SEPTEMBER 15
FORTY MONTHS AFTER THE NOBI DISCOVERY

Hugo Zumthor
Special Agent in Charge of Gloaming Crimes Unit, FBI

The McMaster Nuclear Reactor in Hamilton, Ontario, was a low-power nuclear reactor known as a research reactor on the campus of Canada's McMaster University.[33] These reactors are smaller because they are used for research, not to produce electricity. But they do contain all the elements of power reactors, including highly enriched uranium [HEU].

Goddamn nuclear...well, nuclear anything. Albert Einstein said it best: "The release of atom power has changed everything except our way of thinking...The solution to this problem lies in the heart of

---

[33] "The McMaster Nuclear Reactor is an open-pool type materials test reactor (MTR) with a core of low enriched uranium (LEU) fuel that is moderated and cooled by light water. Primary and secondary cooling systems act to remove the heat that is generated in the core of the reactor, with external cooling towers acting as the ultimate thermal sink. The reactor is housed within a concrete containment building and generally operates weekdays from 8 a.m. until midnight at a thermal power of three megawatts." © McMaster University Website

mankind. If only I had known, I should have become a watchmaker."

Amen, Albert.

I learned all this when a CIA colleague called out of the blue, to request a meeting in my office. I was always a bit wary of such requests. Those meetings tended to be long on cliché and short on workable solutions—the CIA modus operandi. "Why?" I said before I even agreed to the meeting.

There was a pause, and then a click. The line was being monitored. "We need to discuss some Internet traffic regarding a certain group bringing highly enriched uranium or plutonium into the United States," my colleague said. "Easier in person, I think?"

A certain group. Ah. I had a feeling I knew which group the CIA needed to consult me about.

It wasn't until I hung up the phone that it actually hit me.

We were talking about Gloamings, of course. But Gloamings and...

Nuclear power?

Things were proceeding at a frantic pace following the interception of the white paper and I wanted to meet with Lauren Scott to ask her a few questions about the ultimate purpose of the Gloamings. We met at Dulles Airport and sat in the corner of a Starbucks amid the throngs of passengers. Where does all the time go...

"I can't miss my flight," Lauren stated with an annoyed look on her face.

"I know," I replied, "and I appreciate this. The CIA would never let me forget it and then I would owe them one." You never want to be in debt to the CIA.

"So what's up?"

I passed my tablet over to her and she read a summary of the white paper provided by a team of analysts. Lauren's brow furrowed and then she nodded, as if this confirmed all of her fears about the Gloamings.

"What do you think?" I asked.

"Can't say I'm surprised. It's a natural progression of their survival instinct."

I took back my tablet and shut it off. "You believe it? I mean, do you think they're seriously considering this nuclear winter, permanent night scenario?"

Lauren stared at the people crisscrossing the airport terminal. "The good news is that they really need us to survive. The bad news is that they really only need us to feed. I suppose if they ever construct a synthetic blood supply that is identical to human blood, then we better start worrying. Or they could always just imprison us for blood. Probably not feasible, but..."

That's all I really needed to know.

On October 5, an unknown number of individuals entered the McMaster Nuclear Reactor and stole about two hundred kilograms of HEU—about the size of a newborn baby. The reactor fuel at the McMaster reactor consisted of small black pellets which resembled charcoal sticks for drawing and weighed only a few pounds each, so the heat was not excessive enough to prevent transport, or even to prevent holding the pellets in your hands.

The individuals did not leave many tangible clues, other than a knocked-out security guard and a few tire tracks in the snow.

The pellets were traced to the Zemun clan—a large criminal enterprise based in Serbia with about ten thousand soldiers in its ranks. It is thought the pellets were then funneled through New York City and then Dallas, as various radiation detection devices were alerted in those cities. Eventually, the pellets made their way to Uruguay, where they were transferred to the members of the Japanese yakuza gang known as Yamaguchi-gumi, who were thought to have put the pellets on a freighter carrying television and cell phone components made by a Brazilian manufacturer. Then the freighter was docked in Kitakyushu, Japan. The Yamaguchi-gumi clan then transported the pellets to a Gloaming facility in Lisbon, Portugal. While in Lisbon, Gloaming scientists constructed a low-yield but still dangerous tactical nuclear weapon 1.5 feet in diameter, wherein two sides of the highly enriched uranium would slam against each other, causing a nuclear reaction when fired by a specially modified artillery gun, namely an eight-inch howitzer. This inelegant device could be shipped easily by plane or boat.

So much of the media attention—and our efforts—were misguidedly focused on the horror of the Gloamings' "blood banks." Our intelligence agencies were oblivious to the horrifying plans that the Gloamings were conducting under our noses that would change the course of history and lead to years of finger-pointing and investigations. But it would never change the absolute fact.

We never had a chance.

Initial Psychiatric Assessment
March 18, 2:25 p.m.

Patient A is an eight-year-old male and was referred by the school district after frequent outbursts in class, including yelling, crying, and inappropriate slapping of other students. The patient has no previous psychiatric history. The patient's general medical history shows no peculiar illnesses and shows normal functions for his age. Diagnostic tests have been scheduled but not completed. Axis IV of DSM-IV-TR assessment shows that the recent armed conflict in New Mexico has affected the patient. Patient A was asked to write about what causes his stress and generally what he remembers about his first outburst in class.

Interviewer: Tell me what happened when the bombs started.

Patient A: The day of the loud explosion we went under our seats. Mrs. Greer, my teacher, told us not to worry. We stayed there for a while and Lisa held my hand when I started to shake. I was waiting for another one to go but it didn't happen. Mrs. Greer told us to come out and then another bomb went off. This one shook the windows and we all screamed, even Mrs. Greer. We got back under the tables.

Interviewer: Did anything happen after that?

Patient A: Then we got out of class early and my mom picked me up. Mom and Dad yelled a lot about leaving Albuquerque but we don't have a lot of money and my parents have to work. I don't want to go back to school because it's not safe there with planes and explosions.

Interviewer: Did you go back to school?

Patient A: I didn't want to go but the governor gave all of the students at school free gift cards. Two hundred dollars! Mom bought groceries and clothes for me. The governor is a Gloaming and he's a good man.

Interviewer: What do you think about the Gloamings?

Patient A: My friends and me talk about them all the time. They seem really cool and I heard that some of them can fly. My mom says that's not true but she's just never seen it either. She doesn't really like them but she won't tell me why. All of my classmates have seen them. We all think they're pretty cool and nice. My parents and I went to the governor rally at Johnson Park and there were two Gloamings right near me! I begged Mom to walk closer to them until we were right there. I could have touched them. They were a boy and a girl. They smelled so nice, like flowers. I wanted to touch them so bad! They looked at me and Mom pulled me away and we had to leave then. If I could I would be friends with them.

CHAPTER 22

OCTOBER 8
FORTY-ONE MONTHS AFTER THE NOBI DISCOVERY

Hugo Zumthor
Special Agent in Charge of Gloaming Crimes Unit, FBI

My mother once told me that I wasn't a very good son. She only said it once but it stuck with me after she passed away. When I was a child I would run outside to play whenever she wanted to talk to me or hold me. Even when I got older and after my dad died, it didn't change. Her only child ran away to become an FBI agent. I never got over it after she passed. But I'm not the same person I was back then. He doesn't exist anymore...

I was thinking about this as I stood in front of the monument to the children who died here at the gates of the Rio Grande Institute.[34]

---

[34] Everyone was arguing over the Rio Grande Institute situation. The attorney general of New Mexico, the office of Governor Nick Bindon Claremont, the FBI, the Gloaming Council, and every local and national media outlet had a not so thinly veiled opinion about this unprecedented refusal to obey a lawful court order. Sometimes, though, real change happens thanks to a bunch of kids.

In this case, a group of about thirty high school students from different religious backgrounds in the area—they called themselves "interfaith students"—traveled

I didn't believe it when I was first sent the memo two days before it broke on the news: Governor Nick Bindon Claremont, thirty-fourth governor of New Mexico, had died after a blood infection brought on by the consumption of tainted blood. Seemed apropos.

---

to the Rio Grande Institute to protest the experiments conducted there. They left early on a Saturday morning and by noon they were at the institute gates. The kids had packed picnic lunches and held signs advocating for peace and tolerance.

They piled out of the converted school bus and found an area next to the barbed wire fence. The National Guard troops were still in position, in case the Feds decided to show up and make a move. Many of the people in attendance that day spoke of palpable tension in the air.

After about an hour, the interfaith students rose up and started to sing. People could hear the songs from far down the hill, carried by the warm New Mexico winds. Even today no one is certain who began the action or why they moved. But at some point the students began to walk onto the road directly in front of the institute's gated entrance.

The National Guard troops moved in front to restrict access.

The students continued to sing.

The troops stood in their formation, weapons drawn, but the students still sang, with smiles on their faces.

There were no local police on the scene that day for crowd control. That would have been preferable, as local police generally have more experience in handling such matters. Certainly more than state National Guard troops.

The students, young and immature, began to act silly. They danced in front of the troops. A few attempted to hand the troops some flowers picked from the nearby hill. The troops did not acknowledge the students or accept the flowers—until one student decided to approach the guard station at the gate.

Years later, when the House and Senate Select Committee investigated the event, some witnesses stated that one of the students reached into her purse. Other witnesses maintained that all the students simply held flowers in their hands.

However, the fact remained that none of the students were armed with weapons. They only carried flowers and bottled water.

Later, another guard would claim to have been looking out over the sky, losing concentration, when he heard a sound and saw one of the students reach into her backpack, causing him to involuntarily discharge his rifle. Then the other guards acted in concert, following with gunfire as well.

In the moment, as the student veered toward the enclosed guard station, one of the guards stumbled forward.

A gun discharged.

Two other soldiers opened fire on the students.

Of course, his wife, Leslie, then became the new governor by virtue of her being the lieutenant governor. I would never be able to shake the suspicion that she murdered her husband to further the goals of the Gloamings. Her ascension ushered in a new era of cooperation with the federal government. Many people were taken in by the tranquility, but all I could think about was that this new age was simply a temporary cessation of hostilities. I was in no mood to make nice. I was only here to plunder what was left of Nick Bindon Claremont's ambitions. And that would begin at the Rio Grande Institute.

I was on a commercial flight to New Mexico to finally serve the federal search warrant I had been holding on to for a year when I received a message from the New Mexico governor's office, saying that I was welcome to search the facility and if I needed anything else they "were here to help."

So be it.

I called in the Atwater Corporation to helicopter Dr. Lauren Scott to meet me there and help in the search in case we needed someone to interpret any medical data retrieved. She was somewhere in the Southwest chasing invisible microscopic monsters and could meet me there when I arrived.

And sure enough, she was waiting for me in the deserted lobby of the institute, with a large backpack slung over her shoulder.

"Again we meet," she said with a grin. "Your aide-de-camp is present for duty, *mon supérieur*."

That got a smile out of me. We might have some fun out of this yet.

We walked into the main lobby area with its precious artwork still hung on the walls and the marble walls and floors gleaming as if recently polished. But it was all empty. Like a snapshot of a wasteland. Silent, as if one moment there had been the rush and business of people engaged in work and a second later they had all disappeared. Papers strewn on the floor, coffee cups left on tables and shelves. I could almost see the conversations still hanging in the air. It looked like the ruins of Chernobyl or Pompeii.

A small team of agents and scientists followed us in silence as we took the enclosed stairs, with their soft lighting and off-white walls, to the basement headquarters.

Lauren opened the door and I instinctively put my hand on my holstered gun, in spite of the governor's insistence that the lab was safe and had been swept by security. I stepped inside and was shocked by the elaborate laboratory. It had to have been the size of a football field, all white granite and individual lighting. Interior design by way of Apple. File cabinets were open and computers were turned on although I could only imagine that any relevant information had been scrubbed clean before we arrived.

Lauren sat down in front of the largest computer, with three terminals, and cracked her knuckles, which I assumed to be her talisman of entry to any difficult task. I had my own, which involved flicking the trigger of my gun with my thumb. I walked over to rifle through the mess of files that lined the walls.

After two days of trolling through this crap, I'd had enough. This agent wasn't made for the minutiae of parsing words and files in computers. I was meant for shaking down suspects and staring into faces to find out what I needed to know.

Every few hours I would interrupt Lauren to inquire about her progress and she would wave me off. "Almost there…" That was all she would say. I started to think we might be here for weeks or months.

I found Lauren splayed on a cleared-off table like a bird that had just bounced off a window.

"Well?" I asked. "Had enough?"

She let out a deep sigh that sounded like a gust of wind through the trees. "We're always on the verge."

"*Pssht!* Of what?"

"Something really, really important," she replied as she sat up and shook an empty coffee cup. "But that day is not here yet."

"What did you find?" I couldn't wait.

She finally looked over at me. "He was trying to make more money."

"Come again?" I leaned forward as if I couldn't hear so well.

Lauren waved her arms. "This whole operation. It was built for him to capitalize on Gloamings. To make money off the backs of his people."

"Are you fucking serious?" I felt like this information would put me back months. "What about the white paper and human enslavement—"

Lauren shook her head and sat up. "Nothing about that was in here. But that's not to say we didn't find anything interesting."

"Tell me what you found here."

Lauren clicked on the computer and an outline popped up. "They're not as far along as I am in research of their blood, although they have made some interesting discoveries. From what I could gather they were trying to find a happy medium between the long life span and enhanced physical state versus being able to live in the sunlight. They want it all."

"What's their angle on it?" I asked.

Lauren clicked on the mouse and the screen popped up with an image. "This is a 3-D computer model of the NOBI RNA—the ribonucleic acid—which acts as the messenger carrying instructions and genetic information for the virus, in its pore and funnel design with linked residues, double helix infinite strands joined together in movement. Beautiful, huh? It's like any other blood disease, such as Ebola or the Marburg virus. Those diseases were formed in jungles, and one day they jumped that barrier from animals to humans. From monkeys to humans, from bats to humans. How long do you think that took? Hundreds, thousands, millions of years? They want to accomplish the same thing in a year or so."

"Can you determine how far along they are in their research?" I asked, knowing that any success could lead to even more power for the Gloamings.

Lauren turned her chair to face me. "They have come close, but their attempts ended up causing a modified hemorrhagic fever virus that killed many of the Gloaming test subjects. I see what they were getting at. Some coagulate modification that could alter the DNA or RNA."

"But they didn't get that far?"

Lauren shook her head as she grabbed for a couple of empty coffee cups. "Nope. But they did succeed in inactivating certain portions of the NOBI virus through extreme cold and then extreme heat temperatures without resorting to sunlight. They sequenced that RNA and found that afterwards, ten percent of the sequences were disparate from the others. Which gave an altered series of antibodies. Five of these dormant proteins remained attached to the core complex."

I could only nod my head as the words began to run together…

Lauren grabbed my arm as if to make me focus on her words. "They're attempting to find the quintuple complex where the hidden proteins are located. It's like a start-stop sign for the virus. If they can stop the replication they would be much closer to their goal."

"What does it all mean in the end?" I asked. "All these tests and experiments—what does it get them in the end? What do they want?"

Lauren stared at me for a long moment. "They want to be like us..."

The Sun (United Kingdom)[35] **September 25**—Bloody Good Times!

While their mates are in America trying to construct their own Republic, a group of Gloamings decided to take a bite out of the Running of the Bulls in Pamplona, Spain. "Bollocks," you say. "It's during the day!" Ah, but these cheeky Gloamings paid the municipal government in Pamplona to allow a night run. And run they did. Dressed in the traditional white pants, white shirt with a red scarf round the waist, and a red handkerchief round the neck, these Gloamings had the time of their long lives. Then on to Oktoberfest in Munich, Germany. No indication that they donned the lederhosen—oh, that would have been a sight to behold!

---

[35] UK Sunday edition, Living section.

CHAPTER 23

Joseph Barrera
Political Operative

I couldn't believe I was back in DC. I really should have had my head examined for coming back to this town. I always thought that when I came back it would be akin to a Roman general returning to collect his agnomen from the adoring crowds. I would be celebrated by politics and press as a genius consultant with a stringy white beard to stroke and throw over my shoulder with every profound word, like a grandmaster of political thought.

I hadn't lived here since I graduated from college and didn't really think I would be back here unless I was the chief of staff for an incoming president. But financial necessity brought me back to purgatory. After electing Claremont governor, I had been basically exiled from any other campaign—neither Republicans nor Democrats would touch me. A toxic force enveloped me—the result of too many unsavory rumors about that campaign and my hand in it. I hadn't expected all of this. It was all so abrupt. There's a dialogue in *The Sun Also Rises* where Bill asks Mike, "How did you go bankrupt?" He answers, "Two ways. Gradually and then suddenly." I couldn't remember how it happened, how fast or how long it took, but before the grains were sowed and the fodder crops planted, I was broke and alone, with prospects diminished.

I came back to work on Capitol Hill as part of a senator's staff. Not even the chief of staff—only a communications adviser. I wanted to change my name but the word was already out. Hey, we all need a paycheck and health care, right? I wanted to meet some new people so I put myself back into the bars and clubs of Georgetown, Columbia Heights, and H Street. Man, how things had changed. Where were all the normal people? So many hipster scene freaks. I hung out and dated the type crawling all over Williamsburg and Silverlake, all trying to outquirk each other. It was exhausting and I didn't fit in, although in truth the problem probably begins and ends with me.

The only other thing I could do was dive into my work, which was less than exciting unless you enjoy writing press releases to local news media throughout the state of Georgia. Those long days on the phone made me wonder if some people choose to selectively demonstrate their intelligence—or if they are just really stupid. I began to have hazy thoughts that perhaps I was just an underachiever and likely this would be my lot in life.

Three months after my return, I was walking back to my apartment on a cold autumn night after a rousing trivia happy hour at the Angry Donkey when I felt a presence from behind. Something made me feel like I was not alone. It was the middle of the night and I saw that the street was deserted as I glanced back every few steps. I almost felt like I had PTSD from my time in New Mexico, and I had thoughts of never leaving the house at night again. One more glance back and I saw a figure dart behind a car. Maybe. I ran back home...

About a week after that incident, an old acquaintance of mine called me up, saying she was in town and wanted to meet up for lunch. Her name was Becky Owens, and I had met her on an unusual congressional campaign that had received a lot of press. A former president's daughter was running for office, and what would have been another bland congressional race became a national event, with crowded press events and buses filled with journalists following the candidate. Becky had worked for the *Washington Post* and Bloomberg before moving on to the staff of Facebook's recent—although somewhat tentative—incursion into journalism, called Scoop.

We met for a late dinner at a new hip fusion restaurant in Dupont Circle. Pretty much all ambient and accent lighting by candles hung by pendant sconces. I almost tripped a few times. I had no idea it was Italian-Asian fusion until I opened the menu and cringed. I experienced the same emotions when Taco Bell debuted the waffle taco. But hey, the drinks were amazing. After dinner, we sat back and Becky finally got to the point. I knew from her call that she had an agenda in mind with this dinner, but I wanted her to make the first move.

"So what's up?" I asked. She knew what I meant and grinned at the question.

"Well, let's get to the point, then," she answered with a mischievous look on her face. "I'm writing a book and I'd like some help from you."

"Really?" I said, not expecting that response. This seemed kind of normal. "I'll help all I can. What's the book about?"

Becky leaned forward and lowered her voice. "I'm writing the definitive account of Nick Bindon Claremont's election."

I leaned away from her with a surprised look on my face. Okay, maybe not so normal. "Robin Fields wrote *the* book about the election last year. What are you going to do differently?"

A smile played across Becky's face as she tapped her fork on the table. "Get you on record with the real truth."

I could feel my bottom lip quivering. "I gave Robin an interview and told her my perspective." I tried to act casual with a shrug of my shoulders but I couldn't even fool myself.

"I know you want to tell the real story," Becky said with a determined look. "That stuff you gave for Robin's book was crap. Fiction. I want the real scene. I want the rumors confirmed."

We stared at each other in silence for a minute or two. I stirred my sidecar and licked the drops before they fell. "I don't know what to tell you," I said. "The story has been told before."

I walked home later that evening thinking about what she had asked of me. We didn't leave on bad terms—I knew this was just the beginning of a process where she hoped to wear me down. I had doubts as to whether I could actually hold up my end of this unspoken bargain I had made with these Gloamings and particularly Leslie Claremont. I had to be careful and think about what I was going to do.

I opened my front door and I felt that someone was inside, but before I could back out, a hand grabbed me around the collar. I yelled but a voice interrupted me.

"Relax, Joseph," the man said.

"Who are you?" I asked as the hand led me over to the couch and pushed me down. My eyes focused on a figure sitting on one of the barstools near the kitchen. I could smell that sweet scent of Gloaming and my heart beat faster.

"I need to talk to you, Joseph," another voice on the barstool said, and I recognized it from somewhere. Before I could scroll through the hard drive in my brain, the light flicked on and I saw a face that made me feel like a panic attack was on its way: Toshi Machita. Nick Bindon Claremont's former goon.

I swallowed hard. "Hi, Toshi. I hope you've been well. I see you have been re-created. Congratulations." I never thought it would happen. Toshi always seemed more like the help than like the top of the food chain at the Claremont Corporation.

"I have," he replied. "But what I really want to talk about is your meeting with reporters who want to write books about an election in New Mexico."

I jumped up before a hand pushed me back down. "I didn't say a damn thing to her! You can't put that on me. She came to me! You've got nothing to worry about. I told you people that a long time ago!"

"I wasn't finished," Toshi said with a hard edge to his voice. "Actually, what does worry me is the journal you have hidden in a fake folder on your Dropbox drive."

My body became cold. "It's not—I do it for—I have anxiety and my therapist told me to keep a journal but not to show it to anyone."

"Your therapist?" Toshi said. "Well, that's a new one. What things do you confess to this therapist?"

"N-nothing," I said with a loud stutter. "When I was in high school my mom made me go see a therapist, so that started the whole thing. I'm still very resentful of her to this day! I've said nothing about New Mexico."

Toshi sighed, and there was silence. I began to shake before he spoke again. "Stop whining. You're like a paean to emasculation. You have to come with us."

"Look!" I yelled. "I won't say anything to—"

"Let me finish," Toshi said as he rose and walked over to me. "I want you to meet someone. We have some work for you to do. You do like money, correct?"

"I do. Yes. Let's go."

"You must—you must really keep your eyes to yourself. And I can't emphasize this enough: there shall be no talking unless it is initiated. And even in those cases, please approach only myself if there is a need."

The old man stammered and placed his thin gray hands on the table. "She cannot have these tempta—distractions. If you need something, you shall write it on the clipboard I have provided in the hallway. Which will then be read and your request shall be provided to you. If there is a question, your contact shall write it in a note to you to which you will respond on the clipboard if appropriate. Is that something we can agree on?"

The girl in the nurse's uniform nodded but her shaking hands belied any confidence suggested by that nod.

A woman lay on the hospital bed but she was wrapped in a purple velvet blanket that made the scene almost unreal. Three computer monitors were connected to her by wires and tubes, and the screen was lit with the scrolling of vital signs.

The woman opened her eyes and the nurse jumped back a few steps.

"Don't be afraid," the woman said. "Come closer."

The nurse did not move.

"Come."

The nurse took a halting step toward the bed. One more step, and then she leaned against the rail. The woman pulled her hand out from under the blanket and placed it over the nurse's hand. "You know who I am?"

The nurse gave her a shaky smile. "I know."

"It's night now. Can you open the window?"

The nurse walked over to the wall and entered a code on a number pad and a green light came on at the top of the window as a metal cover opened and moonlight filled the room. The woman smiled. "It won't be long before I'm strong enough to be outside and see the stars. One day we'll be able to live in the night without shame. One day."

Darkness.

Joseph blinked his eyes open and the side of his head throbbed with pain. His heart raced, as the scene was flipped upside down. He blinked again and it stayed the same. Then the realization hit him that his vision was perfect but he was hanging upside down. He lifted his neck to see his legs tied to the top of a gambrel. His arms were tied behind his back and he struggled to assess his surroundings in the dim candlelight. But he saw a once familiar figure in a black habit. "Who is there?" His voice was barely above a whisper due to the pain on the side of his head. "What are you doing? Let me down...I don't feel well anymore." He coughed. "The blood is going to my head and I can't feel my legs. My head hurts. Please..."

The old man appeared and moved closer to him; he held a long blade in his hand. Joseph raised his head but he couldn't hold it up and it bobbed from side to side. "What are you doing? I can't feel my legs. Please. I don't feel good."

The old man moved next to him and crouched by his face, as the other figure hovered around the edges of his sight. "You know what I have to do."

Joseph bobbed his head to the side. "Please. What? I told him I would not say anything! I kept my word!"

"I'll start at your Achilles tendon and work my way down…"

He placed the blade at the point of Joseph's Achilles and carefully pushed the knife into the skin and pulled down as the skin opened up like a blooming flower. Blood flowed freely down. The old man pushed his fingers into the wet flesh closest to the calf muscle and placed his index finger and thumb on the femoral artery. He whispered unintelligible words as the artery pulsed in his fingers. Joseph twisted his neck and looked up but didn't believe what he saw. The pain in his legs traveled down his body and he began to shake. The throbbing between the old man's fingers got faster and faster. He pulled up the bloody blade again and sliced the femoral artery as he stepped back.

The blood shot out and down Joseph's body. He looked up again as the blood rained down on his face and he could taste his own blood. He felt the shock of all the blood spurting from his leg and he shook more and harder and his eyes glazed over and he could barely make out the figure of a woman off to the side with an object in her hand. She approached his face. "You should have never agreed to work for the Claremont campaign," she said in a voice barely above a whisper. She licked the dripping blood from his face. "I'm already feeling much better. We're almost there."

CHAPTER 24

NOVEMBER
FORTY-TWO MONTHS AFTER THE NOBI DISCOVERY

Hugo Zumthor
Special Agent in Charge of Gloaming Crimes Unit, FBI

I couldn't get Cian Clery out of my mind. By any measure we had won. Well, excluding the gold heist and me getting sent to the hospital. But hey, I'm the one doing the counting. The score said that Cian wasn't so pretty anymore. And he certainly wasn't receiving the adoration he so desired. The agency knew that his pursuit of gold was only one aspect of a larger goal of a then unknown organization.

And then we received a tip. I have a love-hate relationship with tips. It's very rare that a tip comes in from someone who has no interest in the matter—pure altruism. Most of the time the tipster—whether anonymous or identified—has a justification for the information. And that justification can sometimes determine the fate of the investigation.

The tipster wanted us—specifically the Gloaming section—to

know that police in Chicago were investigating missing blood in various hospitals and blood being drained from cadavers in the morgue. You knew that would pique my interest. I contacted my former supervising agent when I first began my career as an agent. His name was Ringo Janowicz and he was kind of an underground legend in FBI circles. He busted Asian, Italian, and Russian mob operations in Chicago for years while making his name doing undercover work. There was nothing this guy wouldn't do to catch some hood hands-deep in some illegal shit.

Ringo was a great mentor to learn from but kind of an asshole— in all fairness, that's to be expected—who smoked like a chimney. Not e-cigarettes and vaping—he smoked the real thing. Camel nonfiltered. Every second of his waking life. He didn't care that smoking was so out of favor and looked down upon in present society. He would light up anywhere and dare someone to make him put it out. I remember going to his apartment a few times and there would be this foggy haze all over the house. I honestly think it was permanent.

He smoked while he was talking, walking, on the phone, in the toilet, eating...Ringo claimed that he started smoking when he was eight years old. I believed it. He used to have this humongous hubcap from a 1950 Ford Fairlane in the middle of his car console that he used as an ashtray. The fucking thing was always overflowing with butts and ash. Every time we used his car I would have to take the suit I was wearing to the dry cleaners to see if it could be saved. Damn thing looked like it had been in a brush fire.

Ringo told me he would pick me up at the airport. Probably in his own car. There goes another suit...

There was something else about Chicago that left me dreading the trip. Agent Webb's son had moved here after the event to stay with Webb's sister. I was never good with interpersonal relationships.

That's one of the reasons I should never have been married. I know that's a terrible thing to say but no obsessed FBI agent should ever tell another person that they will be with them forever—and will always be there to support them. It's a lie.

I fell in love with Melissa during college, when we had the same political science class—she was probably the shyest girl I had ever met. Eye contact was like winning the lottery. It took more than ten dates to even get a kiss from her. But maybe that's what first attracted me to her. Even after we were married she still acted in a very constrained manner. I attributed it to her being brought up in a very religious environment. Even after the honeymoon she would shower alone and with the door locked and rarely showed her body naked.

My marriage was in embers when Melissa and I hooked up during a couple of days when I was back home between assignments. I say "hooked up" because that was what it felt like—it had been so long since we were together intimately. And then Melissa became pregnant.

I was happy and sad at the same time. Happy to have something beautiful made out of myself but sad because I probably would miss every important milestone of his or her life—until it was too late. So I left…

I had kept tabs on Agent Webb's son and his welfare with a few phone calls and by hitting up other agents who were close to her and her family. I couldn't decide whether to go see him or not. That could only bring up bad memories. I remember thinking of the perfect words. Like most other things, I would probably put it off for another day…

"You think it's the Gloamings," Ringo said, blowing smoke out of his crooked mouth.

"Know anyone else who likes blood?"

We arrived at the Cook County morgue, a disturbingly bustling monument constructed for the dead. Abby Jordan, the assistant coroner, met us in the lobby and walked us to her office. Typical government building: carpet frayed, odd smells, and out-of-date furnishings. I felt at home already.

"Sorry there aren't any chairs," Abby stated as she sat in hers, tapping her pen on the table as if she couldn't wait to get this over with. "Budget crunch, you know. And to think I went to medical school for this. I traded down for sure. So…the police are already investigating this." She sighed. "Why the FBI now?"

Ringo looked over at me, expecting me to take the lead, which brought up some interesting emotions. It's always odd for the mentor to become the assistant. I still felt deferential to him in many ways. "The absence of blood would indicate it could have been done by Gloamings. That's what brings us."

Dr. Jordan stared at me for a moment with an impassive look before she stood up and led us to the main holding area, where new bodies were brought into the morgue either by the police or from hospitals. "We have cameras here at the loading area but not everywhere in the building," she said.

"Could have happened before they got here," Ringo added.

Dr. Jordan nodded. "One of our techs alerted the coroner that every single body in the morgue had been drained of its blood. Then we started taking notes on the bodies that began to arrive, and they, too, were all devoid of blood. We're not sure how long the bodies had been in that condition."

"Or if they were made that way here," Ringo said.

Dr. Jordan shot him a somewhat condescending look. "Fair enough."

"Okay," I said. "Email me the logistics of all the bodies

transported here over the past two months. We'll see you soon."

After we got in Ringo's car, he lit up a cigarette. "Let's go talk to the Chicago detective."

"I'm certain it was Gloamings," Detective MacIntyre stated as he pushed the table away from his large frame and spread his legs out. "Or someone associated with them." He took a bite out of his taco in this cramped taqueria in the Pilsen neighborhood of Chicago. I wondered why we would meet here instead of at the station, but right now didn't seem like the right moment to bring it up. "There's more here than you think." He put down the taco.

"Like what?" I asked.

His eyes looked around as if searching for someone. "Let me show you something."

After five minutes of arguing about which car we were going to take, we finally ended up trapped inside Ringo's smoke machine. It didn't take long...

"My God, man!" MacIntyre cried. "Why not just start a fire in here? There'd be less tar and carbon monoxide!"

Ringo ignored him and drove. "Where are we going?"

"Take 290 to downtown." MacIntyre coughed.

Ten minutes later we were parked in an alley behind the Chicago Theatre. "I'm sure you're wondering why we're here," MacIntyre said.

"That and how many tumors are growing in my lungs while waiting in this car," I said, turning to look at MacIntyre in the back seat.

MacIntyre leaned forward. "People don't know this, but there are over ninety miles of tunnels underneath downtown Chicago. They were built to be freight tunnels back in the late eighteen hundreds.

They're not used for anything anymore. At least until recently."

"What are you saying?" I demanded.

"I think the Gloamings are using the tunnels to take these bodies and drain them of blood. Among other things." MacIntyre sat back with a smug smile on his face, rubbing his hands together as if he had been waiting to tell someone and now that he had he felt better.

"What's Chicago PD doing about it?" Ringo asked.

MacIntyre closed his mouth and shook his head for a moment. "I haven't told anyone."

"Why not?" I asked.

"Chicago PD is in on it," Ringo said with a somber smile. "I know it in my bones."

MacIntyre glared at him and then showed him a satisfied grin. "He's right. I think some in the department are deep into it. Can't trust anyone. The money floating out there is way too much."

"So why the tunnels?" I asked. "Any evidence?"

"Oh, they've been careful," MacIntyre said. "But one of the ambulances that was transporting a couple of dead bodies to the morgue was seen in the tunnel over there." He pointed out the window. "Only takes one mistake."

We left the car and made our way into one of the older buildings—a ten-story granite structure that looked to be over a hundred years old. There was an enormous exterior clock above the entryway. The front was engraved with the words "Marshall Field and Company." MacIntyre explained that many old business buildings in downtown Chicago had basement entry doors to the tunnel network. We made our way inside through the large atrium, and MacIntyre spoke briefly to a uniformed guard. The guard nodded his head and MacIntyre waved at us to follow him past a teak and metal door near the elevators and down two flights of stairs to a small landing lit by one lightbulb swinging from a broken holder. Another door closed off the room.

I took out my flashlight but it was nothing more than a warning sign for trespassers. Then my heart skipped a beat. Ringo pulled out a fluorescent LED UV black light and shined it on the walls and door. They lit up with white streaks from what had to have been cleaned-up blood and other bodily fluids. And written in blood nearest the door handle: "ANOESIS."

"I've seen that word before," Ringo said.

I jerked my head at him. "Where?"

"Some middle-level drug dealer was caught with pounds of DXM and meth at a house he owned near the South Side train tracks. The train would make unscheduled stops or slowdowns and this guy and his crew would put on or take off large quantities of drugs. We busted all of them. When we had him in the box for interrogation, he wrote that on a notepad." Ringo looked at me, expecting to hear my tale.

I was too distracted by this new information to get into how I had come across the word written in blood in that Gloaming safe house in Austin, Texas. More than two years ago. No more reliving that day anymore.

We stepped down into the cool air of the tunnel and walked about thirty yards to where the tunnel branched off into three other routes. I could see tire marks and other evidence of occupation, including lights and some wall stabilizers.

"Gosh darn, something has been going on down here," Ringo said.

"Like I said," MacIntyre added.

I was already walking back to the entrance door. "I want to talk to that prisoner, Ringo. Right now."

* * *

The United States Penitentiary in Marion is a forlorn combination of linked concrete boxes masquerading as buildings. *Too quiet for a prison*, I thought as we walked up through the tangle of fenced walkways, which felt more constricting than a ten-foot hedge maze, like the prelude to a nightmare. We found ourselves sitting in a cramped visiting room with a small table between us, with a curved hook in the middle where the chains were attached from there to the handcuffs.

The chains hooked around the tattooed wrists of Jeff Hughes, who leaned back in his chair like a G—or a reasonable facsimile of one. He was probably too young to carry that attitude but he tried desperately to wear it well.

"The fuck I get out of this?" Hughes screamed, flexing his jail muscles with a pull of his chain.

MacIntyre rolled his eyes and glanced over at Ringo.

"We could talk to the U.S. attorney and get you some points off your time," Ringo said.

Hughes snorted and shook his head in an exaggerated manner. "Gotta do better than that."

I took a sip of lukewarm coffee. Tasted like shit inside a Styrofoam cup. "Jenna—the mother of your children," I said.

Hughes bowed up in his seat. "What about her?"

"She can't visit you because of her being on probation. What if I can make that happen?"

Hughes's tough guy snarl dropped a few degrees and he stared at the table for a moment. "Okay," he said. "What you got?"

I pulled out a piece of paper from my pocket and slid it over to him. On the paper was written "ANOESIS."

Hughes's face turned white and he looked away from the paper. "That—that's not me."

"Tell us," Ringo said.

Hughes sighed and ran a hand over his shaved head. "You can't let anyone know the fuck it was me." He pulled his chains to lean toward me. "Tell me!"

"No one will know," I assured him.

Hughes leaned back, breathing deep breaths, one after another. "My—my brother, Scipio. He got caught up in this group—"

"What kind of group?" MacIntyre asked. "A gang?"

"No no no. Some fucking cult." Hughes looked away.

I glanced over at Ringo, who had his eyebrows raised in surprise. Maybe I was the only one who saw this coming.

"He's fucking obsessed," Hughes continued. "All tripped out on the leader of it."

"Who's the leader?" I demanded, leaning forward.

Hughes slammed his hands down on the table with a clatter of chains. "I have no fucking idea. Some pretty boy. Always talking about his 'beauty' and shit."

I could feel my heart pounding in my chest like a point guard bouncing a basketball up the court. I needed to call Calvin James and get him on this immediately. The smell of Cian Clery filled my nose and I vowed not to lose that scent for a second time.

"You think it's him, don't you?" Calvin James asked as he warmed his hands on a cup of coffee in the passenger seat of Ringo's car. Snow was beginning to pile up on the roof and I could barely make him out with all the smoke in the car, but it didn't matter because my eyes were trained on the front lobby doors of the Washington Lofts—a new downtown living space for all the young professionals wanting to experience the city. It was an old

1928 bank building before it was converted.

"Do the lofts have access to the tunnel system?" Calvin asked.

"No—no access. I checked the original floor plans and there hasn't been any construction. But across the street is the old Chicago Board of Trade building, which has direct access."

"Anyone heard from MacIntyre yet?" Ringo asked from the back seat as smoke billowed out of his mouth.

"No," I replied, and that began to weigh on my mind.

"So this guy has to come out of the building to do his business," Calvin said almost to himself.

We waited in the car, freezing our asses off with only the cigarette smoke to warm us, until about midnight, when a man in a dark overcoat walked outside the loft building as the snow began to fall heavier. "That's him," I said.

The figure trudged through the piles of snow across the street and stopped at the side door nearest the alley at the Trade building. He opened the door and stepped inside.

"That fucker has a key," Ringo said, lighting up another cigarette with the butt of the old one.

"Let's go," I ordered.

We stepped out into the cold and sprinted to the side door. "I should have brought snowshoes," Calvin complained.

"California kid." Ringo laughed.

I reached the door and looked up at a camera. "Guarantee you that's been disabled," I said.

"And no light either," Calvin added.

"And the door is locked," I said with a frown.

Ringo pushed me aside and pulled out his tension wrench and lockpick from his side coat pocket. An old-timer like him and it only took about five minutes with a heater hanging from his lip. *Click!*

Ringo pulled the handle. "After you, gentlemen."

I pulled out my modified Glock 22 with the depleted uranium bullets and took the lead, stepping across the dark hallway, searching for the stairs that would take us to the basement. I found a door marked "Utilities" and looked over at Ringo. He only shrugged. Guess I *was* really in charge.

I opened the door as Calvin pushed his gun and light inside the stairwell and switched places with me. He stepped forward and raised his hand to signal it was clear. We made our way down step by slow step. I switched positions with Calvin and we were making our way to the second flight of stairs when a figure flashed by in my light. I jumped forward and in front of me was a figure kneeling before a bag set against the stairs. He repeated a phrase over and over again: "*Credo in Deo omnipotente. Credo in Deo omnipotente...*"

"Don't fucking move," I screamed.

Calvin stepped around me and grabbed the man by the shoulder as I covered him. He pushed him down and cuffed him to the railing. "What's your name?" The man was silent as Ringo pulled the wallet out of his pants.

He stared at the driver's license and grinned. "Looks like we found Scipio," he said in a coat of smoke.

I stepped in front of Scipio. "Tell me about Anoesis." I could see a flicker of fear cross his eyes.

"I don't know...what that is," he mumbled, casting his head down and muttering words I couldn't hear.

I pulled him up and pulled off his jacket. Next came the shirt. I pointed at Ringo. "You got that black light?" Ringo pulled it out and turned it on. Scipio's arms and torso lit up with convex polyhedron–shaped tattoos with labeled intersections.

"What the fuck?" Calvin said.

"Ultraviolet tattoos," I answered. "Can only see them under black light. And look at that." I pointed at the large word tattooed across his chest: "Anoesis."

"You don't know about it, huh?" Calvin laughed.

"Please," Scipio pleaded. "Don't make me."

"What is Anoesis?" I asked again. "Tell us or we parade you up and down for the cameras as an informant."

"No!" Scipio cried. "I'm almost there. I need this."

I shook my head. "You think they're really going to re-create a nobody like you? No. No. No. You're only a servant. Not a chance."

Ringo kicked Scipio's leg. "What is Anoesis? Spit it out."

Scipio coughed and put a hand over his face. "It's a movement. A devotion to the concept of consciousness as sensation without the intrusion of thought. Nothing more and nothing less. Leader teaches us how to feel this way, every second of the night and day."

Calvin snorted. "What's the goal? What's the endgame?"

"Solipsism syndrome," Scipio muttered, almost a whisper.

"Excuse me?" Calvin said.

"Who's the leader?" I asked.

"I don't know—I swear. He is behind a shroud."

Calvin opened the bag on the ground. "I should have known." I looked over. Inside were vials of blood the size of wine bottles.

"Where are you taking those?" I asked.

Scipio stared at the ground.

"What's going on down there?" I demanded. "Are you taking these down to the tunnels?"

"Please, sir…"

"We're taking you down with us," I said as Scipio twisted in my arms.

"No!" he screamed. "You can't go down there. It is expressly forbidden! You don't realize what could happen. You cannot even begin to perceive what happens in there."

Ringo leaned against the wall to ponder our next move. Calvin moved next to me, with one eye on the prisoner. "You realize we can't go down there," he whispered. "It's not the safe move. Who knows how many Gloamings are down there waiting for their blood—which could turn into *our* blood?"

I thought about what he was saying even as I pretended to ignore it. Even with some meticulous preparation we had barely survived our last encounter with Cian Clery. This was even more sketchy. But we might not get another chance. I looked at Calvin and then Ringo. Ringo smiled his graveyard smile.

"Why not?" He shrugged.

Calvin shook his head and forced down a grin. "I knew the answer already. At least let me run up and call it in."

"Let's do it," I said with clapping hands as Calvin trotted up the stairs to make the call. And he was back down in less than five.

"What are we waiting for?" Calvin said with a twinkle in his eye.

We walked down the stairs until the door stood in front of us. Ringo pulled it open and Calvin moved first with his gun drawn. The tunnel was damp and dark save for a faint flickering light toward the east end, where it split into four other tunnel lines. We shuffled forward, close to the wall, and it became clear that the light was a controlled fire burning near where the tunnels split. The light flickered shadows on the walls and showed a group of at least ten people.

A shout came from the group and we hit the ground. A shot hit the wall next to my leg and I scooted up. Calvin, Ringo, and I returned fire as we rose up and ran to the other side of the tunnel wall that branched out in a westward direction.

A voice cried out, "Everyone stop shooting!" And I didn't know if he was talking to us or them. It seemed like such an odd thing to say at a time like this. We exchanged more gunfire and from the left I could see the golden locks of Cian Clery fighting with another figure in a black cloak, pushing and pulling.

From far behind I heard the thundering stampede of our backup rolling through the only door. With that, the group scattered, with footsteps echoing off the walls of the other four tunnels. I jumped up and ran toward the two fighting men. With a leap, I grabbed and pulled the mask off Cian. A large jagged scar ran down the side of his face, drooping that side like an avalanche. Like someone afflicted with Bell's palsy. He stared at me for a second before wrapping his hands around my neck. My body lifted off the ground with the raising of his arms and I could feel my neck stretching as the gun fell from my hands with a thud. So much for making the most of my second chance...I saw sparklers like the Fourth of July bouncing off the inside of my head before the other man knocked Cian in the jaw, and I was dropped to the floor.

From the ground I saw Cian dash down one of the tunnels as if he were never here. A group of agents tackled the Gloaming who saved my life and I stood up with shaking legs to hold up a hand. "Let him be for a moment."

They stood him up in front of me and I took a long hard look at the man I had never seen before. "Who are you?" I asked.

The man stood there with his mouth open slightly and a confused expression on his face, as if he could believe neither that he had saved me or that he was caught. "My name is Father John Reilly."

CHAPTER 25

Sara Mesley
The Order of Bruder Klaus

A lot of people hate looking at themselves naked in the mirror. But for me, it's how I count the months and years. Bullet scar on my left biceps? May. Knife wound, left calf? December. I am my own living—for now—diary. Ironically, I saw this dynamic a lot when I was a nurse at Johns Hopkins; when you're battling cancer or recovering from major surgery, it's hard to pay that much attention to what's in the mirror.

Once I heard a board member of the order lamenting the night sky and everything that came with it. Not me. Bring on the night. And on this moonless night, I was in Beijing, China, chasing the number one Gloaming on our list: the ten-year-old hermit Herjólfur Vilhjalmsson, who, according to our sources, had left the lava fields of Iceland for an unknown purpose. You would think it would be easy to find a white-haired child who "glowed" like the sun—witnesses were prone to grandiose exaggeration—but his handlers and believers seemed to be doing a masterful job of keeping him hidden.

I wandered through the city for an hour to ensure I wasn't being followed before I found myself in one of the older *hutongs*: Doujiao—"It's the Chinese Williamsburg!" Google stated on my map—where our safe house apartment was located.

Most Chinese, being atheist, did not consider Gloamings to be immoral or depraved, although there seemed to be a certain stigma attached to the few Chinese Gloamings, and they were viewed with caution. So most observers thought that the Chinese government would either treat them with indifference or welcome them as partners. However, for many of the elite in commerce and government, Gloamings were viewed as a threat to their interests. The Gloamings seemed to reciprocate the attitude.

I was therefore pretty sure that Chinese intelligence agencies were looking for Herjólfur Vilhjalmsson as determinedly as I was at the time.

When I entered our safe house, I saw a figure lying on the small cot, arms and legs open like a drunkard. The place looked like a frat house, with a mess of papers and old takeout boxes littering the floor and cabinets. I took a closer look and I recognized that face: Father Reilly. Good Lord, he looked like crap: tattered pants and a frayed dress shirt with a wool sport coat. He looked like he was going on his first job interview after a decade in prison. I kicked him in the leg, and he fell out of the cot and was up in seconds. I flicked on the light.

He recognized me pretty quickly after I took off my wool hat.

"Sara Mesley! Damn! You can't be doing that!"

"Why not?"

"I could have shot you."

I smirked at him and I don't think even he believed it. "With what?"

Reilly shook his head and walked into the kitchen. He pulled out a coffeepot and filled it with water before placing it over a lit range. "What are you even doing here?"

"I prefer my coffee pressed, by the way. I'm looking for Herjólfur Vilhjalmsson."

I could already tell he was in one of his depressive states about the current conflicts in New Mexico and abroad. And why we were so intent on finding this Gloaming child. Our conversations always seemed to bring up more questions than answers...

"Why does the order spend so much time on this kid?" Reilly said. "You're never going to find him. You'll find Liza Sole before you find him. We should be in New Mexico."

"We know where to find Liza Sole. It's simply a matter of getting inside. Anyway, this is the job—some missions are bigger, some are smaller. I'll do what it takes." I wondered how long it would take for that coffee to be in a cup—I could've used the caffeine.

Reilly fixed a stern gaze on me. "And you're not even religious. I can see Bernard and his gang—what they get out of it. But you..."

I straightened up and stared at him. "Not religious? I grew up, on my dad's side, with a family of Pentecostals from Maryland who spoke 'in tongues' for generations. Every week when I went to visit him, we would have to confess our sins in front of the congregation. It was mind-blowing."

"Oh my," Father Reilly said.

"Exactly!" I poked him in the chest. "That was enough religion for me. If I did that nowadays they would probably burn me at the stake. Even my father—devout as all get-out—refused to let me do the confessional after the one Sunday I confessed to the congregation about meeting a boy on a phone sex line—remember those?—and then hooking up with him after we went to his dealer's house to score some meth. And then fucked all night. Needless to say, my confession days were over."

Father Reilly looked up at the ceiling. "Why did I ask..."

"Well, there you go. You're right: it's not for religion. But I'd like to think I'm working for something good here. I'm not just bloodthirsty—pun intended. I do have my own ideas of what's right and what's wrong. And we're probably not that far from each other when you think about it, Father."

"But it's more important now," Reilly said, "with everything going on with that facility in New Mexico. I don't know where this is leading."

"It's leading to where it is now: war. I've been to New Mexico. Nobody knows what's going on there—the public doesn't know. They're stronger than we thought. And the politicians aren't prepared to sacrifice more of their own people over this. So they're trying the 'peaceful solution.' But the Gloamings don't think in those terms—"

"Some of them want peace also, Sara," Reilly said. "I can't believe I'm even saying this"—he looked pained—"but it's something that should be at least attempted."

"No. No, no. We tried that. Look where it got us. Now all the countries are making concessions and the Gloamings are taking them. The Basques and the Bavarians have been trying for a separate homeland for hundreds of years and the Gloamings get it in less than five? Denmark is even floating a proposal to give the Gloamings the Faroe Islands! If they contribute meaningfully to the country!"

"That's why New Mexico is more important." Reilly actually

looked ready to cry. If I had known then where he would end up—what would become of him, who he'd become—I might have paid more attention. I might have saved him from himself.

"I'll weep for the dead before I'll celebrate a land of Gloamings. Even if it means peace."

Around we went. A cluttered rest was all I could hope for this night.

The next day brought me more of a purpose. I was happy to be out on these streets, with just the air and noise around me. Our informants had told us about Herjólfur's recent addiction to cupping, some weird alternative medicine where suction is created on the skin with special cups—it's supposed to help with blood flow and ailments—made from a rare Chinese bamboo. I just knew he wouldn't miss an opportunity to engage in this therapy while he was here, if he was indeed in this country.

My inquiries brought me to an old cupping therapist, who had mastered this art, in an ancient part of the old capital. After searching these streets for hours, I found myself down a dark, crowded alley when I saw a flicker of light amid the darkness. White hair flapping in the wind, body partially covered by a blanket and coat, walking in the middle of a phalanx of large guards.

There. I could smell him. Bring on the night.

By the time events began to move in one direction, I was all in. I felt my own existence tied into the goals of the order. The news came in swiftly: Pope Victor II announced that the prefect of the Congregation for the Doctrine of the Faith, Cardinal Alexander Naro, had been re-created.

Established in 1542, the Congregation for the Doctrine of the

Faith was the oldest of the congregations of the Roman Curia—the administrative entity of the Vatican. The mission of the office was to "spread sound Catholic doctrine and defend those points of Christian tradition which seem in danger because of new and unacceptable doctrines." It was simply the most powerful and influential office at the Vatican, and well known for establishing policy for the Pope in almost all areas. Cardinal Naro was a force of nature on his own: he was conspicuous in his presence and frequently known on various forms of media, in addition to being extremely well traveled.

I felt the anger from my fellow guerrillas, although I didn't have the visceral awareness that they were experiencing. They didn't know if it was from relief that it wasn't the Pope who had been re-created or from despair that Cardinal Naro had. His explanation left them hollow: he wanted to minister to the new species as he did with humans; he wanted to welcome them into the church; he wanted to show that we were all the same species; he wanted to foster an openness among all peoples; he wanted to have many more years to complete his goals for the church…

After a period of mourning came confusion and then rage. This cardinal was much too close to the Pope. The level of influence he had on the church was unrivaled. This is exactly what the third letter had warned the church about, but they did not pay heed. Thus began the era dubbed by Vatican historians as *vulgaris aerae*.

Our biggest concern and opportunity would be the College of Cardinals. The College of Cardinals consisted of the entire group of cardinals in the Catholic Church. Their duties encompassed advising the Pope and, most importantly, choosing a new pope in the event of death or resignation. They were the senior leaders of the church and carried significant respect within the congregations of the Catholic

Church. Of course, I never thought that I would be immersing myself in the inner workings of an established church—struggling with my faith, whatever that was—on a daily basis. Some days I would be accosted by an event or some natural beauty and think, *There must be a Creator who conceived of all of this*. And other days there'd be a similar event and my thoughts would become, *Everything has been a farce; let me just ride it out in my own way*. To quote a wise man: "Oh well. Whatever. Never mind…"

Regardless, it was imperative that we determine the mood of the college regarding the re-creation of Naro.

Pope Victor himself must have realized the precarious position he was in within the church after his announcement. Bishop Thomas himself surmised that Pope Victor could not have known what the cardinals' opinion would be about the re-creation before he condoned it—that would have taken individual calls to each cardinal to gauge their opinion, and if he had done that the information would have leaked way before his announcement. It had to have been a rather impulsive decision coerced by a man seduced by the glamour and promises of the Gloamings. The real question would be how they got so close to him to make their offers.

Years later, an investigation by a *New York Times* reporter, Jon Caramanica, would name one of the papal butlers as the person who made the first attempts to get Cardinal Naro to meet some Gloaming representatives without the knowledge of the Vatican staff. It took a lot of luck, persistence, and coordination, but that was how determined they were to legitimize themselves within society.

Bishop Thomas would attempt to contact every single one of the cardinals—many of whom he had met or knew personally—to understand where they stood on the issue. Thomas felt that the Gloamings would eventually intend to kill the Pope and install one of their own as his replacement. As of that day, there were 222 members of the College of Cardinals, although only 120 of them were eligible to participate in the conclave that was to choose a new pope.

The bishop brought up another wrinkle and obstacle to this plan: a pope is authorized to name new cardinals and also cardinals in pectore—secret cardinals that are not known to the public, or anyone else, for that matter. A new pope may begin to name new cardinals and secret cardinals loyal to him only as a way of stacking the college in his favor. We agreed that going public with our grievances was essential in order to gain momentum and stall any of the new pope's efforts to possibly name new cardinals.

After a few months, the lines began to draw themselves as a distinct majority of the College of Cardinals expressed their disapproval of Naro's re-creation. In fact, it was probably more cardinals than we'd expected, as many declined to comment, which we now can assume was in itself disapproval. News organizations attempted to contact every cardinal to document his disapproval or approval of Naro's re-creation. Pope Victor himself gave a surprisingly muted response to the disapproval from the cardinals. He delivered a message to the church that such divisions would not weaken the church, and that prayer and God's will shall change all minds.

Of course, I didn't believe that. I knew that Naro was using the Pope to bide his time to either coerce the cardinals into supporting him or get rid of them and name new ones that would support him unconditionally. Several of our sources relayed to us that Cardinal Naro was preparing a new canonical judgment entitled "Doctrinal Assessment of the Universality of the Gloaming People *Donum Vitae*." It appeared to be a document to prepare the congregation for the full participation and acceptance of the Gloaming species. There were rumors that the Pope was livid that certain cardinals would conspire against him and Naro. Therefore, the order felt that we needed to intensify our efforts to have Naro resign his position.

Luckily for us there were many Catholics who shared our opinion, and the donations given to the order were more than enough to grow our organization. We soon hired a staff to coordinate our efforts. We were extremely strict in our hiring practices to keep out any spies from the Vatican looking to infiltrate the order. More importantly, we began to have many laypersons and priests come to Phoenix to volunteer for our organization. However, there were some people and groups who, although they supported our goals, did not think we were the proper organization to correct the wrongs of the current Vatican administration and move forward to keep our church free from Gloamings.

I still felt somewhat separate from the organization. It was like I had married into a family that didn't really trust me. And being a woman still left me on the outside of many of the strategic planning sessions.

I suppose at this point you would like me to address how the Order of Bruder Klaus came to be considered a terrorist organization by the United Nations.

The call to arms to protect our church came with an announcement from the Pope that he had named twenty-five new cardinals. This was a month after Naro re-created. We all knew that this meant he, with Naro's influence, was well on his way to stacking the College of Cardinals in his favor so that he, or more plausibly Naro, could be crowned as a new re-created pope for a couple of hundred years with no opposition. This was simply the point of no return for the order.

During this period of time, the Gloamings were still at the height of their persuasive efforts, assuring everyone that they only wanted what was best for the world and engaging in various charitable endeavors. People chose to ignore the fact that most of their membership was increasingly restricted to the top 1 percent—wealth, looks, and talent seemed to be the main criteria. But they were successful in convincing people that they wanted to pursue only positive change as their goal.

Hard to believe when their presence in any given area left a string of dead bodies devoid of blood. Of course, they claimed to have no knowledge of these incidents, dismissing them as local and isolated criminal activity with no connection to themselves. Yet this was exactly how they fed. The Gloamings claimed to feed off what they bought from blood banks and from animal blood, but it was scientifically proven that they needed fresh blood from a human to sustain their lives. They needed to feel the fresh blood pumping into their mouth from a human heart. We suspected for quite a while that their plan was to take over the entire population and use us as feeding farms for their colonizing race. This was proven. In spite of their claims, they never truly prepared to assimilate into proper society.

We began to institute a secret department of the order aimed at finding ways to terminally eradicate the Gloamings. The program started initially as just one of many contingency plans. Only as a last resort. The order began a study of all that was known concerning Gloaming physiology. Given their unique regeneration ability and enhanced strength, it would take various uncommon weapons to terminally eradicate the Gloamings.

The only true surefire weapon was a gun armed with 70 percent uranium bullets. Nine-millimeter uranium bullets, to be exact. No one has yet scientifically determined why uranium bullets to the heart will incinerate a bloodsucker, but the fact that uranium bullets are self-sharpening and flammable may have a lot to do with it. On impact, the subsequent release of heat energy causes the bullet to ignite—at least that's what Wikipedia reported—and they did an amazing job against the Gloamings.

Needless to say, this would be the weapon of choice for our order. The manufacture of the bullets would be another point of contention because of the continued sabotage of the factories that constructed them.

We decided to create the bullets at an underground complex—in secret, of course. It was the only way to ensure the continued manufacture of our only protection. I always thought it was a bad idea—I mean, anything underground helps the Gloamings—but my suggestions went nowhere. They did thank me, though—what a benchmark in gender equality that was.

It wasn't easy, or entirely "legal," to find the depleted uranium necessary for the bullets, but there were many Eastern European Catholic countries that were sympathetic to our cause and more than willing to fulfill our orders for the uranium, although our process was much smaller and therefore the yield was constrained.

We were actually quite proud of our manufacturing process. Many of our monks perfected the casing and molds we used to create the bullet, and the actual design was a closely held secret. The method was not automated, however; it took a significant amount of time to create each bullet. In the facility, there were a series of lathes and monks who worked them twenty-four hours a day on shifts. Another area housed the monks who made the molten metal to create the nine-millimeter bullets. We were ever mindful of the dangers of the uranium and so the finishing mold and metal die were placed in a radiation-protected facility and the workers wore the latest in radiation-protection gear. There was graded-Z shielding on all facilities—a shield that effectively scattered protons and electrons and absorbed gamma rays. It was the safest shielding available. Exits on all facilities had installed radiation monitors to detect any leaks or sudden surges in radiation.

The order began the stockpile of weapons and ammunition for defense purposes originally. I'm not going to pretend that we didn't envision a time when it might be used for offensive purposes, but truly that wasn't the first intention.

Our first mission began with intelligence we gathered at the Vatican. You have to understand that the Vatican bureaucracy is unwieldy—impossible to navigate, let alone scale. The order, from our inception, cultivated many employees of the Vatican—not just priests but support staff as well—to be our sources. Even the janitorial staff were an important avenue of information.

The rumors came first from our priests in the Vatican: the Pope had secretly named three new cardinals ten days before and would be announcing them in three days. Prior to this, the Pope had not been seen in public in about two weeks, which was highly unusual. His nightly speeches had been canceled with no reason given, so the order was already on edge, preparing for any rumor or announcement given this odd silence and behavior, which indicated a major announcement was due.

I myself sat in front of a bank of television and computer screens, all monitoring the news, while taking calls from our various informants at the Vatican and compiling the information into a database so that the senior staff could disseminate the latest reports to everyone.

When we heard the rumor and confirmed that it was true, the order convened a meeting of the executive council. The council discussed various steps that might be taken as a response to this measure—anything from declining to recognize the new cardinals to staging protests at the Vatican and the home countries of the new cardinals.

The department head said that he had some urgent information for all of us: one of our sources had definitively reported that the three new cardinals were to be re-created when they met with the Pope in three days. This, of course, was the final straw. I could see the plan unfolding for the Pope and Naro. Unable to garner the support of the clergy and even the laypeople, the Pope was going to undertake more drastic measures: stacking the College of Cardinals with Gloamings.

I couldn't imagine such a scenario borne to its completion. In practice, this would transform the church as we knew it and not simply from a theological perspective. A Gloaming pope and his acolytes would rule the church and subsequent generations for hundreds of years. I don't remember who brought it up first— probably myself—but terminal measures were raised to the group.

Surprisingly, it took only about half an hour for the council to agree to assassinate the three cardinals before they could be formally named. We probably should have considered all of the legal and moral ramifications of such an act but there simply wasn't the time. The order knew that all members could be held responsible and could face significant prison time—or execution— if our efforts were to be uncovered.

The next surprise was being called into the meeting and told that I would be leading the group on the mission. They thought, and I agreed, that a woman dressed as a nun might be more inconspicuous on a mission that demanded stealth. Maybe I was expendable or maybe they wanted to push for gender equality. Sure…Hey, the order didn't have a monopoly on hypocrisy.

Of course, coming to an agreement proved to be the easiest part. I had three days to prepare a plan—more specifically, a plan that could be implemented successfully.

I contacted our sources at the Vatican to find the private itinerary—where the cardinals would be every hour of their visit. And most importantly, where they would be sleeping. This proved to be quite easy. We knew that there were plots to build Gloaming-safe underground housing at the Vatican, but only the architectural plans had been approved—no construction had begun.

From there we were sent the plans of the house where they would be staying at the Vatican. The security and staff details at the residence were the only questions regarding the plan. Those details were kept highly classified by the Vatican, and our sources could not find out any information about them. Therefore, we did not know what we would encounter upon entering the residence. The preparations had to include a worst-case scenario of overwhelming security.

The order enlisted Father Mark Rogers in the plan. Father Mark eagerly accepted the challenge, and the results if successful. He was still employed at the Vatican but this time assigned to the small Vatican infirmary. Rogers immediately began to establish reconnaissance and cultivate a few more sources among the staff at the villa where the cardinals would be staying.

I was picked up by an Escalade with blacked-out windows in front of a bus stop near a Home Depot. The driver didn't say a word to me as he took me to a private gate located at Phoenix Sky Harbor Airport, about twenty miles away. Things began to proceed quickly as I boarded a private jet owned, I would later learn, by a wealthy stockholder of a fashion design company and a member of our legion of supporters. The plane seemed eerily quiet so I walked to the cockpit and opened the door to see why everything was so silent. The lone pilot glanced back at me and then returned to his equipment. Another professional focusing only on the task at hand. I could relax now.

The coordinator of the plan knew of a small airstrip owned by a farmer and his wife where I could land and have my equipment unloaded without any disruption from the Italian police. As another fail-safe procedure, the farmer had a brother in the Mafia who would be willing to provide the services of corrupt members of the Italian federal police force if they were needed.

The plane arrived without a hitch, seven hours after our initial meeting, in the cover of darkness. The weapons and other materials were housed in large black bags and carried by grim-faced farmhands who placed them in a small VW van; an old barrel-chested man wearing a tweed hat and overalls was in the driver's seat. The old man drove me in silence to the outskirts of the Vatican and stopped at an old stone-and-beam four-story residential building with a pizzeria on the ground floor.

I saw who I assumed to be Father Mark at the street corner downing the last of a slice of pizza, a beer in his other hand, and I could not have been less surprised at the sight. He nodded and walked over to help me take the two bags from the back of the car. After I closed the trunk, the car took off into the night.

"By God—they really sent a woman," Father Mark said with a grin.

"By God—they sent me a drunk," I replied.

Father Mark nodded again. "Well, let's get you inside and see if we can turn you into a nun."

He led me inside the old nineteenth-century building and to the second floor and a sparsely furnished apartment with no occupants. It was filled with a simple bed and couch, with no table. A musty smell pervaded the entire space.

"Who lives here?" I asked.

"Some scumbag monsignor," Father Mark said. "It's where he keeps his young ladies of ill repute." He noticed my disgusted reaction. "Ah, but it's hard for me to summon much outrage when all I can think is that I'm happy he's not trying to suck the blood out of them."

"Very funny," I remarked. "Should be good karma for my mission."

"Since when did you start believing in karma?"

"Today."

Father Mark grinned. "Gallows humor, my future nun. Keep it up. Let's see if you're still laughing when they're pointing guns at us or trying to suck all the blood from our bodies."

I didn't say anything out loud, but he had a point.

We spent the next two hours fitting me into a habit, scapular, and coif. It was more body constricting than any clothing I had ever worn. I didn't know how I was going to have a full range of motion in this ridiculous outfit but it would have to do.

It was at that point that we took the guns and placed them in our holsters beneath our tunics. They would not be easy to pull out but we weren't expecting any surprises before the mission started.

As the sun rose, we took off on foot for the Vatican. I would spend the morning at the Vatican museum, taking in the sights until the late afternoon, when Father Mark would leave work and take me to a vacant office in the communications building. We took a chance doing the operation at night, when the Gloamings were active, but we needed the cardinals to be up and in the residence and not underground sleeping in some pit. In addition, there would be less traffic and light—less chance for us to be seen conducting our plan.

The dark night breeze whipped cold against my face as we walked to the residence next to the villa. Father Mark unlocked a one-room first-floor office that he knew would be unoccupied. He kept the light off and we took seats next to the window. From here we would have a clear view of the villa.

The plan called for us to wait until later that night to make our move. I opened one of the sandwiches from the food bag Father Mark had packed for us to get us through most of the night. I took a sip of the coffee and it was cold but it would serve its purpose for now. Father Mark moved his chair to the corner and prayed. I found it impossible to keep my mind on anything, least of all prayer. I kept running the song "Wouldn't It Be Nice" by the Beach Boys in my head and it was making my heart beat faster, and my nerves seemed to be fraying at the edges.

Of course, drinking cup after cup of strong Italian coffee didn't help either. I glanced at the clock on the desk and it read eleven thirty in the evening. Time to move. I harbored some doubts about the plan but any concern was a luxury at this point. Conducting it at night, when we had strong evidence that the cardinals were now Gloamings, meant they would certainly be awake at this time and on guard. But a daytime attack would mean that the entire Vatican apparatus would be awake and at work. It was a bigger risk to take.

I took out a pair of binoculars and scanned the third floor of the villa. Obviously, the shades were drawn and no light could be seen from any of the windows. In fact, it seemed that the windows were covered in some kind of black paint. I could not make it out.

I felt Father Mark come stand next to me. "I'm guessing no action up there," he said.

"It's locked up tight," I answered, "but we already knew that. I think it's time for us to do this."

Father Mark nodded with a serious look on his face. "No better time." I noticed that he had changed into a mechanic's jumpsuit, the better to blend in as one of the many workers that came in and out of the area.

At this point, I could only think of a quote we had studied in one of my military classes, from the first chapter of Edward Gibbon's *The History of the Decline and Fall of the Roman Empire:* "In the second century of the Christian era, the Empire of Rome comprehended the fairest part of the earth, and the most civilized portion of mankind. The frontiers of that extensive monarchy were guarded by ancient renown and disciplined valor. The gentle but powerful influence of laws and manners had gradually cemented the union of the provinces. Their peaceful inhabitants enjoyed and abused the advantages of wealth, comfort, and luxury. The image of a free constitution was preserved with decent reverence: the Roman senate appeared to possess the sovereign authority, and devolved on the emperors all the executive powers of government. During a happy period—A.D. 98 to 180—of more than fourscore years, the public administration was conducted by the virtue and abilities of Nerva, Trajan, Hadrian, and the two Antonines. It is the design of this, and of the two succeeding chapters, to describe the prosperous condition of their empire; and afterwards, from the death of Marcus Antoninus, to deduce the most important circumstances of its decline and fall; a revolution which will ever be remembered, and is still felt by the nations of the earth."

I feared that if we failed, such words might be written about the Catholic Church and about all other free governments that valued morality and the goodness of their people.

We walked out the service exit of the building. The lights which usually surrounded the building were completely shut off— courtesy of myself and a small old-fashioned BB gun. The darkness was welcome at this point but I would fear it more as we entered the field of battle.

We strolled to the service entrance of the villa. We had no key, so I muscled the door open with a specially crafted door handle screwdriver. The door opened without much of a sound and there was no alarm—it made sense, given the wandering occupants and the temporary residential aspect of the building. Lucky again.

We separated at this point, with Father Mark making his way to the fire escape, where on my signal he would force his way in the window nearest the bedroom where the cardinals were housed.

I walked cautiously down the wooden floors of the hallway, moving on my toes to avoid making any noise. I was surprised by the lack of security even on the first floor, but our sources informed us that the prospective cardinals were attempting to keep an extremely low profile until after the re-creation ceremony. My gun in its holster was stacked with the depleted uranium bullets because I was not sure if there were any Gloamings with the future cardinals—for all we knew even the other cardinals could be Gloamings by now. Additionally, I outfitted a custom silencer in case I had to eliminate any bystanders before I found the cardinals.

Our intelligence was certain that the three prospective cardinals would be occupying the same room at the end of the hallway on the third floor. On the second floor, I dropped to my knees and waited a long ten minutes as I scanned each side of the hallway in the darkness. No one to be seen or heard on the second floor. I peered up the stairs and saw the door that separated the residential portion of the villa.

A few more steps and I reached the door and caught my breath. I guessed there was no AC in these old buildings, along with the lack of security and detection devices. Luckily again, the eighteenth-century lock could be easily tripped with the modified screwdriver. I opened the door slowly and strained to see down each hallway.

This hallway was lit, even though the lighting was dim. I saw one man in a black suit sitting in a chair nearest the last room—the room I assumed to be where the cardinals were staying.

The man in the black suit read from an iPad and the glow bounced off his bearded face. I closed the door and took another deep breath. Feeling a bit steadier, I shook my head, desperately wanting to rip the constricting fabric from my head. I tapped the screwdriver on the door about fifteen times, then stepped to the hinge side of the door. The footsteps came louder toward me on the other side as I pulled the gun from the holster and held it next to my chest.

The door opened and a man's head poked around to stare at the lock and I knew he was wondering why the lock was broken and where that noise had come from. My hand shook as I lifted the gun up to meet his face and pulled the trigger, the surprise shining from his eyes. And I have never forgotten that sight—I remember every single one since the first. The silencer fizzed like a just-opened soda and the blood splattered across the wall and onto my face. I stepped back as the man's body tumbled down the stairs like a rock skipping over a clear lake and hit the iron railing on the second floor.

I leaned against the wall and caught my breath for a few minutes before taking out a handkerchief and wiping the blood off my face for some reason. All it did was smear, as if I were wearing a horrible mask. I hadn't felt like this in a long time, and like all the others I swore it would be the last time. My hand pushed the door open and I skipped down the hall to the last room. Breaking the lock was not an option given that it would be discovered, so I simply knocked on the door twice, hoping that the people inside would assume it was the guard.

After about thirty seconds, the door opened and I pulled the trigger before my brain registered who had their hand on the doorknob. I hit the ground in case my bullets had just ripped through a Gloaming—their tendency upon impact is to have a harmful blast radius of a couple of feet due to their unique anatomical structure and latent radiation. The trigger pulled back a few times and I shot a couple of bullets at the west window— the plan was for Father Mark to be waiting, crouched outside the window, for me to blast it open so he could come inside.

After a quick prayer that Father Mark wasn't dumb enough to stand in front of the window, I pointed my gun at the opening door to the right of me. Two figures stepped out, one holding a bottle of Scotch in a crystal decanter and the other holding two glasses—and I hoped that once this was over someone would be pouring one for me—and I pulled the trigger as Father Mark jumped into the room from the shattered window and the fire escape, with his gun drawn.

At this point, it simply felt as if we were acting out a dream, someone's dream. One of the two figures near the door, struck by a bullet, burst into flames like an ignition or a grenade. The heat blast covered me like a blanket. I rolled over as Father Mark cracked two men coming out of the other bedroom. They fell to the ground without an explosion. I rose up and pointed my gun at the open bedroom door to the right of the sitting room. Father Mark stepped inside the other bedroom and called out that the room was clear.

The only conclusion that could be drawn at this point was that the targets were in this second bedroom. I heard movement in the bedroom in front of me and stepped slowly into the doorframe. One of the cardinals stood in the corner, and as I raised the pistol he let out a high-pitched scream like I had never heard. I hesitated and reeled back from the noise as he leapt toward me and knocked me to the ground and then jumped away. Behind him was another prospective cardinal in red, and he followed the other. Father Mark pumped him full of bullets but he dove through the window with a crash.

Father Mark and I stood looking out the window but the cardinals were nowhere to be seen. A loud siren could be heard coming closer, along with shouting voices from down the street.

"I can't believe we missed that fucking Gloaming," I said almost to myself as I pushed my gun back in its holster. "We need to get out of here."

Father Mark nodded his head and we opened the front door and walked into the hallway. I stopped and held my arm out so Father Mark would not move. Voices from downstairs and the sounds of doors slamming filtered up to us. Father Mark glanced at me.

"Police," I said. "Get to the fire escape."

He nodded and steered me to the middle room—the main room was not safe, given that the broken window would be an inviting target to the police when they arrived on the scene. The door was unlocked and we walked into an empty living room and bedroom. I closed the door behind us and figured we had less than three minutes before Italian and Vatican security started breaking down each door on every floor, including this one. We marched over to the window nearest the large king bed. It seemed to be facing the quieter, eastern side of the building.

Father Mark opened the window as I guarded the door with my gun drawn. I could feel the cold air from the open window as Father Mark scanned the outside area. He nodded at me and stepped out onto the fire escape as the voices grew louder in the hallway and I heard the unmistakable sound of a door being kicked open. I knew they would be kicking down this door in seconds.

Out on the fire escape I thought to close the window behind

me, hoping that they wouldn't notice anything amiss that would lead them to a mechanic and a crazy nun outside on the fire escape. We made our way down the escape in a deliberate manner, taking each step in silence. I was already trying to think ahead. By now I imagined that most exits in the Vatican would be sealed off. We jumped off the metal grate to the ground and slipped down toward the dark trees nearest the medical building.

From there Father Mark opened the padlock on the steel flooring nearest the back service entrance. We both went inside and took the ladder down about twenty feet. At this point, Father Mark removed his one-piece mechanic's jumpsuit and grinned at me like he had just won a ticket to paradise.

"If you're up for it we should do it again sometime," I whispered. And I wasn't sure if he could hear and I didn't know whether I wanted him to, but he gave me one nod of his head as he climbed back up the ladder and then took off on a stroll in his casual priest garb. I was certain he would be nursing a pint within the hour.

I heard the door bang shut and the padlock click in place. He would head back to his apartment in Rome and be back at work the next day—looking a bit more tired but clear of mind and spirit. I'd made a brief and unsuccessful attempt to convince him to return with me to the order's headquarters. He said that his life was still there at the Vatican and that there were many more like him in its employ who supported the true church and could make a difference.

And he felt that if we did this job correctly no one would ever find out he was a part of it. I couldn't have disagreed more as to his safety, but his mind was made up.

As I jogged down the tunnel I switched on my flashlight. After only several minutes the well-made stone tunnels of Vatican City gave way to the earthen tunnels of Rome. I smiled. In the dark and fetid gloom, the brand-new ladder was right where it was supposed to be. I looked up at the open hole and saw the same farmer who had driven me from the airport waving me up with his usual dour expression.

From there it began as the official policy of the order. We decided to take action against any attempt to subvert and alter the beliefs of our church—to take the church back to its original purpose. The bombing of the Windwood Retreat in Mexico City was what really put us on the United Nations list of terrorist organizations. I don't regret that operation. The night creeps were having another illicit gathering designed to stack the College of Cardinals and ensure that the Vatican would be transformed into a haven for the Gloamings. So, no, I don't regret it. But did I feel a sense of accomplishment? Was I proud of killing? I felt what anyone would feel who was caught up in this war—and yes, this is a war—which was that I was building on hope. Hope for a world of truth over corruption, with safety over harm. I was building on the good work of others, I suppose, even if I gave away some of my soul to do so. Maybe if I lost my soul, I still had my integrity.

Chapter 26

Father John Reilly
Operative, the Order of Bruder Klaus

Department of Justice—DIRECTIVE:

SUBJECT: Suspect interview with Father John Reilly
Detainee was captured in **REDACTED** at an undetermined
location of a tunnel underneath downtown Chicago.
Detainee was transferred to a holding facility at
REDACTED. Immediately interviewed by the supervising
field agent.
Detainee was taken to modified Gloaming interrogation
room of which there are five, located in New York City,
Dallas, Chicago, Los Angeles, and Miami.
Following protocol level six interviews, Detainee is being
held for continued interrogation while U.S. secretary of
defense maintains DEFCON 2 status nationwide. Special
agent in charge of Gloaming Crimes Unit, Hugo Zumthor,
has activated all field agents in response and has assumed

control of interview. Top secret security clearance is required for the following transcript.

Transcript tracks with stenographer operator.

Zumthor: Well, you actually are a Catholic priest, it appears.

Father Reilly: I am.

Zumthor: So how does a priest end up with a group of Gloamings forming their own cult? Sounds like the beginning of a joke.

Father Reilly: Or the punch line.

Agent James enters the room.

James: I've been told by someone in the Justice Department that CIA and Homeland Security will be here within the hour. You're gonna be big-time, my friend.

Agent James leaves the room.

Zumthor: Guess we better cut to the chase. When did you meet your first Gloaming?

Father Reilly: You don't know?

Zumthor: Know what?

Father Reilly: I'm a member of the Order of Bruder Klaus.

Agent Zumthor rises from the chair and sits on the table.

Zumthor: Seems counterintuitive, but to be fair, what do I know? Well, then, tell me how you re-created. Let's start there.

Subject says nothing. Holds agent's stare for twenty-four seconds.

Father Reilly: Okay. I'll start in the middle. I was sent to one of our safe houses at Mont-Saint-Michel.

Zumthor: What is that?

Father Reilly: It's a small island off the coast of France. The island is about a mile and a half from the shoreline. On it is a monastery that resembles a castle, like something from Game of Thrones, and one block with some shops and houses. Pretty much takes up the entire island. It's a nice tourist place to visit if you're so inclined. The cool thing about it is it has a natural defense—you can walk to the island from the shore at low tide but at high tide it turns into a natural moat. Got to have a boat then.

Zumthor: Looking forward to visiting. Go on

Father Reilly: I normally sleep during the day, for obvious reasons—at that time I was so worried about being attacked by a Gloaming, I felt I needed to be on guard at night. But it was December, and it was so cold, and I wasn't feeling well, and I was on the run, and jet lag had me messed up—so I fell asleep at about eight in the evening on this old crooked cot shoved up against the stone wall.

Well, I woke up at one in the morning with someone's hand on my chest.

Zumthor: Who was it?

Father Reilly: Liza Sole.

Zumthor: No shit! Bet that was a kick in the gut. Surprised I'm even looking at you.

Father Reilly: Yup. At first I thought I was dreaming. Then I was already giving myself last rites, while kicking myself for slipping so badly. My heart was going nuts. I had many nightmares about this happening.

Zumthor: What did she do?

Father Reilly: She patted me on the chest, then walked over to a chair and sat down.

Zumthor: Hard to believe.

Father Reilly: No one was more surprised than myself.

Zumthor: What happened next?

Father Reilly: We talked, Agent Zumthor.

Zumthor: Really? What could you two possibly talk about?

Father Reilly: [**Sighs**.] Everything. Life. I had so many questions. I wanted to know how she lived. What were her days like? Every day was different to her. Since she is to live so long she has time to see everything around her. To notice everything in existence. To feel everything. She told me about how her concept of time and memory had changed forever. Simple objects and actions seemed to make themselves more aware to her senses. She felt that communication among Gloamings seemed so difficult, and there was a growing concern that many Gloamings were afflicted with solipsism syndrome, which was making them more isolated over time. Oppressive loneliness. They seemed to have a certain detachment illness brought on by all the changes in their minds and bodies—it forced them to concentrate on cultivating and understanding their own minds to the detriment of interpersonal relationships.

They also, which I previously didn't know, spoke in a contrapuntal manner with each other, and only each other.

Zumthor: What does that mean?

Father Reilly: They speak over each other in a fast style, like they anticipate what the other is going to say. Similar to how two music lines are played at the same time in some songs. Like Mozart, or African polyrhythms. Very interesting process.

Zumthor: I suppose she left the part out about sucking blood from innocent humans.

Subject sits in silence. Stares at agent.

Zumthor: So what did Liza Sole do during her travels? Did she say?

Father Reilly: Liza would hitchhike to large and small cities. She never really acted like she was on the run. Her way of living was deliberate—casual, I guess. Nights spent in bars, libraries, or coffeehouses, looking for people to vibe with. Live music got her blood roiling, with musicians being her weakness. The long hair, the weird hygiene, the tortured personality. They followed her like puppies.

Zumthor: Not quite the upstanding lifestyle these Gloamings like to claim they have. So, why were you at the monastery?

Father Reilly: At the time, I was waiting for Sara Mesley to arrive.

Zumthor: Talk about throwing gasoline on a fire. Why?

Father Reilly: I don't know. Still don't. She wanted a meeting. I assumed she was bringing plans for a new mission.

Zumthor: I bet. Okay, so what happened after you bonded with Liza?

Father Reilly: She asked me to leave with her.

Zumthor: Leave with her? Where?

Father Reilly: To her next destination. Obviously she had to keep moving, being the most wanted person—anywhere. There wasn't much time. She initially wanted to go to the village of Courtils, where there was a farm with a large basement so she could stay until it was time for her next location.

I don't know why I said yes. I sat there staring at her for such a long time. Who knows if my mind would have changed given days, months, or years? Today I still couldn't tell you. Maybe it was a chance to see beyond the dogma of my present life. Could faith overcome? Was this the true test I had been waiting for?

Zumthor: So you left?

Father Reilly: If it were only that easy. We had talked for so long that time had drifted from our minds and we were forced to rush in order to beat the sunrise. Liza checked her watch and stood up without a word. She stared at me with a blank expression before a grin broke out and I couldn't say a word either. My mind was clear. I stood up with her and we walked out the door. This was happening. It was then that I realized the high tide was coming in, and then everything changed...

Zumthor: What happened?

Father Reilly: Then Sara Mesley showed up. We made our way to the outdoor stone stairway that circled the monastery from the outside. The moon was bright and you could see the entire island lit up like a stage. Halfway down I heard a shout from above: "Reilly!" I didn't want to look but my head shot up and there was Sara staring down at me from the top of the stairs and viewing platform.

I'll never forget the look on her face.

Zumthor: Anger?

Father Reilly: I wish it were that simple. Betrayal. That was first. Then pain. Then finally anger.

Zumthor: And you left?

Father Reilly: Sara took off like a missile. We all knew she was something to reckon with. The high tide was coming in and the normally walkable sand was taken over by the ocean as we jumped off the island and ran. Neither of us was expecting to be chased by a maniac warrior either.

I couldn't keep up with Liza but she stayed next to me as the water reached my knees, my waist, my chest. My legs were barely churning. It felt like they were weighted down with lead, and the salt water splashed my face and burned my mouth as I gulped for air. In a moment, the water fell over my head and I dove forward into the ocean with my arms cutting the waves in a half-assed swim.

After about ten feet my arms felt encased in cement, and I was forced to stop and float to catch my breath. Three bullets cut through the water near my head, and I could barely be bothered to move as Liza pulled me into her arms and swam forward.

I turned my head and there was Sara, maybe fifty yards away, churning those arms like there was a gold medal waiting at the finish line. We fell upon the shore, drenched in water and covered by sand, and even Liza had to catch a few breaths before moving on. We ran to a motorcycle Liza had parked—

Zumthor: Of course—a fucking motorcycle. How apropos.

Father Reilly: Fits the image, I'll admit. We hopped on and went straight to Andorra.

Zumthor: Never heard of it.

Father Reilly: It's actually—strangely enough—a sovereign city-state near the border of France and Spain. It's located deep within the mountains. Great natural defenses.

Zumthor: All clear, then.

Father Reilly: Not really. Sara must have stolen a car or something, but she was on us from the get. We ended up at a farmhouse in the mountains.

Zumthor: What then?

Father Reilly: We waited for a week until a freighter

arrived to take us to New York City.

Zumthor: New York? Why?

Subject pauses, looks down at his shackled hands.

Father Reilly: To meet with Cian Clery.

Zumthor: Is that a fact?

Subject nods.

Zumthor: Why?

Father Reilly: At the time I did not know.

Zumthor: Did she know him?

Father Reilly: She re-created him.

Agent says nothing. Opens his mouth and closes it. Subject nods slowly.

Father Reilly: I know. Liza was kind of vague about a lot of the details, although she mentioned that when she was on the run, she felt absolutely drawn to the city of New Orleans. No reason given, but she had to go there no matter the obstacle. In late summer, Liza arrived in New Orleans, staying at a late-eighteen-hundreds Creole town house on Saint Charles Avenue. The house contained an extensive and elaborate basement and was owned by a widowed architect who had retired but kept himself busy with different causes and volunteer work. He was also a fervent supporter of Gloaming rights and extremely discreet. After he completed extensive renovations to the basement, his property had been used frequently to house Gloamings who visited New Orleans during the inception of the virus.

Liza spent her nights cultivating oleanders to prepare for her tea. One night she was clipping leaves from the plant in the bright moonlight when Cian Clery appeared before her with a camel hair backpack slung over his shoulder and dirty clothes hanging off his thin body.

"You brought the locusts," Liza said with a smile, showing him the pockmarked leaves she was cutting off.

Cian nodded. "I'll make up for it with this fresh honey I took from a hive in Florida."

From that point, he stayed. During this time, there were new issues that were affecting Liza's situation and her ability to move freely. Now, the order would have you believe that Liza was behind the purchase of property in Borgo—the fourteenth rione, or ward, of Rome. Which happened to be the neighborhood closest to the Vatican. The purchases of various buildings in Borgo was traced to a shell corporation assumed to be Gloaming-controlled. As if she wasn't already number one on their hit list, these events made Liza Sole even more of a target for the order, although it was never proven that she instigated these purchases.

Cian and Liza spent their next few days together, each working to tend the garden at night. No words were said between the two; it was simply assumed that Cian would be re-created. What force of nature could prevent what was always meant to be? I only know what he told me about his re-creation, but he almost did not make it. Liza tends not to proceed with many re-creations because, as the first of this era, she is the most...I don't know...powerful of us all. Not many people can handle such an infusion and replication of the virus on their bodies.

The process took her a week with Cian and included several periods when Cian would have probably been declared clinically dead had Liza taken him to a hospital. Cian's memory of the process is fascinating, almost unbelievable. His mind was taken to a room and locked in a tube made of oak, with bodies below him writhing in pain. A series of complex shapes entered his body—maybe re-created DNA—and he could see his life and all the accompanying thoughts in the shape of a catenary traveling along a type of Cartesian coordinate system, with a circle radius stopping at each memory, which was a mark in the line, which became a curve as it reached his current point in life. He saw parts of his life that never happened. Would they happen in the future? But he realized what we all comprehended in that moment of which I will not speak because you are not one of us: we are all Anoesis, and yes, everything you believe that entails.

And then he woke up, with a peculiar hunger, and he left...

The door opens and the subject is led away.

CHAPTER 27

AUGUST 21
THIRTY-NINE MONTHS AFTER THE NOBI DISCOVERY

Sara Mesley
The Order of Bruder Klaus

Wu-Tang's "Protect Ya Neck" blasted from the bass-heavy speakers of the dingy cab rolling back and forth on the pockmarked dirt road to the village of Listvyanka, near Lake Baikal in Siberia, Russia.

The unforgiving harshness of the snow in this region left me craving a cup of hot coffee as I stared at the white shrouds outside the window competing with the darkness for my attention. It only added to my uncertainty as to what I would find outside Lake Baikal.

The driver hit the brakes and I lurched forward. The cab was stopped near an open gate with a cracked padlock hanging from a loose chain. The driver turned in his seat toward me with a peeved look and a point of his gloved finger. "I go no more!" he shouted above the loud music, in Russian-accented broken English.

I looked up and out the windshield and made out the lights from a cabin about three hundred yards up the path. A foot of snow on the ground, two degrees, blizzard conditions…whatever. I've done harder things. I threw the cabbie some American dollars, grabbed my bags, and stepped out without a word.

The hike to the cabin was a murderous trek in the dark that mirrored the thoughts running through my head. My legs and arms were burning with my muscles demanding rest or nourishment. But at least the trail was flat—I was trying to focus on the positive. By the time I reached the front door I was in no mood for niceties. I kicked the door, holding a bag in each hand.

The door opened and I was met with the newly long-bearded face of Bernard Kieslowki. Never one to throw out a greeting or a smile, he stepped aside and didn't offer to take my bags or ask of my condition—he knew me too well. I threw both bags close to the couch where Father Reilly sat nursing a cup of coffee.

"Welcome," Father Reilly said with a tip of his cup.

"All three of us in the same room together," I replied. "There better be a war going on outside to drag me over here."

Bernard pointed over to Reilly. "This person wants us to go steal some antiques."

Sounded fun so far. "Okay…"

Bernard nodded toward Father Reilly. "Go ahead. Tell her."

Reilly placed the coffee cup on the table. "The third letter of Fátima—"

Oh no. "We've been down this road before," I said, about half ready to call the cab back and return to something important.

"Hear me out," Reilly insisted with a chagrined look on his face. "There's an antiques dealer in Malta who specializes in Greek artifacts."

"Black market, of course," Bernard added.

"But what's the point of—"

"The third secret," Reilly continued. "Some academic—a mathematician—in Brazil analyzed it again and she found that it contained a cipher, that the letter itself was a kind of cipher, embedded and woven in the text. It was dependent on syntax and sound to decipher. We've been reading it wrong."

I glanced at Bernard and he shot me a "What can I do?" look. "Assuming I believe you," I said, "what the hell does it say?"

"That they have always been here, Sara," Reilly said. "Since before the church. Since before *any* church." He sat back and glared at me.

Bernard shook his head. "The point being that this antiques dealer has artifacts that will confirm it. To what end, we can only guess."

"The Congregation of Gibilmanna was an ancient Catholic order in Sicily that apparently was in possession of the artifacts before their monastery was pillaged by the Moors," Reilly insisted. He got up and began to pace the room. "They were then handed down through generations, and then found their way to this particular antiques dealer."

I sighed, wanting him to know how angry I was. "I'll give you three days of my time," I said. "But first you need to get me out of this frozen wasteland.

We took an old Lada Niva that was lent to us by the owner of the cabin. The Niva was one of the most famous Russian-made off-road vehicles ever built. This one was circa 1970 and had a peculiar design that made me doubt whether we would make it five feet in this snow. Picture an old Fiat with large tires capable of all weather and all terrain.

The car bounded up and down with the holes and the snow

and the ever-present rocks and tree limbs, like something in a video game or obstacle course. Have you ever played Mario Kart? Like that but without the friendly mushrooms. I sat in the back next to Bernard, as Reilly was the only one of us who could drive a stick. Needless to say, silent monks don't make the best travel companions. But we made it to Moscow in about four days. Didn't I say that I was leaving after three? Guess not…

From Moscow we took a flight to Palermo, Sicily, a drive to the harbor, and a boat to the island of Malta.

We landed in Malta in the middle of the night and wandered about town until we found a bar open all night. It was an old tavern built into a once-abandoned cave used as a fort back in the seventeenth century. The place resembled a wine cellar with empty liquor casket barrels lining the walls, a mosaic floor, and arched doorways. Oddly enough, there was a small bakery in one of the corners serving hot chimney cakes and *pastizz*. After a couple of hours of beer and cake, we took a cab to a residence about two miles from the coast in the Saint Paul's Bay neighborhood.

Built in 1922, the two-story building was constructed of stone, with exposed beams and iron handrails. The entire block was a row of identical structures of limestone with wooden apertures and Malta tile.

Father Reilly rapped his fist on the door. It creaked open almost immediately, and a young woman answered. She wore a white flowing dress with a blue apron over it and her hair pulled up.

"Can I help you?" she asked in a raspy British accent.

"Are you De'Ann Saxon?" I said.

She nodded with a fixed gaze.

"I'm wondering if you have some time to talk about some antiques we are interested in purchasing," I told her as I tried to look at her and see inside the house at the same time.

Her face betrayed no surprise as she stepped aside. We followed her in. Bernard waited outside, following our protocol of having someone outside to keep watch for any unusual activity. He sat across the street at a coffee stand, probably hoping to hear gunfire or something.

De'Ann led us to a small den with a large sea grass rug covering the stone floor and a tattered leather couch. She offered us the couch as she took a seat next to a wooden desk. With a quick pivot, she leaned toward the kitchen and yelled out, "Lee, watch the pot for me and keep stirring it!"

I turned my head in an attempt to see who was in the kitchen, but the angle of the couch prevented it. It bothered me that I couldn't tell how many people were in there and if they were in there actually cooking or holding weapons, just waiting for the right word.

She turned back to us. "Sorry. I'm making a deer confit. It takes me three days to strain, but is there any other way to make it?" She shrugged. "It passes the time but it also tastes divine."

"I believe you," Father Reilly said. "It must taste wonderful." Almost together, our eyes focused on De'Ann's hands, which were coated with a dark substance that almost looked like part of her skin, contrasting with the alabaster shade of the rest of her body.

She seemed to notice and lifted up her hands as if showing us a picture. "You're looking at my tomato hands."

"What does that mean?" I asked.

"It comes from picking tomatoes—it's a buildup of tomato tar. Happens when you harvest many, many tomatoes. It actually comes from the green part of the vine."

"I've never heard of that," Father Reilly said.

"It's a bitch to get off," De'Ann added. "I'm talking gasoline and alcohol."

"I'll have to remember that," he replied.

"So what types of artifacts were you looking for?" De'Ann asked.

"Greek," I answered.

She cocked her head to consider this for a moment. "Well, of course I can show you some of our artifacts that might be of interest, if you'll follow me to the basement," De'Ann said with a slight smile. She rose up from her chair.

My senses perked up. This felt weird. In this brief moment she had summed us up as serious buyers willing to pay thousands if not millions of dollars? It felt like a trap but there were no other options at this point. Our intel had told us this was the place where we would find some answers. We were in this the entire way.

"Of course," I replied, with a glance at Reilly. His eyes told me he had the same concerns.

De'Ann led the way down the stairs of a confined stone staircase lit by a few hanging lightbulbs to the basement. It smelled like wet stone or some type of cave. As we reached the bottom I was concerned that the lights did not illuminate the entire room.

"This building used to be a garrison, and this basement leads to others down the entire block," De'Ann said.

We reached the middle of the basement and I ran into the back of Father Reilly, who had stopped all of a sudden. "Hey," I cried as I looked around him to see De'Ann holding a gun. A Desert Eagle, in fact. That thing was about the size of a human head, and it could probably have blown a hole in me, Reilly, and the wall behind us.

"Why don't you tell me what you really want?" she asked, her face etched in anger.

"Well," Father Reilly said with his hands up and a slight warble to his voice, "we actually *are* here to see your artifacts."

De'Ann glanced at him with her hand tight on the trigger. "No one knows that I have Greek objects. I'm known for dealing exclusively in Moorish and Roman artifacts. But you know. How is that?"

"A source told us," I replied. "We're here with the Order of Bruder Klaus." I steadied myself and my muscles tensed. I wasn't sure what the reaction would be with that statement and a gun pointed at me, but there weren't many options and the ones I could think of weren't so exceptional.

De'Ann lowered the gun, and I took a deep breath. "My great-grandfather was in the Congregation of Gibilmanna. These artifacts that are in my possession have been handed down to family members in Sicily, Germany, and Poland. All members of the congregation. Families disappear, others acquire different interests, and interest wanes. Soon enough it was all left to me."

Father Reilly leaned toward her with an intense look in his eyes. "These artifacts may match up with a new analysis of the third secret of Fátima. It's important that we see them."

"I think you'll find these particularly interesting, then," De'Ann said. "Come this way."

She led us down another hallway attached to the basement. The ceiling was low and we hunched over as we followed the swinging lamps that lined the walls. The path opened up to a room with a large safe beside a computer monitor in the corner. It seemed so out of place against the ancient surroundings.

De'Ann placed her thumb on the print reader and the safe door clicked open with a climate control *hiss* that filled the room. She flipped on a bright desk lamp near a wooden table with a velvet cover.

She pulled out a 5x diopter magnifying floor lamp, which she placed next to the table. From the safe she pulled out a statue of Pan in marble and put it on the table. She placed the magnifying glass next to the face of the statue and invited me to look.

I leaned over and peered into the glass: two small fangs were in the mouth of Pan. I looked over at Father Reilly, who was grinning at me. "Doesn't prove much," I declared.

De'Ann was silent as she then placed a photograph and a piece of marble on the table. "This was taken from the excavation of the Pergamon Altar in Greece. It tells the story of the life of Telephus, founder of the city of Pergamon. In 1878, a German archaeologist named Carl Humann excavated the site. He took all the fragments to Berlin for reconstruction per his agreement with the Greek and Turkish governments. Unbeknownst to his superiors, he kept many of the most historically scandalous artifacts and donated them to the Knights Hospitaller, a military order of the Catholic Church." She pointed a finger at the photograph, which showed a relief of a man sucking blood from the neck of another man, and a woman collecting blood with a cup. Another section portrayed men with fangs protecting families from invading forces.

I heard Reilly awkwardly clear his throat behind me. De'Ann then presented the piece of marble on the table and placed the magnifying glass over it. I looked at it and the ancient Greek word that appeared: "*Hema...*"

I looked up and De'Ann glanced at me with a knowing smile. "It means—"

"Blood," Father Reilly whispered under his breath.

De'Ann brought out more photos. "These are pictures of the Antikythera mechanism. It's an ancient orrery and complex clockwork apparatus. Some say it was the first computer. Swedish scientists used computer simulation and X-ray topography to read the inscriptions through the corrosion of the artifact. This line at the top. It reads 'A—'"

"Anoesis," Father Reilly said.

CHAPTER 28

Lauren Scott
Doctor and Supervising Researcher, Atwater Corporation

The flight took forever, with two connections, before I stood outside the airport. I was told to take an Uber and then walk a mile to an abandoned parking garage downtown, near a row of run-down strip malls. After the long walk, I took a flight of stairs to the second floor. There were no working lights and the drape of darkness made me shudder and, oddly enough, think back to the warehouse in Melbourne.

The rumble of a vehicle echoed through the structure as it growled through the garage and up the ramp. The lights burned my eyes, and I held up a hand to shield my face. The vehicle stopped directly in front of me. I couldn't tell who was driving, but I moved to the side as a large, fit middle-aged man stepped out of the back and opened the back door without a word. He held out his hand and I gave him my cell phone. I got inside, and

419

as the door closed, I wondered why I had agreed to this.

My stress was compounded when I saw that the windows were coated in such a way that I couldn't see anything through them. The man sitting next to me did not utter a word for the entire two-hour trip. I could not relax at all, and without my phone or paper or a pen I couldn't even pretend to do work.

The car stopped and the man placed a hood over my head. I was led by the hand and walked about twenty feet before climbing some stairs and being taken to a seat. The bag was removed and I found myself inside a small private plane. Naturally, the windows were blacked out on this ride as well.

The same man sat across from me, tapping his fingers on an iPad. The plane took off and I couldn't sleep or relax no matter how hard I tried. All of those meditation techniques Hector had demanded I learn did nothing for me. They only made me more nervous. We were in the air about three hours before landing, which made my adrenaline spike again. The man handed me the hood and this time I placed it over my own head. A thirty-minute drive led to my removing the hood while standing inside yet another garage with a large elevator. It felt as though we were going down instead of up, which seemed odd at the time.

I was led to a room that closely resembled a law enforcement interrogation room with two-way mirrors, a table with chain locks, and a few chairs. Oddly enough, the walls were a strange construction of uneven and cutout wood designs that resembled a maze. It was eerily quiet. The man returned and waved me into the room behind the two-way mirrors.

I stood there for a moment, lost in thought as my adrenaline waned and my body was fighting with my exhaustion, before a voice jerked me awake. "Did they run you through the gauntlet?" a voice said from behind me. I looked to the side to see the stoic face of Agent Hugo Zumthor.

"They sure did," I replied.

"I'm surprised you agreed to come here," Hugo said.

"They told me it would be worth my time," I said, now doubting whether that would be true. "It better be, considering how long this day has been already. What's up with the weird construction in the room?"

Hugo's eyebrows raised up as if he were impressed I had noticed it. "It's an anechoic chamber. It's designed to absorb reflections of either sound or electromagnetic waves. It helps us control Gloamings."

"Really?"

Hugo nodded. "It makes for a weird experience in there." He glanced at me. "They didn't say anything to you about why you're here?"

I shook my head. "Nope. But I guess you know."

"The CIA types barely tell me anything," he replied. "But I think you're going to like this one."

As if on cue, the door to the interrogation room opened and four heavily armed guards in tactical gear led in a man wearing a full priestly cassock in all black. I leaned closer to the glass for a better look as the guards attached the chains to the steel holdings forged to the table. "Is that—"

"Father John Reilly," Hugo whispered.

I turned back to Hugo. "He's a—"

"Yes, he is."

I stared through the glass at every part of him and after a moment Father Reilly's head turned and his eyes met my gaze even through the reflected mirror. "Have you talked to him?" I asked.

"Yes, I have."

Another man came in and introduced himself to Father

Reilly as the interviewer. Reilly didn't seem surprised. His face was impassive. They talked about a journey Reilly had made to view certain artifacts related to the Gloamings, which seemed to indicate they had been here much longer than we thought. But all I could think of was how this would affect my research. This historical analysis was for someone else to consider. "Where is this leading to?" I asked Hugo.

"He wants to speak to you." And as Hugo finished that sentence, Father Reilly turned his head and looked directly at me.

I stood in front of the table on the other side of Father Reilly. The interviewer glanced at me. "I'm almost done here, and then you can ask him a question."

I nodded and he continued.

"So what did these artifacts tell you?"

Reilly shrugged. "They moved my mind in a certain direction. After everyone had gone back upstairs, De'Ann Saxon brought me back down to show me the Veil of Veronica. Used to wipe the sweat from Jesus's brow as he carried the cross. It bears his likeness."

"Is that a fact? So what? Another artifact."

"This artifact had been protected by a band of Gloamings known as the Knights Hospitaller."

The interviewer leaned forward after a pull on his cigarette. "Wait a fucking minute. There's a group of Gloamings out there we've never heard of? Where is their base of operations?"

"This isn't current."

"What do you mean?" the interviewer asked.

Father Reilly gave a slight smile, his eyes wide open. "This was back in the year 1153. They formed the concept of Anoesis—a state of mind consisting of pure sensation or emotion without cognitive content. There is a philosophical theory that states there is no God now, but that doesn't preclude the existence of a God in the future. They conceived of themselves as a type of simulacrum—copies that depict things that had no original to begin with."

Silence. Even I was intrigued. And Hugo's face was creased with a frown.

"So that made you want to re-create?" the interviewer asked.

"I thought Cian Clery was the key. I thought he was the continuation of Anoesis—I plan to bring it back. To conceive of Gloamings as these pure creatures to bring goodness to our lands." Father Reilly stared at his chained hands as if remembering a painful part of his life.

"But?" the interviewer said with a peeved look.

"But he was just a terrorist, intent on demolishing everything having to do with humans. I was wrong and no step closer to the one who would bring back Anoesis." He looked over at me and it was like a jolt of electricity. "Your sister knew about it."

My heart sank for a moment but the feeling was soon replaced by the anger that had filled it so well for so long. My face was grim. "How dare you? What do you know about Jennifer?"

"I met her once and I know she was intrigued by the concept and wanted to explore it."

"Who killed her?"

He stared at me with his head cocked and an almost absent look on his face. "Cian. She wanted to be re-created. It wasn't out of malice. It just didn't take. She knew the risks."

"Bullshit!" I yelled.

He stared at me with a gloomy look on his face. "You know it's true. She loved you and only wanted you to do what is moral."

He was right.

"Tell me about your re-creation."

He was silent for a moment, staring at the table with his lips pursed. "It's not really something we talk about," he replied.

"Like confession, right?" Hugo added.

A slight smile played on Father Reilly's lips. "That's funny. Not really, though."

"Tell me the story," I insisted.

Father Reilly shrugged and took a deep breath. "I assured you of honesty. And I will keep that oath. Liza and I traveled to Brazil for Carnaval. A lot of Gloamings enjoyed the celebrations there for various reasons. I didn't like it there at first. My sleep patterns were messed up from staying up all night. But things aren't always pleasant, so I adjusted.

"We would spend nights walking among the people celebrating, but it was uncomfortable with every person in a mask covering their faces, including the elaborate headdresses that also covered their features. It became disorienting to me, walking among the masked crowds pushing me and the piercing sounds from every direction. Like it was all meant to take me away from who I was.

"When I was young I talked all the time about things: myself, people, love, pain…But now I preferred to be with my thoughts. But that one night, Liza and I walked up into the Rocinha favela in the center of Rio de Janeiro with the stacked houses and winding streets.

"I followed her into a favela at the top of the neighborhood made of brick, rebar, and mismatched wood, with two water tanks on the roof. A Brazilian man and woman led us down into a newly constructed basement and wooden tunnel with a depth of about a hundred feet, with ventilation and electricity. It bottomed out to a large living room with a bar and a few bedrooms that branched off.

The floor was simply dirt from the ground and it smelled moist.

"There were about five other Gloamings sitting on the floor, talking and drinking oleander tea."

I nodded. "What did you talk about?"

Father Reilly's eyes looked at me but it was almost like he was looking past me. "Failure. Whether it's too late to start over. I thought that I should be content to see these faces without their masks and leave it at that. Liza mentioned that now she did not care about why things happen. There was a young beautiful Gloaming in a red shirt who looked exactly like Morrissey on the *Bona Drag* cover. He told me that he still couldn't comprehend this organic life that came from inorganic matter. He heard a philosopher say the same thing and it stuck with him. Everything that has happened before could be thought of as implausible.

"Liza asked me to talk about my family, especially my father. And that's when I remembered it. My father's favorite Bible verse."

"Which was?" I asked.

Father Reilly looked up at me. "Romans 12:2. 'Do not be conformed to this world, but be transformed by the renewal of your mind, that by testing you may discern what is the will of God, what is good and acceptable and perfect.'

"I knew then that I had to be transformed.

"I didn't want to say it out loud, but I felt the continuation of his theory was that to rise above we needed a partially divine creature to appear and take humanity a step beyond where we were now. I believe Hegel talked about the man that could become God—who once was and will be again. Where is the greater intelligence other than what has now been created? I think I felt tears fall down my face, and I glanced over to see Liza Sole staring at me. I didn't have to say a word, but she already knew what I was asking and she consented without a symbol of communication."

"Is that when she did it?" Hugo asked. "Right there?"

Father Reilly shook his head. "It doesn't work quite like that. I lay on a bed and she lay next to me. No words exchanged. I might have fallen asleep and had premonitions. I'm not sure but I remember her mouth on my neck and I began to dream…"

Hugo and I stood there in silence for a moment, just watching him.

"Did you ever find them?" Hugo asked.

"Who?" Father Reilly said softly, as if I had woken him from a daydream.

"The person you were looking for to bring Anoesis back," I replied, my mind still jumbled with thoughts of my sister.

The lines almost left his face, as if he were thinking of something calming and nurturing. "I did. Finally. Someone who had abandoned intention—*via negativa,* as they say. Resurrect me with the dropping of the sun. I'm not trying to be abstract—it's just that no one quite understands it all. Yet."

"Who is it?" I asked.

"Myself."

CHAPTER 29

NEW YEAR'S EVE
FIFTY-FIVE MONTHS AFTER THE NOBI DISCOVERY

Lauren Scott
Doctor and Supervising Researcher, Atwater Corporation

I had never felt so lonely in my life, as this strange, ongoing, unspoken battle continued. I was lonely even with Hector beside me. After the initial victory in the Atwater lab, my anti-NOBI drug failed in many of its field tests. Every week another scientist left Atwater, or a professor at some university would email to inform me that they were no longer conducting research on the NOBI virus. They couldn't take the pressure anymore.

I was assigned a detail of federal marshals as security—essential, given the amount of death threats I received after my research was discussed in a *New York Times* article. I began to work nights and sleep during the day. It was easier than I thought. I couldn't get comfortable enough sleeping at night: I was always feeling as though I was on guard. Every sound outside was someone trying to break in. It was exhausting.

Hector published his book, entitled *The Blood of the Eternal Covenant: Chasing the NOBI Virus*. It was actually a bestseller, with Hector appearing on the *Today* show. Of course, his appearance was marred by an argument between him and the host about whether my research was ethical vis-à-vis altering human genetics to combat the NOBI virus.

Events were moving in a strangely peaceful direction. In conjunction with the Human Rights Campaign and Amnesty International, the Gloaming Council organized a "blood drive for peace," where humans donated their blood as a show of reconciliation with the Gloamings and to demonstrate that armed conflict was not the solution to the present-day issues. The council hoped to facilitate a more mainstream system in which Gloamings could purchase blood donated willingly by humans. Various distribution centers were already planned for cities all over the country to facilitate the logistics of a legal blood bank. A grocery store for Gloamings.

The arguments immediately erupted: many academics likened this process to the selling of organs, and worried about the exploitation of the economically disadvantaged people more likely to sell their blood. But many recognized the need for Gloamings to have food for their survival. However, the moral equation is significant: even in these early days of the blood drive for peace, research is already showing that frequent blood donors have significant health problems. Should we condone voluntary harm to others in order to help another segment that has put themselves at voluntary risk?

Thinking about it only made me feel worse.

I found Hector standing in front of the kitchen counter, head cocked to the side, with a slight smile, tapping his foot to some song playing only in his head. We promised long ago not to discuss the traumas I had faced these past few years on the front lines. No talk of the dangers or of when they were going to happen.

The nervous man I had first met back in Nogales had transformed. He would hand me a cup of black coffee in the morning and calmly ask, "Looking at viruses today?"

And I would smile. No answer. It reminded me of what my dad used to tell me: "Believe half of what you see and none of what you hear."

I took up smoking again, thinking it would help with the stress I faced every day. It didn't seem to help; I started waking up sick, vomiting. This went on for a week, until one afternoon when I was sitting there in the car, tired, at a red light. Then I bolted upright. How could I have been so stupid? I turned into the nearest pharmacy and ran inside.

I quit smoking that day, for good.

I was pregnant.

Of course we waited until after I became pregnant to finally get married. We drove to Nogales—I know: why would we want to relive all of that distress and drama? But it just made sense for us. We married quietly at Nogales City Hall. My parents Skyped in, and when I saw my father crying, I felt the tears coming too. I'm sure they were, like me, both overjoyed and thinking of Jennifer.

Being so close to New Mexico did make me think of everything we had been through, everything that was still in front of us. There were still an inordinate number of military vehicles all through Arizona and the Southwest, so it was hard to think of anything else. A part of me wanted to see the mass grave again but it was now a closed military area. I made do with a tour of the new Nogales autopsy center. What a honeymoon.

We decided to avoid the main highway on the route back to

California, traveling the back roads near the Mexican border. The dusty, vacant roads made me think of my family's long road trip to Disneyland when Jennifer and I were kids. My father had decided to save time by taking these same back roads, and I loved listening to the border radio stations that bled into U.S. radio waves. Mexico, of course, being unencumbered by FCC regulations regarding signal strength and radio wave placement, would line the border with stations, illegally broadcasting any show imaginable along both sides of the border: crazed preachers from every imagined sect, deranged amateur scientists peddling sham cures for any ailment, Spanish rap, hillbillies, lunatics, Tejano, conjunto, Mexican talk radio. Jennifer and I sang along loudly when we recognized the music, but often we just had to listen: a buzz of tunes and voices and static, like a hallucinogenic drug.

Now I thought, what kind of chaotic future were we headed toward? The Gloamings had attempted to enforce a strict method and procedure to govern re-creations, but a new band of savage Gloamings had established their own rules and refused to adhere to the proposed criteria. As more Gloamings were re-created, they searched for more power, more land, more feeding opportunities. Once I had been in the thick of it. Now I was a bystander.

I asked Hector to pull over. I stepped out of the car, and as the warm wind brushed my face, I stared at the vast expanse of desert stretched to the horizon. I covered my stomach protectively. And as the sun began its descent, I felt that familiar foreboding: ever since Nogales, every night always seemed to bring a bit of anxiety with it. But that evening I said a prayer for the morning, and for a sunbeam that would cover us like a shield of light.

EPILOGUE

NIGHT ONE

When I was a child, my family visited the Joshua Tree park, and I wandered away. I became lost in the desert. My parents found me before too long, but I've never forgotten the absolute fear and loneliness I felt, surrounded by boulders and the Joshua trees, the kangaroo rats and jackrabbits scurrying past. Every rustle or crackle terrified me: my father had told me about coyotes that day, and I was certain each noise must be a coyote about to pounce.

But that is not me anymore. I'm standing in the desert. I'm alone, not sure how I got here: I can only feel this new...hunger.

No, not hunger. Thirst.

How hard will it be to control this urge? Do I want to? There is no one stronger than me, so I simply cannot know. I only know that I belong to the future. Not just me—there will be more. And I know we must be prepared to lead, never follow.

My name is Liza Sole, and around me the night air is still.

APPENDIX ONE

The University of Texas School of Law
The Review of Litigation

Condensed version of the article "Can the Gloamings and the NOBI Virus Coexist Within the ADA?"

Fall/Winter

The Americans with Disabilities Act of 1990 (ADA) was passed by Congress and signed by the president "to provide a clear and comprehensive national mandate for the elimination of discrimination against individuals with disabilities."[36] Since passage, courts have struggled to interpret the meaning of the term "disability," with some courts opting for a more liberal interpretation and others preferring a more restricted view of the term.

Within the context of the term "disability" and its evolution, soon another factor emerged to challenge preconceived notions and settled law: the NOBI virus and the persons who emerged from its effects, the Gloamings. As the Gloaming population increased, many of the re-created began to push for more rights

---

[36]   42 U.S.C. § 12101(b)(1) (1994).

to accommodate their unique position in this country. Many of the Gloamings were being terminated from their jobs because employers had less use for employees who could not work during traditional working hours—namely the usual nine to five—and could not be out during the daytime.

The Gloamings were forced to find other occupations when many courts upheld the rights of employers to terminate them for the material change in circumstances. The Gloamings attempted to assert that their condition was covered by either the Family and Medical Leave Act (FMLA) or the ADA. The FMLA basically gives an employee the right to take a certain amount of time off because the employee is incapacitated by a health condition. The time period covered is up to twelve weeks. Obviously, the Gloamings were afflicted with their condition for more than twelve weeks, but attorneys for the Gloamings wanted the courts to expand the amount of time given to them or force the employer to make an accommodation for the condition. The federal courts were unwilling to extend the protections of the FMLA to cover the Gloamings and their new condition.

Many courts argued over terms such as "covered entity" (meaning an employer, employment agency, labor organization, or joint labor-management committee) and "qualified individual with a disability" (identified as "an individual with a disability who, with or without reasonable accommodation, can perform the essential functions of the employment position that such individual holds or desires"). 42 U.S.C. § 12112(a); see also § 12111(2) and (8).

In *Andrew Davis v. Grant-Johnson Advertising*, the Ninth Circuit Court of Appeals went even further by holding that in determining whether an accommodation is "reasonable," one must look at the costs of the accommodation in relation to its benefits and whether accommodating a Gloaming in a work environment would impose an undue hardship upon an employer. The court observed that "[t]he statutory reference to a substantial limitation indicates…that an employer regards an employee as handicapped in his or her ability to work by finding the employee's impairment to foreclose generally the type of employment involved." Ibid. But petitioner had alleged only that respondent regarded them as unable to satisfy the requirements of a particular job, which was as an associate attorney. Consequently, the court held that petitioner had not stated a claim that they were regarded as substantially limited in the major life activity of working and that an employer could not be expected to make a reasonable accommodation for the petitioner and any accommodation would not be considered reasonable. Employing similar logic, the Court of Appeals for the Ninth Circuit affirmed the district court's judgment. 130 F. 3d 729 (2018).

The Gloamings then sued under the ADA for their new protections. The ADA protects a worker who needs to take sick time for a condition that qualifies as a disability under the act. The Gloamings asserted that their condition was a disability as defined by the ADA. And therefore, the employers must make a reasonable accommodation to allow them to keep and do their jobs. All of the employers asserted that to make a reasonable accommodation for the Gloamings would result in an undue hardship to the employer which is a defense to an ADA claim.

The ADA's definition of disability is drawn almost verbatim from the definition of "handicapped individual" included in the Rehabilitation Act of 1973, 29 U.S.C. § 706(8)(B) (1988 ed.), and the definition of "handicap" contained in the Fair Housing Amendments Act of 1988, 42 U.S.C. § 3602(h)(1) (1988 ed.). Congress's repetition of a well-established term carries the implication that Congress intended the term to be construed in accordance with preexisting regulatory interpretations. See *FDIC v. Philadelphia Gear Corp.*, 476 U.S. 426, 437–438 (1986); *Commissioner v. Estate of Noel*, 380 U.S. 678, 681–682 (1965); *ICC v. Parker*, 326 U.S. 60, 65 (1945). In this case, Congress did more than suggest this construction; it adopted a specific statutory provision in the ADA directing as follows:

"Except as otherwise provided in this chapter, nothing in this chapter shall be construed to apply a lesser standard than the standards applied under Title V of the Rehabilitation Act of 1973 (29 U.S.C. 790 et seq.) or the regulations issued by federal agencies pursuant to such title." 42 U.S.C. § 12201(a).

The directive requires courts to construe the ADA to grant at least as much protection as provided by the regulations implementing the Rehabilitation Act.

The EEOC issued an "interpretive guidance," which provides that "[t]he determination of whether an individual is substantially limited in a major life activity must be made on a case by case basis, without regard to mitigating measures such as medicines or assistive or prosthetic devices." 29 CFR pt. 1630, App. § 1630.2(j) (1998) (describing § 1630.2(j)). The Department of Justice has issued a similar guideline. See 28 CFR pt. 35, App. A, § 35.104 ("The question of whether a person has a disability should be assessed without regard to the availability of mitigating measures, such as reasonable modification or auxiliary aids and services"); pt. 36, App. B, § 36.104 (same). The Department of Health, Education, and Welfare (HEW) issued the first regulations interpreting the Rehabilitation Act in 1977. The regulations are of particular significance because, at the time, HEW was the agency responsible for coordinating the implementation and enforcement of § 504. *Consolidated Rail Corporation v. Darrone,* 465 U.S. 624, 634 (1984) (citing Exec. Order No. 11914, 3 CFR 117 (1976–1980 Comp.)). The HEW regulations, which appear without change in the current regulations issued by the Department of Health and Human Services, define "physical or mental impairment" to mean:

"(A) any physiological disorder or condition, cosmetic disfigurement, or anatomical loss affecting one or more of the following body systems: neurological; musculoskeletal; special sense organs; respiratory, including speech organs; cardiovascular; reproductive, digestive, genitourinary; hemic and lymphatic; skin; and endocrine; or

"(B) any mental or psychological disorder, such as mental retardation, organic brain syndrome, emotional or mental illness, and specific learning disabilities." 45 CFR § 84.3(j)(2)(i) (1997).

In issuing these regulations, HEW decided against including a list of disorders constituting physical or mental impairments, out of concern that any specific enumeration might not be comprehensive. 42 Fed. Reg. 22685 (1977), reprinted in 45 CFR pt. 84, App. A, p. 334 (1997). The commentary accompanying the regulations, however, contains a representative list of disorders and conditions constituting physical impairments, including "such diseases and conditions as orthopedic, visual, speech, and hearing impairments, cerebral palsy, epilepsy, muscular dystrophy, multiple sclerosis, cancer, heart disease, diabetes, mental retardation, emotional illness, and...drug addiction and alcoholism." Ibid.

The definition of disability also requires that disabilities be evaluated "with respect to an individual" and be determined based on whether an impairment substantially limits the "major life activities of such individual." § 12102(2). Thus, whether a person has a disability under the ADA is an individualized inquiry. See

Bragdon v. Abbott, 524 U.S. 624, 641–642 (1998) (declining to consider whether HIV infection is a per se disability under the ADA); 29 CFR pt. 1630, App. § 1630.2(j) ("The determination of whether an individual has a disability is not necessarily based on the name or diagnosis of the impairment the person has, but rather on the effect of that impairment on the life of the individual").

In 1980, the president transferred responsibility for the implementation and enforcement of § 504 to the attorney general. See, e.g., Exec. Order No. 12250, 3 CFR 298 (1981). The regulations issued by the Justice Department, which remain in force to this day, adopted verbatim the HEW definition of physical impairment quoted above. 28 CFR § 41.31(a)(1) (1997). In addition, the representative list of diseases and conditions originally relegated to the commentary accompanying the HEW regulations were incorporated into the text of the regulations. Ibid.

As many Gloamings began to be negatively impacted in the workplace and sought redress in the court system, many courts determined that the ADA must be construed to be consistent with regulations issued to implement the Rehabilitation Act. See 42 U.S.C. § 12201(a). Rather than enunciating a general principle for determining what is and is not a major life activity, the Rehabilitation Act regulations instead provide a representative list, defining terms to include "functions such as caring for one's self, performing manual tasks, walking, seeing, hearing, speaking, breathing, learning, and working." 45 CFR § 84.3(j)(2)(ii) (1997); 28 CFR § 41.31(b)(2) (1997). As the use of the term "such as" confirms, the list is illustrative, not exhaustive. However, neither the ADA nor the regulations address whether the intent of the person in acquiring the disability should be considered when determining whether a person should be covered under the ADA.

The most important case in establishing Gloamings' workplace rights was won by the Gloamings when the plaintiff convinced the court that telecommuting was considered a reasonable accommodation. This case was reversed by the Court of Appeals and not taken up by the Supreme Court.

The Supreme Court finally took up the issue in *Kurt Jennings, Petitioner v. Allen and Jacobs, LLC.*, on writ of certiorari to the United States Court of Appeals for the Ninth Circuit. After a lengthy analysis, the Supreme Court determined that "in the end, the disability definition does not turn on personal choice. When significant limitations result from the impairment, the definition is met even if the difficulties are not insurmountable. However, when a person willingly brings changes of a harmful physical nature which are an absolute certainty, then the act should not afford the person the same protections afforded those who have acquired the limitations through no fault of their own. Testimony from the petitioner that his NOBI infection was entirely his choice is unchallenged. App. 22; 721 F. Supp., at 412; 107 F. 5th, at 524. In the context of reviewing summary judgment, we must take it to be true. Fed. Rule Civ. Proc. 56(e). We agree with the district court and the Court of Appeals that no triable issue of fact impedes a ruling on the question of statutory coverage. Petitioner's NOBI infection is a physical impairment which substantially limits a major life activity, as the ADA defines it; however, his impairment is not covered by the ADA because he willingly and with absolute certainty acquired the infection through his own actions.

"The determination of the Court of Appeals that petitioner's NOBI infection was not a disability under the ADA is affirmed. The judgment is vacated, and the case is remanded for further proceedings consistent with this opinion."

APPENDIX TWO

VANITY FAIR
The Gloaming Gambit

Excerpted from The Gloaming Rise to Power *by Edward Ward Jr.*

After failing to sway any state legislature in America to pass Gloaming protection laws, the Gloamings decided to try their persuasive power on a legislative body more susceptible to their unique form of lobbying: the United States Congress.

As often happens during the process of many historical events, the circumstances along the periphery of the proceedings are as compelling as the actual occurrence. Many of the performers of this wide-ranging spectacle carried their own baggage through every scene.

Representative Drew's daughter, Wendy, re-created at age twenty-two, when she graduated from college and fell in love with the famous Gloaming artist Peter Kiyokawa after a torrid affair that culminated in their separation, then reconciliation and subsequent separation. It was the stuff of gossip columns and Internet rumors.

Not surprisingly, a majority of the House considered the bill a nonstarter, and its prospects appeared bleak when the Speaker of the House assigned it to the House Judiciary Committee. Representative Bill Jones, the head of the committee, was a confident and unrepentant opponent of the Gloamings and the process of re-creation. Although his tone and language had softened since his earlier statements advocating a form of quarantine for the Gloamings and denouncing attempts to allocate federal funds for research into Gloaming and NOBI vaccines, he recently expressed concern as to whether the Gloamings were a threat to Homeland Security. Even some of his colleagues questioned whether he could be neutral and consider the alternatives.

Many of the major lobbying firms seemed unsure about how to proceed. Their only concern was to ensure that the potential legislation did not interfere with any private business interests when it came to accommodations. That was already agreed to by all parties, so the remainder of the proposal was left to the devices of each individual legislator. The real effect of that was that the Gloamings' lobbying groups had the field to themselves when exerting their pressures and flattering with campaign donations. Protests from various anti-Gloaming groups were held in cities across the country but they were relatively peaceful.

At this point, everyone in Washington assumed that the bill would never make it out of committee. But Representative Jones, averse to being seen as a complete obstructionist and feeling the influence of other ranking members, allowed the committee to begin work on refining the bill to make it more palatable to the members at large on both sides of the aisle. And this was the point when Marcy Noll, counsel for the House Committee on Homeland Security, was asked to lead the judiciary staff to work on the bill. As this was an extremely high-profile bill pending in Congress, Jones was pleased to lend his input.

They began work with the most controversial parts of the proposed act. The Gloamings envisioned a portion of their bill to be a sort of Title IX for their community. For those who don't know, Title IX is the federal law that prohibits discrimination on the basis of sex in any federally funded educational institution. Basically, it made women's athletic programs receive funding equal to what men's programs receive. But this Gloaming Title IX would cover every aspect of university life to put the Gloamings on equal footing with non-Gloamings in college.

Marcy Noll floated the proposal to the NCAA and a coalition of higher education associations, and the pushback was pretty intense. Most of the universities objected primarily to the cost of keeping a university open with essentially twenty-four hours of classes. Not to mention operating twenty-four-hour stores and cafeterias and retrofitting dormitories or building underground dormitories to accommodate people who cannot be exposed to any amount of sunlight. In addition, the universities would have to ensure that there would be some kind of substance edible to Gloamings on campus. Compromise had to come eventually, but they felt early on that a good way to bridge the large gap would be to allow the universities a considerable amount of latitude in terms of how far they would be required to comply.

The judiciary staff proposed that any qualified university that accepted more than ten Gloamings in a regular school year would be obligated to offer night classes of an equivalent that would keep the Gloamings on a five-year degree plan. The educational institute would be required to offer night classes at a minimum of two nights per week during a semester.

In addition, it was decided to leave athletics and extracurriculars out of the bill and not enforce an accommodation for those types of activities.

The next and most important section of the bill pertained to accommodations for essential government functions. This was one of the more contentious aspects of any proposed bill. Most House members did not want to be blamed for any budget problems that would result from maintaining state offices for twenty-four-hour periods of time. Therefore, the staff actively sought compromises and rules that would be less burdensome on state governments.

The first function would be to restore full voting rights and access to polls for the Gloamings during hours when they could safely be outside. Most members on both sides of the aisle had no concerns about that aspect of the act. No one wanted to be accused of denying a segment of the population the right to vote. Any House member could easily sell this aspect of a bill to his or her constituents.

A subsequent and significant portion of the bill concerned the desire of the Gloamings to prohibit state and municipal governments from denying Gloaming access to essential public facilities. These services could range from the ability to acquire or renew a driver's license to the opportunity to acquire a new birth certificate. This would be the issue of either opening state offices at night or building out Gloaming accommodations to all state government facilities. Either choice would incur significant expense, to be sure.

The Gloaming lobbyists realized early on that any private entity accommodations would have to wait until the national environment changed with the attitudes of the citizens toward the Gloamings. Making private businesses liable for not accommodating Gloamings would lead to no votes, and most legislators knew better than to proceed with any laws impacting business. Therefore, the concentration of the act would need to be focused primarily on governmental accommodations. At this point, the bill began to form into its more complete and final proposal. But there was still work to be done: getting the votes.

APPENDIX THREE

Inside the Gloaming Investigation Unit of the FBI

Although loath to acknowledge a distinct unit to investigate a particular class of United States citizens, the FBI has reluctantly assembled a small unit to resolve certain crimes with Gloaming connections. Named the Division for Undetermined Crime Origins (DUCO), it has taken the lead in many crimes in which Gloaming involvement is suspected.

Agent Hugo Zumthor of the Federal Bureau of Investigation has been at the forefront of criminal investigations with Gloaming involvement. Early in his career, he investigated a Gloaming group known as the Honored Society, which was heavily involved in human trafficking for blood and the illegal importation of blood to certain communities. Zumthor tracked this criminal organization from Chicago to London, where the society peddled the vials of blood collected from various Eastern European countries. The blood was then brought to the United States through containerships, smuggled with legitimate goods. Zumthor uncovered the trafficking scheme during the investigation of a warlord in Benin City, Nigeria, who had been tasked with smuggling the cocaine shipments.

Further DUCO, CIA, and ATF efforts reveal that the Gloaming criminal clans were also heavily involved in human trafficking from various poor economic countries in Latin America, Eastern Europe, and Asia corresponding with the drop in container blood trafficking. The conclusion was that the Gloamings were not receiving the nutrients they needed from degraded blood shipped in canisters and had decided to go straight to the source and begin to procure humans to meet their needs.

Given their lack of true organizational structure similar to that of other criminal entities, the Gloaming criminal clans seemed to operate as lateral parallel groups that coordinated their actions through meetings and digital communications, such as outmoded IM networks and less regulated WhatsApp and UPchat platforms. Similarly, they emphasized a type of inconspicuous lifestyle to their members, so as to not be perceptible as criminals to members of the public. However, "Gloamings were pretty conspicuous to begin with," Agent Zumthor clarified. "I'm not sure it was all that effective as the clans expanded their activities to include money laundering, bid rigging in construction, theft, extortion, and weapons smuggling. Their profits are invested in hotels, restaurants, and real estate. Stolen gold was used, from the start, to safeguard the financial capital of the Nick Bindon Claremont independence regime." Concluded Zumthor, "At least we can see the shape of what we're dealing with now."

Although its budget is small compared with that of other divisions, the DUCO unit has proven its worth on many occasions, apprehending many suspects and breaking up various crime rings known to have Gloaming involvement.

ACKNOWLEDGMENTS

Here is the bottom line: you wouldn't be reading this book if it weren't for my agent, Daniel Lazar at Writers House. I could thank him a million times and it wouldn't be enough for all the support and help with the writing he gave me since the beginning. Thank you for believing in this book and fighting for me every step of the way. Also thanks to everyone at Writers House for all of their help, including Maja Nikolic (awesome foreign rights director) and Victoria Doherty-Munro.

A HUGE (they won't let me use a 200-point font) thanks to my editor, Joshua Kendall, for crafting this book into something more than I thought it could ever be. I can't say enough about our work together and how much I learned about the art of writing. I will always be grateful.

Thanks to everyone at Little, Brown, Mulholland, and Hachette, including Gabriella Mongelli for all of her help in the editing process. To copyeditor Nell Beram: I don't know how you do it, but you have serious editing skills. Also, thank you to Ben Allen for all of his help.

THANK YOU to Michelle Kroes and Jon Cassir at Creative ⸱⸱ts Agency. I wish I could really tell you how mind-blowing it is to have movie agents. You two are incredible people. Also, thank you to Anna Jinks and Michelle McPhillips.

Much thanks to the incredible Mike Ireland at 20th Century Fox for believing in this book.

Thank you to everyone at the amazing 21 Laps Entertainment, especially Dan Cohen and Shawn Levy for seeing something special in this book. Two talented and great people.

All my friends and family in San Antonio.

My sister, Veronica Villareal Mittelbronn.

Bentley.

Mom (Ernestine Folk) and Dad (Raymond Villareal).